RAVES FOR *POINT OF IMPACT*

"The mountains of Arkansas are the setting for *Point of Impact*, a harsh, visceral novel of conspiracy and betrayal by veteran author Stephen Hunter . . . a disturbing mix that plays on our sense of history while at the same time it appeals to our darkest fantasies of rough justice."

—*Chicago Tribune*

"Bob Lee Swagger . . . explodes as a thinking man's Rambo. . . . The characters, plot and courtroom finale will leave readers wrung out."

—*Publishers Weekly*

"A WHIZ-BANG."

—*Kirkus Reviews*

"A HELLACIOUSLY GOOD THRILLER . . . THERE ISN'T ENOUGH PRAISE TO HEAP ON *POINT OF IMPACT.*"

—*Rocky Mountain News*

"Hunter has written a scorcher of a book. . . . It is apparent one is reading a master storyteller. The reader becomes caught up in a relentless surge of excitement. . . . And if when you finish this book, you feel a little tingle running down your back, don't worry. It probably isn't Bob Lee Swagger's crosshairs tickling along your spine."

—*The Tampa Tribune and Times*

The raves continue for *Point of Impact*

"A complex and worthwhile thriller."
—*Milwaukee Journal*

"Stephen Hunter returns the thriller to the individual, making a hero out of a human being instead of machinery and bureaucracy. . . . The combination of exciting action, technical lore and skilled plot manipulation places the novel far ahead of others in its field. . . . *Point of Impact* succeeds in all the right ways. It's a hugely entertaining book."
—*The Sun*, Baltimore

Point of Impact

ALSO BY STEPHEN HUNTER

FICTION

The Master Sniper
The Second Saladin
The Spanish Gambit
Target
The Day Before Midnight
Dirty White Boys
Black Light
Time to Hunt
Hot Springs
Pale Horse Coming
Havana

NONFICTION

American Gunfight: The Plot to Kill Harry Truman and the Shootout That Stopped It (co-written with John S. Bainbridge Jr.)

COLLECTIONS

Violent Screen: A Critic's 13 Years on the Front Lines of Movie Mayhem
Now Playing at the Valencia: Pulitzer Prize–Winning Essays on Movies

Stephen Hunter
POINT OF IMPACT

NEW YORK
TORONTO
LONDON
SYDNEY
AUCKLAND

BANTAM BOOKS

POINT OF IMPACT
A Bantam Book

PUBLISHING HISTORY
Bantam hardcover edition published March 1993
Bantam mass market edition published December 1993
Bantam mass market reissue / February 2007

Published by
Bantam Dell
A Division of Random House, Inc.
New York, New York

Library of Congress Catalog Card Number: 92-27121

ISBN 978-0-553-56351-1

Printed in the United States of America
Published simultaneously in Canada

www.bantamdell.com

OPM 37 36 35 34 33 32 31 30 29 28

TO C.H.
YOU TRIED LIKE HELL.

ACKNOWLEDGMENTS

The author would like to thank the many people who helped him in the preparation of this book, while acknowledging that he alone is responsible for all errors of omission or commission. John Feamster of Tuscaloosa, Alabama, was especially generous in time and effort. Bob Lopez, Randi Henderson, Lenne Miller, Jean Marbella, Joe Fanzone, Mike Hill, and Weyman Swagger, in the Baltimore area, lent support when it was needed. In New York, my editor, Ann Harris, helped me find out what my own book was about and wouldn't let me stop working until I did; and my agent, Victoria Gould Pryor, did her usual splendid job. My children, Jake and Amy, put up with the whole unruly process; and my wife, Lucy, watched me disappear toward shooting ranges, gun shows and my own office for nearly four years without complaint.

ONLY ACCURATE RIFLES ARE INTERESTING.
—Colonel Townsend Whelen

Point of Impact

CHAPTER ONE

It was November, cold and wet in west Arkansas, a miserable dawn following on a miserable night. Sleet whistled through the pines and collected on the humps of stone that jutted out of the earth; low overhead, angry clouds hurtled by. Now and then the wind would rush through the canyons between the trees and blow the sleet like gunsmoke. It was the day before hunting season.

Bob Lee Swagger had placed himself just off the last climb that led up to Hard Bargain Valley, that flat splurge of tabletop high in the Ouachitas, and he sat in perfect silence and perfect stillness against an old pine, the rifle across his knees. This was Bob's first gift: the gift of stillness. He acquired it naturally, without instruction, from some inner pool where stress never reached. Back in 'Nam he was something of a legend for the nearly animallike way he could will his body reactions down, stiller than death.

The cold had fought through his wool leggings and up and under his down vest and begun to climb up his spine, like a sly little mouse. He gritted his teeth, fighting the urge to let them chatter. Now and then his hip throbbed from a wound from long ago. He instructed his brain to ignore the phantom ache. He was beyond will. He was in some other place.

He was earning Tim.

You see, he'd tell you, if you were one of the two or three men in the world he talked to—old Sam Vincent, say, the ex–Polk County prosecutor, or maybe Doc LeMieux, the dentist, or Vernon Tell, the sheriff—you can't just shoot an animal. Shooting's the easy part. Any city dick can sit in a stand, drink hot coffee and wait till some doe goes prancing by, close enough to touch, and then put out the muzzle of his Wal-Mart rifle and squeeze-jerk the trigger and blow a quart of her guts out and find her three counties away, bled out, her eyes still somehow beaming dumb pain.

You earned your shot, Bob would tell you, by letting whatever was happening to the animal happen to you and for however long. Fair was fair, after all.

Through the pines and the saplings, he could see the clearing 150 yards ahead, a little below, coming gradually into what small, low light there'd be that day. A trail ran through it, and at dawn and again at twilight he knew the animals would filter through, one by one, a buck and his harem. Last night, Bob had seen twelve, three bucks, one a nice fat eight-pointer even, and their ladies.

But he'd come for Tim. Old Tim, scarred and beat up, with many an adventure behind him. Tim would be alone, too: Tim didn't have a harem, and didn't need one anymore. One year Tim had had a prong of antler shot off by some lucky city dick from Little Rock and looked out of balance for a whole season. Tim had limped another whole year because Sam Vincent, not as spry as once he'd been, had held sloppy and put a .45-70 softpoint—too much gun, but Sam loved that old Winchester—into his haunches, and only bled him bad enough to kill any normal buck.

Tim was *tough,* Bob knew, and that was the kindest word he had for anybody, living or dead.

Bob was in his seventeenth hour of sitting. He had sat all night in the cold; and when, about four, sleet had started, he still sat. He was so cold and wet he was hardly alive, and now and again a picture of another time would come up before his eyes but always, he'd shake it out, keeping himself set on what lay ahead 150 yards.

Come on, you old bastard, he was thinking. I'm earning you.

Then he saw something. But it was only a doe and her fawn and in their lazy, confident, stupid animal way they came down the trail from the hill and began to move on down to graze in the lower forest, where some lucky city fool would certainly kill them.

Bob just sat there, next to his tree.

Dr. Dobbler swallowed, trying to read the mystery in Colonel Shreck's eyes. But as always, Shreck sat there with a fierce scowl masking his blunt features, radiating power and impatience and somehow scaring everybody in the room. Shreck was scary. He was the scariest man Dobbler had ever known, scarier even than Russell Isandhlwana, the dope dealer who had raped Dobbler in the showers of Norfolk State Penitentiary in Massachusetts and made the doctor his punk for a very, very long three months.

It was late. Outside the rain drummed on the tin roof of the Quonset. A stench of rusting metal, old leather, dust, unwashed socks and stale beer hung in the room; it was a prison smell, though this wasn't a prison, but the field headquarters of an outfit calling itself RamDyne Security on several hundred obscure acres of untillable central Virginia.

The planners sat in front of the darkened room; the brutish Jack Payne, the second scariest man in the world, sat across the table; and that was all, such a tiny team for the immense and melancholy task that lay ahead of them.

On a small screen, four faces had been projected, now glowing in the dark. Each represented a hundred other possibilities; these men had been discovered by Research, investigated at length by Plans, watched by the pros from Operations, and then winnowed to this sullen quartet. It was Dobbler's job to break them down psychologically for Colonel Raymond Shreck's final decision.

Each of the final four had a flaw, of course. Dr. Dobbler pointed these out. He was, after all, still a psychiatrist, if now uncertified. Flaws were his profession.

"Too narcissistic," he said of one. "He spends too much on his hair. Never trust a man in a seventy-five-dollar haircut. He expects to be treated special. We need somebody who *is* special but has never been *treated* special."

As for Number 2, "Too smart. Brilliant, tactically brilliant. But always playing the games. Always thinking ahead. Never at rest."

Of the third, "Wonderfully stupid. But slow. Exactly what we need so far as certain qualities are required, and experienced in the technical area. Obedient as a dog. But slow. Too slow, too literal, too eager to please. Too rigid."

"I hear you flirting again, Dobbler," said Colonel Shreck, brutally. "Just give us the information, without the charm."

Dobbler winced.

"Well," he finally said, "that leaves us with only one."

Jack Payne hated Dobbler. The softy Dobbler, with his big head, scraggly beard and long sensitive fingers, was everything pussy in the world. He had tits. He was almost a woman. He tried to turn everything into show.

Jack Payne was a dour, nasty-looking little man, tattooed and remote, with blank, tiny eyes in his meaty face. He was enormously strong, with a pain threshold that was off the charts. His specialty was getting things done, no matter what. He touched the cut-down Remington 1100 in its custom under-shoulder rig beneath his left arm. In the long tube under the barrel there were six double-ought 12-gauge shells. In each shell were nine .32 caliber pellets. He could fire fifty-four bullets in less than three seconds. Got lots of stuff done with *that.*

"The details are impressive," Dobbler was saying. "He killed eighty-seven men. That is, eighty-seven men stalked and taken under the most ferocious conditions. I think we'd all have to agree that's impressive."

There was a pause.

"I killed eighty-seven men in an *afternoon,*" Jack said.

Jack had been stuck in a long siege at an A-team camp in the southern highlands, and in the last days the gooks had thrown human wave attacks at them.

"But all at once. With an M-60," said Colonel Shreck. "I was there too. Go ahead, Dobbler."

Dobbler was trembling, Jack could see. He still trembled when the colonel addressed him directly sometimes. Jack almost laughed. He smelled fear on the psychiatrist. He loved the odor of other men's fear.

But Dobbler pressed ahead. "This is none other than Gunnery Sergeant Bob Lee Swagger, USMC, retired, of Blue Eye, Arkansas. They called him 'Bob the Nailer.' He was the United States Marine Corps's second leading individual killer in Vietnam. Gentlemen, I give you the great American sniper."

Bob loved their magic. When he had hunted men, there was no magic. Men were stupid. They farted and yakked and gave themselves away miles before they moved into the killing zone.

But the deer, particularly the old Ouachita stags, appeared like ghosts, simply exploding out of brushy nothingness, as if they were superior visitors from another planet. And they *were* superior, in their way, Bob knew: their senses so razor keen, everything focused on the next two minutes. That was their secret. They didn't think about the last two minutes, which had ceased entirely to exist in the second after they were experienced, had evaporated entirely. They only thought about the next two minutes. No past, no real future. There was only now.

And so when Tim materialized with the force of a sharp memory out of the thin Arkansas pines, stunning Bob with his beauty, he did not quite surprise him.

Bob had learned years back in hard places that surprise was dangerous. It made you jerk awkwardly upon the first moment of encounter, and you gave away your edge.

So Bob's initial reaction to Tim was nothing that his body showed.

He was downwind, so no odors would reach Tim's keen nostrils, though Bob of course had washed yesterday with odorless soap; he'd air-dried his clothes; he'd washed his mouth out with peroxide so no tang of toothpaste could hang in the forest air.

The animal's head twitched and turned, and unerringly turned to Bob.

You can't see me, Bob thought. I know how you operate. You can see motion, you're a smart boy at picking out a flick of motion, scampering off to safety; but you can't see pattern. Here I sit, and you're looking right at me and you can't see me.

Bob let the beast's gaze wash over him, then felt it slide away. This was the part he liked the best, the exciting fragility of it all, the flimsiness of the connections that brought buck and man together through the medium of the rifle, but only for a few seconds, and knowing that in a minute, if the buck held, if the wind held, if his nerve held, if his luck held, he'd have Tim in his cross hairs.

He lifted the rifle.

It was a Remington 700 bolt action, lovingly purchased by the Marine Marksmanship Team and presented to him as a retirement gift when he'd been invalided out of the Corps in 1975. It had a heavy varmint barrel which almost neutralized vibration when he fired, though Bob had since replaced the original barrel with a stainless steel one from Hart, which he'd then finished with Teflon so the whole piece had the appearance of old pewter. The barrel, action and even the screws were bedded in Devcon aluminum into a black fiberglass and Kevlar stock. The screws were torqued through aluminum pilars, tightened to sixty pounds. The rifle was purely ugly. It was a .308 Winchester, and one of Bob's own handloads now rested in the chamber.

Bob slid the rifle up in a smooth and practiced motion, economical from long years of repetition. Under slightly less adverse conditions he would have elected the prone, the stablest shooting position, but since he knew he'd have to be still for so long he had been afraid the contact with the cold ground would chill his body numb. Instead, he drew the rifle up to his shoulder, notching his elbows inside his splayed knees, canting his shoulders, locking his arms under the rifle's ten pounds so that it was supported off bone, not muscle; he was building a bone bridge, running from the piece itself to the ground, anchoring it so that no whimsy of muscle fiber, no throb of heart or twitch of pulse, could deflect him at the last moment.

Bob's eye slid behind the scope, a Leupold 10×. The bold optics of the magnification, snatching every bit of light from the air, threw up Tim's head and shoulders ten times the size of life. Again the animal turned toward him, though this time he was projected against the intersection of the cross hairs.

With a thumb, Bob snicked off the safety and settled in to shoot.

I've earned you, you son of a bitch, he thought. And by God I own your ass. You are mine.

His heart seemed to thump a bit. Now he was trying to slip into that calm pool of near-nothingness where the little patch on the tip of his finger just took over as if on auto-pilot, reading the play of the cross hairs, matching their rhythm, anticipating their direction.

Okay, Bob thought, as he made the minute corrections and the cross hairs settled on Tim's spine as he nimbly licked ice-glazed shoots from a tree, okay *now* I own you.

On the screen, the four faces vanished; and then Bob's young face suddenly appeared.

"He's twenty-six, on his third tour of Vietnam," said Dr. Dobbler. "It's June tenth, 1972. He's just officially killed his thirty-ninth and fortieth men, though unofficially the total is far higher."

The slide showed a raw young face, lean and sullen. The eyes were slits, the skin tight, the mouth a hyphen; there was something somehow Southern in the bone structure. He looked mean, too, and very competent, without a lick of humor, with no patience for outsiders, with a willingness to fight anyone who pushed him too far. A boonie hat was pressed back on his head, revealing a thatch of crewcut. He wore rumpled utilities with globe and anchor inscribed on the pocket, and trapped proudly in the joint of his left arm so that it lay along the length of his forearm and was cupped in his hand at the trigger guard and comb was a black, heavy-barreled rifle with a long telescopic sight.

Dobbler looked at the boy on the screen: it was the same expressionless face you saw on the white-trash tough guys, the human tattoo museums and born-to-kill bikers and assault-with-intent pros who did their time in the joint as easily as a vacation, whereas he himself had nearly died from it. That was the first shock of a cultured man: that in such savagery, some people not only survived but actually thrived.

The doctor continued.

"Please note, it's not Robert Lee Swagger; his father named him Bob Lee—he gets quite angry when people call him Robert. And he likes to be called 'Bob,' not Bob Lee. He's very proud of his father, although he must only vaguely remember him. Earl Swagger won the Congressional Medal of Honor on Iwo Jima in World War Two and was an Arkansas state trooper, killed in the line of duty in 1955, when Bob was nine. The boy's mother returned from Little Rock to the family farm outside Blue Eye, in Polk County, in western Arkansas, where she and her mother and Bob managed a threadbare existence.

"Bob is, in many ways, a child of the embarrassing Second Amendment, and he fits the profile of other great American gun heroes—both Alvin York and Audie Murphy come to mind. He grew up orphaned early, in a border state, on a hardscrabble farm, where his hunting was not only natural and expected but necessary. He quickly became a proficient hunter with a single-shot .22 rifle, and graduated, in his teens, to a lever-action deer gun and finally a Winchester in .30 caliber. He was, from the very first time his father allowed him to shoot, an exceedingly gifted rifleman.

"In 1964, having graduated from high school where he got—this is perhaps not as amazing as it seems—excellent grades, Bob turned down a college scholarship and instead joined the United States Marines, just in time for the Vietnam War.

"He did a tour in 1966 as an infantry lance corporal and was wounded twice; he did one in 1968, during Tet, as a recon patrol leader, doing a lot of dangerous work up near the DMZ. In 1971, at Camp Perry, Ohio, Bob Lee was the national thousand-yard center-fire rifle champion. It got him noticed. He returned to Vietnam in late 1971 to the Scout-Sniper platoon, Headquarters Company, Twenty-sixth Regiment, First Marine Division, operating outside Da Nang."

He clicked a button.

The screen displayed a business card with a neat block of print under the silhouette of a telescopic rifle.

It said,

WE DEAL IN LEAD, FRIEND.
—SCOUT-SNIPER PLATOON,
HEADQUARTERS COMPANY,
FIRST MARINES.

"The line was stolen from Steve McQueen in *The Magnificent Seven*. It was his platoon's calling card, part of the First Marine Psywar operations in its region, left in prominent places in the area where Bob and his men were operating, usually in the left hand of corpses dropped by a single bullet in the chest. Scout-Sniper of the First was the most proficient unit of professional killers this country had ever sponsored, at least on an individual basis. In the six years it operated, it is said to have killed over one thousand seven hundred fifty enemy soldiers. Itself, it only counted forty-six men in its ranks over those years. A sergeant named Carl Hitchcock, with ninety-three confirmed kills, was highest; Bob, five years later, was second, with his eighty-seven; but there were several other snipers in the sixties and more than a dozen in the fifties.

"As for Bob, I'll only sketch the high points. He evidently did a few jobs for the CIA's Operation Phoenix, liquidating hardcore infrastructure people, Vietcong tax collectors and regional chieftains and the like. So he is not unfamiliar with the operations of professional intelligence agencies. But his more common targets were rank-and-file North Vietnamese regulars operating in the area. They even had a huge reward out for Bob, over fifty thousand piasters. But most astonishingly, he and his best friend and spotter, a lance corporal named Donny Fenn, once ambushed a North Vietnamese battalion which was rushing toward an isolated Special Forces camp. The weather was bad, and the jungle was triple canopy, so air support or evacuation was impossible. It was out of range of artillery. A thousand men, heading toward twelve on a hilltop. But Bob and his spotter were the only other friendly forces in the area. They tracked the North Vietnamese, and began taking out officers one at a time over a forty-eight-hour stretch in the An Loc Valley. The battalion never reached the Green Berets, and Swagger and his spotter made it out three days later. He killed over thirty men in that two-day adventure."

Even Payne, who tried never to be impressed, had to suck in some air.

"Cocksucker can shoot a little," he said.

The projector clicked.

A man swaddled in bandages lay in a hospital bed, leg locked in traction, face bleak, eyes hugely hollow.

"Bob Lee Swagger's war came to an end on eleven December 1972. He was sliding over a crest line on his way out when he was hit in the hip by a rifle bullet fired from over a thousand yards. His friend and spotter Donny Fenn slid down the embankment to get him. The next bullet hit Donny in the chest, blew through to his spine. Bob lay out there all morning with his dead friend in his arms, until they could call in artillery on the suspected sniper position. It ended his war and it ended his career in the Marine Corps. He was invalided out of the service in 1975, after three years' painful rehabilitation. It ended his competitive shooting, too. Competitive shooting is an extremely formalized sport, involving positions of great physical discomfort, while wrapped tightly in leather shooting garments for maximum body control. With his hip wired together, Bob was never able to achieve those formal positions with the same degree of intensity.

"You could say, I suppose, that Bob Lee Swagger gave everything to his country, and in return, it took everything from him. His heroism was of a sort that makes many Americans uneasy. He wasn't an inspiring leader, he didn't save lives, he didn't rise in the chain of command. He was simply and explicitly an extraordinary killer. Almost certainly for that reason, he never got the medals and the acclaim he deserved.

"What followed, one can almost predict. He was married, but the marriage fell apart. A career in real estate sales outside Camp Lejeune collapsed, he tried to go back to school but lost interest. He was into and out of alcoholism clinics in the mid to late seventies. In the eighties, he seems to have come to some sort of provisional peace with himself, and with his country, if only by withdrawing. And one can only imagine what the excessive patriotic hubris of the Persian Gulf victory has done to increase his isolation and his bitterness. He lives in a trailer, alone, in the Ouachita Mountains, a few miles outside of Blue Eye, subsisting on his Marine disability pay and what's left of the thirty thousand dollars his pal, an old country lawyer named Sam Vincent, won for him in a lawsuit against *Mercenary* magazine in 1986. Alone, that is, except for his guns, of which he has dozens. And which he shoots every day, as if they are his only friends.

"You can see, of course, his ready fund of resentment, his sense of isolation. All these things make him vulnerable and malleable," said the doctor. "He's the man we've been taught to hate. He's the solitary American gun nut."

Bob knew, as the gun jolted into his shoulder and the sight picture disappeared in a blur of recoil, that the perfect shot he'd been building toward all these hours was his. It was as if the image at the second when the lockwork of the Remington bolt had delivered striker to primer were engraved in his mind and he had fractions of a second to analyze at a speed that has no place in real time; yes, the rifle was held true; yes, the scope, zeroed onto two hundred yards with a group size of less than two inches, was placed exactly where he wanted it; yes, the trigger pull was smooth, unhurried; yes, he was surprised when it broke; yes, his position was solid and no, no last second twitch, no flicker of doubt or lack of self-belief, had betrayed him.

Yes, he'd hit.

The animal, stricken, bucked ferociously in its sudden shroud of red mist. Its great antlered head spasmed back as its front legs collapsed under it and it crashed to the ground.

Without unshouldering, Bob flicked the bolt, tossing a piece of spent brass, ramming home a new .308, and reacquired the target. But he saw immediately that no follow-up was necessary. He snapped the safety on, lowered the rifle and watched Tim thrash, his bull neck beating against the sleet and dust. The animal could not accept that it had been hit or that its legs no longer functioned or that numbness was spreading through it.

Go on, fight it, boy, thought Bob. The more you fight it, the faster it gets you.

At last the man stood. His legs ached and he suddenly noticed how cold it was. He flexed his fingers to make certain they still worked. His hand flew to the ache in his hip, then denied it. He shivered; under the down vest, he was bathed in sweat. Numbly, he went over and retrieved the shell casing he'd just ejected.

After shooting, Bob felt nothing. He felt even more nothing than he did in shooting. He looked at the animal in the undergrowth a hundred-odd yards away. No sense of triumph filled him, no elation.

Yeah, well, I can still shoot a little, he thought. Not so old as I thought.

Creakily, he walked down the hill to the clearing and over to the fallen stag. The sleet pelted him, stinging his face. The whole world seemed gray and wet. He squinted, shivered, drew the parka tighter about himself.

The animal wheezed. Its head still beat against the ground. Its eye was opened desperately and it craned back to see Bob. He thought he could see fear glinting out of that great black eyeball, fear and rage and betrayal, all the huge things that something that's just been shot feels.

The animal's tongue hung from its half-opened mouth as the deeper paralysis overcame all its systems. The buck was a brute all right, and its legs were as scarred as a football player's knees. Bob could see a pucker of dead tissue high on the flank where Sam Vincent's sloppy .45-70 had flashed through years earlier. But the horns, though now slightly asymmetrical, were beautiful. Tim wore an enormous rack, twelve points of staghorn, in a convoluted density of random growth, like a crown of thorns atop the narrow beauty of his head. He was all trophy, maybe a record for the Boone and Crockett book.

His flanks still heaved, showing the struts of his ribs. His living warmth and its musty, dense animal smell rose through the plunging sleet. You could almost warm your fingers off of him. His left back leg kicked ineffectually, as even now he fought it. Bob looked at the bullet strike. He could see the impact just where he'd willed it to be and just where the Remington had sent it to go: a crimson stain above the shoulder, immediately above the spine.

Figure I hit you just about dead perfect, partner, Bob thought.

Tim snorted piteously, thrashing again. It irked Bob that he thrashed and splattered the mud up on his tawny hide, spotting it. The animal could not take its eye off Bob as Bob bent and stroked it.

Bob touched the throat, then pulled out his knife, an old Randall Survivor, murderously sharp.

Be over in a second, partner, he thought, bending toward Tim.

"Wait a minute," said Payne.

Dobbler swallowed. In the dark Payne looked over at him with a pathological glare. Everybody was afraid of Payne except Shreck.

"Colonel, I been around a lot of guys like that in the service, and so have you," he said to Shreck. "Proud to say, I served with them in my twenty-two years in the Special Forces. Now, when it's killing time, there ain't no better boy than your white country Southerner. Those boys can shoot, and they got stones the size of cars. But they got an attitude problem, too. They got this thing about their honor. Cross one of them boys, and they make it their business to even the score, and I ain't shitting you. I've seen it happen in service too fuckin' many times to talk about it."

"Go on, Payne," said the colonel.

"They're true men, and when they get something in their heads, they won't let go of it. I saw enough of it in Vietnam. I'm just telling you, cross this man and I'm guaranfuckingteeing you the worst kind of trouble."

"I think," said the doctor in a loud voice, "that Mr. Payne has made an excellent point. It would not do at all to underestimate Bob Lee Swagger. And he is especially right when he notes Bob's 'honor.' But surely you can also see that it's his honor that makes him so potentially valuable to us. He is in fact quite a bit like the precision rifle with which he earned his nickname—extremely dangerous if used sloppily, yet absolutely perfect if used well. He, after all, knows more about what we are interested in than nearly any man alive. He is simply the best sniper in the Western world."

He shot a glance at the silent figure of Shreck, and received in reply only more stony silence.

"But there is a problem. Bob the Nailer, as perfect as he seems, does present one terrible, terrible problem. He has a deep flaw."

Bob leaned over Tim, gripping the Randall in his left hand.

Tim snorted one more time.

Bob spun the gnarled haft of the weapon in his hand, bringing the serrated upper teeth to bear. With the saw blade, he hacked at the base of the left antler, not in the veiny, velvety knob but an inch or two higher, where the horn was stone dead. In a second the teeth cut into and through the horn and Bob yanked as a half of the heavy crown fell into his hand. He tossed it away into the undergrowth, bent, and just as forcefully sawed the second antler off.

Then he backed off to avoid getting trampled.

The beast lurched halfway to its feet.

Bob gave it a hard swat on the rump.

"Go on, boy. Git! Git! Git outta here, you old sonovabitch!"

Tim bucked up, snorted once, shook his unchained head with a shiver of the purest delight and, his nostrils spurting a double plume of rancid, smoky breath, he seemed to gather even more strength and bounded off crazily, bending aside saplings and flinging shards of ice as he plunged into the forest.

In a second he was gone.

I own you, you sonovabitch, Bob thought, watching as the stag disappeared.

He turned and started the long trek home.

"His flaw," said the doctor, "is that he will not kill anymore. He still hunts. He goes to great lengths and puts himself through extraordinary ordeals to fire at trophy animals. But he hits them with his own extremely light bullets machined of Delrin plastic at a hundred yards' range. If he hits the creatures right and he always does—he aims for the shoulder above the spine—he can literally stun them off their feet for five or six minutes. There's a small compartment of red aluminum dust for weight in each bullet, and as the bullet smashes against the flank of the beast, it smears the animal with a red stain, which the rain quickly washes off. Extraordinary. Then he saws their antlers off. So that no hunter will shoot them for a trophy. He hates trophy hunting. After all, he's *been* a trophy."

Colonel Shreck spoke.

"All right, then. It's Swagger. But we'll have to find a trophy this asshole will hunt," he said.

CHAPTER TWO

It was funny how a rifle will sometimes go sour on you. Bob's fine old pre-'64 Winchester Model 70 in .270 had been a minute-of-angle gun for five years, shooting within an inch at a hundred yards, or two at two hundred or three at three, holding ever true to that abstraction of rifle accuracy. But it had suddenly opened up. On today's target, the bullet punctures formed a raggedy constellation over three times an inch.

Yet, baffled as he was, a certain part of Bob was tickled. It was so damned *interesting.* It was one more thing to find out about, another trip deep into the maze that kept him, or so he believed, sane.

Take this damn 70. He could spend a week on it. He'd take it apart, down to its finest screw and spring, and go over each tiny bit of it, looking for burrs in the metal, for pieces of grit in the works, for signs of wear or fatigue. He'd steam clean the trigger mechanism. With his fingers, he'd probe every square centimeter of the stock, feeling for knots, splinters, warps, anything that could lay just the softest finger of pressure against the barrel to nudge the rifle out of true.

And when that was done, if it didn't shoot right, he'd just do it again.

His tiny shop was out back of the trailer, a shed of corrugated tin, dark and oily. Off to one side stood a reloading bench, with a single-stage Rock Chucker for his rifle loads and a Dillon for his .45's, and stacked along the wall, neatly and fastidiously, were his many dies. The back wall had filing cabinets for his notebooks and his targets, and bins for used brass that he'd yet to reload. The smell of Shooter's Choice bore solvent hung in the air like a vapor. A single light illuminated the darkness, and if he wasn't shooting or sleeping he was reading *Guns & Ammo* or *Shooting Times* or *The American Rifleman* or *Accuracy Shooting* or *The Shotgun News* or *Rifle.*

But on this afternoon as he contemplated the delinquent Model 70, he heard his dog Mike barking. Mike, a furious old half-beagle with a mangy coat and yellow eyes, prowled the fence Bob had built around his trailer; in exchange for table scraps and a daily romp through the hills, he'd chase any human thing away, except for the two or three that Bob allowed to call on him. But this day, Mike just kept howling for the longest damn time, and Bob knew that whoever had come by wasn't about to leave.

He slipped a cocked and locked Series '70 Colt .45 out of a drawer and slid it into the back pocket of his jeans, then threw on a jacket and his Razorback baseball hat and stepped out. The sun was a thin wash. Around him, the blue Ouachitas rose bleakly, bled dry of color by the coming of cold weather, and Bob turned the corner to see two men lounging next to what had to be a rented car just beyond the gate, while Mike yowled at them as if he'd kill them if they came closer.

They wore raincoats over suits. But they were soldiers of a sort. Maybe not now, but they'd been soldiers, that was clear. They were carved from the same tough tree, one square and blocky, Bob's own age, but a head and a half lower to the ground, with huge hands and a weight lifter's body; he had a sheen of crewcut hair, and every square inch of him said NCO.

The other was the officer: taller, but husky too, well-proportioned, with a square face and short but not crew-cut hair. He had the look of at least nine of Bob's eleven battalion commanders down through the years, men Bob didn't love but respected, because they put mission first and last and always accomplished it.

"Go on, shuddup," Bob said to Mike, giving him a kick. The dog slunk off to the door. But Bob didn't open his locked fence. He put his hand under his jacket and set it on the haft of the .45, because it's always better to have your gun in your hand than in your pants if it comes to kick-ass time.

"Y'all want something?" he said, squinting up his face.

"You're Mr. Bob Lee Swagger?" said the officer.

"I am, sir." Bob spit a glob of phlegm into the dust.

"You're a hard man to get ahold of, Mr. Swagger. We've sent you five registered letters. You won't even sign for them and open them. You don't have a telephone."

Bob recalled the damn letters. He'd thought they were from Susan, his ex-wife, wanting more money. Or from one of those nutty war groups that wanted to pay him just to come stand around at some motel and tell stories.

"This is private property," he said. "You're not welcome here. You go on back to where you came from and let me be."

"Mr. Swagger," said the officer, "we're here with a business proposition that could mean a lot of money to you."

"I don't need any money," Bob said. "I have plenty of money."

"I was hoping you'd do me the favor of listening to me, that's all. Take five minutes of your time, and then if you're not interested in what I have to say, and what I'm proposing, I'm out of here."

The smaller of the two men had not said anything. He was just eyeing Bob and he stunk of aggression. His big hands were in his pockets and Bob didn't like the way there was a suggestion of bulk under the right arm of his raincoat.

Bob turned back to the officer.

"Why should I do you any sort of favor, sir? I don't even know you."

"Possibly this will establish my bona fides."

With that the older man slipped a jewelry case out of his pocket, and flipped it over the fence. It landed at Bob's feet in the mud.

"It's authentic," said the man. "I won it, all right. In 1966, near Dak To, just off Highway One. I was a major in the Twenty-fourth Mech Infantry. A very busy day."

Bob picked the case up, and popped the lid to discover a Congressional Medal of Honor.

He swallowed just a bit. His own daddy had won one on the Iwo and at least a dozen officers had told him he'd earned one when he and Donny Fenn dusted that main forces battalion in the An Loc, but that it was a shame he'd never get it, as the politics of the moment were such that a sniper couldn't get the big medal. It didn't bother Bob. He'd never wanted a medal. He just didn't like the idea that the killing he'd done was somehow wrong and couldn't be recognized.

"All right," said Bob, trying to put that shame out of his mind. "Out of respect for what you did for your country, I'll hear your piece. Just keep it short."

He unlocked the gate.

Inside the trailer, the two men took off their coats to reveal business suits. It now looked as if the smaller man had some sort of sawed-off pump gun under his arm; but he just sat back, a dullness coming over his face. Bob thought of him as some sort of attack hound; when Bob hadn't been sure whether or not he'd let them in, he was all tense and full of fury, ready to strike. Now that they were inside, the little guy went limp.

The other man, however, did not. Leaning across the small table in the neat little living room of the trailer, he stared, his bright, dark eyes boring into Bob.

"Here, Mr. Swagger. This will help."

He pushed a business card across at Bob, who read:

COLONEL WILLIAM A. BRUCE U.S.A. (RET.)
PRESIDENT–CHIEF OPERATING OFFICER
ACCUTECH INDUSTRIES, INC.

It gave an address somewhere in Maryland, and in smaller type it listed the firm's specialties:

LAW ENFORCEMENT TECHNOLOGY
LAW ENFORCEMENT AMMUNITION
TRAINING SEMINARS AND FIREARMS
CONSULTATION

"Okay," said Bob, "so, Colonel, what's on your mind?"

"Mr. Swagger, after I retired in 1975, I spent the next sixteen years as the supervisor of the Arizona State Police. I retired from that post last year, and now I've started this little business, which means to bring progressive equipment and philosophy to American law enforcement."

"Is that why your boy is wearing a pump gun under his arm?"

The expression on the smaller one's face didn't change; but at the word *boy* his face seemed to lose just a shred of color, as if the man inside were baking in an oven.

"My associate is also my bodyguard, Mr. Swagger. Like anybody who's spent a career in law enforcement, I have some enemies. Mr. Payne is duly licensed by the state of Maryland to carry concealed and he's been authorized by the state of Arkansas to the same courtesy."

"Yes, sir."

"At any rate, this is why I'm here—the newest addition to my product line."

He pushed a yellow box the size of two cigarette packs across the table at Bob.

ACCUTECH SNIPER GRADE, it said in bright red letters.

Under that it said, Law Enforcement Use Only.

Bob saw that it was .308, 150-grain hollowtip. He cracked the box, slid the ammo out to discover it displayed headstamp up in a Styrofoam tray. Twenty perfect double circles peeped up at him, rim-edge and primer, looking like eggs or eyes. He plucked a cartridge from the tray, heavy brass, gleaming brightly, the copper-sheathed cone climaxing in the precise circle of the crater at the tip. It looked like any other .308 except for the bright band of glossier brass at the neck of the cartridge.

"None of the big American ammo companies can touch this stuff," said the colonel. "Not even the expensive grade lines, the Winchester Supreme, the Federal Premium, the Remington Extended Range. I guarantee Minute of Angle in a proper rifle."

"Neck turned," Bob said, his finger touching the bright band. "How can you mass-produce a neck-turned round? That's a handloader's job. I don't see how it can be done."

"Lasers."

"Hmm," said Bob. "Okay, I know some outfits these days use lasers as sighting devices. But y'all use them in the loading?"

"That's right," said the colonel, leaning forward. "Industrial lasers are the coming thing in precision manufacturing. Now, they're used in the manufacture of electronic components, missile guidance systems, high-tech materials. My brainstorm was to try them on ammunition. They can be coded into a computerized program so that you get extraordinary repeatability. You know what the secret of a quality round is. Precision. So all the things that a handloader can do on a very small scale, we can do on a larger scale with brilliant perfection: we buy our brass from Remington in hundred-thousand case quantities; our lasers score the neck of the case both inside and out so that it has the exact diameter all the way around and each case has the exact diameter of every other case. Exactly. Precisely. Then, we can deburr the flash hole, and seat each primer the identical depth. We can manage it with laser-guided machining. In other words, we can code the machines to follow laser tracks as specified by a computer program. We can get the kind of careful quality thousands of rounds by thousands of rounds that you can get round by round on your Lee or RCBS or Wilson or whatever dies it is you use."

Bob looked down at the round in his hand.

"I've gotten some pretty damned fine .308 groups over the years."

"But you've had to *work* to get them, is that right?" said the colonel.

"Yes sir, that's right."

"That's it, in a box. It's a natural for the police market, which is considerable. Later, maybe we'll expand to the civilian if we can establish a law enforcement reputation."

"So what is it you want from me?"

"Mr. Swagger, I'm looking for a professional shooter to fly around the country and put on shooting demonstrations for police departments that are upgrading their SWAT capabilities. But I need a man with a reputation. A man who's been in hard places, kept his head, and come back alive."

"Why don't you get Carl Hitchcock? He's famous. They wrote a damn book about him and made up a poster. He's number one."

"Carl is making too much money on the personal appearance circuit. They pay him two thousand dollars just to appear at a gun show for one day, did you know that?"

"Carl always was a lucky boy."

"We have a facility in Garrett County, Maryland, where we're doing our testing. What we'd like to do is fly you up there for a weekend at our expense, of course. You bring your favorite rifle, your favorite handloads. Okay? Then you can go out on the range with some of our shooters and engineers, fire our rounds and your rounds side by side. We think if you do that, you'll see how our rounds group consistently with your own. That's all we ask. Your forbearance. Give us a chance to let you believe. If you believe, all else will follow."

Bob had no real need or urge to leave his mountain. The fact was, except for getting his hair cut, picking up magazines and his government check at the post office once a month and a chat or two with old Sam Vincent and now and then having a routine checkup on his health or his teeth, he hadn't been down in five years.

"It would be a great job," said the colonel. "I'd fly you around the country and you'd be with men who'd respect you. You know, the world has changed since Vietnam. They say the Vietnam syndrome is dead. We had a war that we won, big time, and now everybody who was in the military can be a hero again. You'd get exactly what you didn't get the first time. You'd get respect and love and appreciation."

Bob made a sour look. He'd believe it when he saw it. But he knew he couldn't stay up here forever. He looked at the rifle cartridge. He was curious. Goddamned thing looked like it would shoot the tits off a mother flea, but there was only proof in the shooting, not in the looking. But he heard it singing to him in a strange way. Poked. He was poked in the head. Hadn't been poked in the head since he'd given up the drinking.

"When?"

"When's convenient?"

"Can't leave now. Got a rifle gone barn sour on me. Say, next weekend?"

"Well, all right. Whatever. You have a credit card?"

"Yes, I do."

"You go ahead and charge your tickets. Keep all the receipts and we'll expense it out. Or, you could sign a contract now and we could write you an advance check and—"

"No thanks on the contract."

"I didn't think so. And do you want to be picked up at the Baltimore airport or rent your own car?"

"I'd take the car, thank you."

"It's done."

"Then that's all there is to it," said Bob. "Now I have to feed my damn dog."

CHAPTER THREE

Bob made his inquiries discreetly. From Bill Dodge's Exxon station on Route 270, he called an old NCO buddy who was a master sergeant going for his thirty, now working Personnel in the Pentagon, and put certain questions before him. The next day, the friend replied with a telegram.

DEAR COOT, it said, YOUR PAL COL. BRUCE IS THE REAL MCCOY. HE LED AN APC ATTACK ON A BUNKER POSITION, WAS HIT TWICE, AND PULLED HIS MEN OUT OF THE BURNING THING HIMSELF. THEY SAY HE DID BECOME A COP IN ARIZONA. SEMPER FI, BUD.

That learned, Bob stopped in at Sara Vincent's travel agency—Sara was Sam Vincent's divorced daughter, and a woman so plain she'd even scare Mike—and bought his tickets, made arrangements with Sam to check his property once or twice a day, and feed the dog, and tried to get himself ready for the world again.

He was all right, too, until the last night. He knew he had to get up early for the drive to Little Rock and just when he'd thought he had everything checked out and was ready for the sack, it came over him. That's the way it came: fast, without preparation, without announcement. It just came and there it was.

It was a bad one. He hadn't had it so bad since the president declared the little war in the desert a victory, and America went on a bender and everybody was happy except himself and maybe another million boys who wondered why nobody put up ribbons for them twenty years ago, when it might have mattered.

Now you hold it on down, he told himself, aching for a glass of smooth brown whiskey to flatten himself out, knowing that if he had one many more would follow.

But there was no whiskey, nothing to blunt what happened in his mind. The memories hit him hard. He remembered the VC he shot who turned out to be an eight-year-old boy with a hoe—it had looked like an AK through the 9× at eight hundred meters in the bad light of sunset. He remembered the smell of burned villages after the Search and Destroys, and the crying of the women and the way the goddamned kids just looked at you during his first tour. He remembered the bellytime, moving through the high grass, avoiding the crest lines, as the ants crawled over you and the snakes slithered by and you just lay there, waiting, for days sometimes, until someone passed into the kill zone eight hundred meters out and you could put them down. He remembered the way they fell when hit, instant rag doll, the toppling surrender, the small cloud of dust it raised. So many of them. The "confirmed" kills were only the ones with a spotter there, to write it in the log and make a report.

But mostly he remembered the sudden shock as his hip went numb and he collapsed and slid down the earthen dam of the perimeter. He looked down and saw the smashed flesh, the pulsing red. Remembering, he put his hand on the wound, and it throbbed some. Then he remembered Donny scrambling down.

"No!" he yelled, "get your young ass back," and the bullet came from so long away it arrived a full second before its own sound. It drilled Donny in the chest and tunneled to his spine. He was dead before he collapsed against Bob and lay across him that long morning.

"Hell of a shot, Bob," the major said later. "We made it over a thousand yards. Who knew they could shoot that good? Who knew they had a man that good?"

You could never forget stuff like that, not really. But he learned somehow not to let it rag him most of the time; he could ride it out in the mountains or in the solitude.

Bob sat at what had passed for a kitchen table. His rebuilt hip ached a bit, all that plastic instead of cartilage. He could feel what he called his own personal night passing over him. Of course the time of day had nothing to do with it. What he called his own personal night was about the feeling of being nothing, of having no worth, of having spent himself in a war nobody cared about, and having given up everything that was important and good. In other days, this was what got Bob off on his drinking, and drunk, he turned mean as shit.

But now he didn't drink, and instead he threw on a coat and went out into the harsh Arkansas night and walked the mile or so downhill. Inside Aurora Baptist, some kind of service was going on. He heard the black people singing something loud and crazy. What are they so goddamned happy for inside that shaky little white clapboard building anyhow?

Out beyond the church was the little graveyard, and

there among the Washingtons and the Lincolns and the Delanos of Polk County was one spindly marker for a man named Bo Stark. Bob just looked at it. The wind howled and roared through the trees, the moon was a raggedy-assed streetlamp, the music pumped and blasted, the black people were singing up a storm, beating the devil down.

Bo Stark was his own age, and the only white man in the cemetery because no other cemetery would have him. He'd come from a fine family and had known Bob all through high school. They'd gone to the same doctor, the same dentist, played on the same football team. But Bo's people had money; he'd gone on to the university in Fayetteville and from there had joined the Army and spent a year as a lieutenant in the 101st Airborne, another fool for duty who'd believed in it all. And after that, nothing. Bo Stark had gone a man and come home a no-account. The war got inside him and never let him go. One bad thing turned to another; couldn't hold a job, wouldn't pay back loans, was searching for the death he'd only just missed in the Land of Bad Things. Two weeks after the war in the desert was over, after the mighty victory and the celebration, one Sunday night he'd finally killed a man in a bar with a knife in Little Rock and when the police found him in his daddy's garage in Blue Eye, he'd blown a .45 through the roof of his mouth.

So Bob stood there as the wind brought cold memories from the cold ground out at him, and looked at the marker: BO STARK, it said, 1946–1991. AIRBORNE ALL THE WAY.

He came here when he was frightened, because in the radiance of the glowing church, standing over the body of the man who could have been and was almost him, he could see it in the stone: BOB LEE SWAGGER, 1946–1992 USMC SEMPER FIDELIS.

Now he looked at it, and realized it was time to do that which could kill him fastest of all possible dangers: to go back. He wondered if he had the Pure-D stones for it.

He still thought of it as The World. It was the place where all things were, where women and liquor and pleasure and temptation commingled. Now he was back in it. He landed at Baltimore–Washington International Airport after a crazed flight that took him to St. Louis from Little Rock, then east. He was worried that his rifle, with the bright orange airline tag on the handle of the gun case, hadn't made the trip; you always worried that some person in the airlines system would see the thing and snap it up.

But sure enough, the case came out of the luggage chute and moved along to him on the rubber belt so that he could pluck it up.

"Damn," someone said, "hunting season's long over, pardner." It was early January, though surprisingly mild.

"Just a target rifle," Bob said easily to the man, scooping up the case. He felt a little silly with the long, hard thing, so weirdly shaped among all the other luggage, and knowing that he himself looked so cowboylike to these Eastern people, in his best black Tony Lamas, a nice pair of Levi's, a pointed-collar shirt with string tie and a black Stetson, all under a sheepskin coat, his best coat.

Getting the car turned out to be no problem at all as the reservation in his name was waiting and the girl at the counter was especially ingratiating. She thought he was some kind of cowboy hero; her eyes lit with joy at what he took to be his incredibleness and when he called her "ma'am," she was doubly pleased.

He left the airport, found his way to the Baltimore–Washington Parkway, from there to the Baltimore

Beltway, and then west out I-70, across Maryland. Even in the yellowed state of high, dead winter, he could see that it was a lovely place, rolling, not so savage as Arkansas. Soon he came to mountains, old, humped things, ridge after ridge of them. In three hours, beyond Cumberland, he found himself in Maryland's wildest pastures in its farthest, westernmost regions, not wild like the Ouachitas but nevertheless free of the poison taint of the city and just barely tame enough to accommodate the most provisional sort of farming. It looked to be fine deer country, way out in Garrett County. He was searching for a town called Accident, and halfway between it and nowhere, just where they'd said it would be, he found the small Ramada Inn nestled under the mountains. He checked in, his reservations all made and an envelope waiting for him with a hearty welcoming letter and detailed instructions on how to reach the headquarters of Accutech at its shooting facility a few miles down the road. There was also his per diem, ten crisp twenty-dollar bills.

Bob went to his room and lay down on the bed and didn't go out anymore that night. He just thought it all out, trying not to be bothered that he had been followed his whole long trip out from the airport by a very good surveillance team.

Like everything associated with RamDyne, the trailer was small and seedy and cheap. The outfit never did anything first-class and seemed only to have cretins of the prison guard mentality working for it, like the horrid Jack Payne. And now it was jammed with men Dobbler was supposedly briefing.

The doctor sighed, looking at the dull faces in his audience.

"Er, could I have your attention please?"

He couldn't. They paid him no attention at all. He was irrelevant to them.

How far he'd fallen and how fast! Once the youngest member of the Harvard Medical School psychiatric faculty and the sole proprietor of one of the most flourishing private practices in the Cambridge–Greater Boston area, he'd had the life he'd dreamed of and worked for so furiously. One day, however, when he was tired and his resources nearly depleted, on a last appointment, he'd let his discipline slip. He'd touched a woman. Why had he done it? He didn't know. In the nanosecond before he did it, it hadn't even been in his mind. But he did it. He'd touched her and when she looked at him he realized that she wanted him to touch her more, the sexual savagery that spilled out stunned him. He made love to her right there in the office. It was the start of his out-of-control phase, abetted by a severe amphetamine habit. He seduced nine patients. Inevitably one had gone to the police; the charge was rape. The squalor played itself out over six melancholy months, climaxing in his acceptance of a plea-bargained second-degree assault conviction, which delivered him, courtesy of a feminist judge, to the ungentle ministrations of Russell Isandhlwana. The symmetry was perfect, even awesome—justice at its finest: Dobbler had fucked nine neurotic women in his office; in prison he was fucked by an immense man, who called him his dickhole.

And now, he was Raymond Shreck's dickhole. Not sexually, of course, but even Dobbler found a certain black humor in the irony: he'd gone from the ignominy of the prison to somehow secure a position in subservience to a man with the same (though somewhat modulated) sense of physical power and ruthlessness as Russell Isandhlwana, a man whom, like Russell, he totally feared but whom he needed for protection and strength.

"Earth to Planet, Doctor!" It was the horrid Payne.

"What?"

"Hey, get with the program. You lost it there, man."

Ah! He'd lost his place again, wasn't sure what question he was answering. It was the last briefing before the subject showed up.

Oh, yes, he was holding forth on Bob's unique capacity for utter near-death stillness, explaining to Payne's perplexed listeners why it was that Bob, though in his room from five-thirty P.M. on the previous evening, had simply ceased to exist for their listening devices. He was trying to get them to see how *important* this was, for it got to the very nature of Swagger's uniqueness.

"Ah—yes, he has an ability to shut down and let the world go about its business while he's frozen; and then when he's become a part of the environment, then and only then, will he strike. But like any skill, it's a skill that simply has to be practiced. He was practicing nothingness."

Somebody yawned.

Somebody farted.

Somebody laughed.

"All right," said Shreck, vigorously, climbing up front and by sheer body heat exiling the doctor to the wings. "Thanks, Dobbler. Now, listen up, I want eyes front, Payne, get your people to pay some attention for once. It's very close to the most sensitive part of this operation, the next thirty-six to forty-eight hours."

Shreck's dark eyes seemed to beam with strange force.

"Let me tell you who you're dealing with, so there's no misunderstanding. This guy is mule-proud Southern, as stubborn as they come. He doesn't want to be pushed and he won't stand to be insulted. He's also still got some gung-ho Marine in him. He'll be a fucking ramrod; you try and bend him and he may kick your ass. So the way we play him is slow and steady. You don't push; you don't order. You just smile and go along. Any questions?"

Shreck's sudden dramatic appearance had its desired effect: it silenced the troops.

They were fools.

"Sir?"

Someone had leaned in.

"Yeah," said Shreck.

"Sir, it's 0730 hours. Surveillance called; subject just left the motel. He's on his way."

"Okay," said Shreck, "I hope you were listening to the doctor, because if anybody screws up I'll have his ass. Now let's get cracking, people. First day on a new job."

If nothing else, it had a comforting feeling. It was, after all, a rifle range, one of those peeling, flaking, sagging, yet grand places where men have always gathered to plunk themselves down before a piece of paper with a black circle imprinted on it and discover the secrets of their own rifles and their own selves. Bob had spent a lifetime, it sometimes seemed, in such a place, and always the talk was good and the feeling among the shooters easy and generous.

He stood on a concrete apron, before a series of T-shaped shooting benches, green, always green, on every shooting range in America they were green. Bob could see the place had been built sometime in the thirties, the private preserve of some hunting and shooting club or other, and he knew that under the sagging roof that shielded the apron and the benches there'd been many tales told of deer that had gotten away and of loads good and loads bad, and rifles worth as much as a good woman and rifles worth as little as a dog with the clap.

The only unusual thing about this place, a mile or so off the main road by a series of convoluted gravel tracks, was a trailer off to one side, which while not new looked as if it had just been dumped there. Before it stood the sign of the sponsors of this day's labors, Accutech.

He could see the targets across the faintly sloping yellow meadow beyond the line of benches, a black dot at a hundred yards, a black period at two hundred and a black pinprick at three hundred.

"Coffee, Mr. Swagger?" asked the colonel, still in his raincoat. Next to him was the morose little noncom who always looked ready for a fight. Everybody else was a gofer, except one pear-shaped city boy with a goatee who looked like he had a finger up his ass.

"No thanks," he said. "It jitters the nerves."

"Decaf?"

"Decaf's fine," he said, and Colonel Shreck nodded to a man who quickly poured Bob a paper cupful from a thermos.

It was surprisingly temperate, around sixty, and a gentle breeze pressed over the range; above a pale-lemon sun stood in a pale-lemon sky. It was the false spring, a phony of a day, too sweet to be trusted this month.

"All set, then?" asked the colonel.

"I suppose," Bob said.

"Do you want to recheck your zero before we start the testing rounds?"

"Yes sir."

"All right, gentlemen, let's move away. Eyes and ears on."

Bob uncased his rifle, lodged it on a sandbag rampart and slid the bolt back. He cracked open a box of the Lake City Match rounds, threaded five, one after the other with a brass clicking, into the magazine, pushed home and locked the bolt which flew forward and rotated shut with the gliding ease of a vault door closing on ball bearings and grease. He pulled his Ray-Ban aviators on, hooking them behind the ears, and slid his earmuffs down across the top of his head, clamping his ears off from the world. He felt the roar of blood rushing in his brain.

Bob slid up to the rifle and found his bench shooter's position, his boots flat upon the cement apron of the range as if making the magic construction of stability up through his body that would translate to the rock-hard hold of the rifle itself.

He pulled the rifle up, and in, chunking it against his shoulder, placing his hand upon the comb tuned so just the faintest smudge of fingertip caressed the lightened trigger, adjusting a bunny-ear bag underneath the butt-heel. His other arm ran flat along the shooting bench, under the rifle which itself had been sunk just right into the sandbags.

Bob found his spot-weld, and closed his left eye. The image was a bit out of focus, so he diddled with the ring to bring it back to clarity and for his effort was rewarded with the black image of perfect circumference, quartered precisely by the stadia of the scope, ten times the size it had been, now as big as a half-dollar at point-blank range.

He exhaled half a breath, held what he had, and with that wished the end of his finger to contract but a bit and was rewarded with the thrill of recoil, the blur as the rifle ticked off a round. As he was throwing the bolt, he heard a spotter.

"X-ring. Damn, right in the middle, perfect, a perfect shot."

Bob fired four more times into the same hole.

"I guess I'm zeroed," he said.

A man called Hatcher briefed him on the test.

"Mr. Swagger, one of my associates will load your rifle with five rounds. You'll not know if you're shooting your own handloads, the Federal Premium, the Lake City Match or our own Accutech Sniper Grade ammunition. You'll fire four groups of five rounds each at a hundred yards, four at two hundred yards and four at three hundred yards. Then we'll compute the groupings and see how the ammunition stacks up. Then, this afternoon, we'd like to run a similar series of tests, but from offhand or improvised positions, with a stress factor added in. I think you'll find it quite interesting."

"You're paying the bills. Let's get shooting," Bob said.

Bob shot with extraordinary concentration. What separated him from other shooters was his utter consistency, his sameness. He was a human Ransom rest, like the mechanical gizmo they use to test pistols, coming each time to the same strained yet perfectly built position, cement to bone to wood, bone to rifle, fingertip to trigger. Each time, the same: his cheek just so against the fiberglass of the stock, the same pull of rifle into shoulder, the same cant to his hand on the grip, the same angle and looseness of his off-hand, the same distance between eye and scope, the same half-breath held, the same three heartbeats in suspended animation, the same infinitesimal backwards slide of trigger as the slack came out, the same crispness like a grass rod snapping as the trigger broke, the same soundless detonation and blur as the rifle shivered under the ignition of its round.

"X-ring, little high, maybe a third of an inch high at two o'clock."

"X-ring, within an inch."

"X-ring, inside an inch."

There were no flyers, no glitches, no mistakes. Bob

found the groove and stayed there, throughout the long morning, hardly moving or breathing or wasting a second or a motion. It pleased him queerly that the rifle was taken from him empty, then brought back loaded, that regularly someone ran to record and change the targets.

He lost count. It was like the 'Nam. You just shot and watched the bullet go where you sent it, with the tiniest of deviations. It became almost abstract, completely impersonal; you didn't brood on it, merely broke it down into small rituals, small repetitions. And on and on the score mounted, so that nobody could stay with him and he got closer and closer to Carl Hitchcock's legendary figure of ninety-three.

"X-ring."

"X-ring."

"X-ring."

When he was done, had shot all four five-shot strings at all three ranges, he put the rifle down, while technicians ran out to secure the targets and calculate the group sizes.

Of course Bob had made the loads early on, by the slight difference in the kicks. He knew his own rounds right off, and was just a bit slower in marking the difference between the Federal and the Lake City loads, but in time he could tell; that left by process of elimination only the Accutech Sniper Grade ammunition. It shot a mite high, he felt, and he had the impression of the shots clustering just over the X-ring, carrying a bit. Lots of ooomph though, a hot round, very consistent.

"Mr. Swagger, would you like to see your results?" asked Hatcher.

"Yes, I would," said Bob.

He went over to a bench where the results were being tabulated, by two men with a set of dial calipers.

"Okay," said Hatcher, "I think you'll be pleased. I've

marked each target according to the distance and the ammunition you fired. At a hundred yards, you fired Federal Premium, Accutech, Lake City Match M852's and your own handload, in that order. Here are the targets."

Bob looked at the mutilated X-rings, the small spatters of perforations dead center where the bullet holes had cloverleafed.

"The group size, as we make it, is as follows. Federal, .832 inches, Accutech .344 inches, Lake City Match .709 inches and your handload .321 inches."

Bob examined them; yes, the Accutech stuff was about as good as his own handloads, and quite a bit better than the two best factory loadings. He nodded.

"Let's see how she holds out a bit," he said.

"Okay, at two hundred you drop the four and a half inches the ballistics table says you'll drop but you'll see the group sizes remain under a minute of angle, though the Federal begins to push it."

Again, Bob saw the neat clusters of punctures; this time, however, cloverleafs were rarer, almost a function of coincidence. Each group was between one and a half and two inches in diameter, and each about two inches off the X-ring, as the bullet had dropped. The Federal, surprisingly, yielded the sloppiest grouping with the holes spread out at almost two inches exactly; again, Bob's handloads held truest, at .967 inches, center of outer hole to center of outer hole, less than half a minute of angle, but the Accutech lot was pressing him closely, with a .981-inch rating, also less than half a minute of angle, and Bob felt he might have done better because he sensed his own round immediately and relaxed, having the confidence in its ability to perform.

"And now, our *pièce de résistance*," said Hatcher. "Mike, the three-hundred-yard targets, please. Mr. Swagger, I think you're going to see why we call our ammunition 'Sniper Grade.' You, above all others, should grasp the significance."

He handed the four targets out.

When Bob was impressed, that respect took the form of a low, involuntary whistle. He whistled.

At three hundred yards, cloverleafs were a thing of fantasy. At three hundred yards, the groups fell between nine and eleven inches from the X-ring, at six o'clock, outside of the black. The groups opened up and the Federal revealed its fraudulence: it had exploded beyond minute of angle to a full 4.5 inches.

Bob shook his head with an evil snort, deeply disappointed. The group looked like the random pokings of a child.

The Lake City did a bit better, but not much; it was just at the minute of angle limit, the group playing across three inches, though in truth one of them might have been a flyer, because if you subtracted it the group fell to 2.5 inches.

And Bob saw that the Accutech stuff had beaten him. His own group still had the illusion of a circle, the punctures clustered within 1.386 inches; he was sub-minute of angle still, but the damned Accutech was 1.212 inches, with one three-shot triangle within .352 inches!

"Damn," he said.

"That's shooting," someone said. "That's *fine* shooting. Most men can't see at three hundred yards, even with a 24×."

"No," said Bob, awed. "That's ammo. That's *fine* ammo."

It *was* fine ammo. Only fifty to sixty men in the world could handload ammo that fine, Frank Barnes maybe, a couple of the sublime technicians at Speer or Hornady or Sierra, a few wildcatters of a dying breed, old gnarled men who'd lived with guns in machine shops their whole lives. A few world-class benchrest shooters who agged in the 1's. A few Delta or FBI SWAT armorers. Whoever put this stuff together knew what he was doing. Bob had an image in his head of some old man who'd done it a million times, working the brass down to the finest, smallest perfection. It took more than patience; it took a kind of genius. He felt him. He felt him on the range: the presence of an old shooter who knew what he was doing.

Bob knew then. He'd suspected before but now he knew. They were playing him, guiding him; they weren't what they said. Then who were they?

Bob smiled.

"Now what, colonel?"

"Well, let's eat; then, this afternoon, we'd like to take you to another range, where you'll be gunning for targets at even farther ranges . . . beyond five hundred yards. Out as far as a thousand."

"Sounds good to me," said Bob.

"Then, tomorrow morning, Mr. Swagger, I'm going to give you some *real* fun!"

That night, Bob turned down an invitation from the Accutech crew for a nice feed at a restaurant in Thayersville, and instead took his rented car and simply drove alone until he found an unpretentious place farther out, away from the built-up areas, a country place where he could sit by himself and not be paid any mind.

They didn't follow him. They now kept their distance, thinking sure they had him.

And maybe they did. He was damned curious where all this was headed. He knew in a general sense, of course, what it had to be. It had to be about killing.

His reputation had preceded him. People in certain zones knew of him. Occasionally something weird would come his way—a nibble, a veiled hint, just the slightest indication that some really nice money could be his if he'd only meet so-and-so in St. Louis or Memphis or Texarkana and listen to a certain proposal. These offers came from strange sources, over the years. Certainly, some were from what he took to be organized crime interests. Others came from what had to be intelligence sources—Bob, after all, had done two jobs against civilian targets in the 'Nam, when ordered to in writing by higher headquarters. Still other approaches were simply well-off men with pathological inclinations who wished to use him, in some way, to solve a business problem, to right a wrong, to avenge an infidelity.

No, Bob always explained. It was against the law.

Go away, please.

Most of them did. Though occasionally, one didn't: there was one breed of hater it took special effort to drive away—those who knew that the country was entirely theirs, and that all good things would flow if others were removed. Of course what they meant, usually, was the black people. Bob had served with too many fine black NCOs in the 'Nam to listen to this kind of shit, and though he had more or less given up on violence, he had broken the nose of a fellow from some outfit calling itself the White Order. The man had said through blood and anger they'd put Bob on The List too, and Bob had grabbed the man and thrust the blunt muzzle of his Colt Government Model down his throat and explained simply, "Mister, if you can't do your own killing, you don't scare me worth a drink of spit!" The man had pissed in his pants and disappeared off Bob's mountain but fast.

But now—these others, this damn Colonel Bruce with his medal and his little bird dog Payne. Rich enough to buy this whole spread, bring him way out here, have someone make up these excellent cartridges.

Who were they? Who was worth killing to go to this much trouble?

Agency.

He could smell it all over them. This was how the Agency worked, at odd angles, never quite out in the open, bringing you halfway in so that by the time you figured out what was what it took more effort to get out than to stay.

So? He sat and considered, perplexed, aching for a taste of liquor, a cold splash of beer against his throat, to soften up his mind so that he could think better. But he knew one drink and he was lost, so he fought his way through stone-cold sober.

Agency wants me hunting again.

But who?

Bob thought and thought on it in the little restaurant, his head and hip aching, and got nowhere and only after many hours did he notice the place was about to close, and the waitress was making hungry eyes at him. He'd have no part of that, no thank you. No women, no liquor, never again. Only rifles and duty.

But what was duty?

Who was worth hunting?

Who had loaded the Accutech ammo?

Bob got in his car and drove back; he slept dreamlessly, still setting course by a single star: nothing is worth killing.

He'd tell them tomorrow after hearing them out. He would not kill again.

CHAPTER FOUR

The next day they met at the three-hundred-yard range, but without explanation the colonel was absent. Without his intense presence, his people seemed a little more relaxed. The man Hatcher seemed to be in charge, though only barely. He was a wiry fifty-year-old redhead, with spaces between his teeth, a pocketful of pens nested in some kind of plastic envelope in his breast pocket, and the distracted air of a man who knows too much about one thing and not enough about a lot of things. He herded Bob into a black Jeep Cherokee and with two others, including the stolid Payne, they drove over a network of back roads, around the hilltop, to another area.

What he saw shocked Bob some—a large, clear

field on the down slope of a hill, at one end of which stood a jerry-built scaffolding, pipes bolted together, the whole mad structure held stable by guy wires sunk into the ground at a variety of points around its perimeter. It looked like a circus tent without the canvas, or the skeleton of a building without the cement.

Bob saw a series of ladders to its upper reaches, and up there he saw a platform where a shooting bench and a chair had been installed.

"It's a building in Tulsa, Oklahoma," said Hatcher. "Or, rather, the height and the distances equal exactly the height and distances of a building in Tulsa, Oklahoma. See the car?"

At one end of a dirt road that ran before the whole ridiculous structure there was an old limousine chassis, its engine long since gone, its body rusty, but its passenger compartment reasonably intact; it was attached by chain and winch to what must have been an engine a half mile away.

"Now what the hell is this?"

"It's our SWAT scenario," said Hatcher. "We've gamed out a situation where we're going to ask you to fire on a moving target in a hostage situation. You'll be operating off cues—you'll be earphoned into a network and you'll get an okay to fire at a bank robber who's fleeing the scene surrounded by hostages. You'll have an envelope of about five seconds to go for a head shot. It's based on an event that took place in Tulsa in 1986, where an FBI sniper had to take the same shot."

"What happened?"

"Ah, he hit a woman hostage in the spine, paralyzing her. The bad guy shot two other hostages to death and then killed himself. It was a horrible thing, just a horrible thing. Man, that agent trained for that shot his whole life, and when it came, he blew it. A shame."

"They were in a limo?"

"No. It was the back of a pickup. We got a deal on the limo."

The Cherokee parked, and various people stopped scuffling about and came over to greet the team. Hatcher checked with technicians, radios were issued and handed out and they took Bob to a blackboard under a lean-to.

"You know, Mr. Swagger, in the past fifteen years, by our computations, law enforcement authorities, federal and local, have taken over eight hundred fifty precision shots. That is, through scopes at armed felons at ranges from between thirty-five and three hundred fifty yards. Do you know what the one-shot stop ratio is?"

"I'd bet it's low."

"Thirty-one percent one-shot drops. Hell, just last year in Sacramento, California, a police sniper took a clear shot at an unmoving gunman through the door of an electronics store and missed him completely. The guy shot three hostages to death before they settled his hash. Do you know why?"

Bob thought a while, took his time, and then delivered an answer.

"Some tiny percentage of the misses might be due to round deviation or equipment failure. But I'd bet the most usual cause is shooter failure. In the 'Nam, I missed my first shot. And my second. It takes practice to get used to staying relaxed while taking the trigger slack out on a man."

You have to find a little cold place and be there by yourself for a while, he was thinking.

"That's right," Hatcher sang out cheerily. "So our theory is that if we can increase their confidence factor even by a tiny margin, it's a great thing. You want that guy on the rifle knowing what he's got in his chamber's going to do its job if he does his. And one reason he'll believe it, we're hoping, is because you've told him so and showed him how."

Bob nodded.

"Can I see the vehicle?"

"No. Think of it this way, did the FBI agent see the vehicle any time before he had to fire? No, he didn't and we want to put you where he was. And we're not going to tell you the range either, that's something we'd like you to dope out on your own. No, what we'd like is to put you up there on what's supposed to be the fifth floor of the Tulsa Casualty and Life Building. It's October tenth, 1986, and a bank robber named Willie Downing with a cheap Star 9mm and three female hostages is being driven toward Tulsa International Airport where an airliner is waiting, he thinks, to fly him to Africa. You're Special Agent Nick Memphis of the FBI, SWAT trained, the best rifle and pistol marksman in the office. Sometime in the next few hours, Willie Downing will be before your sights, having killed a policeman and a bank guard and wounded two more, and now demonstrating serious signs of a PCP-induced psychotic episode. Your supervisor has determined that yours is the best shot; you have the angle and the opportunity. The real Nick Memphis was firing a Remington 700 in .308, but without the heavy varmint barrel—"

"Shouldn't have mattered," said Bob, "not for one shot."

"Anyway, we're going to tie you into a radio net and a lot of the information you'll be getting is based on the actual transcripts, so you'll be in about the same situation as Nick Memphis was. I'll be on the mike down here, reading you the radio commands to play you just the way his supervisors played Nick Memphis. You'll have plenty of time to set up, just like he did, and plenty of time to acquire the target while you're waiting for the green light. So, Mr. Swagger, now that you've seen it—do you want to play?"

Bob looked up the teetery structure of rods and lumber. It didn't seem too damn steady. But it had him. His vanity was pricked. Could he hit this shot, especially where some federal fool had failed, using up several lives in the process?

Suddenly, for the first time in his stay in Maryland, Bob let the tiniest hint of smile crease his face.

"Let's do it," he said, for the moment not giving a damn about Accutech but eager to the point of glee to take on Willie Downing and Nick Memphis.

They told him the real Nick Memphis had fired off of sandbags in a fifth-floor windowsill, and way up in the scaffolding, after a long climb, he discovered that setup, necessarily jury-rigged, but stable enough.

He put on the earphones and hands-free mike, and switched as instructed to Channel 14, the FBI Control Channel.

There was the hiss and crackle of static, then he heard, "Ahh, Charlie Four, do you read, Charlie Four, do you read?"

"Am I Charlie Four?" he asked.

"Affirmative," came the response. "Charlie Four, please advise as to your position." It was Hatcher, play-acting Base.

"Well, I'm up here, dammit."

"Bob, let's put ourself in 1986 for the sake of the exercise," said Hatcher over the earphones. "Just reply in standard radio argot."

"Read you, Base. Ah, I'm situated in the fifth floor of Tulsa Casualty, I have a clear view east down—" he tried to remember from the map the name of the street down which Memphis took his shot, "down Ridgely."

"Ah, okay, that's an affirmative, Charlie Four, you just hold steady now."

"What's the situation?"

"Ah, Charlie Four, we have suspect heading your direction down Mosher. He's gone through two ambushes but on-site command wouldn't authorize a go because nobody could get a clear shot at the suspect. He's surrounded by these damn hysterical women and we think he may have tied himself to them."

"Read you, Base."

"Please stand by."

Bob took a second to look at the rough "street" down which he'd be shooting. The problem, of course, was range. Known-distance shooting was easier, because then you can calculate the bullet drop by the ballistics tables and your own experience. But Bob had no natural feeling for range. Some men could look at something and by the weird mechanics of the brain simply know what the distance was. Not Bob. So he had worked out a crude naked-eye system in Vietnam. If he could make out eyes, he knew he was inside a hundred yards—the rare shot. If he could make out face, he was under two hundred yards. If he could just make out head he was under three hundred. If he could make out only legs, he was under four hundred. If he could make out body, he was under five hundred; if he could only see movement, he was under six hundred.

From his vantage point, he watched as technicians scurried over the killing ground beneath him, examining the chain that would tow the car, fussing with the engine that would pull it, adjusting video cameras mounted on tripods down the roadway. He fixed them in his mind, reading their shape and making his calculations off them. He figured the shooting site would be about 320 yards out.

Meanwhile, the crackle and hiss played against his

ears, as he heard other reports from police and FBI units checking in for instruction; it was a constant chatter, a torrent of loose noise. Why hadn't poor Memphis had a spotter with him, someone to run interference and to shelter him from the hundred distractions?

Though Bob could only see blue-humped mountains and rolling forest and though the breeze played against his skin, cooling it, he had no trouble imagining Memphis in the hot little office behind the sandbags and the rifle, his tension and agitation growing as he waited alone, his excitement bounding as the situation drew nearer and nearer to him.

It was the excitement that fucked him, Bob thought. You don't shoot from excitement or haste or urgency. You shoot out of calm professional confidence, rooted in the belief, built up over a thousand hours' practice and a hundred thousand bullets fired, that if you can see it you can hit it.

"Charlie Four, you there?"

"Affirmative, Base."

"Command advises that suspect vehicle has just turned down Lincoln, entering your district."

"I have that, Base."

"ETA four minutes."

"Read you, Base, back to you."

"Ah, Charlie Four, I'm getting real bad reports from people in the field, they're telling me this guy is waving his gun and screaming at the hostages and that every time he sees a police vehicle he acts a little crazier. He's bad news, bad, bad news."

"Reading you, Base."

"Charlie Four, you think you'd be able to make that shot?"

Bob squinted through the scope at the road down which the hostage vehicle would travel.

"I have it big and clear, Base. The shot is there for me if it's there for you."

"Charlie Four, this guy could go off at any moment and hurt some more people."

"I read you, Base. You got an ETA for me?"

"He's at Lincoln, Charlie Four, Lincoln and Chesley, and a uniformed officer says he's really flipped out. Makin' me nervous, very nervous."

"Base, I make the shot three hundred twenty yards. I can put it in a fifty-cent piece at that range. Confidence is high here."

"Ah, Charlie Four, I've been in contact with command and it's getting real hairy in that car. We're, um, we've decided to authorize a green light for you, Charlie Four."

"I'm reading you, Base, and making ready to shoot. I'll be off the air now."

"Ah, Charlie Four, that's a negative. I've got two spotters here; I'll be notifying you when suspect gun is pointed in safe direction and you can go for a head shot, Charlie Four. We can't risk a spasm shot, do you read?"

"Negative, Base, I can't be concentrating on anything but my shooting."

"Then, stand down, Charlie Four, I won't authorize a green light unless I've visually verified suspect's gun position, just like the book says."

So there Nick Memphis had had it. Caught right on the horns. He'd have some guy yelling in his ear as he was shooting, or he'd have to stand down and walk away from it.

"All right, Base, you talked me into it. I'm sliding into shooting position now. You sing out when your people say it's clear."

Bob slid the rifle into his shoulder, watched as the scope came up big and bright and clean, a movie-screen world, all in primary colors bold and furious.

"Charlie Four, he's turned down Ridgely, he's coming into your kill zone right about now."

Bob threw the bolt, feeding one of the Accutech .308's into his chamber. He drew the rifle to him, found the hands-free mike got in the way of his spot-weld, and thus quickly and savagely bent it out of the way, to take his place behind the gun.

It was a modified sitting position, with the weight on his left ham, his body canted slightly as the rifle was pulled to him, while resting solidly on the sandbag barricade. It felt completely moored to the bags, its weight entirely on them. His upper body supported itself on elbows, and the rifle rode a fulcrum of the sandbag, guided by his hands pulling it tight against his shoulder. His hip flared a bit under the strain, but it wasn't anything he couldn't handle.

As he looked through the scope, Bob made subtle corrections in his grip and body position, trying to find, given the circumstances, an equipoise: one position where everything was tucked just right, where he felt most comfortable, less stressed, where his breathing was natural and loose, and yet through it all he still felt anchored into his chair and the bench and the bags.

Through the scope, he watched the slight tremble of the cross hairs, matching his breathing. That was the enemy, really: not Willie Downing or Nick Memphis or Accutech or anything—no, it was his own heart, which he could not quite control (nobody could) and which would send random messages of treachery to the various parts of his body. At these last moments, the heart could betray anyone, firing off a bolt of fear that would evince itself in a dozen tragic ways: a trigger finger hitch, a breath held too long, a weirdly detonating synapse that caused the eye to lose its sharpness or its perspective; an ear that suddenly heard too much or not enough; a foot that fell asleep and distracted its owner from the serious business at hand.

Bob blinked quickly, ordered himself to chill out, and tried to see in the lazy tremble in the cross hairs not something to hate (his own weakness) but something to make peace with—something to forgive. Self-forgiveness was a large part of it: you can't be perfect all the time. Nobody can: accept your weakness, try to tame it and make it work for you.

Bob breathed slowly, letting the air hum half into his lungs, then humming it half out. He didn't want a lot of oxygen in them, ballooning out on him at the awkward moments. But dammit, he still didn't quite feel comfortable. It was all so strange: sitting up there in the pretend building, pretending to be an FBI agent, pretending it was 1986, trying to pretend it was real.

There is nothing to pretend, he told himself. There is only shooting, and that's never pretend.

He'd figured the math out much earlier. Having memorized the ballistics table, he knew that at 320 yards the 150-grain bullet was programmed to drop about ten inches and would have slowed, by this distance, to a velocity of about 2,160 feet per second. But he also knew that this Accutech stuff was a bit hotter than the standard. And so he figured it would only drop eight inches. But he was shooting downhill, a slightly different problem than shooting flat; this meant he'd add more of a drop, because bullets fired at an angle fall farther; he took another inch out of the equation. That put him nine inches low at 350 yards, except that the wind, just a slight breeze, would move the bullet as it traveled perhaps four inches to the left. So he had to hold nine inches lower and four inches to the left. Then he had to lead to compensate for the speed of the car; and he had to do it on cue, when he got the green light command over his earphones.

"Charlie Four, do you read?"

Fuck it, thought Bob, what does *he* want?

He said nothing. The mike was bent under his chin and to pull it back into place was to blow his spot-weld, his hold and his peace. He would not give that up.

"Charlie Four, goddammit, where are you?"

Bob was silent, awaiting the arrival of the vehicle in the bottom right quadrant of his scope.

"Charlie Four, goddammit, get on the air! Do you acknowledge? Call in, goddammit, Charlie Four, I need you authenticated."

Bob was silent, trying to flatten out that bit of tremble from the reticle. He tried to make his mind blank and cool and drive out any sensation of his own body. There should be only two things: finding the right hold and preserving it through the trigger pull.

"Charlie Four, you don't call in, I'm not gonna green light you, goddammit, I have to have you on the air so I know you're reading my commands!"

Bob held silent. His breath was rougher now; he felt like tossing the earphones away! Talking to him! Now!

He tried to clear his head, to make everything go away except the shot. He could not.

"Charlie Four, green light canceled. Abort it. Hang it up, if you're there, Charlie Four. Do you read? Shot authorization is canceled. There'll be no shooting, goddammit, Charlie Four."

And now he saw it.

The limo body, hauled by the chain, slid into view. Its angle from him was not acute but more like forty degrees; the car appeared to be moving at about twenty miles per hour; Bob had no trouble pivoting the rifle on the bag through a short arc as he tracked the car, looking for his hold. He tried not to note the details, but he could hardly help it. Downing, for example, was, preposterously, a watermelon; the four hostages around him were balloons. It was crude but effective, especially in the way the wind made the balloons waver in unpredictable ways and the bump and grind of the two made the melon queerly elastic, nearly human. Bob almost laughed. All this money to shoot a melon! And he knew it was absurd, too. A hundred men could hit a melon like this, but only one of them could hit a head.

And then that was gone too, as, suddenly, Bob had the position, had it, knew it, had the shot, had it right, had it perfect. He held as the car continued to slide and involuntarily, without having consciously decided to disobey orders, he began to take the trigger slack out. He was going to shoot anyway, fuck it.

"Charlie Four, gun is down, green light, green light, green li—"

But Bob had fired already by then, having already made the decision at some subconscious level. His brain had yielded to his finger; his finger had decided and in the instant before the blur took it all away from his eye, he saw the melon detonate into a smear of red against the green Maryland countryside as the bullet tore through it and mushroomed. And when the scope came back from the recoil he saw all four ballons still waving in the wind and the melon blown in half.

"Congratulations," said Hatcher. "You win all the marbles. You solved it."

Bob said nothing, just fixed him with a cool eye. He had climbed down from the tower, to be surrounded by admirers.

"When did you decide to shoot?"

"It just happened."

"You were so fast when you got the green light. Damn, you were so *fast*!"

Bob didn't tell them he was halfway through the pull when the word came.

"Here, you can read the transcripts yourself." He handed them over to Bob, who looked at them briefly, enough to satisfy himself that yes, indeed, Base had been on the earphones to poor Memphis until almost the last second.

BASE: Have you acquired the target?

AGENT MEMPHIS: Yes, sir, uh, he's at the bottom of my scope, he's rising into my cross hairs, uh, he's—

BASE: Hold your fire, Charlie Four, until I have a confirmation that his piece is down.

AGENT MEMPHIS: Base, goddammit, I have him, I *have* him, I—

BASE: No authorization. Hold it, Charlie Four, I can't let you shoot, I—

AGENT MEMPHIS: [garbled]—have it, dammit, I can—

BASE: Negative, negative, Charlie Two, can you give me a visual?

AGENT O'BRIAN: I can't see his gun, Base, I, oh, Christ, he's going to fire—

BASE: [garbled] Shoot, green light, fire, goddammit, take his ass down—

AGENT MEMPHIS: [garbled]

BASE: God, you hit the girl, he hit a girl, oh, Jesus, in the back—

AGENT O'BRIAN: Suspect is firing on his hostages, Jesus, will somebody hit him, Nick, hit him, hit him, *hit him*!

AGENT MEMPHIS: I can't see, he's behind, oh, Jesus, he's shooting them, I can't get another shot, oh, Jesus, help them, help them, somebody, *help them*!

AGENT O'BRIAN: He just blew his own head away. [obscenity], Nick, he put that gunbarrel in his mouth and blew his [obscenity] head away, he—

BASE: Get those people medical aid, get those people medical aid, Jesus Christ, get those—

AGENT MEMPHIS: Shit.

That was enough. Why hadn't Memphis had a spotter, someone sitting next to him up there? Sniping was a two-man job, or it was a one-man, on his lonesome, job. It wasn't for a guy with a radio playing in his ear. And Base. Base was the real enemy; Base had made it impossible for the guy to hit that shot, blabbering away like an old woman.

"They fucked him, but good," said Bob through tight lips. He thought of the poor jerk, watching the great Tulsa massacre through his scope, helpless, enraged, and most of all unforgivingly furious at himself for having missed the shot and hit the woman.

"What happened to him?"

"He married the woman he hit. He quadded her, and he married her. Still in the Bureau, with a poor woman in a wheelchair to care for the rest of his life."

Well, here's to you, Nick Memphis, thought Bob. If I were still a drinking man, I'd lift a glass to you, and if I ever become one another time, then I'll lift one for you too.

"It's remarkable how institutions reveal themselves under stress," said Hatcher. "See, the Bureau is basically a bureaucracy, and under everything it does, there's a bureaucratic imperative. So Base had to monitor Memphis, even at the moment of firing. *Had to,* neurotically, pathologically. That was Base's first operating principle, to cover his own ass. And poor Memphis, being a team guy, even though the solo artist, poor Memphis played along. And in so doing, completely compromised his shot."

There was a pause.

"But Mr. Swagger, you didn't. Because you're not a member of a team, and you have no norms and traditions to live up to. You can just go for it. You see through to the necessary which is utmost concentration. That shot was probably within the furthest reaches of Memphis's envelope, and under perfect circumstances, he'd have made it. But he got fucked. We tried to fuck you, and you just sailed on through it. Man, you whacked Willie Downing good."

There were several other fans clustered around Bob, besides the gooney Hatcher. He could sense their admiration, and despised them for it.

"Now, Mr. Swagger, we've got one more test for you. Do you still want to play?"

Bob launched another gob into the dust, queerly uncomfortable but not entirely displeased with the awe that was being thrust upon him.

"I'll take another shot," he said. "Maybe I'll get lucky again."

"This one is straight up your alley. It's pure sniper war. This one is based on an incident that took place outside Medellín, in Colombia, in 1988. It's highly classified so I've got to ask you never to disclose specifics to anybody. Fair enough?"

"I'm just here to shoot, not talk."

"As I explain it to you, I think you'll understand the need for delicacy in the matter. It involves a DEA agent who took a fourteen-hundred-yard shot at a drug dealer who was responsible for the murder of a DEA team. The guy had fantastic security, bunches of Colombians packing a lot of automatic heat. And the word was out, if anybody tried to take the guy down, the Colombians would just start blasting. So, reluctantly and unofficially, DEA decided to take the guy out with a minimum of fuss. Highly illegal, but it was felt a message had to be sent to certain parties in Colombia."

"So it was a straight hit?" Bob asked.

"Yes. Your kind of work. No hostages, nothing. Just a man and a rifle and a hell of a long shot."

"You're not making any fourteen-hundred-yarder with a .308, I'll tell you that."

"You're anticipating us again. The DEA shooter used a .300 H & H Magnum, with a Sierra 200-grain slug. Here, here's the rifle. The same one."

He nodded, and one of the technicians brought a rifle case over and opened it. Bob only saw a rifle.

But what a rifle.

"Goddamn," he said almost involuntarily, "that's a honey of a piece. Damn!"

It was a bolt-action Model 70 target, pre-'64, with a fat bull barrel and a Unertl 36× scope running nearly along its entire barrel length. Its dark gleam blazed out at him in that high sheen that was now a lost art but had reached its highest pitch in the great American gun-making days of the 1920s and '30s. It was almost pristine, too, clean and crisp, well tended, much loved and trusted. But it was the wood that really hit him. The wood, in that slightly thicker pre-'64 configuration, was almost black; he'd never seen a walnut with such blackness to it; but it wasn't like black plastic for it had the warm gleam of the organic to it. Black wood?

"That's a hell of a rifle," he said. He bent quickly to look at the serial number: my God, it was a one followed by five beautiful goose eggs! 100000. The hundred-thousandth 70! That made it infinitely desirable to a collector and marked it as having been made around 1950.

"From the Winchester plant in 1948. The metal was heat-treated at higher temperatures to give it the strength to stand up to a thousand-yard cartridge."

"Okay, let's give it a whirl. You have the ammo?"

Hatcher handed over a box of Accutech Sniper Grade .300 H & H Magnum.

LAW ENFORCEMENT USE ONLY, it said in red letters.

Bob opened the box, took out one of the long .300 H&H's: it was like a small ballistic missile in his hand, close to four inches of shell and powder and bullet, heavy as an ostrich's egg.

"What kind of ballistics?"

"It's a thumper. We're kicking it out off 70 grains of H4831 and our own 200-grain bullet boattail hollowpoint. About three thousand feet per second."

Bob thought numbers and came up with a 198-inch drop at a thousand yards; figure maybe 355 for fourteen hundred yards.

Bob took the rifle. His first love had been a Model 70, often called the Rifleman's Rifle, and he now owned several, including that recalcitrant .270 that had consumed him before coming up to Maryland, and whose problems he hadn't quite mastered. So the rifle was like an old friend.

"Where can I take it to zero?"

"Uh, it's zeroed. One of our technicians has worked it out to the yard. It'll shoot to point of aim at the proper range."

"Hold on, there, sir. I don't like to shoot for money with a rifle I haven't tested."

"Ah—" said Hatcher, embarrassed at Bob's flinty reluctance. "I can *assure* you that—"

"You can't assure me of a thing if I haven't done it myself."

"Would you like me to get the colonel?"

"Why don't you just do that?"

"All right. But I can tell you that the man who zeroed the rifle to that load and range—he won a thousand-yard championship with it in the mid-fifties. It'll shoot. I guarantee you it'll shoot. He's got the trophies to prove it."

Bob squinted.

Finally he said, "Goes against my principles, but, goddammit, if it says Winchester, I'll take a crack at it."

Bob lay in a spider hole. It was cramped and dirty. The walls seemed to press in. His view of the world consisted of only a slot, maybe six inches by four inches, and through it he saw a series of low ridges. Far, far away, there was a raw wall where the earth had been bulldozed up to form a bulwark.

"He waited in that hole for two weeks," Hatcher had told him. "Just be glad we don't put you through that. And after all that waiting the shot came, and he missed it. A shame."

Garcia Diego, for this was the dope dealer's name, was a careful man, and had extended his security arrangements out a thousand yards from his hacienda. He was the most hunted man in Colombia after wiping out the team in Miami. Now DEA had tracked him down and knew that if he slipped out, it would be at dawn, over the back wall of his hacienda, and he'd be visible for just a second or two before he scurried away to his ATV and disappeared into the jungle.

"What you'll see, Bob," said Hatcher, "is a remarkably lifelike human form. It's an anatomically correct dummy. We're pulling it over the ridge on guy wires that won't be visible to you, and it's suspended in a frame, but it should, from this distance, look startlingly like a man. You'd best go for a center body shot."

Now, alone, Bob settled in behind the rifle. The old Winchester was the rifle he'd learned to shoot on all those deer seasons back in Arkansas. It was like a letter from home, or from the early fifties, and it made him think of his old dad. Earl Swagger was a dark and hairy man, with a voice like a rasp being drawn over bare iron, a man of solemn dignity and quietude, well packed in muscle, who nevertheless never ever raised his voice or struck anybody who hadn't first broached the issue of violence himself and who treated all men, including what in those days everybody called niggers, with the same slow-talking courtesy, calling everybody, even the lowest scum of earth, sir.

He stood over Bob patient as the summer sun, endlessly still and steady.

"Now, Bob Lee," Bob could remember him saying, "now, Bob Lee, rifle's only as good as the man using it. You use it well, it'll stand by you come heaven or hell. You treat it mean and rotten like an ugly dog, or ignore it like a woman who complains too much, and by God it'll find a way to betray you. Hell hath no fury, the good book says, like a rifle scorned. Well, the good book don't say that exactly, but it could, Bob Lee, you hear me?"

Bob Lee nodded, swearing that he'd never mistreat a rifle, and these many years later, that was, he felt, the one claim he could make: he'd never let a rifle or his father down.

He looked down to the firing ground.

There was no movement at all. It was quiet, except that the wind had picked up; he could hear it thrumming like a cicada, low and insistent.

Beyond a thousand yards, you're in a different universe. The wind, which under three hundred yards can be a pain in the butt, becomes savage. The bullet loses so much velocity on its down-range journey that its trajectory becomes as fragile as a child's breath. The secret is to make the wind work for you, to read it and know it; it's the only way to hit.

Beyond a thousand yards, even with a scope, there's no chance of bull's-eye, no talk of X-rings; you're just trying to get on the target, though an exceedingly gifted shooter with the best rig in the world can bring his shots in within four inches.

With his thumb, he snicked the safety off the Winchester, locked his hands around the grip and pulled it in tight to his shoulder, and ordered his body to relax as he looked for his spot-weld.

Scrunched into the spider hole among the stench of loam and mud, he was in something as close to the classic bench shooter's position as he could get, rifle braced on sandbags fore and aft, with just the softest give in the rear bag so he could move the piece in the brief period of time he'd have to track the moving man. His breath came in soft wheezes, half a lung in, half a lung out, as he adjusted to the lesser stream of oxygen.

Finding the spot-weld at last, he was amazed at how bright and clear the world looked through a Unertl 36.

Good thing he was indexed in the right direction. The bigger the scope, the smaller the field of view; if he'd had to hunt for it through the little bit of world the scope allowed him, it could take all day.

And then he saw it. It was just a shimmer of motion, right at the crest line of the earthen wall fourteen hundred long yards away. A man's head peeped over, and peeped back. He was coming.

Bob felt the tension in him begin to rise.

And then he realized, suddenly, though not in words, for there was no time for words in the blaze of the moment, that this shot was what it was all about. The rest of it, Accutech, Sniper Grade ammo, Nick Memphis in Tulsa, a DEA mission against a dope king—all that was prelude. This was the moment they'd been nursing him toward, by slow degrees, an inch at a time, coming onto it the way a man would come upon a final, and much waited for, much anticipated, threshold.

It was a terribly long shot, he now saw: almost nobody

in the world could make it. He calculated the ballistics roughly and quickly, because he'd done it a hundred thousand times before, trying at least to bracket what the bullet ought to do at the range from what other bullets of similar weight and trajectory had done, and felt the wind, and tried to dope his way toward a hold, tried to instinct his brain into the shot. But he felt that he was way out there. He was in undiscovered territory. Nobody had ever been where he was before. Who'd risk a shot like this? It was criminally dangerous, dope king or not.

All these thoughts, of course, fired through his head in nanoseconds. The man emerged from the wall, slithered over the top, and stood there, for just a moment, sloppy as shit, happy as a lark. He was a dot, a period, a pill. He was so very far away.

Bob made half a hundred minute corrections in a time span that has no human measure, found his spot in that weird moment of clarity, and felt the trigger go back on itself and break, and lost the picture from the scope in the blur of the rifle's buck, and knew he'd sent the shot home, for he'd had a flash of the figure going instantly limp on him, and it fell and rolled without dignity down the slope.

Now Bob saw what he had done—what they had made him do.

And for the first time, Bob felt as if he'd blasphemed with a rifle.

Their enthusiasm didn't mean a great deal.

"Mr. Swagger, by God," burbled Hatcher, "do you realize we've had twenty-eight men in here. We've had some ex–Delta Force shooters, some top FBI people, the top gun on LAPD SWAT and half a dozen other big city SWAT teams, we've had the top shooters from the NRA thousand-yard championships, and nobody, none of them, not a one of them, has hit that shot! You put that bullet within an inch of the heart. A one-shot kill at fourteen hundred yards."

Bob looked at him, squint-eyed.

"It's a nice rifle," he said. "And whoever you got loading for you knows what the hell he's doing. Yes, sir."

Even Payne, so unimpressed yet curious, now looked at him with some strange glint in his eye.

"Hell of a shot," he said, in a voice meant to suggest that in his time he too had seen, and maybe even taken, some hellacious long shots.

But Bob still felt tainted. It was like waking up after a night with a low woman, and hating yourself for what you sold to have her.

"Mr. Swagger, you all right? Damn, if you'd have been with DEA, Diego Garcia would be historical right now, instead of the richest man in Colombia."

Bob smiled, trying to pin down the peculiarity he felt.

Daddy, what did I do? he thought, remembering when he'd taken his first shot at a deer, and gut-shot the poor creature and he'd felt shame and hatred for himself. His daddy had told him that it was all right, and tracked the creature down himself to finish it off, three long hours of following blood trails up and down some of the roughest slopes in the Ouachitas. His daddy had told him God forgives the bad shots if God knows that in your heart you were trying to put meat on your family's table and that you truly loved the creature you were hunting and were making it and yourself a part of nature.

If God didn't want man to hunt, why did he give him the brains to figure out gunpowder and the Model 70 Winchester rifle?

"Oh, I figure I know where I stand," he said, because

it just flashed into his head and he knew what they'd done to him.

"And what I figure is, you'd best go get that phony colonel of yours, and get him fast, so he can explain to me why it is you went to all this trouble to turn me into the gook who hunted *me*!"

He turned, glaring.

"You motherfucker, you turned me into the sniper who crippled me and then killed my best friend."

He felt like fighting. He turned and drove the Model 70 rifle butt into Payne's mouth, literally lifting the man off the ground with the blow, and driving him to earth leaking shattered teeth and blood. He hated to tarnish the rifle's glowing wood with such dreadful matters, but certain things demand to be done. The blow sounded like somebody hitting a haunch of beef with a steel pipe and it completely destroyed Payne's fat ugly face and put fear into his little pig eyes. Then Bob reached down and yanked the hidden cut-down Remington 1100 from Payne's shoulder holster, jacked the six red shells out into the dust, and tossed the piece behind him.

"My dog doesn't like you and I don't like you, Payne. I don't like a man who carries a sawed-off semi-auto 12-gauge full of double-ought because he doesn't want to miss."

He turned back to Hatcher to find the educated man's stunned disbelief at the rapidity and absoluteness of the violence.

"You still here? Get your colonel or I'll whip up on old Payne here till the sun goes down."

Then he watched them scamper.

CHAPTER FIVE

Myra died on Tuesday at 11:43 A.M. The hospital called him, right there in his office. It was Dr. Hilton. Nick just said, "Yeah, oh, okay. I should have been there."

"Nick, she wasn't conscious. Okay? Don't hold that against yourself."

"Yeah, but I should have been there."

They'd said it would probably come at the end of the week. The vital signs were very low and she hadn't come out of the coma for nearly ten days. So it was not unexpected, but when these things happen, they carry a sort of devastation with them that is impossible to imagine. Nick was stupefied at how hard it hit him, sitting there in his office, listening to the chatter and hum of life going on about him.

He remembered that on one of her last clear days she herself had told him to be strong, to get himself ready, that her time was near.

And, of course, she told him not to feel bad. He'd done as much as any man could do, he'd paid all his debts, oh, lord, he'd paid them. It was worth it, she said. There'd never have been a Nick for her any way except the way it happened, and she was glad that it had happened the way it had happened. Now he was to go have some fun.

That was Myra. Never asked for much, and certainly didn't get much, but somehow made her way through it, never picking up the bitterness some people who have far more seem to acquire. He wished she were with him now, because over the years he'd come to rely on her in special ways, almost as much as she'd had to rely on him. But that was stupid; he wished his wife were here to help him get through the death of his wife!

Instead, Nick got up and found Hap Fencl, and told him he had to go out for a little while. And that maybe he was going to take some time off now.

"Myra?"

"Yeah, finally. Boy, she fought."

"You want a Valium or anything, Nick, old son?"

"Nah, I'm okay."

"What you got ticking? Anything hot I can look over for you while you're gone? Got a bust or two coming up? I love the hairy stuff, you know me. A commando type."

This was a joke; Hap stood five feet eight and weighed about 150 pounds, while Nick was a wide man, thick and strong and a judo champ, black belt, and still the best shot in the office. But Nick didn't laugh, because he'd sort of phased out there for a second. He blinked, and pulled himself back.

"Oh? Uh, nothing, no. The usual. Following Colombians all over the town with Mickey Sontag, that's all. Mickey's out at the cop range today on that SWAT qualification. I was just going to push some paper, more or less, until he comes back."

Hap was the supervisory agent in charge here in the New Orleans office, and a very good guy, easy to work with. He specialized in organized crime, while Nick worked drugs, usually in liaison with the DEA, mainly because he had a diplomatic touch and got along well with what most of the other men called the DOA boys.

So it was no problem for Nick to drive out to the hospital. He got there in fifteen minutes, on a drive so blank it could have lasted for fifteen hours and taken him from Omaha to Tallahassee.

They hadn't moved her.

"Do you mind? Could I be alone with her for just a minute?" he said to the nurse.

"Sure. But we'll have to take her to the mortuary soon enough."

"Yeah. I know."

They scurried out. Nick looked around, hating the goddamned room. It was like all the rooms he'd spent his life in, anonymous, personalityless, some fake paintings on the wall, the smell of plastic and disinfectant heavy in the air. Yet, hating it, he knew Myra wouldn't have minded it. It was never her way to mind such things.

"I was meant to die that day," she once told him, "like the other two girls, and that man. But your bullet saved me. It delivered me. It gave me you, Nick Memphis, it made me Mrs. Nick Memphis, and so what I've got is all gravy. It's dessert. Six years of dessert."

Well, dammit, now he was crying, wasn't he? She'd forbidden that. When it became clear that her collapse was accelerating and Dr. Hilton said there was almost no chance at all, she'd told him she couldn't have him crying.

You should be happy. No more lady in a wheelchair. You're still a young man. Go out, get drunk, throw a party.

He went to the bed where she lay under a sheet. He'd seen corpses, of course, at crime scenes, in morgues, and when his mother had died in 1977, while he was at Quantico. And of course he'd seen them in the Tulsa street that day. But still he found himself shuddering and had to make himself pull the sheet back, wondering if he should. But he wanted to. He wanted to see her once more.

Of course the coma had drained the flesh from her face, and her eyes, those hot, bright, fascinating eyes, were closed, and some time ago they'd cut her red hair short, almost as a boy's. But it was Myra.

She looked like a little bird. Her skin was pale, and her bones were as fragile and precise as doilies. But the pain was gone. Myra had pretty much lived in pain for six years. No arms, no legs, plenty of pain. So her face had a kind of repose it never quite achieved in life.

Oh boy, he thought, honey I am really fucking up. You said not to cry and I've just lost it, lost it, lost it.

"Nick?"

It was the doctor.

"Nick, you want us to get you anything?"

"No, I'm okay."

"We have to take her now."

"All right."

He stood back and let them have his wife.

Nick went out into the sun, blinked, reached for a cigarette before he remembered he'd quit. He put on his sunglasses, because he felt his eyes swollen and pouchy. He tried to think. Then he remembered there wasn't much to think about. They'd made plans, he knew where she was going, and when the funeral would be. It would be in two days, which would make it, let's see, Thursday. Between now and then, it was all automatic, all of it.

He supposed he ought to go home, maybe some people would come by or something, some guys from the office, maybe their wives. He'd taken Myra to some of the parties over the years, and once they'd gotten over their clumsiness about The Tragedy, as he knew it was called, they got to like her, and some of the wives grew close to Myra and had the habit of dropping in.

But he shook the image out of his head, feeling the temptation to slide back into the good old days. He knew that way was craziness, he'd end up in another crying jag. He tried to get hold of himself, thought the best thing might be to go for a long drive, just point the car toward Biloxi and go, maybe spend a couple of days lying at the beach. Jesus, maybe find a girl, like Myra said, get laid, for crying out loud.

But he knew he couldn't and he wouldn't do that. He didn't know what to do. That was the hardest part. He just didn't know what to do. Then he thought about going to the movies or something, anything to just take his head out of here for a few hours. But movies were usually filled with people getting killed or maimed and he didn't feel up to it.

At last he hit on the lake. He'd just drive over there down by the water where it would be calm and cool and he could sit there and enjoy the scenery and let the sun melt on his face for a couple of hours, and just chill out, flatten out, drift a bit. But he figured he ought to call in, what the hell, just in case.

He found a pay phone and dropped the quarter.

Fencl answered.

"Hey, Hap, I think I'm shorted out for the day. I'm going to fade, okay?"

"That's cool, big guy. Hey, the guys want to take up a collection."

"No flowers. She didn't want flowers. And don't break any arms, okay? They want to give, fine. If not, that's fine, too. And give it in her name to some charity. That would be very, very nice, I'd like that a lot."

"Great, no problem. By the way, you got a snitch named Eduardo?"

"Huh?"

"Guy calling himself Eduardo calls in, 'bout half an hour ago. Said he had to talk to you. Very shook. Latino accent. Probably nothing, but you can't tell."

Nick ransacked his head. Eduardo? He had about fifteen investigations going, mostly small-time drug runners, most of them thought to be working for Gilly Stefanelli, the capo of the New Orleans organized crime branch. But he could place no Eduardo in this catalog of losers, grifters, sharpies and angle-players, though indeed the name sounded familiar.

Then, yeah, he had it. It was a pass-over. Wally Deaver, who'd just left DEA for private business, had told him he'd given his name to a few of his snitches and contacts, because he didn't want the guys in *his* fuckin' office making supervisor off of *his* snitches.

"What's the number?"

"Ah, lemme see, nine-eight-eight, twenty-twenty, room fifty-eight."

"From the exchange, I'd say it's out by the airport, isn't it?"

"Yeah, I could hear jets overhead. You know, Nick, why don't you pass on it? It's no big deal, these guys call in with shit all the time, that's all. If it's important, he'll call back. Take some time, sort it all out. Put all your pieces back together, it's no problem. I'm sorry I even mentioned it."

"No, I ought to give the guy a call. You never know. Talk to you."

Nick hung up, fished for another quarter, and dialed the number quick before it vanished from his head. He got a desk clerk, identifying the place as the Palm Court, and asked to be put through to room 58. The phone rang and rang and rang.

"I guess he ain't there," said the clerk.

"Hey, where are you?"

"It's just off I-ten at the airport exit. We're on the left, two down from the Holiday Inn."

"Great, thanks," said Nick, looked at his watch, and with a sigh decided to go back to work.

The Palm Court Motel turned out to be a shabby nonchain budget joint familiar by type out of half a hundred third-rate dope deals that Nick had either watched or busted or simply listened to. It was one of those cinder block places painted in gaudy, once-fanciful colors and built in the early fifties when Americans were just discovering their automobiles and the seductions of a bright band of highway to ride to the horizon.

He pulled into a stall, found room 58, near the stairway on the first floor, bathed in the fluorescent glow of two Coke and two Pepsi machines. He knocked hard on the door. Nick was a big man, almost two hundred, and though extremely strong, never quite looked it. He had a soft, mulchy body and wore his hair in a longish crewcut. He was wide, really, rather than big; and the hair was a bit blond and the eyes bluish. He looked more like a junior minister or a soap salesman than a federal agent.

His gift was for friendly perseverance—a virtue learned from Myra. He thought of before as his Hot

Days. There'd been a time when he'd burned to lock criminals away, to test himself in the streets and sewers, to save America from itself. In service to that dream he'd driven himself monastically for close to his first five years in the Bureau. He was always pushing himself, and yearned to go on the raids, the big busts, to get assigned to the Counter-Terrorism Squad or the Bank Robbery Rolling Stakeout Team. He wanted to kill a bad man in a fair gunfight, that was his goal.

Then it all came apart in Tulsa. Since then he'd surrendered both his body and his career in making up for that one botched moment, in trying to drive it from his mind.

But sometimes, lying there, hearing Myra's tortured wheezing next to him or seeing, in the moonlight, the skeletal silhouette of The Chair, it would come back over him with the force of an unexpected blow.

God, you hit the girl.

That's what Base had said.

Nick would get up and be physically ill. He'd stagger into the john and blow his food for an hour, and come out reeking and shaking and so full of hate for himself and his botched moment, leaden with infinite, futile regret.

He realized his fingers were bleeding from pounding on the door.

"Mister! Hey, mister, I don't think he's there!"

Nick looked up from his fade-out to see a maid.

"Oh, yeah," he said, "sorry. Say, you see the guy? What kind of guy was he?"

"Older guy, you know. Nothing special. Just another traveler."

"How long ago he leave?"

"I didn't never see him leave. They came to visit him. Then they left. You a cop?"

"I'm with the FBI. Who came to him? What kind of guys?"

"Guys in suits, you know. Like you. Younger maybe. Darker maybe. That's all. Left, oh, maybe, ten minutes ago."

"Do me a favor, go get the manager."

The manager was a geezer in a Hawaiian print shirt so garish it looked like a nuclear nova, hurling gobs of orange light off into the universe. It was quite a shirt for such a scrawny old rat who smelled of bourbon and deodorant.

Nick flashed badge and ID and told the guy to pop the door.

"You got a warrant or anything?"

It amazed him, the lip he had to take. It was television and the movies. Ten years ago it was all, Yes sir, thank you sir, what can we do sir. Now everybody thought the FBI was a bunch of fascists and had an attitude to throw.

"What are you, a lawyer?" Nick asked. "The guy wants to talk to me. Maybe he's sleeping. Come on, you don't need a hassle here. Just do me the favor, okay?"

"No, it's that this guy was a bastard. He insisted on this room. The one next to the Coke machines. It wasn't even made up yet. But he threw a horror show. So that's why I didn't want to come crashing—"

"Just pop the lock, and let me do the talking," Nick said.

The old guy made a face, and let Nick know how reluctant he was, and Nick realized he was being played for a ten-spot, but he just put his dumb, patient look on, and waited the performance out and finally the man unlocked the door.

The first thing Nick noticed as he stepped inside was the blood. The blood everywhere. On the walls, on the bed, on the mirror, on the ceiling. Classic arterial spatter pattern.

"Aghhhhhhh!" the maid screamed.

"Holy fuck," said the manager.

"All right," Nick said, "you two, out. This is a crime scene. You go on in and call eight-eight-five, three-four-three-four and ask for Agent Fencl. You give him the address, tell him it's a real bad eleven-twenty and that he should get the troops out fast before the city boys get here. Tell him Nick is already here, do you understand?"

The old guy's eyes were broadcasting Station P.A.N.I.C. but he ran off to do what he was told.

Nick edged into the room. It was a slaughterhouse.

Most of the killing had been done on the bed. It was soaked in blood and there were jet sprays all over the wall above the headboard. Nick thought they'd hit him with axes and from the gore on the walls figured that maybe two or three whackers had gone to it. He could see blood-soaked adhesive tape where they'd splayed him to the bedpost to work on his soft areas with the axes. But Eduardo wasn't there.

Nick could see a blood trail leading off the room into the bathroom. Jesus, the guy chopped and mangled like that, he had somehow tried to crawl into the bathroom.

Nick could see his bare feet now, pigeon-toed in that loose way that prerigor bodies often have, where there's no will or dignity, and the limbs just arrange themselves into random patterns as defined by gravity. He walked delicately over to the bathroom doorway and leaned in to look down at the body. He noted a broad but old bare back and sinewy muscles. Eduardo still wore his suit trousers, blood-soaked white linen. The head was skewed to the right and Nick could see the profile of an elegant, perhaps aristocratic face with balding white hair and an aquiline nose. A bondage of electrician's tape crudely encircling the lower head locked a wad of cotton into his soundless mouth. The visible eye was open wide, in horror, and the face—as did the whole body—seemed almost to be floating on a tide of blood. So much blood.

Nick stared. Why the hell would he crawl in here? Why die on a bathroom floor instead of in a bed? Why roll off the bed and crawl, dragging your guts and lungs and organs into the bathroom? But then he followed the man's splayed left arm and at the end of his hand Nick saw his finger pointing—no, writing. He'd written something in his own blood on the white linoleum floor.

But as Nick watched in horror, the tide of blood seeped farther out in satiny, blackish splendor from the ravaged body of Señor Eduardo, and it engulfed the word that he had written. Just as it vanished, however, Nick made it out.

It said ROM DO.

The forensics people had been there an hour and the body had finally been carted off and Hap Fencl was still yelling at and being yelled at by a captain of homicide in the New Orleans police department in the never-ending turf war between local and federal agencies, particularly on crimes that seemed initially solvable, when, finally, Nick, down the hall on a pay phone, made contact with Wally Deaver.

Deaver was now head of security for a large pharmaceutical firm in Boston and it had taken the better part of the intervening time for Nick to track him down.

"Walter Deaver."

"Wally? Hey, Wally, you'll never guess—"

"Nick Memphis, man, I'd know your merry tone anywhere. How the hell are you? How's Frenchtown? Gumbo still hot?"

"That it is, old pal. Now listen, there's a little something that's come up I wanted to—"

"Nick, you ought to give up the Bureau and join me out here. Jesus, Nick, money, money, money, there's so much money to be made, it would be great for Myra and you could—"

"Yeah, sounds great, this is no line of work for banking any bucks, that's for sure, not if you stay straight. Listen, Wally, there's some old busine—"

"How's Myra?"

"She's great," he lied. "Anyway, you remember just before you left you gave me a list of snitches you said might call. You'd given 'em my number instead of any of the guys in your own outfit because you were so pissed off about policy?"

"Yeah. What, did one of them go sour on you?"

"Boy, did he go sour. Somebody whacked him, but good. He looks like that Panther Battalion got hold of him." He was referring to the Salvadoran Ranger Unit that had shot up a village and killed almost two hundred women and children, a story that was all over the news a month or so ago when the investigation drew so much attention. "I figure couple of guys worked him over with fire axes. Whacked his action like you wouldn't believe."

"Oh, Jesus. He must have crossed the Colombians. Those guys are barbarians. You mess with them and they mess with you right back."

"Yeah, maybe."

"So which of my bad boys was it?"

"Guy named Eduardo. He tried to call me, but I was out. By the time I tracked him down, they'd totaled him in a sleazoid motel out by the airport. I'm there now."

"Eduardo?"

"Yeah."

"Oh, yeah, Eduardo," Wally said unconvincingly.

"I made him to be about fifty-five, maybe sixty, kind of an aristocratic-looking guy. Ring any bells?"

"Yeah. Eduardo Lanzman. But guess what? He's not a Colombian, he's a Salvadoran. And the news gets worse. Here's the punch line. He's a spook."

"A spook?"

"Yeah. I met him down there, you remember when Bush had the drug summit in Cartagena? Lots of DEA guys went down, mixed with their opposite numbers as part of the deal. He had it in Colombia, of course, but there were guys there from all over Central-A. So I meet this guy. He was in their National Police Intelligence Section from Salvo. Seemed like a decent guy. So, you know cops, we exchange cards, I tell him if he gets anything hot headed my way, he gives me a call. But someone later said he was an Asset. You know, Agency pork. Agency not as in DEAgency but as in CIAgency."

"Hey, if he had something, why wouldn't he call his own team?"

"You never know, Nick, in that world. Maybe it *was* Panther Battalion that hit him, and didn't have anything to do with drugs, but was political. That's a serious league down there; you piss off the wrong guys and the Comanche with the Darkened Windows comes calling at midnight."

"You did give him my name? I was right on that?"

"If it's the same guy, maybe. Just before I left, I went through my Rolodex and sent out a form letter. To all my snitches and contacts."

"Great. And one more thing. You got any idea what 'ROM DO' might mean? His last message. Maybe what he was trying to lay on me. Any idea at all?"

"Doesn't mean a thing to me, Nick."

"Okay, thanks, Wally."

He put the phone down, turning the information over in his head.

"Nick, we got something. His passport." It was Fencl, calling him from room 58.

"Guy's name is Eduardo Lachine, of Panama City, Panama. He had a ticket stub from a flight in from Panama this A.M. Plane stopped in Mexico City. As we make it, he came straight here, probably by taxi. According to the hotel, he made one call—"

"To me."

"Yeah. I guess. And that was it."

"Are we going through his luggage?"

"That's just it. There isn't any luggage. The room clerk said there wasn't any luggage either. This wasn't a trip. He came here to see just one person. You."

"And it killed him," said Nick.

CHAPTER SIX

The colonel had attitude, that was for certain.

Not a twitch of regret touched his tough face, not a shred of self-doubt. What he got from Bob—furious rectitude, and the concealed threat of violence—he paid back in spades.

"All right, Swagger," he said. "You've seen through us. What do you expect, congratulations? You were supposed to. It's time to put the cards on the table."

"Why'd you do that to me? Why'd you set me up to take that shot on myself and poor Donny?"

"They say you don't trophy-hunt anymore, Swagger. I wanted to let you know that there were still trophies worth hunting."

They were now in a small, crummy conference

room in the trailer that wore the Accutech sign near the three-hundred-yard range. The colonel glared at Bob; the others were some kind of bearded sissy Bob had seen at the range, and the suckass Hatcher. Weirdly, dominating the conference table on which it sat was a large Sony TV with VCR. Were they going to watch a show?

"What is your name, sir?" said Bob.

"It isn't William Bruce," said the colonel. "Though there is a Colonel William Bruce and he did win the Congressional and he was supervisor of the Arizona State Police. A fine man. I'm not a fine man. I'm a man who gets things done and I usually don't have the time to be anything except an asshole, and this is one of those times."

"I don't like being lied to. You'd best come clean, or I'm on my way out of here."

"You'll sit there until I say so," said the colonel, fixing those hard, level eyes on him, asserting the weight of rank.

It was a sense of command that he'd seen in some of the best officers, the men who pushed the hardest. It wasn't inspirational, except by deflection; it was instead a gathering of will, a fury to win or die. It was a gift, too, and without it in battle an army was lost. But Bob had seen its ugliness too—that rigidity that could conceive of no other way but its own, that willingness to spend other men's lives that came from holding one's own cheaply but the mission dearly. This guy stunk of duty, and that's what made him so fucking dangerous.

"We're after a man," the colonel said. "He's a very special man, a very sly man. We think we're going to get a shot at him. We're after the Soviet sniper who has hit many great shots in his time, among them the fourteen-hundred-yard job that blew out your hip and the spine shot on Donny Fenn."

It was amazing, Dr. Dobbler was thinking. His self-control was astonishing. No gasp, no double take, as if it didn't matter. Swagger simply took it in, and went on, his concentration unmodified, his glare unblinking. No signs of excitation as were common to the species in moments of conflict. No rapid breathing, no facial coloration, no lip-licking, muscular tension. *No excitation!* No wonder he had been such an extraordinary soldier in battle.

Dobbler wondered how rare this was. Was it as rare, say, as the ability to hit a major league fastball, a gift given to about a hundred babies a year? Or was it extraordinarily rare, such as the ability to hit a major league fastball for an average of .350 or better, which arrives to a baby once in a generation or so? Dobbler knew he'd come across something rare and it gave him a thrill. It scared him, too.

Bob was leaning forward.

"You don't give a shit about Donny Fenn. There's only two of us left in the world that remember that young man. And you don't give a shit about my bad pin."

"You know what, Swagger? You're right. I don't give a shit about Donny Fenn. And I don't care about your hip. But I care about this Russian. Because he's back. He's hunting again."

Nick put fifty cents in and after a bit, somewhere inside the machine there was a shifting and a clunking, and after another bit, a can of diet Coke rolled down a chute and banged into the bin. He pulled it out, peeled the pop top back and took a long, bracing swig.

"Damn," said Hap Fencl, "fifty cents. In our building the goddamn things cost seventy-five."

But Nick didn't respond.

"I can't think why a guy would *want* to be next to a Coke machine," he finally said. "Hell, two Coke machines, two Pepsi machines, an ice machine, and a machine that drops bags of stale peanuts." He gestured to the little arsenal of vending equipment clustered in the alcove just outside room 58.

"Maybe the guy had a sweet tooth. Never wanted to be away from the machine."

"No, it's the last room you'd take, you got guys dropping quarters or rattling through the ice all night long. It doesn't make a lot of sense."

"Nick, he thought he was being followed maybe. So, he wants a room where there's a lot of action outside in the hallways, figuring it might scare the hitters off. These guys, though—*nothing* would have scared them off."

"Yeah, but—"

"Hey, Nick, you're not thinking straight. You've seen a dozen of these things, not quite so bloody. It's a straight drug-trade wipeout, the Colombians or the Peruvians or whatever sending the word out that they are not to be disobeyed or nasty things happen. This guy got caught snitching; went underground; they caught him and whacked his butt good. Okay?"

Nick nodded. Still, it bothered him.

Why me, he thought. Why would this guy call *me* of all people on the day my wife dies.

He emptied the Coke can in one wet, sweet swig.

"Here he is, Mr. Swagger," said the colonel. "The man who shot Donny Fenn. And who crippled you."

Bob looked at the face that the colonel had brought to the television screen with the snap of a remote control. He tried to see some special thing there, something that said shooter, something that said sniper. What he saw was a lean hard face, a face that had no nonsense in it. The eyes were slotted and dark, like gun slits; the cheekbones were streamlined knobs; the hair a tight military sheen. There was a streak of the Orient in him in the slight flare of his cheekbones—he looked like a Mongol.

"Solaratov, T. We think that's his name. But nobody knows what the T stands for."

Bob just grunted, because he didn't know what else was available.

"T. Solaratov, as photographed from quite a distance away by an agent code-named Flowerpot in Kabul, Afghanistan, in 1988. Our last picture of him, and our best. He's fifty-four years old, in peak condition. Runs twelve miles a day. He was in Afghanistan advising Spetsnaz units on sniper deployment. He's an expert on sniper deployment; he's hunted men all over the world. Whenever the Soviets needed a shot to be taken, he took it for them. How many men have you killed, Sergeant?"

Bob hated this question. It was nobody's business; it didn't matter.

"All right," said the colonel, "you can be strong and silent. But the official records say eighty-seven and I'd bet you hit lots more. Lots."

Bob knew what the figure was. He sometimes pretended he didn't but he knew, exactly.

"We figure Comrade T. Solaratov has sent over three hundred fifty suckers on to a better world. Head shots, mostly, his trademark. No pussy center-of-body shit for this boy."

Bob grunted. That was serious shooting.

Nick flashed his ID on the woman and in a few seconds, he was led in to see Mr. Hillary Dwight, vice president, the Coca-Cola Bottling Company of New Orleans, in charge of vending sales. Mr. Dwight was a florid man in a white tropical suit who perhaps drank so much pure

Coke that it had affected his ample waistline. But he had a monk's shrewd, devotional eyes and an office so neat it spoke of a tidy, precision-oriented mind.

"So what is it I can do for you, Mr. Memphis?" he asked. "I hope one of my drivers hasn't gone and done something wrong. Those boys have access to all sorts of institutions and, frankly, the quality of personnel just isn't quite what it once was."

"No, sir," said Nick. "No, it's just a little mystery I'm trying to get a handle on. We have a fellow who got himself killed in a motel room out near the airport—"

"Good heavens," said Dwight.

"But before he got killed, he specifically asked for the room near the Coke machines. You have two Coke machines just outside and Pepsi-Cola has two. There was also a Handy-Candy Dispensing Machine for candy bars and nuts and the like. Now, what are the properties of a Coke machine that might make a man who suspects he's being trailed by killers seek out their presence? Or am I barking up a wrong tree entirely?"

"Hmmm." Dwight's plump face knitted up densely with the process of thought.

"What was the motel?"

Nick told him.

He stood, spun to face a desktop computer terminal and tickety-ticked in some instructions. Nick watched as obediently, in electro-yellow, the program rose before him. The fat man studied it.

"Well now, Mr. Memphis, you see we're in the process of replacing our Vendo-Dyne 1500 series with the more advanced Vendo-Dyne 1800. You've seen them. They talk to you. You can put dollar bills into them and get change. A very sophisticated piece of machinery. And powerful, too."

Nick nodded, enjoying the arcana of Coke Culture.

That was one of the many things about his job he liked so much: it took you into new worlds all the time.

"Ah, yes. Yes, we'd just serviced that place and, yessiree, we'd replaced the fifteen hundreds with eighteen hundreds just last month. A great advantage is size. The eighteen hundreds hold two thousand cans while the fifteen hundreds only hold five hundred. Means we don't have to service them nearly as much, and we can pass the savings on to the consumer."

Nick remembered. Fifty cents a can.

"So what does that tell us?" he asked, remembering the glossy, blinding brilliance of the new Coke machine in the hallway.

"Well, sir, one of the properties of the eighteen hundred happens to be its field generation."

Nick waited on the explanation.

"The eighteen hundred really encompasses a small computer chip and it needs power to run it. So it generates an electromagnetic field. We had two of them there? Well, they were putting out a blanket of electromagnetic pulse, that means."

Nick shook his head, cursing his own stupidity.

"I don't get it," he said.

Mr. Dwight smiled, and then explained.

"All right, Swagger, here's what we've been able to turn up on the guy. T. Solaratov, according to an Israeli team that went after the fucker and almost nailed him when he was instructing Fatah in sniper techniques in the camps of the Bekka Valley in the mid-seventies—our best source of information on him, I might add, and a damned shame for all of us that as close as they got, they weren't able, quite, to get their man. When he was eighteen, in the Soviet Naval Marines, his shooting abilities were first discovered and cultivated. In the years 1954 to 1959, he absolutely ruled the Eastern Bloc shooting matches. He was an extraordinary target marksman. We believe he got his first kills, however, in Hungary, in 1956; both Nicholas Humml and Pavel Upranye, Hungarian nationalists arguing for further resistance to the Soviet troops, were dispatched from long distance by Moisen-Nagant bullets at rallies. No trace was ever found of their killer.

"By 1960—after certain exploits in the Congo—he had obtained a commission and been selected out of the Soviet Naval Marines for an even higher elite, the Spetsnaz, the Soviet special forces. He more or less retired from competitive target shooting in 1962. Then, he disappeared, except for the occasional sightings and some other rumored guest appearances.

"And in 1972, when a gunnery sergeant named Bob Lee Swagger bounced Number Three Battalion of the Fifth People's Shock Infantry in the An Loc Valley, killing thirty-six men over a heroic two-day encounter and thus saving the lives of twelve Green Berets and a hundred indig troops on an eavesdropping mission up near the Cambo border, the NVC freak and send to Moscow for a pro. So Comrade Solaratov arrives. He's searching for one guy. You. It takes him a week to infiltrate in, but he can't get closer than fourteen hundred yards. He studies you, living and pissing and shitting in that little hole, for a week. Then when everything's perfect, he takes the shot you took today. Oh, but fourteen hundred yards is a long way."

"He didn't get the drop right," said Bob.

"That's right. So he takes you low, in the hip. But that gives him the range. And when Donny comes over, he hits it. Center chest. Then he's history. Solaratov's a big hero! He gets the fifty-thousand-piaster reward on your head, and two days later he's in Moscow, having strawberry blintz and getting laid."

Bob looked at the shooter's face on the television

screen. Yeah he'd heard the rumors. Guys came back said a white guy had nailed him.

The colonel continued.

"We have him next in Angola in the seventies, we've got him in Nicaragua instructing Sandinista shooters, we've got him in and out of the Middle East, as I told you, where the Israelis laid on a napalm strike just for him, and missed him by less than an hour. He's very big in the Middle East. Does a lot of work for some nasty boys over there. We've got him in Afghanistan for a long long time. He ran a unit of Spetsnaz snipers there, they dropped their targets in the hundreds. Make you and Donny look like Sunday school teachers."

Bob's hand went to his hip, to quell a little flare of pain down there.

Nick called a guy he knew in DEA who had a brother who worked for Defense Mapping in Washington but who had at one time worked for a certain outfit quartered in Langley, Virginia. It was a complicated exchange, involving a lot of billing and cooing, and finally begging on Nick's part, but finally the brother said that, yes, he knew some people in the outfit still and he could make a certain, highly unofficial call to an old buddy and ask Nick's one question. He would only ask the one. He would ask no others and he would deny till the day he died that he ever knew or heard of a Nick Memphis. He would call Nick back . . . well, he'd call Nick back when he was good and ready to.

"Why would a Russian be back in this country hunting somebody?" Bob said.

"I said he *was* a Russian," said the man. "I didn't say he was hunting *for* the Russians. Solaratov was ousted, unceremoniously retired, when the Red Army downsized last year, after the Soviet Union broke up. Pissed him off. He felt discarded. He felt bitter. Know anything about an old war-horse who feels discarded, Sergeant Swagger?"

Bob just stared at the prick.

"He was spotted in July. Guess where?"

"I don't like games, mister."

"It would have been your first and only guess. Downtown Baghdad, in the presence of a General Khalil al-Wazir, who is head of Al Mukharabat, the Iraqi secret police. Now, Sergeant, into the present. Let me tell you about Rainbow. Do you know what Rainbow is?"

"I don't know what Rainbow is," said Bob, wanting the man to be done with it.

"Hardly anybody does. It's a satellite, exceedingly sophisticated, stealth impregnated, that sits in very high orbit above the Middle East, seeing all that it can see and sending the pictures back to us. Very helpful the past few years. The Iraqis and the Syrians and the Libyans suspect it's there, but they can't verify it because they can't pick it up on their cheap Eastern Bloc radar. But they're careful. When they do their secret things, they do them at night, when Rainbow isn't nearly so effective. But strange things do happen. Who would play lotteries if they didn't? Now look at this."

He snapped the picture control and brought up a series of photos. They appeared to show, one after another, a hazy series of markings on the earth as seen from high up.

"That's Rainbow working over central Iraq about two hundred miles above Baghdad, near a military installation at Ad Dujayi late one night a few weeks ago, trying to get a line on our old friends, the Medina Division of the Republican Guard. And what do you see? You see almost nothing. And then . . . a miracle."

He clicked again.

The photo was dramatically clearer. What Bob saw was towers, very like the one he had perched in that morning, overlooking networks of roads or amphitheaters at varying distances, the geometry of each setting subtly different from its brothers.

"Lightning. Nature's flashbulb, something nobody could predict; it lit the ground at the instant that Rainbow was snapping away. And yet the clouds weren't sufficient to blot out our view of this rather elaborate arrangement.

"But what's *really* interesting about this setup is they take it down every day. It must take hundreds of men. And just to keep our satellites from getting the snapshot we've just seen. Look, here's what the daylight reveals."

He clicked again; what Bob saw was simply a random pattern of roads across a desolate plain.

"Now can you solve the puzzle, Swagger. These photos. Solaratov in Iraq. Do you see it yet, Swagger?"

"Sure," said Bob. "They're prepping a shot. Those are buildings and streets. He'll have handled the range and angle solutions already. It'll be familiar to him."

"We should have come to you in the beginning. It took a young man in the Agency, a photo analyst, *weeks* to come up with the same answer, and those are lost weeks. But he finally had the bright idea of coding the grids of buildings to streets by angle with the help of a computer and having the computer run a check on those same streets and angles. Swagger, it's the Inner Harbor from the U.S.F.&G. Building in Baltimore, it's the back porch of the White House from a roof at the Justice Department—the Justice Department!—and it's Downing and Huguenot streets in North Cincinnati, and finally it's North Rampart and St. Ann in New Orleans."

"All right," said Bob. "So it is."

"Sergeant, those places have one thing in common. They are all sites of speeches to be given over the next several weeks by the president of the United States."

Dobbler watched the two of them. They were both children of the superego. They had nothing in them that would ever tell them to stop, hold back, wait, consider. They were both forceful men, without ideological underpinnings, who approached the world simply as a set of problems to be solved.

He remembered when the colonel had found him working in a mill clinic in Rafferty, Massachusetts, prescribing aspirin and bandages to the children of mill workers.

The colonel had simply walked in, so vivid a presence that no nurse would hold him back, laid down the *Boston Globe* front page that carried the news of Dobbler's sentence the year before across three columns, and said, "If you can keep your dick in your pants, I can get you some really interesting work. Lots of money. Fun, travel, adventure. Some of it's even legal."

"W-what do I have to do?"

"Supervise recruitment. Analyze prospects from a psychological–psychiatric perspective. Tell me which of 'em will jump when I say boo."

"Nobody can do that."

"No, but you ought to come closest. Or would you rather stay here and hand out bandages for the rest of your life?"

"It's part of my arrangement with the cour—"

"Not anymore."

The colonel laid a parole board exemption before him.

"Are you with the government?" asked Dr. Dobbler.

"You might say that," said the colonel.

Bob let the silence hang in the air until it seemed to crack.

"They're still trying to win that war," said the man. "They think they can win it with one shot. And Solaratov's the hired gun."

"What do you want from me?"

"Swagger, you've done something damn few men have done. You've stalked and hunted men, hundreds of them. You are one of the world's two or three best. Maybe an Israeli or two, maybe an SAS man somewhere, this Solaratov, Carl Hitchcock, but nobody else in the world is in your class. We need a man who'll attack our problem for us the way a sniper would. We want to know how he'd put an operation together, where he'd shoot from, what sort of ordnance he'd use. We want you to brief our security people, who'll find ways of making sure the information is inserted into the federal security mainstream and acted upon. Because we want to catch this piece of terrorist shit and turn him and empty out all his little secrets and use him as a club against his masters in Baghdad. We'll smart-bomb them back to dust and cinders."

Bob said nothing for a time. He was thinking things through and still he didn't like all this, didn't like the fact that these boys still had *Agency* on them like a smell. He wasn't sure if he trusted them enough to have a cup of coffee with. But then he knew he didn't really have a lot of choice. It was all set up, set up years ago.

He remembered the numbness and collapse as he went down and the way Donny scrambled down after him, his whole life ahead of him, and the way the light vanished instantly from Donny's eyes as the bullet bit through to his spine. He finally turned to the colonel.

He said, "Put me on the rifle, Colonel. And I'll body-bag this sly old boy for you."

For the first time in many years, Bob the Nailer smiled, feeling just a bit reborn.

Aroused, Dobbler wrote.

CHAPTER SEVEN

The funeral was on a Thursday, with all the office guys there, and most of their wives, even some of the office girls, and maybe a few dozen other people from the law enforcement community in which Nick moved, and their wives too. And some people who'd simply read of Myra in the *Times-Picayune* obit.

There must have been fifty or sixty. They stood quietly in the sunlight, not really moving or talking, but just by their radiance being there with him, trying somehow to help him and do something for Myra. It pleased Nick that so many showed up. Myra had been such a quiet little mouse about her life, taking what she was given; there should be medals for the Myras of the world but somehow there never were, so a graveyard crowd was the next best thing.

The cemetery was out in Kenner, fifteen long miles west of the city, a place Nick had chosen on his own because it was so open and grassy. None of those looming, dark, jungly trees and the soupy ground sheathed in thatches of reeds that seemed everywhere in what passed for "country" around New Orleans, just an expanse of green overlooking some tract houses and, in the far-off, the lake. Nick liked it because it seemed midwestern to him, and he liked all the sun, the grass and the trees that weren't cypress or fern.

And of course it was a bright and shiny day, a bit chilly, everybody at their best. It was formal in the most meaningful sense; it gave Myra the idea of having counted and being part of some larger, more organized whole, a society.

He even spoke a few words over the bier, after the minister had finished.

"Look, um," he mumbled, "I wanted to thank all of you and your wives for taking time off to come on out and help me say good-bye to Myra. Uh, she was a terrific gal, as you all know, and it's real great that you guys came on by. I know it would have made her real happy. So, uh, thanks again for, you know, coming on by."

It sounded lame but he didn't care.

Then they filed by and shook his hand and said dumb, stupid things and he nodded and watched them go.

"I'm so sorry, Nick," said Sally Ellion, one of the pretty girls in the Computer Records Section.

"Oh," he said, somewhat startled to see her here. "Yeah, well. Uh. Thanks for coming."

"You were so brave," she said.

"Huh? Me?"

"Yes, you, Nick," and then she moved on.

One of the last in the line was Hap Fencl.

"Nick, take some time off, for Christ sakes. You been through a lot. Give yourself a break."

"Hap, the best thing for me is to get back to work, you know? I'd just get bigger and dopier if I hung around the house. And there's all the things to remind me. So I'll see you in an hour or so."

"Nick, you take care of yourself, you hear?" said Hap's wife Marlee. "You need any help, you let me know."

"Sure," he said.

Then he watched them go, until he was alone with the box, except he could see some old black guys standing way off with shovels. They'd wait and wait until he left, and then they'd lower her and discreetly cover her over. With dirt. That was all. That was it. That was what had to be faced.

Okay, babe, he finally said. The guys with the shovels are here. Time to go. I'll always remember. Goodbye.

"Now, people," Hap was saying when Nick showed up, late, still in his dark blue suit, "we're getting the buzz out of Washington on these Colombians still and DEA all over the goddamn board is howling that we're not putting them in our loop so—"

"But if you give it to those guys, it's all over the street in fifteen seconds—"

"Okay, DEA has a slightly different agenda than we do, you all know that, they're going for the quality bust because they don't have enough guys to burn small fry like us, so once in a while, yes, Mike, they do let a little something loose so as to turn it for something bigger. Still, what I'm giving you is the official word from on high, you guys *gotta* share with DEA."

There was a murmur of disapproval from the twelve

agents of the New Orleans FBI narcotics squad. Outside, in the bright afternoon sun, the traffic snorted and honked up Loyola Street in front of the Federal Building. Nick slid in next to his partner, Mickey Sontag, who'd held a seat for him.

"I miss—?"

"Same old," the Mick whispered, "just shit on paperwork flow, on some new buy-money regs due out, some news on qualifications and SWAT applications, the same old same-old."

"Great," said Nick.

The meeting continued, the usual early Thursday afternoon ordeal and Nick wondered why Hap didn't just cancel. But Hap was old Bureau, no matter how much a one-of-the-guys type he pretended to be, with a dad and an uncle having retired as supervisory agents, and so he'd always play rules, rules, rules. That was the FBI way, as Nick knew better than most.

Then they moved to cases, as one by one the agents briefed their pals on what was hot and what was not, all of it standard and routine. The point was that in give-and-taking like this on a formal basis every week, maybe somebody would notice connections between cases, make quantum leaps or free associations, and it sometimes happened. But it didn't this time: just droning men in their law enforcement–dud voices ripping fast as hell through stuff that nobody else much cared about, no patterns in it anywhere. Nick couldn't pitch in, having not really leaned into his job since Myra died and that goddamned guy got whacked in the Palm Court Motel. But he made a noise when it came to Questions One and All.

"Questions one and all?"

There were a few, nothing much, and finally Nick got his hand up in symphony with Hap's glance in his direction.

"Say Hap, on that guy whacked at the Palm Court, what's the disposition?"

"Not much. DEA has no record on him in the dope loop and NOPD can't commit any real manpower, thank you, you know how those guys are in throwing bodies at cases that look like they're not headed to an arrest."

"So where does that leave us? Guy was trying to reach me, he—"

"You know, Nick, it's not really our bailiwick if he's not fleeing a federal charge or committing a federal crime. I think it'll end up in NOPD's I-hope-some-body-tells-us-who-did-this file."

"Come on, Hap, you know we can ride hard on any-thing if we can find the angle."

"Yeah, but it doesn't look remotely promising. Drugs, maybe, but there's no evidence anywhere in the system. The guy's not from here. You say he's Agency, but the Agency doesn't say he's Agency."

"The Agency *never* says they're Agency. According to the Agency, the Agency doesn't exist. But this guy's not a Panamanian, Hap. My source told me he was a Salva-doran."

"Yeah, well, the paperwork doesn't bear it out. That was a legit passport."

"Which could mean he's major league spook."

"Which probably means he's minor league nothing. And if he were spook, you damn well know the Agency would be here running a damage control operation. They freak when we're talking national security, you know how that bends them out of shape. They don't care. No leads, no nothing. It could be jealous hus-bands, squabble over profits, family problems, that sort of thing. It's interesting like a mystery novel, clues, that 'Rom Do' bit, yes, I give you that. But there's gonna be two hundred fifty unsolved homicides in this area this year, and I'm looking at one of them, eh, pardner? It's just not *interesting*. You know in D.C. they want body bags to brag about, indictments, convictions, that sort of scalp hunting; so I can't commit to big maybes."

"You know—"

"Nick, I got something for you I think you'd like, you give me a chance to get to it."

"Well, let me just throw a fast possibility at you. Okay? I've been thinking it over."

"It's late, Nick. And there's some other—"

"Please!"

"Oh, go ahead. Shoot. Fire away."

Nick cleared his throat.

"First, I have to ask myself, how'd those guys get in that room. The hitters? Guy was scared, guy was on the run, guy thought he'd been made, guy was sending out signals of catastrophe. But he's only in the room maybe ten minutes before they're on him?"

"Maybe he ordered out for room service and—"

"No room service in a crappy joint like the Palm Court. Plus, he wouldn't have. No way. He was just going to sit tight until he talked to somebody he trusted, that being me, because he had my name from a guy he knew in DEA. Me, Bureau, rather than somebody in DEA, because, like we all know, DEA isn't tight. We just joked about it a few minutes ago. They're not tight, he doesn't trust them, doesn't that tell you the guy knows what he's doing?"

"Okay, so go on," said Hap.

"Here's a second thing. He asks for, no he *demands*, a room next to all the Coke machines. Very weird, you have to admit. Now why would he do this? I mean really, Coke machines?"

"Maybe he liked Coke, Nick," somebody said.

When the laughter died, Nick said, "The Agency says he's not one of theirs? But let me tell you something very interesting. Not two weeks ago, this Agency which doesn't exist, it puts out a routine what's called Technology Memo for field usage, about the useful properties just discovered in vending machines that would especially help a guy on the run in an industrialized city. I went over to the Coke company a couple of days ago. Coke machines, especially the new, powerful ones, guess what? They put out a low-frequency electromagnetic force field. Enough to screw up a TV, radio, a small appliance. Or a parabolic mike for acoustical penetration."

He looked at them, let it sink in.

"He knew he was being hunted by pros. Pros who'd have the latest audio stuff. The Agency had just told him how to beat it. Don't you see?"

"Nick, I—" started Hap.

"But it gets even *more* interesting. Know why? See, they had very good stuff. Not crap stuff, like we have, but state-of-the-art eavesdropping gear. So he thought he had them beat, but they had him beat. And that's how they got in."

"What's the eavesdropping have to—"

"Only way they could get in without a struggle or leaving pick marks on the lock or any physical evidence of entry is with the magic two words. The magic two words were 'Nick Memphis.' Eduardo Lanzman or Lachine or whatever he calls himself, he calls the office, asks for Nick Memphis, leaves a message. Ten minutes later knock comes at door, somebody says, 'Nick Memphis.' Eduardo opens, they're on him very fast, and they whack him. Fair enough? So how'd they get my name?"

The guys looked at him silently. Mike Farthing lit a cigarette. Hap was making like a couch potato. Mickey Sontag, another bruiser but a young one, scratched his nose.

"They couldn't run a tap, they didn't have time. How'd they get my name?"

"Okay, what're you saying?"

"They *had* to have a parabolic mike. They acoustically penetrated his motel room. It wasn't hard-sealed, of course. But they could beam through the electronic interference of the Coke machines and hear what he was saying. Okay? It's the only adequate explanation of the event."

They were looking at him.

"And the significance of that—if their equipment is that good, then it's one of those jobs that costs out at about two hundred thousand dollars. We're talking an expensive piece of equipment. *We* don't even have one, you guys know. If we want one, we have to petition Washington, make the case that our bust is that important, and they send it over from Miami or down from St. Louis, in a van with two technicians, that is, if we can get the highest approval. So what's a piece of the space age like that doing being deployed in some low-ranking drug hit? I'm telling you guys, the signature all over this one is that it involves some big-time heavy hitters, some intelligence people maybe, or at the least some very, very big drug operators."

Hap considered.

"Nick, it's thin. You don't have any hard evidence, you have nothing to take to court. You only have your interpretation. And the word of some guy from Coke."

"Hap, just give me a week or two, it's the silly season, and if now and then it runs thin I'll drift over to Robbery Detail or shag paper for Bunco-Fraud or run stakeouts here on narc so these guys can take a day off now and then."

"What's your angle?"

"I want to ride the mike thing. Who makes these things, how are they dispersed, who owns them? How would people get hold of them? We can justify it by saying that it's a possible stolen government equipment thing, if you get any heat on it. But just let me attack it through that angle, and in a week or so, I'll let you know what I've come up with."

"Ahh," said Hap, "it's not making me happy, Nick, I have to answer to Washington and you know what pricks they can be. Tell you what, you do me a favor, I'll do you a favor, and we'll see how we shake down end of the week."

"Name it."

"Well, your favorite Mickey Mouse outfit, our old pals in the Secret Service are—"

A chorus of groans. Secret Service personnel were arrogant, reputedly the best shots in federal service, very showy, very touchy, and always hard to deal with because they put their agenda up front of everything.

"—hold the cheers, girls—anyway, they're sending a security detail down because, in, um, three weeks, Flashlight is coming. Yep, the man himself. Anyway, Washington wants us to cooperate up the kazoo with Secret Service and the bad part is the people on Pennsylvania Avenue are sending a heavy hitter down to run the liaison because yours truly doesn't quite carry enough weight. But we have to provide support. So I need a gofer to run errands for this big guy and keep him out of the office's hair and make my life easier. So here's the deal, Nick, you fill this guy's coffee cup for him and kiss his butt just where he likes it to be kissed, and dovetail with the assholes from Secret Service, and I'll cut you some slack to run this investigation."

It was a deal Nick couldn't say no to, and so he said yes, happily, but the happiness only lasted a second.

"Yeah, now I got you, buddy. Guess who the Washington shot is?"

Nick had a presentiment of tragedy.

"No."

"Sorry. Yeah. Guy's a comer, what can I say. It's Howdy Duty."

Howdy Duty was the nickname of Howard D. Utey, special assistant to the Director, former head of counterespionage, staff director of counterterror, former assistant director of organized crime, one of the hardest-charging law enforcement executives in the Bureau and a man much loathed and feared by all who knew him.

But especially Nick, for in 1986, Howard D. Utey, Howdy Duty, on his way up fast, had been supervisor of the Tulsa office. Howdy Duty had been on the other end of the mike when Nick took his shot.

Howdy Duty was Base, howling in his ear as he blew out the spine of the only woman he'd ever love.

CHAPTER EIGHT

Bob made a fast check from outside; if they'd been in, they'd been damned careful and very professional; he could find no trace of entry, no tracks or disturbances in the dust, no sign even of scuffing where they might have wiped out tracks. Most important, the dog Mike was slightly mangier for wear, but not dead, and Bob knew that if anyone had tried to enter the trailer compound, Mike would kill or die himself. Sam Vincent had kept the beast fed while Bob was gone, and Mike, part sloppy beagle and part God-knew-what from deep in the Ouachitas, was on him when he unlocked the cyclone gate, tongue wet and gloppy, eyes warm yet mournful. Mike was another solitary creature, a great pal who could seem to make no other friends and simply gave himself wholly to Bob's service.

Bob rubbed him and made him sing for joy, then got him some food as he opened his various padlocks—the trailer first, immaculate and pristine as he had left it, the gun vault, all guns gleaming in their patina of oil (he quickly replaced the Remington 700 while doing this), and finally the shop out back, where the problematic Winchester 70, damn its stubborn soul, still sat disassembled.

He looked at it, felt a yearning to lose himself once more in its intricacies and try to get at its secrets. Why was it now betraying him? Had it grown bored with loyalty and not enough attention? Had it a weak character, was it not a piece to be trusted when things turned dark and hairy? Or was it just tired, being fifty years or so old, an ancient piece of steel that had lost some inner fortitude?

But as he stared at it, he knew he could not give himself to it, no matter the ache involved. He had something to do now, something he wanted so bad it hurt him in places where he didn't think it would hurt ever again or that he even had.

He remembered himself lying with Donny's heavy stillness atop him, Donny's warm blood flooding over him, mingling with his own as the flies came and feasted on the stuff and from just inside the embankment the major was yelling, "Don't you move, Bob, goddammit, we got a fire mission coming in, we'll smoke his fucking ass." He remembered remembering while he lay there the time in the An Loc Donny had stood out in the motherfucking green open with his M-14 calmly shooting at gooks and drawing lots and lots of fire as poor Bob, busted from cover downslope like a covey of quail, scrambled up to the safety of the crest amid a sleet of destruction, his 700 flapping stupidly in the breeze, the jungle floor erupting from the misses around him until he finally made it to the top and the two of them fell behind the crest, laughing like maniacs, just spared death, high and nuts on danger, so in love with the great fun of their profession and the sense of the edge that made all pleasures so infinitely tasty.

"Oh, Christ, Bob, you shoulda seen the look on your damn face coming up that hill, damn, I near to bust a gut."

"You dumb sonovabitch kid, why didn't you get your ass down, no sense both our asses getting wasted."

"Fuck, Bob, it'd been worth it to die to see you lookin' so scared," and he dissolved in laughter.

He remembered his old dream: he and Donny and Donny's beautiful young wife Julie, a few dogs, some good old Arkansas whiskey for cold nights, all of them somehow living together in the Ouachitas, away from civilization, with their rifles, hunting every day, drinking every night. It was a stupid dream, he now realized, stupid as they come, because there was no way the world would permit such a thing; but he'd been young and dumb when he'd thought it up.

And he remembered when the major came in and saw him, his leg slung above him in plaster, the whole left side of his body immobilized.

"Didn't know they had someone who was that good," the major had said. "It was a hell of a shot."

Oh, yes it was. It was a hell of a shot.

I want him! Bob thought. Oh Jesus I want him. But it was a year before his body was well enough to hold a rifle again, and by that time he'd heard the rumors: white guy. Specialist. Someone brought in for just one job. But by that time, too, his war was over.

So now he thought he'd tremble or cry. The dog's warm tongue came slopping across his open hand, jarring him back from there to here. He shook his head a bit to stir the memories and make them flee, and was aware how rocky he suddenly felt.

Oh you Russian, how I want you for what you took from me!

Then he got hold of himself, felt his remade self fly back inside his body; he was all right. He was Bob again, who never talked but to three or four men in Blue Eye, Sam and Doc LeMieux, Sheriff Tell, the late Bo Stark when he was sober, and who shot at least a hundred rounds a day, rain or shine, and had given himself up entirely to the rifles so that he could live out his life and feel nothing at all.

He was all right, he had work to do, it was fine, now he was ready.

Bob worked it out, on decaf coffee and TV dinners, his own way. That is, eighteen, twenty, twenty-two hours at it, nailed at the kitchen table under a dim wash of bulb or a gray wash of thin January sunlight, with only the morning walk with Mike and the few hours' sleep to break up the journey. He did it slowly, carefully, never speeding up, never slowing down, looking through the maps and plans, drawing diagrams, taking measurements off his calculator, studying the architectural renderings of the buildings, making notes to himself.

He was a jungle shooter of course, an outdoorsman. But it seemed to him nevertheless that a city was a different kind of jungle, so that the same lessons would apply. A shooter would need the same requirements, the same perfect harmony of elements before taking a shot. And by this knowledge, he steered himself.

A shooter would need, first off, a clean theater of fire. By that Bob meant more than just a lane of fire. He'd need a line to the target, of course, but equally important he'd not want a formation of buildings either to the east or the west, to funnel the prevailing winds and generate unpredictable shears of energy that could take the fragile trajectory of the shot and make a pretzel of it. He'd want the sun behind him when he shot to kill the possibility that his scope would pick up a beam of light from the sun in front of it and toss it somewhere someone was looking—and the Secret Service would certainly be looking.

And then there was range. The Secret Service Worry Zone, tragically nonexistent in 1963, would almost certainly be a half mile out by this time—that's 880 yards where no windows could be open, where there'd be cops on every rooftop, circling helicopters, security checkpoints. The Russian would be at least a thousand yards out, maybe more like twelve hundred. He'd need a place to shoot from three-quarters of a mile away. And it would have to be a secure place, too, with an easy, unobservable entrance and exit, with access to an escape route. And it would have to be high for visibility to the target, but not too high. Shooting downward on an angle always played tricks on bullet trajectory too, particularly at extended ranges, but there was a cutoff point beyond which the trajectory became too irrational and was uncontrollable. Bob figured Solaratov would be at least three stories high, but could not be any more than five.

And the temperature was important too. A heavily humid climate could affect bullet trajectory too, but a frigid one would be even chancier, the near-to-zero weather making the gun's action stiff and awkward and subtly transforming the vibratory patterns of the wood of the stock and the metal of the barrel to say nothing of the fiber of the man behind the trigger. Bob had heard a hundred stories of good men taking that most important shot at a twelve-point buck on a frozen winter day and watching in horror as the bullet puffed harmlessly against the bluff ten yards away, and the beast took flight, leaving the hunter to face a bitter winter. He didn't think the Russian would shoot in any kind of cold weather, or in a particularly damp climate—too many ifs, too many maybes. If you're going to do it right, you do it where the earth itself is your ally, where the climate and the land and the sun and the sky are your friends.

He looked for a shot to take place where it was between fifty and seventy degrees out, on an overcast day, but a coastal city, where the wind was tempered by offshore fronts, and didn't howl in off a frozen midwestern plain or a frozen lake.

Then there was the question of noise. No matter what weapon Solaratov chose this time, he could not use a silencer that would only work with a subsonic round; he'd have to be at velocities of over two thousand feet per second with a weight of at least 150 grains and more likely 200 to have a chance of making a twelve-hundred-yard head or torso kill. They'd have to build him some sort of nearly soundproof room or chamber, a shooting bunker with acoustic baffling and only the smallest aperture for sighting and shooting; but he himself would have to be back from the aperture, so that the muzzle blast would be absorbed by the acoustic baffling, with some sound leakage from the aperture, but not enough to get a real fix on, as the sound would be generalized and diffuse. So Bob thought of a rooftop structure, a disguised heating plant; and from that he calculated there'd have to be nothing jerry-built about it; they were working on it even now, a structure of some sophistication and complexity, easy to disassemble perhaps, but nevertheless convincingly stable.

They could use any thousand-yard rifle, from a .308 on up to a .50 caliber sniping rifle of the sort now said to be in the inventory of elite units. Surely the Russian would have access to a .50. That possibility blew the distance factor out close to seventeen hundred yards, and it opened up the circle of possibility even further.

Bob moaned, rare enough for him; the job seemed huge; his head ached. He looked and couldn't tell if it was day or night, checked the jungle Seiko he'd worn since he'd bought it for twelve dollars in an Army PX in 1971 and saw that it was almost midnight. He sighed, and went back to work.

Location, time, distance, weapon. These were the points of his compass. As he studied the documents and tested a hundred shooting sites against them, he came up dry the first time through. He tried again, harder, sinking deeper into it. He tried to imagine the man, a shooter like himself, sunk in his sandbags, in a little dark room a mile out, watching through the scope as the president of the United States did this thing and that thing, and then his head blew off in a big red gout of tissue, a blizzard of bone and blood and brain. It would take weeks to find the room if he were firing from a mile out. They might never find it.

He worked it through, over and over and over, in slow, grinding degrees, sinking so far beneath the surface he wondered if there was a surface. Was there a solution? Could it be done? Where could he find everything. He—

Hey!

He watched it appear, watched it organize itself before his very eyes, saw it all fit together.

He saw in that instant how it would happen, how it had to happen. He knew where.

It was the third day, late, well past midnight. All right, he thought. You motherfuckers think it's 1972, fourteen hundred yards outside the Da Nang wire as Sniper Team Alpha slides over the berm.

It won't be.

Because this time I'll be waiting.

CHAPTER NINE

"Nicky, Nicky," said Tommy Montoya, "oh, my boy, this is not like you."

Montoya was Cuban, deep into spook life, who occasionally came across tips that he passed Memphis's way as he did his jobs for various agencies of the federal government and perhaps for other customers as well. He was one of those edge-masters, a bit too clever for his own good, who'd some day be found in the Big Muddy or Lake Pontchartrain with a diesel crankcase wired to his ankle and a school of guppies living in a thoracic wound cavity. But until then, Tommy Montoya would lick the oyster dry and now he smiled, holding an opened bivalve in one fat hand, and his thick tongue darted out to nudge the gelid thing loose from its tray of shell, so that he could suck it down in one intense, sensuous moment.

Nick tried to avert his eyes. Christ, how could anyone eat one of those things? Nick was of the opinion that if it didn't bleed when you cut it, you didn't put it in your mouth. But the Cuban still had his uses. He knew things nobody else knew—the business, for example.

"Nicky," he said again, "you know you go through channels. DEA's got priority on those big eavesdropping rigs, you apply through—"

"Come on, Tommy," said Nick, in a hurry to get through Tommy's coy games, because Howdy Duty was due in that afternoon and he wanted to be ready when the old Base got there, because if you got off on the wrong foot with Utey, you never got back to the right one, as Nick knew only too well.

So he was nervous and not handling this brilliantly. Besides, the bar on the riverfront was dark and seething with exotic men, and Nick, in a Stay-Prest blue poplin suit and a white shirt, felt as if he had FED stenciled between his hairline and his eyebrows in letters three inches tall and knew the long grip of his Smith 1076 was printing through the coat.

He plunged ahead, all illusion of finesse gone. "Say I needed one fast. I gotta circumvent the red tape. I got a big bust coming up but I'm afraid, say, there's a leak, either in DEA or my own shop. I want ultrasophisticated listening technology and, just to make it worth somebody's while, let's say I liberated enough cash from a bad dealer to be able to pay the going tariff. So what's my best move?"

"You ain't wearing a wire, my friend? You're not trying to bug a bugger or con a con man? You always seemed to me to be a pretty straight kind of guy."

It was said of Tommy that he'd gone ashore with 2506 Brigade at the Bay of Pigs, and spent two years in

Castro's prisons—and that he had scars like star bursts on his back. He had that Latin thing—*cajones,* machismo, whatever—that lurid but nonneurotic willingness to do violence that radiated out of every pore of his ample body.

"No, I'm clean, man, that's all. I just have to figure out how some guys got some powerful listening equipment into play out by the airport a couple of days ago. Where they got some stuff and got it quick, to set up a hit."

"That guy had his insides cut to ribbons?"

"Yeah, that guy."

"Ooooooo, Nicky, that's a strange one. You know, you always hear things. Always. You know, the players, the teams, when something like this goes down. Except now. Nicky, my friend, would you believe, I ain't heard nothing. It's strictly from out of town. It's got nothing to do with us, I'll tell you."

"Maybe not. Still, it's kinda personal. Come on, Tommy. I'm just playing up the equipment angle. I have a source who swears the guy was some kind of Salvadoran spook, and I'm also hearing Agency on him, but the Agency won't play ball with me and his records are so suspiciously clean it makes me wonder how come a guy could lead a whole life without ever getting a parking ticket."

Tommy made a sour face, then with his tongue liberated another oyster. How such a thick man could do such an obscene thing with such quick delicacy really amazed Nick.

"I'm trying to figure how the hell the guys got in to whack the john. They *heard* him trying to reach me. With some gear. Now, where the hell you get stuff like that around here?"

"Well," Tommy finally said, "what I think you want would be one of the Electrotek 5400 models. It's a portable directional parabolic microphone, very state of the art, known for its capacity to penetrate even hardened rooms. We're talking over a million the unit. Far as I know, only seven were built—four for DEA, two for the Agency, and one for a foreign client, very hush-hush."

"What country?" asked Nick.

"Oh, I wouldn't want to say, my friend. But they had themselves a nasty little war going on."

"El Salvador! That's it. Son of a bitch."

He saw pattern before his eyes. It's what he lived for: the magic connection between parts of a case.

He was thinking in great leaps: Electrotek *goes* to El Salvador in what year? Say, late eighties, when we're pouring aid in. Okay, so this guy Eduardo Lanzman, he's spook, but he learns something? Something big? Something dangerous? Scares his butt. So he thinks, who the fuck can I call? Obviously, it's got spook business all over it, so he doesn't want to go to his old pals in the Agency, right? Because he hasn't shaken it out, doesn't know quite who's doing what to whom, who's on which side—oh, I know how shadowy it gets—so he has to find someone outside—someone *safe*, someone he can trust—to tell. So he thinks of an old pal in DEA who might have some kind of perspective, except that guy is not in the life anymore. So, he then thinks of this FBI agent the DEA guy told him about. So he takes off. But now they know he's gone. So he cools his heels somewhere, just to throw them off the track. But somehow they know he's headed toward New Orleans, so that gets them time to get the unit up here and set up a surveillance at the airport. Where they spot him. They follow him. They've got the goddamn thing in play. They find the room; they penetrate it electronically, these Salvadorans. They get my name, they pop the room and turn poor Eduardo inside out.

Tommy looked at him.

"Nick, you look like you just had a religious experience. The Virgin, did she talk to you?"

"Somebody did," Nick said. Not normally religious, he had a brief impulse to make the sign of the cross for Eduardo, who opened the door expecting to see dull old Nick but instead caught three bad hitters in the face and died the death only a Mandarin torturer could have invented . . . and yet who cared so much that even after the executioners had left and his guts were like dirty socks in the bed and the shock had worn off enough for the pain to be the fifth act of every opera ever written, this guy still had the machismo to crawl to the linoleum and pass on the message.

ROM DO.

ROM DO?

What did it mean? What was this clue, so tantalizing, so goddamn cute?

"I got another weird one for you. This guy, he left a message written in his own blood. ROM DO, in caps. What's the words *Rom, Do* mean to you, Tommy. Anything? I spent thirteen hours in the library the other day, just going through books on crime and espionage, looking for something. I asked the big smart guys at Quantico in the Behavioral Science Department, you know, our intellectuals. They came up with nothing. Any idea?"

"Rom Do? Could be anything, man." Then he laughed. "Funny, it reminds me of something."

"Okay," said Nick, "so sing. Tell me."

"Oh, it's crazy."

"Crazier the better, my friend, that's where I'm at."

"You know I was on the island in sixty-one? *Bahia de Cochinos*, huh, my friend? The Bay with the Piggies?"

"Yeah, so it's said."

"Okay, my battalion was first ashore at Red Beach, you know, near Playa Larga. Okay, we used Army call signs, just like the American army, because we believed in America and we believed in that cocksucker JFK, man, we loved him and we loved our little invasion." The bitterness spurted out and clouded his words. Then he caught himself.

"Anyway, later they changed it. Okay, they changed it and made it more jet age. The *D*, I mean."

"What are you talking about?"

"The *D* became Delta. *D* for Delta. Not Dog no more, but Delta. You went on the radio and your call sign was a *D*, you were Delta. Delta Company, Delta Flight, Delta squadron, Delta Force, that sort of thing. But in the early sixties, they hadn't changed. *D* was Dog. *R* was Romeo. It was call signs and I was in Second Battalion, 2506 Brigade, *La Brigada*, and we were Romeo Dog Two, there was a Romeo Dog Three, Four and Five, the guy running the show, the *patron*, out there on the ship, he was Romeo Dog Six. 'Rom Do'? Your guy's hurrying on that floor, his mind ain't working right, he's dying. He's sending you a message from the past. Romeo Dog. Get it?"

"Romeo Dog? No, I don't get it," Nick said, turning the info over in his head.

What the hell was Romeo Dog?

Howdy Duty hadn't changed; he was one of those men who couldn't change. But then Nick hadn't changed, either. Nick would never change: he'd always be a special agent, and never a supervisory agent. Maybe he didn't really mind that, because in his own heart he knew he wasn't cut out to give orders and he wasn't interested in power and a fine home in the Virginia suburbs of Washington. But having the no-promotion tag on his record would at least keep him off of the really interesting squads and out of Washington forever. He'd never get Anti-Terrorist, which was the crème de la crème in the eighties and probably would be well into the nineties; it was fast-reacting jungle gym stuff, guns and SWAT tactics, and interfacing with some extremely interesting other agencies, the fastest league of all. He'd never get a Hostage Rescue Team. Now those boys were the elite: HRTs kicked down doors and smoked bad guys when it came the time to walk the walk. And he'd never get Organized Crime either, and that was hot stuff, sinking through the membrane of the Mafia, entering that twisted, yet fascinating world; if you got that, you were *doing something.* It was true of counterespionage too, only the hard part of that was simply following Cubans around Washington and wiretapping embassies. But also interesting.

No, Nick would stay forever in out-of-the-way, B-city offices; Baltimore or Richmond or Frederick were as close as he'd come to Washington and though less than a hundred miles each way from the Big Town, they were still universes away, and the leap from one to another, without a validating stop in New York or Miami or L.A. (where Nick would never go, either) was a quantum leap . . . impossible by the physics of Bureau culture.

Yet for all of that, he did not hate Howdy Duty. Utey had simply faced the hard decision of sorting out the Tulsa incident so that it would do the Bureau the most good, and if he identified himself and his own career as "The Bureau" in some way, it wasn't a selfish decision so much as a helpless one. That was how it went; that was how he thought.

And so, when Nick picked Howard D. Utey up at the New Orleans airport, it wasn't a particularly tense or awkward thing. They both understood.

Howard stood on the curb outside the American terminal and waved when he saw Nick in the gray government Ford. He even had a little smile as he ducked to come in, tossing his bag in the backseat.

"Hi, Nick. Boy, you're looking great. Still keeping that hair, huh?"

"That's right, Howard. It just won't fall out, I don't know why."

"Nick, I was sorry to hear about Myra. Was she in any pain at the end?"

"No. She'd been in a coma for a long time. She just stopped breathing. It wasn't a hard end. She had a hard life but she had an easy end."

"Well, thank God for small and tender mercies."

"I know, Howard," said Nick, dully, concentrating on not calling him Howdy, though it occasionally happened, and Utey, who knew his nickname well, always pretended not to notice.

Howdy Duty was quite a small man, actually, small and ferrety, but not stupid or slow. He had simply given himself totally to the Bureau, and had set about to rise with the patience and the fury of a poor boy. He managed it with certain political gifts, to be sure; but also by working as hard as it was possible to work.

"They still call me 'Howdy Duty,' Nick?"

"I'm afraid they do, Howard," said Nick as they drove in from the airport.

"Well, that's all right, as long as it's behind my back, and as long as I never hear that it's gotten to Secret Service, Nick. That I would have to regard as an act of treachery, not to me personally, but to the Bureau as a whole. You know, everybody here likes you, Nick—everybody *everywhere* likes you, that's one of your gifts—and it'd do everybody a lot of good if you'd pass that information around. I know that informally passed information is sometimes more efficiently communicated than office memos. Fair enough?"

"Yes, Howard," said Nick. That was Howard. He established the rules and played by them—unless it suited his purposes to change them.

"Now, Nick, a lot of what we'll be doing in the next few weeks is liaison, which again is why it's great to have you on the team. You have a wonderful gift for getting along with people. Don't think it hasn't been noticed. And you'll need all your affability, all right? All of it. Every bit."

"Sure, Howard. So what'm I going to be doing? I heard the pres—"

"That's right, Nick. On March first, the president will be flying down from Washington in the morning for a speech and presentation in downtown New Orleans. He's going to be giving Archbishop Jorge Roberto Lopez the Freedom Medal—you know, the Archbishop of Salvador who won the Nobel Peace Prize?"

Nick knew, of course. Archbishop Roberto Lopez was a validated Great Man, the heir to the martyred Archbishop Oscar Romero; he had worked tirelessly at getting the two sides in that bitter war, exacerbated so terribly of late by the Panther Battalion massacre, to talk.

Nick remembered the news footage: Bishop Roberto Lopez walking among the dead children by the riverbank in his humble black cloth with a humble silver cross about his neck, his eyes wracked with tears behind the wire-frame glasses. A poet, an expert on medieval Latin alchemy, a complete apolitical, who had the love in his heart to tell NBC, "I do not hate the men who did this. I love them and I forgive them. To hate them and to demand their punishment is to guarantee that such horror will be perpetuated."

"The president's popularity has slipped a bit since the war, Nick. I think he wants to get on the Bishop Roberto Lopez bandwagon. It certainly won't do him any harm."

"Maybe he just admires the guy," said Nick. "A lot of people do."

"Anyway, I know you're not aware of this down here, you know"—he meant, Nick knew, at *your* level—"but recently relations between the Bureau and the Secret Service have not been very friendly. In Chicago three months ago, we ran into a problem of intersecting investigations—counterfeit money drew Treasury in and we were working it from an organized crime standpoint, and somehow we never knew the other was there. An arrest sequence got confused and one of our people shot one of theirs. Didn't kill him, and they say he'll probably be on his feet in six months or so, but it left bad feelings."

Nick shook his head. It sure as hell must have. No one really liked working with the Secret Service, particularly on security details, where the guys in the sunglasses were absolute pricks, and by informal fiat took command of any situation. Feelings always were rubbed raw; no ten-year Bureau man liked being told what to do by a twenty-three-year-old boy in shades with an earpiece, a lapel pin, and an Uzi in a briefcase. And yet that's the way it always happened.

"It's the same drill, Nick, you know it. Secret Service will provide the manpower and the close-up security; they'll run their own security investigations; but we're there to back them up, to run interference with the locals with them, and to handle any investigative work that won't fit into their time frames."

To be their gofers, Nick thought bleakly.

"Now the director is adamant," Howdy continued. "We've got some fence-mending to do. And that's our job. Fence-mending. You and I, Nick, we are the fence menders. Through you, I'll be turning over the resources of our New Orleans office to Secret Service; in turn, we're to be granted a bit of security authority ourselves and indeed, we'll be part of the operation on the day Flashlight arrives. It's a good chance, Nick; it's something I thought you'd enjoy, and if it goes well, I'll certainly mention you prominently in the reports. You'll have a great deal of latitude too; the freedom to do what best you can do. Who knows? Things can change. This might just get you out of your rut."

"Sure, Howard. I appreciate the chance."

But Nick knew Howard would be on him like a cheap cologne; that was Howard's way, that was the Bureau's way; it had happened in Tulsa; it was happening now.

"So, Nick, you've got a clean desk? You're ready to swing away? Hap Fencl said you'd come to me with nothing hanging over you. Is that right?"

"More or less. I've got this one little thing going, a murder that was probably facilitated by some high-tech military equipment. You know, it's funny, the guy was also Salva—"

"Don't we turn here?"

They had just sailed by a sign that pointed to downtown off a left-hand turn.

"Huh?"

"I'm staying at the Hilton. Weren't we supposed to turn here?"

"Oh, uh, no, Howard, not that way. That'd get you there. But this time of day, it's faster to stay on Sixty-one, then cut over to Ninety. See?"

"Oh, all right. It's your town. But I would have turned there," Howdy Duty said. He didn't mean to sound displeased, Nick thought; but he did anyway.

CHAPTER TEN

In each of the four cities, he presented the same phenomenon: a tall, lanky man in boots and a blue denim shirt, pressed and buttoned to the top. He wore a down-filled field coat, suede Tony Lamas and his black, wide Stetson but in Baltimore he felt out of place with the hat and left it in his room.

In each city he checked into a middle-range downtown hotel after taking a cab in from the airport; he ate modestly and never drank and when he wasn't in his room, studying his maps, he discreetly toured the shooting sites, taking notes, walking off the distances, watching the fall of the light and the way the shadow angles changed as the sun moved across the sky; feeling the temperature, the push of the prevailing winds, looking at the traffic patterns in and out, at the theaters or stages where the president would be speaking when the shot was to be fired; he walked endlessly around the buildings, into their lobbies, but he never pressed his luck, and made no attempt to get into places where he was not permitted. His only eccentricity most people mistook for an elaborate camera. In fact, it was a Barr & Stroud prismatic optical rangefinder, with two lenses eighty centimeters apart. It enabled him to measure distances with unerring accuracy.

In each city, he learned things no map or guidebook could tell him. He discovered small discrepancies in the elevation grids of the Cincinnati hills, not much, but just enough to throw a shooter off. He'd be higher than he thought he was and his bullet's trajectory therefore more subject to the pull of gravity.

In Baltimore, he noted the persistence of wind off the harbor; he'd never associated Baltimore with wind at all and the information irritated him. The guidebooks never said a damned thing about it, but the gulls hanging like helicopter gunships over a burning village told the story. He imagined a bullet riding those winds, drifting this way and that in their grasp, perhaps true to its aim, perhaps not.

In Washington, he saw the trees. The shot indicated in the picture of the Soviet shooting mock-up would have to pass through trees. Admittedly, this time of year the visibility was fairly good. But Bob thought the problem was a bullet-deflecting sprig of limb; it would be like firing through a labyrinth, and even the smallest of obstructions could send a heavy-caliber bullet moving at close to three thousand feet per second spinning off in the craziest ways.

Then, too, in Washington the shooting platforms were exceedingly iffy; Justice was closest but the angle into the back lawn of the White House was extreme, and if he were shooting from there—about 450 yards—T. Solaratov would have a quarter profile as a target, always the hardest angle into major body structures, a devilishly hard shot, though Bob had dropped a few that way. Almost a full mile out, from the Department of Agriculture, the sniper would have a much wider target, and presumably a much stabler one, as bodies don't move laterally during speeches nearly so much as they moved up and back. Still . . . shooting through trees a mile out from atop a government building—this said nothing of the extraordinary deception operation that would have to be mounted to get him in and out—seemed the longest of long shots, purely from a technical point of view.

New Orleans was a Southern city, which he appreciated; the air was balmy, the breezes mild. Of all the cities, he liked it the best, and quickly found that only a sliver of it was the fabled block or so of Bourbon Street where all the movies were filmed. The place itself had a sleepy, nondescript way to it and the black people still carried themselves with that elegant dignity that is only possible in the true South.

But the problem with New Orleans was the air, which was heavy with the tang of salt water and the acrid, dense musk that miles of mushy swamp produced. It was almost a jungle climate, and though it could be shot through with accuracy—Bob had done it, after all—it produced the sort of accuracy warpage that would have to be planned for and practiced in. This was most interesting; if they were going to go for a .50 caliber shot a mile out in New Orleans, it occurred to Bob that they'd almost have to build themselves a mile of range here, because each swampy ecosystem has its own peculiar climate, depending on the density of the salt water, the gassiness of the swamp, the prevailing winds. You couldn't prep a New Orleans shot in Iraq or even Russia, except in its most inconsequential aspects; you'd have to do it over a period of days in a period of weather conditions to see what hob the moisture would play on the bullet.

Might be interesting to check out, he thought.

His travels finished after ten long days on the road, Bob flew back to Arkansas and returned to his trailer. Again, it was as he left it, unentered; again, Mike's slobbery love greeted him and he took some time to work with the dog, to pet him and make him feel wanted, to rub those velvety ears. You didn't want to spoil a creature with too much attention, but Mike had such need it moved Bob. It was the longest time he'd ever been away from the dog; the dumb love poured up to him from the eyes and the hot breath. Its paws were flung upon him as Mike went nuts in bliss.

"Hey, boy, your old man's back," he said, again surprising himself with a kind of laugh. Truth was, he felt pretty damned good. He'd been in The World, tested himself against it, and come back in one piece, not destroyed. The work was fascinating and what he'd found pleased him; he was eager to get on with the next bit.

He went to the icebox, found some chili frozen in a square like a brick, and set it to warming on the stove; then he showered quickly, changed into clean jeans and shirt and boots. Then he took Mike for a good four-mile walk. By the time he was back, the stuff was hot and red, as he liked it. He ate it quickly and economically, with large glasses of iced tea, only momentarily missing the beer that had once been his chief sensual pleasure with hot food.

Then, though tired, he felt nourished. He went over to a typewriter that had been in the family since his grandfather was sheriff of Polk County back in the twenties, and began very slowly and carefully to write.

Bob always surprised people with his literacy; they expected an ex-Marine gunnery sergeant from Arkansas to be a complete fool when it came to letters, not knowing, say, capitals from small letters, or what a paragraph was about, or the difference between a period and a colon or the meaning of that great puzzler, the apostrophe. But he knew all that; more, he knew he had a small, quiet gift for expressing himself clearly and it always pleased him to do so. And he did so now.

He wrote a twenty-two-page document explaining his analysis of the four shooting sites and his prediction of T. Solaratov's preferences. He knew, of course, where he'd shoot from himself; it scared him a little, because he saw how easy it would be, how in spite of all the advances since 1963, how despite the extent to which everyone had entered the era of maximum paranoia and security, it was still nearly impossible to stop a man with a rifle and the will and the skill to use it.

It was not an eloquent document, but it was direct, after the military fashion.

> It is my feeling that the subject will most likely attempt his shooting of the President on 1 March of this year at Louis Armstrong Park in New Orleans. He will be shooting a 750-grain copper-sheathed .50 caliber round from approximately 1,200 yards out. The bullet will be traveling, when it strikes the President, at over 1,500 feet per second, and that should, with the bullet weight, defeat any body armor the President is wearing. The time of the shooting will almost certainly be near the end of the President's speech, which is scheduled to begin at 11:30 and last 45 minutes. There are three reasons for this. First, a shadow falls across the podium of the shooting site

between 10:30 A.M. and 2:15 P.M. on that day (give or take a few minutes) and the President will be deepest into it at the end of his speech, which will mean that the glare from the contrast between the light and the dark will be at its minimum during the time of his exposure. This would not be a factor under normal ranges, but the extreme distance of the shot will make even the most incidental considerations important. Second, midday is by weather bureau records the calmest time of day; the prevailing winds tend to be at their gustiest during the morning hours. The Russian will almost certainly know this, if he's studied carefully. In fact, of the four shooting sites, only New Orleans puts the President in the zone of exposure during the calmest part of the day, with Cincinnati a distant second. And finally, the New Orleans site offers at least three escape routes. If he shoots from the steeple of St. Louis Cathedral in the French Quarter, which is located 1,200 yards from the site of the speech, and he uses some kind of external (by that I mean nonballistic) noise suppression system, he can very easily retreat down the (closed) stairway, step into the crowds on the square and melt away. It is unlikely that discovery of the site would be made for several minutes, perhaps hours, because the site is so far from the bullet strike. From the church he could very quickly walk to the Mississippi, which is less than half a mile away, and flee by boat down into the bayou system, and it would be almost impossible to locate him in there. He could also depart down Decatur, a major thoroughfare unlikely to be burdened by heavy traffic at that time of day. Or finally, in desperate straits, he could be picked up by helicopter in the open space of Jackson Square, just in front of the Church.

Then Bob made his recommendations.

1) Secret Service should be informed at earliest possible date of the Soviet attempt and brought in on our side. But they have to be made to understand that the point of the operation is not only to safeguard the President's life but to apprehend and interrogate the Soviet–Iraqi shooting team and its support units.

2) Radio networks should be authorized and interjurisdictional limits set, so that SS knows exactly its responsibilities and this agency knows what it can do too.

3) Monitoring of St. Louis Cathedral in New Orleans should begin immediately; almost surely the shooting team will begin to modify and adapt it prior to 1 March. At the same time surveillance should be extremely discreet, so as not to scare away "the bird." As enemy investigation of the site will almost certainly be thorough, it is further recommended that no direct observational devices or planted listening devices be employed. They would be onto those in a second. A very good way might be to observe from above—F4Js at 20,000 feet orbiting in circle—with infrared cameras for heat signatures, in the way the Air Force did in Vietnam when it was interdicting the Ho Chi Minh Trail.

4) An aerial search of greater New Orleans bayou and swamp area should be commenced immediately in order to locate the site of Russian preparation. In order to adjust to climatic conditions in late winter/early spring, the shooting team will almost certainly hold several live fire run-throughs under circumstances as exact as possible so that Solaratov knows exactly what to expect as to load performance and so forth.

5) The President should of course be warned, but

if he is as courageous as he proved to be in the war against Iraq, he will insist upon taking part in the exercise to lure the shooting team onward, rather than using a double or canceling the event. His earliest participation is necessary.

6) On day of event, counter sniper teams should be stationed concentrically from the President's speaking position as indicated on map. These positions are located roughly 600 yards out and are oriented away from, rather than toward, the President. Each unit should be equipped with one Remington Model-40A1 rifle with Unertl 10× scope and carry duty load of M852 Match Accuracy Lake City Arsenal 7.62mm NATO cartridges, in order to engage the Soviet–Iraqi team in the event of actual shooting. (I would like to lead one of these units, and I prefer to locate myself at the starred site on the map on the day of the event; if necessary, and given the proper command authority, I can take out the Soviet–Iraqi team before any harm is done. I'll shoot the shooter through center mass and the spotter—if there is one—in the left body quadrant; a quick reactive team can almost certainly get to him before he comes out of shock and begins self-destruction procedures. He should be an interesting intelligence source.)

7) Debriefing of captured Soviet and/or personnel should begin immediately so that we may act on their intelligence immediately; in Vietnam, interrogation information was sometimes squandered when we reacted too slowly.

He stopped typing.

That was it.

What else was there?

Well, of course there was one other thing and it was the thing that no man could plan for. Luck. One only prayed for it, and maybe it would be there and maybe it wouldn't.

He looked at his watch. Time to sleep; tomorrow he'd send the report to the people he now believed represented the Central Intelligence Agency.

He stripped and crawled into bed. Mike bounded up too, for the big soft stupid dog liked to touch him ever so slightly through the covers in sleep.

But at four he awakened and went back and read the document over. It seemed good. He couldn't sleep however. He knew it was absurd but he felt he was being watched or something. He sat back and tried to work out his feelings about his new employers.

He didn't trust them. But they were all he had.

And then he thought: I need an edge. I need a way to keep these boys from turning on me if things go wrong. He tried to think of what that might be, but he couldn't come up with a thing.

CHAPTER ELEVEN

It was humiliating. Nick had become a complete and total gofer, a clerk, a fool. He bustled through the corridors with files and coffee and doughnuts like Hazel the maid. Howdy Duty hardly let him talk to the Secret Service people at all, leaving that delicate task to himself; Nick had been appointed head eunuch.

"Hey, Memphis, your slip is showing," his ex-partner Mickey Sontag yelled out as Nick raced from the file room to a former storage room now bearing the important title on the door JOINT SECRET SERVICE/BUREAU MEETING GROUP, where the federal bodyguards and the sanctimonious Utey had set up shop.

"Yeah, yeah" said Nick helplessly, knowing he

was running late, pissed as hell that Ginny Feany, mistress of the files, had not found the dope on one Clark Clarkson, White Knight of the Lafayette Parish Ku Klux Klan, quite fast enough.

"Boy, they running you ragged, old Saint Nick."

Nick was thirty-four; this *old* shit had to stop.

But "Yeah, yeah" was all he could think to say.

In the meeting, the senior Secret Service guy, Phil Mueller, was sounding off as usual like General Patton for a squad of his own troops and for Howdy as well.

"And this is the last of them?"

"He says it is," answered Utey for Nick, before Nick could answer for himself.

"Even the inactives, the discontinueds, the imprisoned and the dead ones?"

"All of them, Phil."

"So with your files, with our information, and with the stuff from the National Crime Index, we got what, total maybe two hundred fifty names? Triaged into three categories, Alphas, Betas and Charlies, for bad risk, possible risk, and should-be-checked-out. How's the numbers on it? You getting through the Alphas?"

"Uh, Phil," said one of the Secret Service joes, "we're working them pretty hard. I've got three teams on them, that's six guys for fifty-six of them, I've got a Beta team, and we've got a hundred twenty-four Betas, the rest Charlies."

"How's it shaping up timewise?"

"I think we'll make the Alphas, no sweat, if we bring some of our other people in. I think we'll make most of the Betas, too, we get a break or two. But it's those damn Charlies that have us worried. I just don't think, manpowerwise, we're going to get very far into them."

"Um," said Mueller.

"A thought, Phil," said Howdy Duty.

"Yes, Howard."

"Maybe Nick could work the Charlies. Most of it's phone, no? Checking up?"

"Hmmm," said Mueller.

"He'd be more than willing, right, Nick?"

Nick just sat there, stewing.

Great. What these guys were doing—what they *always* did prior to a visit by the Man—was developing, in coordination with local law enforcement and cooperating federal agencies, a regional list of known wackos, screwballs, right- and left-wing dingbats, survivalists, and others fitting the potential risk profile. These people were then investigated by teams to determine location and current situation; if some signal of instability was detected by the officers, then surveillance was sometimes mandated; more frequently, the guys were simply rousted savagely, detained, had the shit scared out of them, then sent on their way. It was painstaking, boring work, absolutely the dullest. But it was Secret Service policy to know where all the nuts were stored before the Man got into gun range.

"But the bomb—" Nick began.

"Can wait," snapped Mueller. "You get digging into the Charlies, okay, Memphis?"

"He'll do it," assured Utey. "Nick, you won't mind putting in the extra time, will you?"

So what do you say? Well, the good Bureau man doesn't say anything; he doesn't let anything show; he just nods and knuckles under and gets behind the team.

And that's what Nick committed himself to doing, biting down his anger that he'd missed a shot at the Secret Service bomb detail. Now those guys were pros. He'd wanted to see them work, they were so legendary. They did site preparation, and when they were done working an area over, you knew it was sanitized, that the dogs had sniffed no explosives or wires, that the spectrometers had uncovered no unusual radio waves for command detonations, that no sniper's nests or shooting platforms had been uncovered.

And it was outdoor work! It was doing something! It was getting back into the field, away from all this political nonsense and being just a clerk-jerk. And, the truth was, what Nick hated most of all of it was sitting in the office. He knew he wasn't thorough enough, that he tended to make small mistakes. He cursed, silently, as his fate overtook him. But he kept his face flat and mild.

When it was over, Herm Sloane, who wasn't too bad a guy, slid by and said, "Too bad, Nick. Know you wanted to slip out tomorrow. We're just bogged down."

"No problem," said Nick, trying for cheer, which was his usual way of dealing with adversity.

"I don't know who's worse," Sloane added conspiratorially, "my guy assholing it all over the place or your guy sucking it up all over the place."

"It's pretty fucking pathetic," Nick said. "You got those Charlies for me?"

"'Fraid so, old pal."

Sloane handed over the stack of files that he had triaged into the Charlie category. Nick looked at them sadly. It was hours and hours of work. He knew his investigation on the death of Eduardo Lanzman was falling apart. It wasn't happening, because he couldn't get to it.

The names were prosaic, pitiful, and as he glanced through the files, he saw the usual litany of failure and hatred, the usual roundup, the usual suspects. Little men with large grudges and imprecise grips on reality, who were only to be reckoned with because they had or could get guns.

And then Nick saw the name of his hero:

Bob Lee Swagger.

Bob the Nailer, he thought. Jesus Christ!

In three fourteen-hour days, Nick managed to eliminate fifty-six of his seventy Charlies. It was exhausting work, sitting there, phoning this office or that, tracking down that parole officer or this one, going through phone books and the state prison records division, talking to cops and lawyers and the various parish morgues. Of the fifty-six, more than half, twenty-nine, had simply died since, for whatever reason, they had been placed on the Secret Service Active Suspect List. Nick suspected therefore that the list was very old; so many old men. Another sixteen were serving jail time. Five were currently in mental institutions—these were the real crazos, whose difficulty in dealing with authority over the long term had finally gotten them classified pathological and who were now rusticating in some picturesque bayou bin. Six more had vanished, left the city or the state, simply disappeared off the face of the earth. They were now, happily, somebody else's worry. That left fourteen to be accounted for, tracked, located, what have you; it was not easy work but he went at it with a great deal of effort.

And it left Bob the Nailer.

Nick had first heard of the great Marine sniper sometime in the early eighties, in an article in one of those *Soldier of Fortune*–type magazines that he used to read at the time. He remembered the cover photo of the lean young man in the camouflage paint and the intense eyes, and the beautiful Remington rifle he was carrying and the cover line: THE MOST DANGEROUS MAN ALIVE. The stories were incredible; whatever the guy shot died. Bob the Nailer had eighty-seven confirmed kills in Vietnam; he did some jobs for the Agency, it was said; and, his masterpiece, he'd hit a North Vietnamese battalion moving on an isolated Green Beret camp and held it down for two days, killing thirty-odd men in the process, saving the Special Forces' bacon.

That was when Nick himself was trying to be the great shooter, back in his ass-kicking SWAT days, before Myra and Tulsa. Thinking back now, it all seemed so clear and innocent; you were a trained man, you went against bad guys, and because you were so good, they got nailed.

That was when he'd sold his soul to the rifle, when he was, however briefly, an acolyte in the cult of the sniper. He shivered a bit at the vanity of it, remembering what his pride had turned into in Tulsa.

Still, all these years later he had a place in him full of respect for Bob. Bob had never wavered, had let nothing stand between himself and what he wanted to be, and Bob had tested himself in the crucible of the actual, while Nick had only tried once and failed spectacularly. His bullet had gone exactly where he had not wanted it to.

So it was with a sense of facing his old self and his old beliefs and the mistakes of his own youth that he set about to track down Bob the Nailer. And like many memories, this one proved easy enough to unearth. Bob was not hard to find, that is, the traces of Bob. He'd checked into the Robert Oliver Hotel in the French Quarter on February 3 and checked out on February 4. Two days. Nobody much remembered him; the only vague reports Nick could scare up told of a tall western-styled man, very leathery, who said nothing, kept to himself, was gone all day, and left without fuss. Had a funny camera with him, some expensive Jap thing probably.

Business of some sort, Nick thought. He'd heard that Swagger hadn't been able to stay in the Marines because of his injuries. Probably today he was some kind of traveling salesman or something, or an Arkansas farmer into the big city for the hell of it, a wild few days or something, take some pictures like any tourist, and go on back to the South Forty.

But it occurred to Nick to ask a more fundamental question. Why was the guy on the Suspects List at all? Who put him there? What gets you there?

He ran Swagger through the FBI computer and learned he had no record, at least no felonies listed anywhere. He checked him against the National Crime Index and again came up with nothing. Calling the Department of the Navy, he learned that Bob had retired at the rank of gunnery sergeant with physical disability pay after twelve years active service and close to three years in the hospital undergoing joint reconstruction and extensive physical therapy and had no blemishes on his record. He checked with the Veterans Administration and found out that Bob had never sought or received any kind of psychological testing, or counseling or anything like that. There seemed to be nothing on him at all. Now why the hell had he ended up on this list? And who was tracking him enough to note that he was here in New Orleans?

He called Herm Sloane.

"Hey, Herm—"

"Nick, we're really pressed for time up here? What is it?"

"I just have one question. These Charlies, where do you get them? How does a guy get on the Charlie list?"

"Well, the Alphas are usually developed from intelligence, usually from the Bureau investigations of dangerous groups, from other Justice Department or DEA sources and our own intelligence unit; um, the Betas are usually guys with minor criminal records, guys who've made lots of public threats, who have an authority complex and tend to attract attention; and your Charlies are letter writers. We keep all the threatening letters the president gets, or threatening-seeming letters. Why?"

"Oh, there's a Charlie here that surprised me."

"Listen, call Tom Marbella at Treasury in DC. He collates the letter files; he'll let you know what's what."

Some minutes later, Nick managed to track down Marbella and Marbella said he'd check it out, let him know, and some time after that—it was the next day, actually—Marbella called back.

"Okay, I've got the file up on my computer terminal now. Your boy seems to think he should have won the Congressional Medal of Honor," said Marbella.

"Hmm," said Nick, a noise he made when he wanted to indicate he was on the phone still, but that he had no attitude or information to convey.

"Three weeks ago, he writes a letter to the president, explaining that the Marine Corps screwed him out of the Congressional Medal of Honor that was his by rights, just like his dad's, and that he now wanted his medal, and would the president please send it on?"

"And that gets him on a Secret Service list?"

"Hey, after sixty-three, *anything* gets you on a Secret Service list, friend. We take no chances. We win no friends, but we take no chances."

"Is there anything threatening in the letter?"

"Uh, well, our staff psychiatrist says so. It's not an explicit threat so much as a tone. Listen to this. 'Sir, I only request that the nation give me that which is my due, as I served my country well in the jungles. It's quite important to me that I get this medal [exclamation point]. It is mine [exclamation point]. I earned it [exclamation point]. There's no two ways about it, sir, that medal is mine [exclamation point].' "

Nick shook his head. Like so many others, the great Bob the Nailer, the warrior champion of Vietnam, the master sniper, had yielded to vanity too. It was no longer enough merely to have done the impossible on a routine basis and to know that you and you alone were of the elect. No, in his surrender, Bob, like so many others, wanted celebrity, attention, validation. More. More for me. I want more and I want it now. It's my turn.

That's what Nick ran into all the time on the streets. Somehow in America it had stopped being about us or we or the team or the family; it was this me-thing that turned people crazy. They expected so much. They thought they were so important. Everybody was an only child.

But it seemed so un-Bob-like somehow.

"It sounds pretty harmless to me," Nick said.

"It's the exclamation points. Four of 'em. Our reading is that exclamation points indicate a tendency toward violence. Not an inclination, but a *tendency,* a capacity to let go. That's the theory at any rate, though the truth is, we've found that letter writers almost never go to guns. They just don't. For most of them, writing the letter is the thing that satisfies them, they sit back and everything is nice. Still, this guy is supposedly a hell of a shot, or was at one time. He used four exclamation points. And we do have it on record that he did go to New Orleans—"

"Yeah, I've confirmed that—"

"And so we put him on the Charlie list. Check him out, see if he deserves an upgrade to Beta—"

"That's what I'm doing."

"I know the Charlie list is shit, Memphis. Nobody likes to do the Charlie list. Usually the guys just out of training end up doing Charlies. You sound, um, a little old for Charlies."

"Look, I do what my boss says, that's all."

"We appreciate it. Glad to have the Bureau's help."

"How did you know he was in New Orleans?"

"Huh?"

"You said, 'And he *was* in New Orleans.' How did you know that?"

"Uh," said Marbella, "it says so. Right here in his file."

"But where did that information come from? I mean, a snitch, another agency, a cop shop, the Pentagon, the VA?"

"Hey, it doesn't say. You know, this stuff comes in from all over, some of it pretty raw. What's the big deal?"

"Is somebody *watching* Swagger?"

"Shit, man. I'm the last guy to know. And it doesn't say a thing here. It's just raw data, Memphis. Some of it's accurate, some of it isn't. It's up to you to check it out, okay, bud?"

"Yeah, sure. Hey, thanks a lot," Nick said. He hung up.

What should I do? I should do *something.*

He called Directory Information for the state of Arkansas, learned quickly that Bob Lee Swagger had no listed or unlisted phone number. He called the Arkansas State Police, and found that Bob Lee Swagger was not under investigation or indictment of any sort, but from that he learned Bob's address, which was simply Rural Route 270, Blue Eye. Finally, he called Vernon Tell, who was the sheriff of Polk County, Arkansas, and after giving the FBI identification code, quickly got to the sheriff himself.

"Bob Lee? Bob Lee just lives up the mountain by himself. That's all."

"Any problems with him?"

"No, sir. Not the most sociable fellow in the world, no, sir. Bob Lee keeps to himself and don't like people picking at him. But he's a good man. He done his country proud in the war, and his daddy done his country proud and Earl's daddy Lucas was actually the sheriff back in the twenties. They're all old Polk County folks, and wouldn't hurt nobody didn't hurt them first."

But it bothered Nick that Bob lived alone, away from society, with a lot of guns. The profile of the loner gunman had proved out too many times to be coincidental.

"Any drinking or substance abuse problems?"

"Mr. Memphis, believe me, it would be a lie if I didn't tell you some years back, Bob Lee had a problem with the bottle and had some wild times. He's always in pain, you know, because of the way he was hurt in the war. But I believe Bob Lee has found himself in some way. All he wants from life is freedom and to be left alone."

"What about medals? Has he ever said anything about medals? Are medals important to him?"

"To Bob Lee? Let me tell you something, son—were you in the war or anything?"

"No sir, I wasn't."

"Well, son, the only people that are interested in medals are the ones that are fixing to run for office some day. I went from one side of Burma to the other with General Merrill's Marauders in 1943 and 1944, and the only man I ever saw who wanted a medal or cared about a medal later became the only governor of Colorado to be impeached. No, son, Bob Lee Swagger don't give two damns and a jar of cold piss about medals. I've been out to his place a time or so and you'd be hard pressed to find an indication anywhere that this man was one of the bravest heroes our country ever produced."

Somehow, that pleased Nick.

And that night, when Herm dropped by, he said, "Nick, you got any Charlies to butt on up to Beta or Alpha classification?"

Nick answered, "Yes," and he had three names, men

who seemed dangerous but whom he had not been able to turn up.

Bob Lee Swagger was not on the list.

At last he was out of the office. Sitting in a swamp, as a matter of fact, but at least, indisputably, out of the office.

He sat in the back of a Secret Service van, with Herm Sloane and his partner Jeff Till as Till, the expert, fumbled and cursed at a control console. The van was all dressed up with electronic gear.

"Not a goddamn thing," said Till.

"Are you sure it's reading?" said Sloane.

"I'm not sure of a goddamn thing," said Till, a little neurotically. "All the lights are red, we're on the right directional beam, but believe me, I am getting absolutely nothing but hum and static. It's making me crazy."

Nick let the two chums take turns cursing the equipment that flickered wanly in front of them.

Outside, there was nothing but bayou and hanging cypress and the swish and rustle of swamp water and small, mean creatures squishing through the mud. Somewhere three hundred yards ahead—at least in theory—there was a farmhouse that doubled as the headquarters of the White Beacon of Racial Purity, a rabidly antiblack group said to be floating around the fringes of the New Orleans loonies culture. These were fat-bellied white guys with tattoos and Ruger Mini-14's, their favorite piece, far to the right of the Klan, good old, mean old boys who'd dropped out of the Klan because it was too dang *soft*. That is, if they existed. Nick was privately of the opinion that it was a policeman's fantasy, or rather an easy out; any inconvenient crime could be blamed on the White Beacon, and thereby consigned to the unsolved files without much in the way of an investment in time or energy. He had once spent a week trying to get a fix on them, concluding that there was nothing but vapors of hate and rumors feeding on rumors.

But, on a tip that Sloane had gotten from a detective in the New Orleans Gang Intelligence Division, he and his partner and, as local representative, the reluctant Nick Memphis had come out well past midnight in the Service's electronic monitoring vehicle in order to penetrate the farmhouse—no warrant was necessary if the penetration was done via parabolic microphone—and see what the White Beacon boys were up to, if there were White Beacon boys and if this was the farmhouse where they were meeting. Nick knew at least three sly old Cajun detectives who'd drink themselves goofy in merry recollection of having sent three Northern federal whiteboys out into the swamps for a night, listening to the cicadas. But he said nothing.

"It can't be a goddamn overlapping signature," said Till. "It's just junk equipment. It isn't even digital, for Christ's sake."

"Maybe the beam isn't getting through the trees," said Sloane.

"Maybe it's the goddamn junk equipment," said Till again.

But Nick felt as if he was in the space cruiser *Enterprise*, it was so high-tech.

"What's wrong with the equipment?" he asked. "Man, if we have a big bust, we have to requisition our EV from Miami."

"We been trying to get an upgrade for years," said Till. "This piece of shit always goes into a zone two weeks before the Man does. But it was built in the sixties and it's so far from being state of the art, it can't even pick up HBO! It's a piece of shit!"

"You need an Electrotek 5400," Nick said innocently.

"Jesus, yeah!" said Till. "Sure, but I don't have a million bucks lying around to spend on listening in on people. Hell, all I'm trying to do is protect the life of the president of the United States, that's all. How'd you ever hear of an Electrotek? That goddamn thing's top secret."

"Guy told me. Said there were seven in the world."

"No, they built five or six more. Yeah, wouldn't it be sweet if we had one. Man, we wouldn't have to go to this fucking swamp. We could go to the parking lot and tune in."

"It's the Agency and DEA that have them, right?"

"And certain overseas clients with very high and tight connections."

"I heard some guys got them in Salvador."

"Wouldn't surprise me. No death squad would be complete without them. Meanwhile, guys like us who are trying to work for a living, we get a piece of sixties shit like this. Man, I think I'm getting Country Joe and the Fish on these earphones."

Nick shut up for a while then, as Till jimmied and dicked with the equipment.

"I got something," he finally said.

"Tape rolling?"

"Tape rolling fine. Ah, let me see if I can amplify it and bring it out . . ."

Nick heard a babble of voices chattering over the loudspeakers:

"You know, dem boys, dey be, you know, um, dey be hawmping in de woods fer ole gata, lemme tell you, um, dey be hawmping da swamps, shooooo-eee, boy, wif dem, like lights, you know, you know what I'm saying, *lights*, like, and when dem boys git in reals close, *wham*, *wham!*, you know—"

"I hate to tell you," Nick said, "but I don't think

those are the Beacons. Not unless they started an equal opportunity program."

"Shit," said Sloane.

"Man, what are they talking about?" said Till in wonderment.

"Gator hunting, I think. These old backwoods blacks, they go out late at night and attract gators with light, then bop 'em over the head with ax handles. Highly illegal, but they eat the meat and sell the skins and teeth. Poaching. It's poaching. You guys want to bust 'em for conspiracy to poach? It's three to five and it's federal."

"Shit," said Sloane again. "I know that guy said it was thirty miles out Parish Five-forty-seven, then left at the dirt road for thirteen miles."

"I think he was chain pulling," said Nick. "These old Louisiana cops, you know, they love their pranks."

"I'm going to report his ass," said Sloane hotly.

"No, don't do that. See, he's got you. You can't prove it was anything but real and if you make a fuss, *you're* the one that looks like the ungrateful ass. Listen, my first year in Gumboland, I spent half my nights on wild-goose chases. This is what passes for sport down here. Those guys are sitting in the back room at The Alligator Club right now, laughing themselves sick, I guarantee you. But you did your job, right? That's the main thing."

"Christ, Memphis, you're a walking testimonial to the human power to forgive."

"It's so much easier than being a hard guy. Especially in *their* town. Now I get along with them pretty well, because I paid my dues and never complained."

"Ah, let's get out of here," said Till.

"Just think, Till, how silly you'd feel if you'd been parked out here in a million-dollar Electrotek 5400. All dressed up and no place to go."

Both the Secret Service agents laughed, and then Till said, "No way I'm getting hold of an Electrotek unless I go to work for RamDyne, which I just might do."

Nick said, "RamDyne?"

"You never heard of RamDyne?"

"No."

"It's Fed heaven. You fuck up bad, or you get fucked bad, but you're good, you know, really *good,* maybe RamDyne gives you a call one night. Then you are on easy street. And you get to do all the stuff the CIA *used* to do. Interesting stuff."

"Ah," said Sloane, "it doesn't even exist. I hear guys talking about it now and then, but I don't know a single guy who's ever gotten that kind of nod."

"But it's nice to think of the money, isn't it?" said Till, dreamily.

CHAPTER TWELVE

Bob came over the rise and looked down the wet tarmac to see the trailer a mile ahead, and the car parked next to it. He drew his parka tighter; the wind pushed into and through it. Next to him, Mike poised, taut, his sloppy jowls tightening, a curl of angry low sound slithering out of his throat.

"Easy, boy," said Bob, trying to rub some softness into the animal's tension. He stroked the hard neck and the velvety ears and after a second or so, Mike broke contact with the strangers at the trailer and cocked his head, looking at Bob, puzzlement showing in the deep lakes of his eyes.

"There, guy," Bob said in a low mutter, "it's all right. They're friends," though a sardonic tone crept into the last word.

He had wondered when they'd be in touch. It was a sleety day; the weather had rushed over the Ouachitas; low clouds rolled angrily by; pellets of ice fell diagonally, cutting the skin, collecting in puddles on the road, while the wind sliced through the trees.

Bob shivered, not quite warm, and pressed ahead.

The colonel sat in the car, reading a newspaper. Payne lounged on the fender.

"Howdy, Payne."

"Hi ya, Bob. Nice dog."

"Dogs aren't nice, Payne. They're either good or they're bad, meaning either they stick or they cut. Mike sticks."

Payne just looked at him, something like a smirk on his dark, blunt features. Bob felt the hostility, but it didn't particularly bother him. Payne didn't worry Bob a bit.

"How's the mouth?"

"My old man hit me harder. He didn't give me no warning either."

Payne smiled, showing new dentures.

"All right," said the colonel, stepping out of the car.

Payne immediately stepped back.

"Get inside, Payne. Wait for me."

"Yes, sir," said Payne, sliding obediently into the car.

"Hello, Swagger. How are you?"

"Fine," said Bob.

"Nice dog," said the colonel.

"He sure is."

"Some kind of beagle?"

"Beagle and something."

"Well, anyway. Can we talk?"

"Sure."

Bob unlocked the gate and Mike ran to his hut like the obedient creature he was. Bob took the colonel inside.

They sat down at Bob's table and the man pulled out a well-thumbed copy of Bob's report.

"I don't mind telling you, this is an excellent piece of work."

Bob nodded.

"You might be interested in knowing that independently we came to many of the same conclusions. We've also had some further information on Solaratov. We think we have a very solid sighting outside of Huarte City in Cuba. Now why would that be significant? The reason is that it's a swampy region whose weather and proximity to the sea and humidity tendencies almost exactly match New Orleans's. So they may be prepping the shot down there, rather than, as you guessed, trying to put together a range up here."

"I see."

"But we agree that almost certainly they're going to go for him in New Orleans."

Bob just nodded.

Then he said, "So are you going to let me be on the rifle that day?"

The colonel looked him in the eye. Bob respected a man who gave you the bad news straight up, no bullshit, no fake sorry.

"No. No way. Forget about it."

Bob said nothing.

"Higher people have decided. He has to be taken alive, discreetly, and debriefed; he's a treasure chest of information. It's more than personalities, it's politics and policies. It's duty."

Bob nodded.

"I know you want a crack at him. We all do. But we have to be professional. We have to see him as an asset. It's not about justice or anything. It's about doing what's necessary."

"This johnny isn't going to be so easy to nab clean."

"We'll let the FBI and the Secret Service worry about that. They're pros."

"So, I'm out, that what you're saying?"

"You've done your part. We *needed* you. And now that time has passed."

Bob grunted. It was sort of like Vietnam. Thank you and fuck you.

"There'll be a check."

"The money isn't necessary. It was an honor."

"It's not a lot. We didn't want to insult you. It's a month's pay at gunnery sergeant rate."

"Fine. Much appreciated."

"Swagger, when I walk out this door, that has to be it. It has to be left alone, do you understand?"

"Yes, sir."

"I've taken a chance, a big chance, telling you this much. You've learned things no private citizen has ever learned. We have to be able to trust you."

"Sure," said Bob.

"Swagger, if you show up in that area with a rifle, if you do something stupid to get at this Solaratov, you could blow the whole thing. You could get yourself killed, you could mess up our whole operation, you could let this bastard get away. We expect your discipline, your best help."

"Yes, sir."

"And that means just sitting tight. Do you understand? Can you be professional?"

"I've always been a professional, sir."

There was another curious pause in the conversation. The colonel looked away, clearly troubled. Bob just stared at him, conscious of the slow tick of time, the settling of atoms in the room. He needed a drink. First time in years, he had the extraordinary urge to open a bottle of Tennessee drinking whiskey and float away on its torrents, to drift and bob and see where he ended up next morning or next week or whatever, in whose bed, in what prison.

Shit.

"But I don't—"

"What?"

"What secrets can this guy have? He's a shooter, that's all. He's going to kill a great president. Let me be there and I can nab him with a .308 hollowpoint. That's the nabbing he deserves."

The colonel looked off.

"I'm going to tell you why we have to take him alive. I'm going to tell you why it's absolutely imperative that we take him alive. It may turn out that you weren't the first American he shot and that Donny wasn't the second."

"He had an earlier tour in 'Nam?"

"He had an earlier tour, all right. But it wasn't in 'Nam. We have a very good authenticated sighting of him in Mexico City, Swagger. It's on film, Mexico City. November eighteenth, 1963. Our people trailed him. They lost him at the airport. There were three flights from Mexico City on November eighteenth, 1963. To Dallas, Texas."

The colonel held him in his eyes for a long time.

"We've been working on this a long, long time, Swagger. We want this boy. We want him so bad. He's an old dog, and we want him because then we can find the answers to some very interesting questions."

"I understand," said Bob. "I was out of line. I apologize."

"All right," said the colonel. "For the record my name is Raymond Davis. I'm a senior plans officer in the Central Intelligence Agency, as you have no doubt guessed. This operation is code-named Ginger Dragon, and it involves over three hundred men. Do you understand that *everything* I've told you is absolutely top secret?"

"Yes, sir."

"We'll need seasoned spotters, Swagger. Men on scopes who can find Solaratov for us so that we can take him. Nobody's better on a scope than you."

"I suppose that's true."

"No rifles. Just give us your eyes and your brains. Be on our team. No solo work. You just work with us to take this guy. Pay him back for Donny Fenn that way. Pay him back for all of us. That's how you nail him, Bob. Can you nail him like that?"

"I'll nail him," said Bob.

He had another of his bad, sleepless nights, and woke up swaddled in drenched sheets, his hip aflame, the image of the light gone from Donny's blank eyes forever strobing in his mind.

Goddamn him, he thought, thinking of the man hunting him as he had hunted so many others.

He felt greedy for vengeance and he knew it could make him stupid and sloppy, and he wished again he had a way to protect himself, not from *them*, whoever they really were, but from himself, his own greed and self-indulgence.

And then an idea came to him. It was so simple really: it involved a few minutes' welding, a certain adjustment, and at least from one angle he was protected from their use if they tried to use him in a certain way.

He laughed about it after he was finished. It was such a little thing. He reassembled the Remington .308, wiped it down with Sheath to keep the moisture away, and replaced it in his gun vault. Like to see the look on somebody's poke when they pulled the trigger on that one!

He slept dreamlessly.

CHAPTER THIRTEEN

Beneath the Presidential Security Detail and the Site Preparation Team, at the furthest reaches of the security pyramid, was that blur of extra bodies known as "Cooperating Agencies" and it was well within this blur, sitting in an automobile with a cold cup of coffee, a red lapel button and an attitude problem, that Nick Memphis found himself at nine-thirty in the morning on the day of the president's speech. He was one of several thousand cops, FBI agents, military personnel and the like who had to surrender their weekend because the president, ever mindful that his popularity ratings in the Latino communities, so high after the war, had begun to slip just a bit, and so he had chosen to give the

Freedom Medal to the Salvadoran archbishop Jorge Roberto Lopez.

Nick was by himself, which didn't please him much; he'd somehow expected more, having kibitzed so valiantly with the Secret Service advance detail over the preceding three weeks, been loyal and obedient as any dog, doing Howdy Duty's bidding whenever possible and with a smile on his face. But at intense moments all institutions default to turf warfare, and Nick was pained to discover that Secret Service did not want the Bureau anywhere near the zone of its highest visibility and responsibility, so he'd been exiled to a further outpost of the empire of security. Worse, Mickey Sontag, his most recent partner, was sick; so poor Nick had to spend all of game day by himself.

He now sat a good four blocks off the motorcade route and the site of the speech, parked on St. Ann Street in the Quarter, a block or two down from Bourbon's luridness and the crush of tourism. Around him were old brick residences, all quaint, all pastel, all shuttered. Ahead, in the far distance, he could see the grotesque wrought-iron arch that signified the entrance to Louis Armstrong park on North Rampart, one reason why the White House had chosen the site: access to it, through that gate, was so limited. There were still worries, left over from the Persian Gulf War, about terrorists. The sun above was bright and now and then people would stream by, in hopes of getting a good early location on the president's motorcade or a good seat for his speech.

Idly, Nick listened to the security network, Channel 21 on his radio unit, as Phil Mueller held the whole thing together from a Secret Service communications center on the roof of the Municipal Auditorium, which was just off the site of the speech.

"Ah, this is Airport, we have Flashlight on the ground and taxiing toward the hangar."

"Reading you, Airport, this is Base Six."

Nick recognized Mueller's authoritarian voice over the radio; he knew that Howdy Duty would be standing right next to him, really there more for public relations, to keep the Bureau's profile high, than for any meaningful security reasons. Nick tried to generate some feeling for Utey, pro or con. But he couldn't get himself to hate the guy, even after Tulsa all those years ago. Hate just wasn't in Nick, not a bit of it.

"All teams in place, we are waiting momentarily for Flashlight to disembark."

"Thank you, Airport, please confirm when Flashlight is out of plane and motorcade is proceeding."

"Reading you and roger that, Base Six."

"Uh, people, Game time coming up, I want to run a last security check, make sure everybody's on station. So by the numbers, I want you to check in and give me a sitrep."

One by one the security units checked in, a torrent of radiospeak and bored, commanding voices crackling and soupy over the distorting radio network—all of them, because Mueller was a stickler. That was three helicopter teams, over fifty men spread around on rooftops, maybe seventy-five police units at various intersections on and nearby the motorcade route, all the high-powered lookout posts in the immediate vicinity of the site, and of course the hot dogs of the Presidential Security Detail, many of whom had come ahead and were already in position on site.

When it came time for Nick, he was on the ball.

"Ah, Base Six, this is Bureau Four, I'm on station on St. Ann, ah, all activity normal, I've got nothing on rooftops or any visible window activity."

"Affirmative, Bureau Four, keep your eyes open, Nick," said Mueller.

The touch of personal recognition pleased Nick, not that it meant a damned thing.

"Four out," he said, and went back to eyeballing whatever was around him, which was not much. He squirmed uncomfortably, because the Smith 1076 was held in the Bureau's de rigueur high hip carry in a pancake holster above his right buttock, and though the pistol was flat, unlike a revolver, it still bit into him. Many agents secretly kept their pistols in glove compartments when they drove around, but it was Nick's law to always play by every rule, and so he just let the thing gnaw on him under his suitcoat.

As he sat there, Nick phased out the rest of security check-ins, and tried to reassemble his thoughts on the Eduardo Lanzman case, because he wanted to really get cracking on it as soon as Flashlight was out of town. The report from Salvador, just in, had been a disappointment: the Salvadoran National Police had no Lanzman on their rolls, and who up here could prove different? And Nick also had the Bureau research people trying to find something out about this RamDyne outfit he'd picked up on from Till and he thought that—

But then the message came rumbling across the net, "Ah, Base Four, Flashlight has debarked and the motorcade is about to commence."

"All right, people, let's look sharp," said Base Six. "Game time."

"Ah, Base Four, Flashlight has debarked and the motorcade is about to commence," Bob heard over the radio. Then, "All right, people, let's look sharp. Game time."

"Bob, that's it, the show's begun." It was Payne nearby.

"Okay," Bob said, "got you clean and simple and am all set." But he wished he had a rifle and in fact felt like a simpleton without one.

He was a good four hundred yards from the president's speech in the fourth-floor room of an old house on St. Ann, but he didn't look toward the park; he looked back, toward and over the French Quarter. Seated at a table, he stared through a Leupold 36× spotting scope that he had carefully aimed at the church steeple still another thousand yards out. It was the steeple from which he'd predicted the shot would come. Payne and a New Orleans uniformed cop named Timmons were with him, Payne on the radio, Timmons just more or less there.

He heard the security people on their network.

"Ah, Base Six, this is Alpha One, we are progressing down U.S. Ten at approximately forty-five miles per hour, our ETA is approximately 1130 hours, do you read?"

"Have you, affirmative," said Base Six. "Units Ten and Twelve, be advised Flashlight and friends are moving through your area shortly."

"We have it under advisement, Base Six, everything looking fine here, over and out."

Bob thought it was like a big air-mobile operation in the 'Nam, an orchestration of elements all moving in perfect syncopation and held together by some command hotshot on the radio network, as the various units through whose sector Flashlight moved called in their reports.

"Ah, Base Six, this is Ginger Dragon Two, we have all quiet in our secure zone at present," he heard Payne speak into the phone.

"That's a roger, Ginger Dragon Two, we're reading you, our apprehension teams are on instant standby."

"Anything yet?" Timmons now asked him. He was a

large, dour man, whose belly pressed outward against his uniform; he seemed nervous.

Bob's eye was in the scope. Though the target was so much farther out, he could see three ramshackle arched openings under the crown of the steeple, each louvered closed, each dirty and untouched.

"It's the middle window," Payne now said calmly.

"I know what window it is," Bob said. Why were these guys *talking* so much? "I have no movement."

"Maybe he's not there yet," said Timmons.

"Oh, he's there. It's too close to time. He's there."

If he's anywhere, Bob thought, he's there. He's sitting very still now and though we can't see him, he's drawing himself together for the shot. He's probably taken as close as can be constructed to this shot a thousand or so times, maybe ten thousand times. I know I would if I were in his shoes. But he's a little nervous; he'll want to be alone and he'll want it quiet. If there are others in the room with him, then they're just sitting there, not making any noise, letting him accumulate his strength.

According to Colonel Davis, a very skilled FBI embassy penetration team had discreetly planted light-sensitive sensors in the belfry, and the sensors had recorded data to suggest that every night between four and five A.M. a working party of five men entered the room and made preparations. Bob assumed they were soundproofing the walls and building a shooting platform to get the proper angle into the president's site fourteen hundred far yards away. At the precise moment, three or four of the louvers would be removed; he'd scope and shoot and the team would replace the louvers. The window of vulnerability was maybe ten seconds.

"Ginger Dragon Six, we are beginning our apprehension maneuver."

"Keep it discreet, apprehension teams." Bob recognized Colonel Davis, who was running this operation, the one concealed within the larger drama of the president's arrival and security.

"Fuckin' A," said Payne, "they getting ready to nab the sucker."

Bob looked at his watch; it was only 1115 hours now, still an hour from the shooting event.

"Man, I hope your Federal team has got it together. This is a very nervous cat, he's got spotters himself making sure he hasn't been blown."

"These are the very best guys," Payne said. "These guys have been training for this one a long time. Lots and lots of dues gonna get paid off today, I can tell you. It's payback time."

Something melodramatic and movielike in Payne today irritated Bob.

"Ginger Dragon Two, you have the best angle on the target, you have anything to announce?"

"He's talking to you, Swagger."

"That's a negative. But if they're there, they probably came in late last night; and they'll be real quiet. Tell him that. Lack of activity is to be expected."

"Uh, Ginger Dragon Six, this is Dragon Two, uh, spotter has a negative so far."

"Is he sure?"

"Oh, Christ," said Bob. "Tell him they're there, goddammit, and that I'll sing out when I get a visual confirm, and that that will be at the point of shooting, and goddammit, he better get set to bounce his people in there fast."

Now wasn't the time to begin doubting the scenario. They all believed in the scenario, they'd discussed it dispassionately all afternoon yesterday.

"Uh, confidence here is still high, Dragon Six," said Payne.

That's what ruined operations and that's what killed people in the field—that sudden, last-minute spurt of doubt, like the lash of a whip: it made people morons. So many times Bob had seen it; it was exactly what sniping wasn't.

"We may have to go early," said Ginger Dragon Six.

"Do that, and you got nothing," said Bob. "He's there. Goddamn, I can *feel* him. Oh, he's there and he's on his rifle, and he's just settling into it."

He wished he had a rifle too.

"Okay, Alpha Team, this is Base Six, Flashlight's ETA is now just five minutes."

"Base Six to Alpha, Flashlight is now in your zone."

"We have Flashlight, thank you, Base Six, good job."

"Roof Team, this is Base Six, any activity?"

"Negative, Six, all clear except for our people."

"Keep me informed, Roof Team, we are near maximum vulnerability now."

"Have you, Six."

"All teams, Max V condition, on your toes, people, on your toes."

On his toes! Nick felt so out of it he almost had to laugh. This is your life, Nick Memphis. He sat in the car alone in a zone so barren of life it seemed despoiled, or some vista in a sci-fi movie set after the end of the world. All the tourists had hustled on by to get a looksee at the president. Here he was, on the far outside.

Now he saw it. The motorcade hurtled down North Rampart, and just briefly the gates to the park were opened, and through it sped Flashlight's three-million-dollar Lincoln which no bullet could penetrate, sixteen New Orleans motorcycle cops, the Security Detail quick reaction van, and two cars of reporters and TV people. And then they were gone.

Man, he thought, I'm so far to the outside there is no inside.

He tried to stay alert out of respect for the ritual, and the big Smith in the pancake holster was some help. It gouged him but in his curious way he enjoyed it.

Yet always he felt a little guilt. He'd gotten the easy part: for he knew that the forty minutes of Max V as Flashlight was exposed were absolutely the most terrifying—and exhilarating—for the Secret Service agents who now ran the show.

"Ah, Alpha Four to Alpha Response, I have a squirrel in the fourth row left, can we get a team on him, please, like really fast, guys."

It was the Crowd Squad, working the people.

"Alpha Four, the Hispanic guy, right, black overcoat?" came Mueller's response from the roof of the Municipal Auditorium just beside the podium that had been erected in front of a wading pool.

"That's my squirrel. Guy's got a shifty, stressed look and his hands are in his pockets. I can't tell if he's by himself."

"Ah, okay, Alpha, we're moving in."

The crowd squad maneuvered quickly to neutralize the guy they'd ID'd as a possible. Nick envied them the action even if, as it did 999 out of a thousand times, it turned out to be groundless.

"Okay, Alpha Four, the squirrel just lifted his little girl up to see the Man, and he's got three other kids with him."

"Back off then, Alpha Four, good work."

Nick heard cheers and laughter echoing through the empty streets; the president had made a joke. He checked his watch. They were running a bit behind schedule. It was almost noon and the speech was scheduled to have started at 11:45, but it had just gotten under way. He'd seen the site plan, amazed at how precisely these things are choreographed. There'd even been a rehearsal for the Security Detail to get them used to body moves, to the look of the situation, so that if something ungodly happened, the place at least would be familiar to them.

But Nick could remember from the site plan where Flashlight would be standing, where the archbishop would be, flanked by his own bodyguard. The rest of the guys up there were Service beef, two staff assistants, and Mr. Football, as they called the Air Force staff colonel who was always a discreet ten feet from Flashlight with a briefcase full of that day's nuclear go-codes. Nick could imagine them up there in the love and glee of the crowd, these happy men who ruled the world, and who would not even in their older age remember this day.

"Ah, Chopper Four, this is Base Six, can you take a right-hand circle about half-mile out? I have a New Orleans police report of some roofline movement. I'm looking at Grid Square Lima-thirteen-Tango, I got a cop in that area says he thinks he saw something. My countersniper team in that zone has called it a no-show, but take a look, will you, big guy?"

"That's a big rog, Alpha Six," came the voice from the chopper, and Nick heard the thing roar overhead, a black Huey.

"Ah, Base, I've got an all clear, your cop must have seen a mirage."

"Okay, Chopper, good work."

"I'm out of here, Alpha Six."

The bird's roar fluttered and diminished.

Nick was alone again, on the face of the moon.

"Time," asked Bob, and lost the answer in the roar of the chopper.

When the bird cleared, he asked again.

"Eleven-fifty-six, pal," came Payne's answer.

Bob breathed out heavily, a stupid move, because it somewhat jittered his eye's placement against the scope; he blinked, lost his image, came back to find a black half-moon of eye-relief error cutting into the cone of his vision because he wasn't properly aligned. His heart was pumping.

Goddamn! he told himself, be cool, man.

And there it was again, the arch in the steeple, in perfect clarity, its black dullness sealing off his vision, simply a maze of ancient slats. He stared at it as if pouring himself through it, willing what he wanted to be there to be there, so far away, fourteen hundred yards from the target but just within the range of a world-class shooter like T. Solaratov.

Where are you, you bastard?

And then he saw him. He saw the sniper.

It was a subtlety in the light behind the slats, a shifting, a certain tightening, a certain coming together. As his mind raced to put the various molecules of light and dark together into a picture, he realized that fifteen or so feet back, the sniper, at a bench like any rifle bench, was feeling his way into position. And in the next second or so, the whole thing assembled in his head; for now he saw also the solemn drift of the others in the room, very slow, very steady, but moving ever so slightly, a man on a scope next to the shooter, two men well back from the window. Then he watched as one by one, with the slowness of a glacier's move, a slat and then another and still a third was removed. The diagonal slash in the arch was three inches wide. Behind it, he saw something move or tighten.

Very quietly, Bob said, "Payne, he's there, I got his ass, he's a minute or so from shooting, send the boys in, now goddammit, send 'em in, he's there, he's there."

"Ginger Dragon, we've got him, go, go, go, go," said Payne.

"You got him," yelled Timmons, the cop, "you got him."

"Send those damn boys fast," said Bob, "he's set."

Christ, he wished he had a rifle. It was his shot. It was a shot that kept him alive all these years—to have the motherfucker there, the man who did Donny Fenn, the man who blew out his hip and ended the life he was born to live, to have him right where the Remington wanted to go, right where he could put it. His trigger finger began to constrict and he imagined the buck of the rifle as he fired. He could take the trigger slack all the way down and ship a .308 hollowpoint out there and send that fuck straight to hell, drive his heart and spine all over New Orl—

"Goddamn, where are they, get 'em in there. He's going to—"

"All elements, move in, Ginger Dragon, go, go, go," he heard Payne on the radio.

Where were they? There should be a chopper overhead, FBI SWAT guys in black rappelling down it, men moving in from all the hidden parts of the universe, men with guns and purpose, moving swiftly to stop—

"Where are they?"

Bob saw the spurt of flame as Solaratov fired.

"Bob?"

He turned and Payne shot him in the chest from a range of six feet.

Nick yawned and—

He heard the sound of a shot.

It froze him. The universe seemed to halt and his heart turned to stone.

Then the radio exploded.

"*My God, Flashlight is down!*"

He sat up; swallowed again.

The shot came from close by.

"We are under fire on the podium, Flashlight is hit and down, my God!"

"Alpha Actual, Alpha Actual, all units, Alpha Actual."

Actual was the code word; it meant somebody was shooting at or had shot the president.

"Medics, vector in those medics, get these people out of here!"

"Medevac, this is Alpha Four, we need you ASAP, the man is down and hit, oh, Christ, oh, Jesus, get him fast, there's some other people up here hit, oh, Christ!"

"Off the air, Alpha Four, your medevac is vectored in, are you still under fire?"

"Negative, Alpha Six, I think it was two, maybe three shots, I don't, oh, God, there's blood all over—"

"This is Base Six, all units are cleared to fire if you have targets, this means you, countersnipers."

"Where's that fuckin' medevac, we have blood everywhere, guys are down."

Nick listened in horrified fascination.

"Do we have an isolation on the shot?"

"It was a long one, Phil, a sniper, I think it came from someplace out there beyond Rampart, in those fuckin' houses, maybe that tall one."

"SWAT people, let's get going."

"Negative that, this is Base, goddammit, we've got to get that chopper in and get the Man out of here."

But me, Nick thought. I have to move. *I have to move.* He was out of the car, hating himself for the five seconds or so he'd lost.

Without willing it, the Smith came up into his hand from the pancake. His big thumb snaked out and pushed the safety up and off.

He ran toward the sound of the shot, which was on the left, the big house at 415 St. Ann.

Payne dragged him into another room. He felt the blood on his chest, warm like urine, so much of it. It felt like the last time.

In the blaze of light, as his head lolled and his limbs went limp, he could see a shooting bench, rigged together of cement blocks and weathered pieces of wood, and on it, there lay a rifle, slightly atilt on a brace of sandbags, a heavy-barreled Remington 700 with a Leupold 10× Ultra scope.

The New Orleans cop was talking urgently into his radio unit.

"Base Six, this is Victor Seven-twenty, I have shot suspect white male with rifle at five-one-four Saint Ann, please send assistance, I say again, Base Six, this is Victor Seven-twenty, I have shot suspect in the attic of five-one-four Saint Ann, please send assistance."

Then Bob looked at the rifle.

It was his rifle.

"I have wounded suspect," said Timmons. "Get people here fast. Get me ambulance, get me paramedics, get 'em here ASAP!"

"Okay, dump him," said the colonel, stepping out of the shadows as Bob slid off into stillness, "and let's get the hell out of here."

Bob sat there, feeling again what he had felt on the ridge line when the bullet tore through his hip: shock, hatred, pain, but mostly rage at his own stupidity.

It was winding down on him. His breathing came with the slow, rough transit of a train that had run off its tracks and now rumbled over the cobblestones. His systems were shutting down, the wave of hydrostatic shock that had blown through him with the bullet's passage upsetting all the little gyros in his organs. He felt the blood in his lungs; there was no pain quite yet but only the queer sensation of loss, of blur, of things slipping away.

Then something cracked in him.

No you aren't going let it happen

You been shot before

You can fight through it

You be a Marine

He took a deep breath, and in the rage and pride he found what would pass for energy and without exactly willing it, he stood up, again surprised that there was no pain at all, and with a strange, determined gait began to move toward the door.

"Jesus, he's fuckin' *up*!" he heard the cop's anguished cry, and another shot rang out, hitting him high in the left shoulder, glancing off the bone—a heavy impact and a red sear of pain—but then he was out the door and there were only two steps to go toward a window and he launched himself, felt the window shattering, and amid a rain of glass he fell through bright sunlight toward God knew what.

Nick was looking around in a spasm of confusion. He'd entered the courtyard of the large brick house because he'd heard the cop over his earpiece claiming that he had hit a suspect. But that was a block away, at 514; he was at 415. He heard a helicopter's roar as it whirled and darted; he heard sirens rising.

But he stood in the sunlight wondering if he should go back to the street to check the address. He thought maybe he was in the wrong area. It was a maze to him; the building scruffy and dilapidated, lots of other houses close by. Jesus, any one of them could have been the location of the call-in.

He froze, wondering what the hell to do, where to go, what he should be doing, who was in command. The gun grew heavy in his hand. He felt idiotically melodramatic, and at the same time wished he were wearing sunglasses, because the sun was so bright.

Then, immediately above him, he heard what sounded like the breaking of a hundred ice cubes and he looked up into the radiant sun. Amid a sleet of glass, a man had launched himself crazily from a fourth-story window and Nick watched him fall with a sickening acceleration toward the ground, except that fifteen feet into it, he landed with another stupefying, dust-rising whack on the slanted roof of a bay window, rolled akimbo down it, and fell again, this time by some miracle of grace and agility gaining enough control over his body so that he landed on his feet, more or less on the wooden stairway which ran up the side of the house. He lurched down the steps.

Nick stared at him dumbfounded.

The guy looked like death itself, a lean-boned, blond-headed man with squirrely-slit eyes and a deep tan. He was in blue jeans, boots and a blue workshirt. There was blood on him everywhere, and as he tried to stand, he fell back, then got his feet under him and lurched up.

Nick threw out the 10mm and screamed, "Don't move, don't move, FBI, goddammit, don't move!"

The man went to his knees as fatigue and blood loss overwhelmed him and his head pitched forward; he seemed almost to collapse and Nick raced forward, yanking his cuffs from the compartment on his belt, got behind him, and got one cuff on a limb with his one free hand, holding the Smith 10 in his other, even as he smelled blood and sweat and felt the man shiver and groan.

"Fucked me," the man kept saying, "fucked me so bad, fucked me, fucked me, fucked me." The voice was cracker-South, a twang drawn over a banjo string.

Holding the cuffed hand up and tight, Nick slid the 1076 back into his pancake, and reached for the other wrist to bring it up to the cuffs.

For just an instant Nick knew he had him, and then the whole thing turned shaky as the man, with a force that stunned Nick, drove up and under him, and Nick felt his center of balance going, reached back for his Smith, but by that time had somehow lost leverage as well as balance as the man beneath him turned into nothing but snake.

The world splintered as Nick, judo-flipped expertly, hit the ground, his breath driven from him. He tried to right himself, but what he saw instead was the man above him, filling the entire horizon of his vision, but now coiled like a cavalry trooper with a saber, except there was no saber but only an elbow, which exploded into Nick's cheekbone.

In the next second, amid the roar in his head and the shock, he felt a hand groping on him and as he tried feebly to prevent it through the throbbing that had overwhelmed his face, he felt the pistol being slid from his holster.

"No, God!" he shouted, grabbed the hand, but even then failed.

Now the man stood above him, the pistol leveled at his head, its bore a ravenous black mouth that would in an instant spit flame and that would be all.

Nick was dead; he accepted his own death, felt it swell in him, but then was astounded to look past the gun to the man's looming and anguished face, as if he were looking up at a man hung out to die, his face mottled with suffering and despair, and yet in the gray eyes something terrible and abiding.

Compassion, Nick thought, but he could not believe it even as he recognized it.

Then the man was gone, scuttling off in a half-run, leaking blood.

Nick stood to give chase but a bullet whistled by his ear, fired from above, and smacked up a cloud of dust at the fleeing man's feet. Two more came, two more misses and then the man was out the gate and in Nick's car.

Oh, Christ, he thought, because in his urgency he knew he'd left the key in it.

The car started, revved and was gone.

"Goddamn, goddamn, missed him, shit, hit the fuck twice, dammit."

Nick turned to see a fat and sweaty New Orleans cop racing toward him down the steps and yelling, Beretta waving about in a fat hand.

"I'm FBI! Call it in," Nick yelled, noting the man's radio unit.

"Ah, Base Six, where the hell are you, this is Victor Seven-twenty, I have hit the suspect twice, but goddamn, he's still running, and he jumped some guy and got his car. What's the number, bubba?"

Ah! Nick didn't know. He'd checked it out of the interagency motor pool that morning.

"It's a goddamn Ford, beige, don't know the number. A Taurus, I think. They'd have the number at the pool. But it's got a radio in it, he'll be listening. Who are you?"

"Timmons, Traffic Division. Seen something up on the fourth floor moving up near the goddamned roof line. Called in that chopper, but they didn't see nothing. Went in, heard the goddamn shot, and bounced the guy. He made a jump at me and damn if I didn't put a Silvertip right through his chest and knock him down. And two minutes later the guy is up and running. Took another shot, hit him in the shoulder, and then he's out the fuckin' window. Took three more shots after he decked you, but missed."

Nick just shook his head. He tried to figure it out, but one thing he knew for certain, and that was he was in big trouble. Getting your piece taken from you by a presidential assassin who'd already soaked up two bullets was a definite bad career move.

"Man, I'm screwed," he said in a little burst of self-pity.

"Shit, no sweat," said the cop. "I seen 'em hit like that before. You may not get 'em with a one-shot stop but they bleed out in ten minutes. He's a dead guy right now. They'll find him half a mile away, piled up against a dipsy dumpster in an alley."

"No," said Nick, knowing that the fates would not be so kind to him. "Not that guy."

He turned.

"Get on that thing and put out an all points bulletin. Bob Lee Swagger. Of Blue Eye, Arkansas, and the United States Marine Corps."

"You *know* him?" the cop said.

"Yeah," said Nick, suddenly feeling all sorts of pain begin to fire away all over his body, but the physical pain wasn't so much as the anguish for the terrible days ahead. "Yeah. I know him."

Bob drove through waves of hallucination, skidding left- and right-hand turns, watching alleys fly by, terrified most of all of the bird. He knew if a bird had him, he was dead and gone, because a bird could stay with him.

But no bird came. In a second, over the car's police radio, he learned why.

"Base Six, that medevac all set with Flashlight and other wounded aboard, let's clear the air so we can ASAP to Shock Trauma."

"Roger, Shock Trauma, I want all birds to go to ground level while we get the man to the hospital. Any word, Alpha?"

"Lots of blood, that's all I can tell you, Base Six, and we got paramedics working hard. You let us worry, he's in our hands now."

Then other messages broke in and the whole thing degenerated into a cascade of possibilities, of rumors, of men yelling for attention and assistance. He heard a couple of references to "five-one-four Saint Ann" and the fleeing suspect, but that baffled him; he'd been in 415; 514 was a block away, on the other side of the street. Where did they get that number? What was going on? Then he had it. Sure, that's how well planned it was. Timmons gives the wrong address, as if he's flustered. The whole outfit goes to the wrong house a block away. That gives Payne and the colonel the time to slip away.

He drove onward, down deserted streets, and now a new problem began to eat at him. His head kept trying to float back to Vietnam. He fought with it, feeling very much two men, a weak one who wanted to return and a strong one who would not let him. He'd been hit in Vietnam too, and once you've been hit, it always feels the same. He slid for a second, unrooted in time, the dead past floating up big as a movie in front of him. There was an enormous amount of pain that day, and the pain he now felt brought that back. But this wasn't anything like it. The pain of the hip had been absolute.

This pain was stunning and pointed but he knew he could beat it. He'd had worse pain than this, plenty of times. This was nothing. He snorted, trying to get out of the 'Nam, and made himself concentrate on old Jack Payne and the happy glint in his pig eyes as he pulled the trigger.

He felt himself slipping into numbness and stupidity. He hated himself for that moment of utter strangeness when he'd been shot.

Gun-simple fool. He'd been easy for them because he wanted Solaratov so bad, that was it. That was the best trick, how they played on what he wanted. These Agency fucks had somehow found out about him and

Donny and how they got nailed by a Nailer coming over the crest, and they used it on him like a club, used his most private thing. Agency hoods, working on something big and dark and complicated, meant to turn on his stupidity and his vulnerability and his need.

Now, I got to stop the blood or I die. He looked about him. On the seat was a bag that said Dunkin' Donuts. He reached in, pulled out a wad of waxy paper. He tightened it into a ball and stuffed it into the entrance wound, the one that was bleeding so badly.

There. Wasn't much, but it was what he had.

He knew exactly where he was going, if he could only stay smart enough to get there.

He'd studied it, after all. There was only one escape route. Now, he had only one problem and that was the fact that he was dying.

Or was he? Shouldn't he be dead by now? The first bullet had gone right through him, for some crazy reason, and he suspected that it was a ball round, overpenetrative, it had missed major body structures, taken out no arteries, whatever. As for the shoulder hit, that part of his body had gone to numbness, but there wasn't much blood and he had a sense, maybe illusory, it didn't matter, that no bone had been broken. So on he drove, by this time calmed down and no longer roaring. But he had to dump the car, that was the thing. The car was death.

He drove toward water.

In water there was safety.

"Attention all, units, we have a definite confirm, we have Government Interagency motorpool car, a beige eighty-eight Ford Taurus, plate number Sierra Doggie one-five-niner-Lima, that's Sierra Doggie one-five-niner-Lima. Suspect is armed and dangerous, a white male, about forty, wounded but considered dangerous, and an early ID for the name Robert Lee Swagger, I say again, all units, he's armed and dangerous, approach with caution."

Oh, shit, he thought.

But Bob had seen the water.

He rolled off the road, raising a cloud of dust behind him, slewing through weeds and mulch. Suddenly it was before him, the vast band of blue-black Mississippi, a sinewy, bending thing. He had no real idea of what he was doing because of blood loss. And of course the rage which was making him insane. He had no sense of making a decision. The car just surged ahead and he felt a sense of liberation, of release, similar in fact to the one he'd felt as he blew through the window, and then suddenly there were bubbles and blackness all around him, pulling at him. In the pocket of the cab, the water line rose as the car sank. He rose with it, until his head struck the ceiling. He felt the torrent blasting through the car's open windows as he sank, and he knew he'd die now, trapped beneath the surface.

But again his rage helped and it released a last pump of energy and adrenaline, and with half a body and the thrust of his legs, he managed to get the door open. He was almost born again. The water was warm and green now and he rose toward sunlight, and then suddenly tasted the air. The plunge off a dock had carried the car maybe fifteen feet out; overhead a helicopter made a sweep of the river, the way the Hueys had buzzed the Perfume during Tet. But it was far off and couldn't see him.

He flipped to his back, and propelled himself toward shore. Drifting, he eventually found himself among green reeds weaving in the current. Barges plied the water a half-mile or so away, but the river was so wide here it looked to be a placid lake. Bob waded woozily, his hair plastered against his scalp, his wet shirt heavy against his skin, his body drugged with fatigue. He couldn't believe he was still alive and able to move. It seemed a miracle.

He found a rotting log floating in the weeds. If he stayed there he'd die or get caught and he knew if he got caught, he couldn't kill them all, kill Payne and the colonel—and kill Solaratov, who made it all possible. If it was Solaratov. And if it wasn't, he'd kill whoever it was. That's what he wanted.

Bob got his belt off, stopping momentarily to discover with surprise the gun he'd taken jammed into his waist. Thank God it was stainless steel and probably wouldn't rust. As for the bullets, would they corrode? He didn't know. What choice did he have? He slid it to his jean pocket, a tight fit that would hold good. Then he buckled the belt around the log and wrapped his arm through it, and pushed off. With surprising swiftness, the log carried him into the center of the river, and the current picked him up. But he felt amazingly good. Now and then a chopper buzzed by but he wasn't visible against the log and when darkness came, he swore at the flashing lights here and there along the shore. But Bob just let the current carry him along through the afternoon and the night, and when the dawn broke, he was right where he wanted to be. He was in the jungle.

CHAPTER FOURTEEN

The lead editorials mourned the passing of the great man, of course, but the off-leads quickly got to the matter of blame.

And so he returns, ran the piece in the *Washington Post* the next day, *the seedy little man with the grudge and the rifle.*

> The grudge does not make him special; only the .38 caliber rifle does. Like a figure from our darkest, most atavistic nightmares, he returns, and writes himself into history. If, as the Federal Bureau of Investigation has alleged, the perpetrator of yesterday's shooting tragedy in New Orleans turns out to be Bob Lee Swagger, the Vietnam War hero fallen on

> hard times and embittered because his country would not award him the Congressional Medal of Honor he felt he deserved, or if he turns out to be another man with vainglorious notions of what he deserves but could not get, it really doesn't matter. What matters—what has mattered since 1963—is that in this country alone history can be written with firearms precisely because firearms are available; small men can become, momentarily and delusionarily, big men, because firearms are available. In the case of Lee Harvey Oswald it was a cheap Italian war surplus rifle. In the case of yesterday's tragedy, it was a high-powered American sporting firearm, manufactured by Remington. Again, it doesn't matter. What matters is that guns have no other purpose but to kill, and that they kill so frequently has begun to erode the illusion of the "American sportsman." Isn't it time for everybody, in the terrifying wake of another bloody American tragedy, a *typical* American tragedy, involving guns and dreams that would not come true, to begin to work toward the day when only policemen and soldiers and a few forest rangers have guns?

The *New York Times*, by contrast, took a more geopolitical view:

> The terrifying events in New Orleans yesterday merely reconfirm that as a nation we have not yet recovered entirely from the great cataclysm that was the Vietnam War, no matter our nearly bloodless victory over Saddam Hussein last year. A veteran of Vietnam, much

decorated and held in great esteem by his peers, perhaps propelled into bitterness by the glory of the recent battle in distinction to the lack of glory in his own, evidently descended in hatred to the point where he could commit a terrible act, and thereby blaspheme his own well-established heroism and the cause he fought so valiantly for 20 years ago. It is to be hoped that Robert Lee Swagger, the Marine gunnery sergeant and champion sniper who yesterday apparently achieved his 88th kill, may be captured alive, his psyche examined, the seeds of his violence exhumed. The first interest here must be justice. If Sergeant Swagger is indeed guilty of this crime, he must be punished. But we hope that the punishment is tempered with mercy. Like few other men, Sergeant Swagger was a product of his times. The wounds from which he has bled internally over the past two decades were wounds inflicted by his own country and its vast and careless disinterest in his struggles and the struggles of the men with whom he served. That is why, although he is not a victim, he is certainly a tragedy. When he is apprehended—if he is not already dead, as some law enforcement officers have conjectured, given the gravity of his wounds—perhaps these issues will be answered; but perhaps they will not. And perhaps finally, the largest perhaps of them all will be if Bob Lee Swagger comes at last to have some peace himself. When that happens, perhaps we as a nation can also have some peace, when we at last accept the evil of our enterprise in Vietnam, and the squalor of our position in the world as we

> attempt to impose our way on other nations. Once again, our way, the "American way," has been shown to be the way of death.

The Baltimore *Evening Sun* wondered:

> Who needs a long-range assault rifle capable of shooting a man dead at over 400 yards? Certainly not the thousands of children who perish accidentally at the hands of such militaristic-styled guns each year nor the thousands more innocent citizens killed by such multi-shot long-range guns when carried by drug dealers on our city's streets. Nor do the innocent animals slaughtered by such weapons in our nation's forests. Only the powerful gun lobby, drug dealers, the demented men who kill animals for pleasure . . . and assassins, as yesterday's tragedy in New Orleans proved, need such a gun. Congress should act immediately to ban telescopic-powered long-range multi-shot assault rifles. That way, we can give life a chance.

In fact, it was not the murdered man's face that appeared on the cover of *Time* and *Newsweek;* it was Bob's. In an instant, he had become a world celebrity, by virtue first of the killing and second of the miraculous escape, and third for what he represented: the Dixie gun nut with all that trigger time in the 'Nam, gone off on his own twisted route. He was Lee Harvey Oswald and James Earl Ray and Byron De La Beckwith all squashed into one mythic figure, the sullen white trash, yankee-hatin' shooter, a character out of Faulkner, a Flem Snopes with a rifle.

The case had been swiftly developed by the FBI;

Nick Memphis's visual ID of the suspect minutes after the shot had been fired only hastened matters by an hour or so, and the media and police computer networks were far faster and more sophisticated than they'd been in 1963.

The rifle, for example, was quickly tracked by serial number to the Naval Post Exchange system, where it was identified as having been purchased in 1975 by an officer in the Marine Marksmanship Unit for presentation as a retirement present to Bob Lee Swagger, Gny. Sgt., USMC. Bob's signature upon a receipt was uncovered. It followed quickly that the new barrel, a Hart stainless steel model, had been installed by a custom gunsmith in Little Rock named Don Frank; Frank had the serial number in his records, and verified that the job had been done in 1982 for Bob Lee Swagger.

With that information in hand by eight P.M., agents from the Little Rock office of the FBI obtained a search warrant and journeyed out to Blue Eye, cut through the padlocks at his property and examined his trailer and the contents of his life with a great deal of care.

There, they found even more incriminating evidence —maps, drawings, sketches and notes of the four cities in which the president of the United States was scheduled to speak in the months of February and March, with diagrams of the speaking sites. The notes were particularly damning: "Wind, how much wind?" Bob had written. "What time best to shoot?" Bob had wondered. "What range? Go for a long shot, or just try and get up close?" And, ".308? .50? What about some sort of .308–.50?" They also found ticket stubs and hotel receipts indicating that he'd traveled to all four cities, and other teams of agents quickly verified his presence in each. And finally, they found a Barr & Stroud rangefinder, for calibrating the exact distances between shooter and target, an invaluable aid for any sniper.

They also found thirty-two rifles in his gun vault and seventeen handguns, and an empty space where the Remington 700 had rested before he removed it for his trip to New Orleans, and over ten thousand rounds of ammunition.

And they found one other sad thing, much remarked upon in the press for many weeks: lying in a shallow grave, the body of Bob's dog Mike, his brain blown out with a 12-gauge shotgun, because, as the senior agent in charge told NBC news, "He knew he probably wasn't coming back and there was no one to take care of Mike, who was probably the only creature Bob loved in this world."

On the issue of the dog, there was one demurral, from Bob's friend the old ex-prosecutor and war hero Sam Vincent, who never for a second believed Bob had taken the shot, and who had once helped Bob sue *Mercenary* magazine.

"I'll tell you this," he said to the newsmen who had tracked him down. "Whoever done this thing to Bob did a good job. He framed him, he took his reputation from him, he made him an outlaw and the most hated man in America or the world. And he's got you boys putting your lies about him in your magazines and newspapers and on the TV. Well, I tell you, he done a good job, but he made one mistake. He killed Bob's dog. Well, around these parts, we consider our dogs family. And that makes it *personal.*"

This quaint bit of Arkansas lore made the evening news, but nobody paid it much attention because nobody wanted to get into the bitter old man's delusions.

Other witnesses were located to discuss the phenomenon that had become Bob Lee Swagger. His father's legendary heroism was hauled out of the files, and his father's death on U.S. 67 the night of July 23, 1955, as a sergeant in the Arkansas State Police and one of Arkansas's seven Medal of Honor winners from the Second World War. A number of old Arkansas salts who knew both men made television news appearances.

"Hard to b'lieve a son of Earl Swagger's could end up like this," they said to a man. "He was one of the bravest, fairest, most decent men to ever walk the face o' the earth. We-all thought Bob was a true-blue type too, but you can't never tell how a boy's gonna turn out."

A few ex-Marine snipers who'd served with Bob were located; only one would go on television and say "interesting" things—and only with the proviso that his face not be shown. He was now an automobile salesman.

"Bob was just a great shot but he had the coldness," the man said, "the coldness of heart that makes a killer. Of all of us, and there were over fifty men rotated in and out of that platoon over the three years it was operational, he was certainly the best. But as far as I know, we all went back to civilian lives convinced we'd served our country as well as we could. And most of us readjusted."

The man went on to detail his own psychic difficulties with living with his own evil, his own fascination with violence. He'd been in and out of programs, he said, had a long history of alcoholism and only just lately had gotten his life together again. Later, when it was determined he was a fraud, the story ran only on *Entertainment Tonight.*

On the third day, the ballistics report was issued by the FBI. It began with the bad news that the bullet—which had mushroomed considerably as it plowed through bone and brain, then veered free and struck something hard, perhaps a nail in the podium—was unreadable as to its rifling marks. However, preliminary results of tests on the bullet's metallic structure via a neutron activation analysis revealed that it matched perfectly with traces of copper residue found inside the

Hart stainless steel barrel on Bob's Remington action. Two partial fingerprints were lifted from inside the weapon's barrel channel; from Marine Corps records, they were quickly verified as Bob's. The empty shell found on the floor had indeed been fired in the chamber of the Remington; all its marks corresponded exactly to the markings of the chamber. The shell itself probably came from an order of brass—.308 Winchester Match Nickel Plated, Lot No. 32B 0424, manufactured by the Federal Cartridge Company, Anoka, Minnesota—which Bob had purchased, mail order, from Bob Pease Accuracy in New Braunfels, Texas. The matching shells, some loaded, some yet untouched, were found in his workshop.

And last, there was the letter. Poignant, desperate, awkward and naive, it swiftly became the most famous letter in American culture: Bob telling the president he wants the Congressional Medal of Honor because he's earned it. It was the letter that got him on the Secret Service's Charlie list, and had not an idiotic FBI agent blown the assignment, it was the letter that might have saved a man's life. But there it was, the crucial issue of motive.

In all this, there was not one public doubt raised about the guilt of Gunnery Sergeant (Ret.) Bob Lee Swagger, of Blue Eye, Arkansas, in the matter of death by gunshot in New Orleans, Louisiana, on March 1. That was finally uttered, for the first time, on the fourth day, when a reporter from WKNU-TV finally tracked down Mrs. Susan Swagger Preece, of Highland Junction, North Carolina, who had once been married to Bob Lee Swagger and was now the wife of a hardware store owner.

She was a bitter little woman, her face almost completely concealed under a headscarf and sunglasses.

The reporter caught her rushing from her husband's Cadillac toward his lawyer's office.

No, she had no idea where Bob was, and doubted very much, if he was alive, if he'd try to make contact with her. That was all over, she said, and life was too short to be involved with Bob Swagger more than one time.

But she had a last thought.

"I'll say this, though," she said, turning for just a second, "if Bob Lee Swagger took it in his mind to fire a bullet at the president of the United States, then the president of the United States would be a dead man, and not no Salvadoran archbishop. You're telling me Bob Swagger aimed at a man and missed and killed another man? Bob Lee Swagger never missed nothing he aimed at his whole life and that's the Pure-D truth."

CHAPTER FIFTEEN

Millions of people saw it within minutes. But Nick Memphis did not see it for three days, and then only by accident.

He was at hub center of the Swagger manhunt in FBI headquarters, going through leads, keeping his head down in the seething atmosphere of the place now so totally locked into finding the sniper that it seemed unable to pay attention to some smaller details . . . such as himself. But he knew Mother Bureau would get around to it. He knew the inevitable could not be avoided, and that he was riding in a bubble of illusion. The ax would fall. On him. Soon.

But for now he'd lost himself in the minutiae of the reports, and the sightings that now extended over seven states. Bob was everywhere. Bob was in Alaska. Bob was in California. Bob was really Lee Harvey Oswald's brother. Bob had held up a gas station in Tuscaloosa, Alabama. Bob was a dance instructor in New Haven, Connecticut. He had what appeared to be an amusing sighting in Everett Springs, Georgia, where an ex-Marine, who said he knew Bob in the war, swore he'd run into him on a back trail in the Blue Ridge Mountains, and Nick was trying to figure out how the hell Bob could have gotten from New Orleans with two nine-millimeters pumped into him to Everett Springs, Georgia, in the damn Blue Ridges.

But from the investigators, not much at all had surfaced. The car had simply vanished. No snitch had any word at all, and the pressure was on but good. Helicopters cruised the highways and a hundred agents had been flown in to handle the pursuit, on which considerable professional pride rested. But a thousand roadblocks and a hundred thousand photos had yielded nothing at all.

Where had the damned guy gone?

Suddenly, Hap Fencl was leaning in.

"Hey, Nick, we finally got the CBS version, you wanna look?"

"Ahhh—" Nick paused. Something weird in him ticked off. No, he didn't really want to see it, even if, by chance, the CBS cameraman had been best situated to record impact and collapse and poststrike scramble, and even if the pricks at CBS had been snooty about playing ball with the poor old Feebs, who were only in charge of tracking down the motherfucker on the trigger, and even though NBC and CBS and the three New Orleans affiliates who'd had tape on the ultimate moment had shipped it right over, that is, *after* airing it. Despite all that, Nick was reluctant. His whole misfortune was tied up in it: the terribleness of his own missed shot now somehow replicated by the strange pattern in the life and times of his hero. And a certain secret part of Nick couldn't yet believe that the Great Bob the Nailer, the champ of Vietnam and eighty-seven or so odd man-on-man encounters in the boonies, the man who never missed, had, somehow, some way . . . *missed.*

Bob the Nailer might have been a lot of terrible things but he was a great shot. He never missed, that's what Nick thought, along with Bob's wife and two or three others.

"Come on, pal, you might as well see what all the shouting's about. The shouting's gonna be in your ear sooner or later, old buddy."

Hap said this with a malicious grin, not quite meaning to be cruel but rather to be bluff and hearty and masculine and to undercut the tension, because everybody knew Nick was a gone goose. So Nick could hardly turn down the invite.

He walked into a dark room a few minutes later, to a batch of catcalls and hoots—everybody had been working so hard, three eighteen-hour days in a row that Nick-baiting was a treat for them all.

"Hey, hero, where you been hiding?"

"Nicky, whyn't ya shoot the motherfuck when you had the chance, I haven't been able to touch my wife in three days and I am getting very very horny, old boy."

"Nicky, don't let these dicks turn you around, you done good, except for letting him get away, that little minor detail."

"Yeah, yeah," he said in answer to his jolly tormentors, "just wanted to see if you clowns were as good as you say you are. Three days and you guys haven't found your nuts yet."

"Ooooo, brave words from the land of the walking dead."

"All right, gentlemen," said Howdy Duty, who had

gotten himself appointed coordinator of the Swagger manhunt, "let's close it down and watch. Go ahead, Hap."

"Okay, guys," said Hap, "this is raw, unedited TV tape, courtesy of our good friends, the assholes at CBS who make more money and do *lots* more damage than we do. You'll notice the time sequence at the bottom right of the screen that's blocked out for TV showings, but very helpful for our purposes. I've got it cued to thirty seconds before the first shot—assuming, and we're still not sure, there was more than one shot."

The television screen leapt to light and there was Flashlight, his good-looking, rather bland and characterless face knitted up in a slightly unconvincing mask of passion. It was a tight shot, only him and he was singing fulsome praise of this Latino who'd done so much to repair the damage between, as Flashlight put it, "our two great countries," and had worked so tirelessly to effect "reconciliation, reconstruction, and recognition."

And so, Flashlight concluded, what a great pleasure it is to award Archbishop Jorge Roberto Lopez the highest award we have in this country for civilian accomplishment, the Medal of Freedom.

The tape dropped back to a two-shot and the cleric, in modest black, with a beatific smile on his face, comes up to the podium on the president's right to take the president's hand and to genuflect to accept the silky garland with its little hunk of gold plating around his fat neck. He turns, giving his back to the audience, then bends as the president lifts to raise the thing over his—

"That's it," said Hap Fencl, as the image froze. "What we're gonna hear a lot of once the conspiracy boys figure out how to make a bundle on this, is how come Bob doesn't shoot when the president is talking and he's got an easy frontal or brain shot. Why does he wait till he's turned to his right and the Latin guy is moving into the line of fire? Answers, anybody?"

There was silence. But Nick knew.

"Hap?"

"Yes, Nick."

"Ah, the reason is that a headshot is too far to risk from, what, five hundred yards out? Not because he can't hit a head at that range, you can bet your ass he can. But because the head is the most animated part of the body and most of the body movement begins at the head; so the head is never really still and it moves so quickly because the neck muscles are so articulated and because the reaction time between impulse and action is nearly instantaneous. So the head's a no-go, at least for a pro. But at the same time he's worried about body armor so he can't quite take a full frontal, center-of-mass shot. See, he's waiting for Flashlight to turn slightly, to raise his arms, and he's going for a raking shot into the sleeve vent of the body armor. He wants a translateral chest shot, putting it into him right in front of the armpit on about a forty-five-degree angle. The bullet will traverse left to right, expanding as it goes, and it ought to clear out all the chest structures. He'd be dead in a second, before he hit the ground. Was Flashlight wearing body armor?"

"Secret Service won't say. That's very good, Nick."

"Too bad you're a dead man," somebody said anonymously in the dark.

There was some laughter and even Nick had to smile.

"Okay, let's get to the good stuff," said Hap. "Brainshot time, boys and girls."

On some twitch, the archbishop lurched up as if a back spasm suddenly struck him and Nick thought that he'd been hit or something; but no, it just seemed to be the random play of events in a very small compass that for whatever reason, instead of lowering his head to take the president's garland he raised it and pushed his head into the kill zone where Swagger's bullet hit it full force, back right rear quadrant.

The moment, frozen in the stillness of the videotape was staggering: ripeness is all, said Lear, though Nick had learned it from Joseph Heller in *Catch-22* when Snowden died in the back of the plane, but here it was again, that message. Man was matter. Light him, he'll burn. Sink him, he'll drown. Shoot him in the head, his head will explode.

The head seemed to disappear in a sudden flame of motion, a smear across the lens as if the atoms were individually decomposing. In actuality, of course, it was a .308 caliber 200-grain bullet hitting at about fourteen hundred feet per second, breaching the cranial vault, opening like a steel tulip inside, veering crazily through the whorls and confusions of the august archbishop's gray matter and blowing crazily out his left eye socket and in so doing spattering tissue into the horrified face of the president of the United States.

"He's a complete rag doll the microsecond the bullet goes through him," said Hap.

There was a moment of almost holy silence as the man's death loomed in frozen grandeur on the screen.

"It's a little tough to tell from this angle, Hap, but are we sure the president was the intended target? Jesus, that's a dead center hit to me," somebody said.

"Now I don't want that kind of talk," Howdy Duty said, asserting himself for the first time and quick to deal with the apostasy. "That's exactly the kind of nonsense that got started during 1963 and haunts us to this day. Yes, absolutely the president was the target, you can see the way the head rose into the line of fire."

But Nick just sat there staring at the moment of death, the brains like a breaking red wave emptying themselves in the face of the president who had not yet begun to react. He'd thought so much about shooting a person at long range—it had been his life once, before Myra, his vanity that he could do it, do it well, save lives, become a hero—and something now reached him that disturbed him.

He tried to fix on it, to sift it out of the data but—

"Nick? Nick? Hey, somebody poke Nick, he's sleeping!"

"Oh, yeah. Sorry, what's up, Hap?"

"Nick, you did some sniper time on SWAT, any way he's not shooting at Flashlight?"

"Ahh—" Nick paused.

"Well, Nick?" asked Howdy Duty.

"Can you get an angle reading from the point of impact and the wound channel and trace it back to a source and make sure it came from that house?"

"No. Just got the report from Washington. They ran it through their big ballistics mainframe program, and the best they can do is pinpoint a rough semicircle of about seven degrees. And there's over nineteen buildings with windows opening onto the shooting site from there. We've been over each of them, though, and the only one that had blood and a rifle in it and an empty shell happened to be the one where Bob the Nailer walked on a nine-mil and took your Smith," Hap said.

"Well, that's it then," said Nick, letting it slide, knowing he'd hoard his doubt at least a little longer, rather than risk Howdy Duty's ire this early in it, and hanging on to his career by a pubic hair.

"Okay, let's go on," said Hap.

Impelled by the force of the bullet, the cleric now plunged forward and smashed into the president, and the two went down in a terrible heap.

"Archbishop Roberto Lopez crashes into Flashlight, after spraying him with tissue and blood, but by this time the bullet has exited and smashed into the wood of the podium slat," Hap continued to narrate, "where it will be recovered by our ballistic technicians, too damn mutilated for a ballistics signature reading. Still, one bullet, two men down, elapsed time four one-hundreths of a second. It's a hell of a piece of shooting."

The drama continued to unfold, now in real time. In seconds, Secret Service men of Alpha Security Team, pulling Uzis from God knows where, are surrounding Flashlight so that no other bullet may reach him. Mere anarchy is loosed around the podium, but the Alpha guys stay very calm and completely purposeful.

"Hey, these Alpha guys know how to operate," said Hap.

"Too bad they're such pricks," came a jokester's voice.

The drama then seemed to devolve into pulsating patterns of light and color. Evidently, a Secret Service Alpha guy pushed all the cameramen back and for just a moment the world went all to blur. When it came back, a small knot of men is gathered around Flashlight who is supine, but trying to struggle to his feet. Archbishop Roberto Lopez is almost in his lap, that head with its queerly deflated look, as if it were a balloon and not a skull. The Secret Service guys are dancing around; then a medic comes atop the podium, and they bend to let him in. A few seconds later the world dissolves; this time it's under the torrents of air that the standby medical chopper radiates as it settles with lazy urgency out of the sky. The camera shifts to it as paramedics and stretcher teams race over to Flashlight and the Alpha team. Screams, shouts, confusion. It reminded Nick of a pickup game of basketball, all frenzy and nonsense.

And then he had it, what was weird about the shooting.

"Could we go back to the hit?" he asked.

"What are you, a ghoul?"

"Come on, Hap, let me see the hit."

There was some grumbling but Hap rewound the tape, then punched PLAY, and the drama reinvented itself up there on the screen, the lurch of the old man, the sudden, stunning, boltlike arrival of the bullet, the sleet of bone and tissue, and Nick was thinking about his own shooting.

I overcompensated, he thought. I knew the bullet, traveling downward, would drop farther. That's the effect of the angle. So I overcompensated, missed high, and hit Myra. Now this Swagger, he knows shooting like he knows his own two hands and the smell of his own sweat. He knows where the bullet will strike. That means the bullet drift is going to be vertical. He'll hit high or low on a vertical range; if he's shooting at the president's armpit, if the bullet goes too high it hits the president in the neck or head; if it's too low it goes into his ribs or hip.

But *this* shooting error was lateral. It was on the same damn level as the president's armpit, for the man was kneeling . . . but it was a lateral error, an aiming error, which had nothing to do with the shot's most difficult aspect, the play of the downward angle over the long eight hundred yards to the target. Could a gust of wind have just nudged it off target?

He remembered that March 1 had been an unusually calm day, with the wind under five miles per hour. It was possible but not probable.

It suddenly occurred to Nick that the shooting error made no sense at all. He would shoot over the president, he would shoot below the president; he would not miss to the right. Not this boy.

Nick swallowed. He'd arrived at a place he didn't want to be: it could only be that Bob Lee Swagger was shooting for the archbishop all the way.

And then he realized what bad news this was for everybody: currently the only theory available to unify the events was that that mean-ass, sullen, pissed-off Dixie whiteboy Swagger was shooting the president. It made sense. It held together—but only if Swagger were shooting for Flashlight.

If Swagger wasn't shooting for Flashlight . . . a dizzying realm of possibility opened up.

Nick had a weird moment here, as his whole life traveled its fucked-up way before him and he suddenly saw that he was about to diverge from the path.

Because he now knew Swagger was innocent, and that the reason he saw compassion in the sniper's eyes as he stood above him with the big Smith was because the sniper was still, by his own lights, a moral man, an honorable man—a man who did not shoot the innocent and Nick, stupid and bumbling, had been of the innocent.

"Nick?"

It was Howdy Duty.

"Nick, I'm afraid I'm going to have to ask you to see me sometime today. All right?"

Oh, shit, thought Nick.

The cow was not frightened of Colonel Shreck.

Her eyes were placid and dull, though huge. There was something tenderly stupid in them.

The cow chewed her cud, occasionally scuffed one hoof in the straw, or bent her great, gentle head down to seize another bunch of hay from her bale.

"Shoot her," said Colonel Shreck.

Hatcher kneeled, squinted, then found what he was looking for. He raised a 9mm Beretta 92 and shot the cow in the chest, hitting her square in a painted spot.

Dobbler winced at the report, even through the high-decibel soundproof earmuffs; and he thought he'd be sick, though he'd been feeling woozy since the event. He forced himself to look back at the animal. He'd never seen anything die, much less anything so huge and warm-blooded.

But the cow didn't seem interested in dying. She'd twitched just once when the bullet drove through her and a tiny track of blood opened up from the black pucker of the entrance wound. But her head came back up, she continued to chew and to gaze at her audience benevolently.

"Of course she has one great advantage," said Hatcher, rising. "She has no conceptual ability. She cannot understand what has just happened to her. Swagger, of course, saw the gun, and knew what happened. Thus his collapse and initial response to shock. But physiologically, that's it. That's the shot on Bob. Same range, same ammunition, same angle, through the center chest."

Dobbler studied the animal. The animal appeared to study him back until he bored her. Then she lowered her head for another thatch of hay. He thought he would puke. He struggled to keep his focus, but could feel the sweat running down his face.

Dobbler watched as Shreck stared at the creature. The colonel seemed bent in some furious, one-pointed crusade to absorb all the life from the animal, his dark eyes gobbling up her destruction with no remorse whatsoever, only great curiosity. She paid him no attention.

"She's hit and the bullet has gone down through her thoracic cavity and exited the other side," said Thatcher. "But it's not stopping her. It's not even *irritating* her. This happens all too frequently. You may recall the famous 'Miami Shootout' of May 1987, where a creep named Michael Platt was hit ten times, once through the lungs, mostly with Winchester 9mm hollow-tips and kept firing long enough to kill two and wound five FBI agents."

"I thought the *point* of a hollowpoint bullet," said Colonel Shreck, "was to open up and rip the shit out of the tissue and organs."

"It didn't open," said Hatcher. "If it had, he'd have never made it to the car, much less dumped that FBI agent. We know because Payne's report says he saw blood on the back of the shirt. It had to go through without opening up."

"Why didn't it open up?" Shreck asked.

Finally, Hatcher answered. "In our research, we've found that most of the stopping problems with 9mm Silvertip came with first-generation ammunition. They first started manufacturing it in the mid-seventies. The real bad stopping problems took place then; subsequently they changed the circumference of the cavity and the composition of the copper sheathing the lead, and since then the results have been much better, up to about seventy-three percent one-shot kills. But Timmons had to draw his ammo from police sources. Otherwise, there'd be reason to suspect some kind of frame-up. And we think the police issue was an older lot, purchased back in 1982. But we *had* to go with police issue, because if he used an unauthorized load it led to very dangerous ground. We simply trusted him—or Payne, who insisted on doing the actual shooting—to place a mortal round. If he'd hit the heart, it wouldn't have mattered. If it had opened up and he missed the heart, it wouldn't have mattered. Unfortunately he missed the heart *and* it didn't open up."

"Shit," said Shreck. "And why did Payne miss the heart?"

"You'd have to ask Payne, Colonel Shreck."

"I did."

"Bear in mind, sir," said Hatcher, "that in the expanse of the chest, the heart is a fairly difficult target. It's much smaller and to the right of where people think it is. I talked with him about anatomy, but in the dark, and the crisis of the second, he . . ."

Hatcher let the sentence end.

"You're a doctor, Dr. Dobbler. What's the medical prognosis?"

Dobbler cleared his throat. He'd researched this.

"Swagger could die of blood loss or infection. But it's possible that the bullet just rushed through doing minor tissue damage and left him largely intact. If he was smart enough to stanch the bleeding right away—and clearly he *was*, having been wounded before—he'll heal up and if he doesn't get infected, he'll be good as new in two weeks."

Shreck looked as if he were going to laugh.

"Now," said Hatcher, "let me just show you, by contrast, a later 9mm."

"Of course," said Shreck.

"This is a Federal 147-grain Hydra-Shok, with a post in the center of the cavity, to help expansion. I think you should see some dramatic results."

Suddenly, Dobbler was nauseous. He didn't want to watch the man shoot the animal and then talk about the weight of the bullet and the angle of the wound and the size of the temporary stretch cavity. It seemed obscene to him: it was killing, after all, not to any ends, not to purpose or point, but just to satisfy some arcane curiosity.

Dobbler looked away. Outside, through the barn door, he could see the rolling Virginia hills.

"Just a second," said Shreck. "Dr. Dobbler, would you mind paying attention?"

Dobbler smiled and turned his face to watch. The bullet was fired. She kicked, an amazing burst of energy from so stolid an animal. Then her heavy head twitched once. Subtly, her lines changed as she shuddered, and her knees went as the bullet, a ragged nova of hot metal, ruptured her heart, and she surrendered. The great head slid forward and lay atilt, eyes blankly open. She was still in a dark and spreading pool of blood.

Dobbler smiled weakly, afraid he'd lose face in front of Shreck, but thought for just a second he was all right. Then he vomited all over his clothes.

But Shreck did not even notice. Instead he watched the animal die, then turned to Hatcher and said, "Now at least I know what to tell them."

"Ahhh," said Howdy Duty, regretfully. He looked up at Nick over half-specs, his face haggard with fatigue. He'd been working like the rest of them, eighteen on and six off, and was beginning to wear a bit thin. But he would be polite, Nick knew.

"Come on, sit down, Nick."

Nick sat down. The gray light of the office turned Howdy Duty's skin the color of old parchment; his eyes were lost behind the crescent specs. He had a slightly distracted air.

"Oh, Nick, what are we going to do with you?"

Nick didn't know what to say. He'd always suspected that he didn't prosper in the Bureau because he'd never been much at coming up with charming answers to rhetorical questions agents in charge tended to ask at awkward moments. So, as usual, Nick said nothing; he just parked his considerable bulk into the chair, breathing hard.

"Nick, tell me about the Charlie thing to begin with. The Secret Service is making all kinds of trouble. You know what an asshole that Mueller can be."

"Well," said Nick, swallowing as he began, "maybe I did screw up. But Jesus, Howard, there were over sixty names on the Charlie list, and they were way down in importance. The Secret Service guys themselves said that; they won't admit it, but they made it seem like it was strictly business as usual. But I worked it real hard, Howard. What's his name, Sloane, he told me himself I'd done a good job. I located most of them or accounted for them; I recommended three be moved up to Beta classification, and they didn't like that one bit, because it meant *they* had to do more work."

"But you did miss Bob Lee Swagger?"

"Not really. I picked him out, and made inquiries. I called Sheriff Tell in Polk County to find out if he'd had any recent troubles. He'd been sitting pretty, off by himself. They say the pattern with these guys is they begin to destabilize in the days before they make a hit. There was no sign of that. He didn't fit any pattern and his sheriff vouched for him. Also, the only reason he was on the list was for that letter and the only reason the letter got him there was because it had four exclamation points. Four exclamation points! It seemed like a safe call to me. I can't say I'd make it any different way now."

"All right, Nick. I suppose you performed *adequately*. We can't expect *distinction* twenty-four hours, seven days a week. Nick, I think I can save you from Secret Service, because they want some Bureau blood to let them off the hook. It was really their operation, and they got beaten."

"They sure did."

"But, I've talked to the director and we feel our position is strong. They could complain that we didn't do a good job on the Charlies and we could complain that they were so poorly managed they couldn't deal with the Charlies themselves. Mexican standoff, and I think they'll back down. Now, Nick, I have to say, that arrest; it was badly bungled."

"I know, Howard. I screwed up."

"It looked so bad in the newspapers. And it looks bad inside the Bureau, too. We're supposed to be able to handle situations like that."

"I don't know what to say, Howard. It was a desperate situation. Maybe I—I just don't know, Howard."

"Nick, you were in a desperate situation in 1986 in Tulsa and you mismanaged that, too."

Nick was silent. Then, finally, he said, "Howard, I just want to be an FBI agent. That's all I ever wanted."

"Well, Nick . . . the director has left this call to me."

Nick hated the fact that he was begging. But he tried to imagine a life without the one thing that mattered as much as his wife, which was the Bureau. He had to live a life without Myra now; but he couldn't imagine one without the Bureau.

"Please don't fire me, Howard. I know I haven't been sharp lately. But I just lost my wife a few months ago . . . it just hasn't been an easy time."

"Nick, we need bodies on this thing. I'm going to suspend you without pay for a week, but it won't go into effect for three months. Then I'm afraid it'll have to."

Nick nodded. It meant that within a month afterwards he'd be rotated back to the sticks and he'd never get out. It had taken him years to get to New Orleans. But it also meant, however provisionally, he'd be able to stay.

"I suppose I'll be transferred then."

"Nick, you know how it works. And I'm going to have to put a letter in your file. Like the other one."

"Yes."

"Nick, I don't want to."

"Okay, Howard."

"I'm trying to cut you as much slack as I can."

"Sure, I appreciate it," Nick said.

Sure, I appreciate it! You prick, if you'd have kept your fucking trap shut six years ago, I'd have nailed that fuck right between the eyes and I'd be where you're sitting and you'd be on your way back to Tulsa.

"You're still in the Bureau, Nick."

"I appreciate that, Howard."

"But, Nick, no more mistakes. Do you understand. There can't be another slipup."

"There won't be, Howard. I promise."

CHAPTER SIXTEEN

When Bob crawled from the water just before dawn on the day after the shooting, his head seethed with rage and flashing pictures and hallucinations. His body was numb as the log under which it had floated and slightly swollen and soft from the long immersion; he smelled of diesel oil from the barge scum that coated the surface of the river below New Orleans. He reckoned he'd drifted fifty or so miles; around him were scrub pines, an infinity of them, and boggy marshes, a maze of them, and dense, interlocking cypress trees. Small things scurried and then went silent; far off, a bird made a strange and mournful sound, a screech of pain; then it went silent too.

You're going to die, he thought.

There was nothing here but the sameness of jungle, its merciless face. And there'd be men in it too, soon enough, hunting him.

You're back where you started, only you're older and weaker.

He stumbled a few feet, went to his knees. When was the last time he'd eaten? Must have been yesterday, breakfast. He'd been shot twice, used his last drop of adrenaline in getting out of there, and floated in the sullen river for eighteen horrible hours, slung upside down under the goddamn log, only his nostrils flaring above the water.

So there it was: eat or die.

Didn't matter if the wound was infected or not; if he didn't eat he'd wear down fast, and the jungle would feed off him in a matter of hours.

Been in tougher fixes, yes I have, I do believe.

But he hadn't. There was no chopper waiting to air-evac him if he could just make the LZ. There was nothing but this jungle and outside it a whole world set to do him in.

It must have been a bit after dawn. The air was very crisp and clean and smelled fresh as baby breath. The sun was still weak. It was feeding time, he knew it soon enough.

Then Bob happened to feel something hard against his leg, and realized the hardness had been there all night. He slid the pistol from his jeans pocket. It was a big stainless Smith & Wesson .45 automatic, their new Model 4506. No. No, by God, it wasn't, it was that fancy new 10mm the FBI had started using. He wondered about the round. He'd trust his life to a .45, having fired a hundred thousand .45 cartridges in his time through a variety of Colts. But this new thing, a 10-mil? He didn't know.

Man without a gun has got no chance, Bob thought. Man has a gun, he has a chance.

With a thumb as big as a brick, he pawed the magazine release. The mag fell out and he saw the agent had it loaded brimful with hollowpoints, like little brass Easter eggs down there. He sneaked a look to see if the man had the chamber stoked, and the gleam of brass from the seated cartridge answered him. Would they stand up under a soaking? Only one way to find out. He slid the magazine back, felt it lock and with a same brick thumb got the hammer back and locked.

He sat back, wishing he had more strength to find a position, or a trail, some place to hunt from, a good place to shoot from, a brace, anything. He had none of it. Only the gun. Overhead, the sun filtered through the dense tree cover, thin, not yet eight he reckoned. The shadows were blurry. Or was it his eyes going? Was he sliding off into nothingness, bled out like a deer shot quickly and not well.

He was hallucinating again. Strange, at this time he thought of Donny Fenn and all the scary moments in the boonies, and how at the real crazy-ass seconds, Donny'd begin to laugh a little, a hysterical giggle.

Donny, boy, you'd be laughing today if you could see old Bob and what's become of him, sitting on his wet ass in some bog waiting on death or a creature.

But Bob couldn't laugh. He tried to settle back. Seemed like there was a dim memory of sitting in the rain a while back a whole night through, waiting on Tim, the whitetail buck with the twelve-point spread. That was a long wet wait, wasn't it? Oh, that was a hunt! He remembered the way Tim came blasting out of the foliage, like a ghost or a miracle, and how the rifle came up to him and he fired and knew how well he'd fired. That was a night, wasn't it? Hit Tim above the spine with a bullet cast from epoxy; must have weighed less than 25 grains, atomized when it hit the flank but the shock knocked the sense out of Tim for a good five minutes.

He remembered sawing the antlers off.

Nobody going to kill you to hang your head on a wall, he thought.

Go on, boy. Git.

He remembered the creature leaping away when it came out of its coma, full of juice, crackly with life.

He laughed crazily.

They sure tried to hang my head on a wall.

Then Bob looked up and there it was. Late, it was drinking late. Maybe so deep here in the swamp there were no men and so there was no fear. Bob didn't know. He just heard the rustle of twigs snapping, saw a flash of color.

It was some sort of ugly spotted pig. Bob watched it emerge from the dapples of the trees maybe seventy-five yards out. It was ugly as an outhouse on a hot day, and yet when Bob saw it he almost cried for the second time in his life, the first being when he was alone at nine and had gone off onto the hill after Major Benson had come to tell them his daddy was dead out near Fort Smith.

But Bob didn't cry. He made ready to shoot.

The damned gun was new; suddenly it felt different than his old Colt automatic, as if it were fighting him. Squeezing his left hand around the right, printing down on his right thumbnail with his left, his elbows locked between his pressing knees as he sat in a modified isosceles, fighting the tremors of exhaustion that nuzzled through his wrists and tried to betray him in their treacherous way.

Front sight. Front sight. Front sight.

That was it. That was the key, the rock upon which the church was built. You had to see the front sight with a pistol, and let the target be a kind of hazy blur in the far distance. Otherwise, nothing good happened at all.

Front sight, front sight, front sight.

In the notch of the rear sight, a frame, he saw the huge red wall of the front. There was only front, rock steady, big as Gibraltar or Mars, Bob bending into it with every last thing, and the pig a kind of soupy blur, its details lost in the distance, just a splotch of movement against the stability of the greenery.

He hoped that damn cop had zeroed it well. He hoped the water hadn't deadened the primers or ruined the powder in the case.

Bob was so poured into the shot he didn't hear the noise at all or feel the recoil, as the big pistol whacked back. What he saw was the pig speared through the spine by the lead, which, entering its tough hide, ruptured; it hit and broke the spine.

The animal squealed as death closed it down, then a spasm of fury rocketed through it. It tried to climb to its now stunted and shaky legs but, having a broken spine, was unable to direct the last part of its body to obey. Then, with a last quiver, it went quiet.

Bob got himself up. Still woozy, still soaked, he felt death in his own limbs, stalking through his body, hunting him. But he walked onward, dazed, kept sane only by the smell of the burned powder that his nose picked up in the riotous odors of the swamp, a familiar thing onto which he could lock. He wobbled to the pig, then collapsed as he reached it.

It weighed about forty pounds. It was about three feet long. It smelled of manure and offal. Its snout was curiously delicate, as if designed by an angel; its lashes, fleecy at the closed slots of its eyes, were also delicate, like a child's.

The bullet hole was an ugly blister over the shoulder, but there wasn't a lot of blood seepage. It hadn't come out, unlike the bullet Payne had put into him, which is why he had lived and the pig had not. Served Payne right for using something tiny like a nine. Payne had broken the one true moral law of hunting: use enough gun.

Some day, I'll use enough gun on you, Payne.

Swiftly he got out his Case XX, still secure in the watch pocket of his Levi's, thanking God for a good Case knife that would hold an edge all down the many years and thanking God also for his own stubborn ways that made a small knife as much a part of daily dressing as boots and socks.

Turning the dead animal so that its soft belly was finally exposed, he had a moment of crisis. Felt as if he'd fallen out of his own body there for a second. A wave of hallucination crashed over him. He forgot everything. But then it came back and he found himself with the knife and the dead animal and he butchered it swiftly.

Bob wanted the liver, which he found, a treasure amid the gore, and ripped it out, feeling it hot because it was so soaked in oxygenated blood.

The liver was richest in nutrition and tastiest this side of a fire. Bob tore off a bite, stunned at the intensity of the flavor and the sense of richness; it made him dizzy it was so powerful. He ate some more, chewing ravenously, amazed at how hungry he was; how desperately he needed it. He ate and ate until the liver was gone.

I am alive, he thought.

Then he heard the roar of a chopper, and dropped. A Huey sped low above the riverbank, blowing the trees left and right as it hurtled along.

They're looking for me, he thought, with a wave of regret at the complications of his life. Then he picked up the carcass, slung it over his back and headed deeper into the swamp.

CHAPTER SEVENTEEN

Dobbler always found Shreck's occasional absences frightening. The customers here at RamDyne were tough guys, like cops or soldiers, or if not tough, they were distant, techno-nerd types, and both groups looked upon the large, soft psychiatrist with an attitude characteristic of their professions: either contempt or indifference, depending. So the doctor tended to sit in his grubby little office when Shreck wasn't around to act as his sponsor in this strange world.

The RamDyne offices—offices wasn't exactly the right word—were located amid the cargo terminals and warehouses of Dulles International Airport, just south of Washington, D.C. They were a shabby warren of jerry-built light-industrial units sequestered behind double Cyclones that wore double spirals of razor wire, guarded viciously by armed men. The sign next to the guardhouse at the sole entrance said only BROWN EXPORTS, without corporate logo or escutcheon. It had a prosaic, unexceptional quality to it, and the guard who always looked fiercely at Dobbler, as if he never recognized him after a full year on the payroll, went with the outfit's bunker mentality.

Dobbler's office was a dingy closet unbecoming an assistant professor at a junior college in Idaho; with concrete floors and surplus wardroom furniture, it looked like the office of a doomed teacher who never would get tenure and would live forever on the hook of his department chairman's whim. Everything in it was junk, from the sagging bookcase to the desk scratched with strange initials to the ancient safe for confidential documents. It even had bars at the window, an irony not lost on Dobbler. The fluorescent light was imperfectly calibrated, and threw shadows no matter how you sited yourself in it, that is, when it wasn't flickering wanly.

But it wasn't as if Dr. Dobbler had the worst office; Colonel Shreck's, in another building, was equally crummy; it was just a bit bigger, with a moth-eaten sofa near a window that yielded a vista of cargo planes taking off or landing. It didn't even have a bigger safe, but exactly the same beat-up model as Dobbler's. The doctor often wondered if it had the same combination!

Dobbler now sat in his office, trying to focus on the problem before him. He found the silence ominous, as if a spell had been cast by the freakish escape of Bob Lee Swagger. And that, in fact, was the problem Dobbler now faced.

The last words from Shreck had been simple.

"Doctor, go back over the documents. Tell me where this asshole went."

Dobbler answered tentatively, as he always did.

"Y-you don't think he's dead?"

"Of course not. Now, I've got to go out of town for a few days," said Shreck. "Try and let me have a report when I get back. I have the utmost confidence in you."

Before Dobbler the material fluttered in and out of focus.

Concentrate, he instructed himself. Man on the run. No friends. Where does he go? Where can he go? Who would have him?

He had the files of data assembled by Research in its first evaluation of the subject and his own psychological reports.

Breathing heavily, he began to shuffle through them. Bob's life in the years before his recruitment seemed comprised of two things: his guns and his long walks through the Ouachitas. He was hiding from the world, Dobbler thought, feeling himself unworthy of it.

The detritus of Bob's life spoke of no warm personal relationships, at least not outside of Polk County. His only friend was that crotchety old Sam Vincent, who'd helped him sue the magazine. If he were alive, he might eventually try to return to Polk County, and maybe to Sam. But now, on the run, where would he head? There was no indication—no sisters, no brothers, no old Marine buddies, no women, not a thing. The man was too much like some kind of exiled warrior—Achilles sulking in his tent came to mind—to need companionship of any kind.

Even the financial records, uncovered by a credit agency, confirmed this pattern. Clearly, Bob kept his finances in control by iron discipline—he could live off his fourteen-thousand-dollar government pension because his expenses were low and he had no creature comforts, no interest in clothes beyond their function, no travel or diversion. There was no record of what he'd done with the thirty thousand dollars he'd received from the magazine in his out-of-court settlement. He had a credit card—a Visa, from the First National Bank of Little Rock—but the reason seemed to be convenience; he could make telephone purchases of reloading components and shooting supplies, thus saving himself time and trouble writing up orders. He bought his clothes from Gander Mountain, Wisconsin, his powder from Mid-South Shooter's Supply and a couple of other places. He lived to shoot, that's all; and, Dobbler supposed, he shot to live.

Would he run to shooters?

This was an alien world to Dobbler, so he tried to imagine it. Then he realized that from what little he knew of shooting culture, there'd be no place in it for Bob. Those folks tended to be conservative rural Americans; they'd have no sympathy for a man whom they thought had winged a shot at the president of the United States. Which left him with . . .

In several hours of close scrutiny, he came up with nothing. He looked around; it was late in the afternoon. The place was quiet. There were no answers anywhere. He was ready to give it up. Maybe tomorrow he'd notice—

And then he saw it.

He looked, blinked, squinted, looked again. It was so little. It was so much nothing. It couldn't be.

It was a telephone billing on Bob's December 1990 Visa bill.

A place called Wilheit's, in Little Rock. The phone number was given.

It seemed . . . *familiar*.

He rifled through the credit report, looking for the other Visa bills, and found nothing until . . . December 1989. Wilheit's.

Quickly he found December 1988 . . . Wilheit's.

The bill was roughly the same, seventy-five dollars.

What was Wilheit's?

He called the number, and waited while AT&T shunted the connection through dialing stations and off satellites, and the phone rang, sounding far away, and then was answered.

"Hello, Wilheit's, c'n ah hep you?" was how Dobbler heard the Little Rock accent.

"Er, yes. Um. What do you sell, please?"

"Whut do we *sell*?" said the voice.

"Yes. What sort of establishment are you?"

"We're a florist, son. We sell flowers."

"Ah," said Dobbler, hanging up.

Now who on earth would Bob Lee Swagger be sending flowers to every December? A Christmas thing? But Bob wasn't a Christmas sort of guy.

Jack Payne was not a happy camper.

Like the other two men who had been in the room at the time, he was haunted by the resurrection of Bob Lee Swagger.

Since then, Jack had stayed clear of the colonel, knowing he'd probably have to answer for the blown shot.

But how could it have been blown?

Well, someone on the team had said, the damn Silvertip probably didn't open up, that's all, so it just went on through, and old Bob fought his way through the shock, and was up and running. He was a Marine, see, Marines are tough.

No, Jack thought there was something else. It was his own rotten luck with a handgun. In truth, he hated pistols. That's why he carried the cut-down Remington, because almost was good enough with six 12-gauge double-oughts at your fingertips. In Vietnam once, his first tour, '62, Jack just a scrawny corporal, he had been on the way to the shitter and looked up in horror as a gook came at him with a bayonet on an old French boltgun and sheer murder in his eyes. Jack had left his carbine somewhere and pulled a .45 and squeezed off seven quick ones as the little man charged crazily at him. He missed all seven. Missed them all, fell to his knees and waited for the blade. What happened next was that from thirty yards some guy with a grease gun cut the gook in two—literally, into two pieces—and Jack lived to fight another day. But he hated that moment because he had pissed and shat in his pants as he went to his knees, knowing he was finished and too weak to do anything.

"Hey, Corporal, you'd best git yourself a pair of diapers," his A-team leader had said to him after the firefight, and the whole goddamn team erupted in laughter. That's what he hated the most, the fury of the humiliation. And that's when he swore he'd never carry a handgun again and he'd never humiliate himself again.

But now Swagger had humiliated him twice.

That's all right, Payne had told himself. I'll get me another shot at you and this time I'll put two, three, maybe all six double-oughts into you, motherfucker. Some of these kids on the team think you're some kind of bull-goose macho motherfucker, some kind of super-cracker, a Dixie boy full of piss and leather; not me, Swagger. Double-ought cut you down to your rightful size real good.

Then Jack snickered, remembering.

I already started having my fun with you. I killed your fucking dog.

A thousand leads, a thousand nothings. The man had just vanished. Nick, now more a glorified clerk than an actual federal investigating officer, sat in the office for twelve hours at a stretch and watched every single lead dissolve into wisps, every report fizzle, every trace turn up counterfeit.

The other men didn't like to be seen talking to Nick. They'd deny it, of course, but he noticed that when he joined a knot of kibitzers on the rare down minutes, one by one the guys would peel off and he'd be stuck facing a blank wall. Only Sally Ellion always said hi because she was too pretty and popular to run any danger of career contamination. She once even told him she was sorry he was having troubles.

"I'm sure it wasn't your fault," she said.

"I'm sure it *was*," he replied.

"I heard that you might be going to another office."

"Yeah. Well, not for a while, not until this thing gets done. They need bodies now. *Somebody's* got to wash out the damned coffee cups. But I'll probably be heading out. Maybe not such a bad thing. New Orleans hasn't really worked out. I'll get a start somewhere else."

"I know you'll do well, Nick," she said, "wherever you go."

He smiled; she was a nice girl.

Meanwhile the office pool was running odds of eight to one that Bob was dead; no man could disappear so completely from the largest federal manhunt in history, leaving no traces at all. Especially a man who, as reports developed, hadn't a friend in the world, had no network of allies, no organization, no peers. The complete and absolute loner.

But meanwhile Nick clerked and cleaned for the first-stringers, bearing his humiliation with as much dignity as he could muster; and maybe it was while he was washing out the coffee pot that he had his bright idea.

Don't do this, he said to himself.

You are in deep enough trouble already.

Man, they are going to eighty-six your ass out of here if they catch you.

And it's so unlike you to do anything at all contrary to official policy.

But . . . it was such a *good* idea.

And like all good ideas, it was simple.

He couldn't stop thinking about the man he'd found cut to pieces in the motel three months before the Roberto Lopez shooting. It struck him as something more than coincidental that the man was Salvadoran, as Wally Deaver had told him, even if his credentials and the Bureau ID'd him as an Eduardo Lachine of Panama City, Panama. But one man had seen Lanzman. That was Deaver, in Boston, back when he'd been a DEA agent at the Bush drug summit in Cartagena, Colombia, in 1990.

Why not fax Wally a morgue ID of the stiff? And that way find out if . . .

He tried to think of what it would mean if a Salvadoran secret agent had been murdered in New Orleans a few months before the assassination of a Salvadoran archbishop unloved by his own country's regime. But it gave him a headache, and he went back to work.

The general leaned forward, proposing a toast, his white teeth gleaming, his eyes radiant with joy.

"To our friend, *Colonel* Raymond Shreck. A very great man. A truly wonderful man!"

He raised his glass, which was filled with an expensive wine.

The general was a sleek, smiling man named Esteban Garcia de Rujijo, and at thirty-eight, through great ferocity in a multitude of hardfought campaigns, he had become the commanding officer of the Fourth Battalion (Air-Ranger), First Brigade, First Division ("Atlacatl") of the Salvadoran Army. His unit was nicknamed *Los*

Gatos Negros, or Panther Battalion, for their jet-black berets.

"Thank you, sir," said Shreck, in Spanish.

Shreck, eyes hooded, wore his old uniform with Ranger tabs, Special Forces MACV lightning patch, his Corcoran jump boots glossy black, the trousers bloused into them. He carried his green beret under his epaulet. The uniform still fit perfectly and its creases were razors. The Combat Infantry Badge dominated a chestful of ribbons, including the Distinguished Service Cross and the Purple Heart and the Silver Star with two Oak Leaf Clusters, all of which were his.

Shreck and the general—and a third man—sat at a dinner table in a large museum of a house, on two thousand prime acres in the hills just north of the seaport city of Acajutla, in northern El Salvador. The house was not the general's, at least not yet. It belonged to another man also named de Rujijo—the general's father. It had been owned by the de Rujijos since the Spanish had conquered the region in 1655.

The third man, who was sitting next to Colonel Shreck, was a small, merry, elderly gentleman named Hugh Meachum, formerly of the Central Intelligence Agency's Directorate of Plans and, since his rude retirement from the Agency in 1962, a fellow at the Buddings Institute of Foreign Policy in Washington, D.C. If the general was *el gato negro,* then Hugh Meachum, a connoisseur of pipes and wines and ironies, was *el gorrión,* the sparrow.

"The general is very pleased with you, Raymond," said Meachum. "He should be. You certainly saved his bacon."

"Yes, bacon," said the general, who had been educated first at El Salvador's National Military Institute, and then at the National War College in Washington,

D.C., and the Command and General Staff College at Fort Leavenworth, Kansas.

"It is not an easy thing to kill a priest," said the general. "Not even a communist priest."

"The general believes that Archbishop Roberto Lopez was a communist," said Meachum. "He truly does."

Shreck knew this was the sort of thing that amused Meachum. Meachum often privately marveled at the sheer barbarity of these people. They were capable of anything, and it took a great deal of skillful handling to prevent them from going hog wild. They were capable of killing in the thousands. The general *had* killed in the thousands.

"A most excellent operation," said the general. "*Muy excelente.* The world thinks that a crazy American tries to shoot the president of the United States and accidentally hits this pious bystander. And nobody knows it's really justice reaching out to kill a communist priest."

He had a pockmarked face and a dark mustache. He was dressed in evening clothes, including a red plaid cummerbund. He wore a high-polish stainless steel Colt 10mm Delta Elite in a shoulder holster. Shreck had noticed its ivory grips when the general had bent to pour the wine.

"It was an expensive operation," Shreck said.

"Cheap, whatever the cost."

"And oh-so-very necessary," said Hugh Meachum. "That archbishop was going to get the Panther Battalion investigation opened again. And he had the president's ear, too. And how very, very embarrassing for many people *that* would have been."

"It was wonderful," said the general. "Tell me, though, *Colonel* Shreck. The great shot that brought this communist priest down. A *great* shot, no?"

"A great shot, yes," said Shreck.

"Who do you have who could make such a shot? What a shot! It is truly an amazing shot."

"It was," said Shreck. He himself wished he knew who hit that shot. Whoever he was, the guy could shoot, maybe better than Bob Lee Swagger.

Shreck looked over at Meachum, who only twinkled, as if he'd had a bit much to drink.

"I would someday," said the general, lifting his wine, "consider it an honor to shake this man's hand."

So would I, thought Shreck.

"We will convey your sentiments, of course," said Hugh Meachum.

"It was *muy excelente*," said the general. "*Perfecto.* Number One."

Shreck almost said, Yes, except for the asshole who got away. But Meachum had warned him not to raise the subject. The general was somewhat touchy.

Shreck took a quick glance around the baronial dining room of the de Rujijo estate; outside, in the twilight, a vast garden undulated over rolling land down to a pond, a perfect oval, inscribed into the earth so that the setting sun would reflect dazzlingly off of it at twilight. Beyond was the jungle; and beyond that, the sea, a gleaming band some two miles or so away.

"You should know, *Colonel* Shreck, that for us it did not go perfectly."

"Oh?" said Shreck.

"But not to worry."

"Oh my," said Hugh Meachum. He took another sip of wine.

"A traitor. Yes. A traitor."

Shreck nodded, waiting, thinking, oh shit, what now?

"Who learned of our arrangement. And fled."

"Messy," said Hugh Meachum. "Very messy. Certain people will not be pleased."

"Not to worry," the general repeated.

"And why not, sir?" asked Shreck.

"The traitor was betrayed himself. He was hiding in Panama. When he finally thought it was safe, he flew to New Orleans. To the FBI. But we were waiting. Do you remember the wonderful electronic surveillance vehicle your organization provided to our intelligence service?"

"Affirmative," said Shreck.

"With this, we tracked him. We made certain it was our Eduardo, and we eliminated him in a manner that communicates to all who know of such matters our seriousness of intentions."

Shreck nodded.

"And now I drink," said the general, "to my brave *compadres* and to the glorious future of our two nations."

"Hear, hear," said Hugh Meachum.

Fuck you, thought Shreck.

The next morning, waiting for the helicopter that would take him to the airport for the jet back to the United States, Shreck stood in the meadow before the great house and looked at the sea. It was a gray day, windy and moist, with a chill in the air surprising for the tropics. The chill made him think of the mornings in Korea, when he'd been just a kid, and all the times he'd sworn in Korea that no matter what happened to him, he'd never be cold again in the morning.

But he felt cold.

"*Colonel,* you are all right?"

It was General de Rujijo, now in his camouflages with his black beret. The high-polish Colt automatic hung in a shoulder holster under his left arm.

"I am fine, sir," said Shreck.

"You look under the weather, *Colonel.*"

"No sir. Not at all."

"Good. I have a little present for you. From my very own archives."

He snapped his finger and an aide brought over a briefcase. The general reached inside and pulled out a black plastic box that Shreck recognized as a videotape cassette.

"I record all my battalion's operations," said the general. "For training purposes. This is a copy of the action on the Sampul River. You should find it educational, how well our troops mastered their lessons."

Shreck had an impulse to smash the man's skull in. But he smiled grimly and took it from him.

"I have many more," said the general. "You may have that one."

"Yes sir. Thank you, sir."

The general smiled with courtly dignity, saluted and when Shreck returned the salute, he turned and walked away.

Shreck looked at his watch; the chopper was late, nothing ever happened on time in this goddamned country.

"Colonel, you seem especially morose today."

Of course it was old Hugh, who was never quite as drunk as he seemed, even if, at eleven A.M., he had a gin and tonic in his hand and a pinkish hue to his face.

"That asshole just presented me with a tape of the Sampul River job. I guess the point he's trying to make is that we're all in this together, like it or not. If he goes down, the tape reaches somebody important and we all go down."

"The general is a practical man."

"It makes me sick that a motherfucker like de Rujijo thinks he's got us. He reminds me of some of those shit-ass gook generals in their fucking jumpsuits who made it out in seventy-five with a couple of hundred million bucks in the sack."

"Raymond, I've always appreciated your tact. You never say what you think, do you?"

"I don't get paid to think, Mr. Meachum. I didn't go to Yale, like you did. We both know that."

"Of course not. Well, the general. The general has his uses. He's a dreadful man, a war criminal most certainly. A great importer of *la cocaína*. But he and he alone was not responsible for what happened with the Panther Battalion troops on the Sampul River. We made that mess, too. You, Colonel, too. You were there. Those were your trainers in the field. And, if we are to be responsible adults, we must clean it up."

That didn't really satisfy Shreck of course: it was too easy.

"We did what we did," he said, "in perfect awareness of the consequences and the risks—and the costs. We did it because we believed in the long run it would save far more lives than it took."

"Indeed we did. That, after all, is the sort of calculus they pay us for, isn't it? But that same principle extends to this last operation, which you implemented so well in New Orleans. It costs us two men—an intellectual bishop with a surprisingly intractable moralistic streak, and a beat-up war hero who's a complete gun nut. If we don't use those men, and somehow the archbishop's will prevails and it comes out about Panther Battalion, and who did what and why, then the left and the right in this bloody little country will never *ever* get together. There will be no treaty; the fighting will go on, the thousands will continue to die—"

"Come on, Mr. Meachum, that's not what worries you. What worries you is that the lefties might win here, even as communism is crumbling or has crumbled all over the world, and we've kicked ass bigtime in the Persian Gulf. That's what sticks in your craw."

The old man smiled one of his mischievous Meachum smiles, then faded behind a mask of remoteness.

"Well, Raymond, believe what you will and for whatever reason you wish. But agree with me on this one sound operating principle. That this man Swagger must be found and destroyed."

"We'll get him."

"Speaking of which, I had an idea. The Electrotek 5400. State of the art, is it not?"

"You know it is."

"It seems a shame to let it sit up in New Orleans until the general figures out how to get it back through customs. It occurs to me how very useful it might be to you in your quest."

"Jesus," said the colonel.

"Yes, I thought you'd be pleased. You see, Raymond, even though you don't think so, we do take care of our own. We always have. We always will. And I'd destroy that tape if I were you."

"I will," said Shreck, looking at the goddamned thing in his hand.

CHAPTER EIGHTEEN

He drove through brightness. There was brightness everywhere. The sun was a blaze, a flare; the white sand picked it up and threw it back. He drove squint-eyed because he had no sunglasses. He drove straight on because he did not want to stop to rent a room, knowing his face was the most famous in America. He lived on candy bars and Twinkies and Cokes from desolate gas station vending machines and thanked God he had had a couple of hundred bucks in his wallet. He drove through the pain and the anger; he just committed himself to driving and he drove.

Now it was hot. He was in desert. The spindly cacti that played across the low rills looked as if they could kill him; in some religious part of his brain they looked like crucifixes, though of course he was not a Catholic but some sort of Baptist back when his daddy had been alive. Ahead, the road was a straight, shimmering band in the heat; mirage rose off it in the light and dust devils swirled across it. Onward he drove.

He held right at seventy, just five miles over the speed limit. He was in his third stolen car, a 1986 Mercury Bobcat, but always before he stole a car he switched its plates with another vehicle's. That was an old trick he'd heard about on Parris Island, from some tough young black kid, probably now long dead in Vietnam.

It was strange: from the long, wet haul across the swamp, hoarding cartridges, hunting to live, taking only the surest of shots; then, when he was down to his last, he came across something like civilization. He threw the gun away and nabbed a car; and then a long eighteen-hour driving stretch that brought him to desert. Ten hours in Texas. New Mexico was shorter. He was now in Arizona. Texas was long past, though it had been a long, long stretch in Texas. He knew he was almost there. And what was *there*? Maybe nothing. Maybe this was it. But there was no other choice. He'd thought it out. No, no other place to go that would not get him caught because they'd be looking for him everywhere. But here there was a chance.

He came over a rise. A little town in the desert, a spread of buildings, with bright tin roofs glowing in the sun, lay just ahead. There'd be some kind of law here too, but he didn't care. Far off, he could see the purple crests of mountains, but for now just this spread of buildings in the desert. He slowed.

The town came up fast.

AJO, ARIZ., the sign said, POP. 7,567.

He drove through, shielding his eyes against the dazzle. Bank, strip mall, convenience store, two gas stations, one main drag, what looked to be some tract houses where a lot of water had produced what passed for green, a McDonald's, a Burger King, another gas station, Ajo Elementary School, and then, yes, finally, Sunbelt Trailer Park.

Bob pulled in. Drove all this way for such a scruffy little place, huh? Maybe a hundred trailers, maybe a hundred palm trees, it all looked the same to him.

He almost lost it right here at the end. Some pain fired up behind his eyes and his whole body felt itchy or patchy, as if he'd come down with a terrible skin disease. The entry wound hurt something terrible; a low throbbing against his nipple where the bullet had driven through him.

Am I going to make it? he wondered.

He drove up and down the little streets of trailers and saw people out of cartoons, fat Americans in shorts, women with their hair in curlers, lots of sullen, rude little children.

I must look a sight, he thought.

But nobody noticed; they were all sunk into their own dramas.

Then he saw her name on the mailbox, followed by R.N., her profession.

He knew the address from memory. All the letters had been returned unopened, placed in a slightly larger envelope. The flowers, every December, around the fourteenth. She probably just threw them out; she never sent a note of thanks. Yet she had never moved. She had not changed her name or made any attempt to become who she wasn't. She just wouldn't let him in. He was the rotten past and it carried too much hurt.

Bob looked at her place: the trailer was shabby but well tended, with trim little window boxes, with flowers in them. That was a woman's gentle way. The trailer was brown, edged in white trim, plastic. Neat, very neat.

And suppose she was not home? But the car was there, what had to be her car. And the name was hers, just as he knew it would be. Suppose there was a man there? Why not? She was a woman, didn't there have to be a man?

But he didn't think there would be.

He turned off the engine, and managed to lurch to the door. He knocked.

He'd never seen the woman before, only her picture. But when she opened the door he recognized her instantly. He'd always wondered what she looked like in the flesh, all those times off in Indian Country, looking at that picture. She had been a young beauty then and now she was a not-so-young beauty, but she was a beauty.

The face was a little too tough, some wrinkles, but not too many; the eyes, behind reading glasses, were gray, and miles beyond any kind of surprise. The hair was blond, but just blond. The lanky tall woman before him looked at him with eyes that stayed flat as the desert horizon.

She wore jeans and some kind of a pullover shirt and no makeup and had her hair pulled back in a short ponytail. She held a book in her hand with a bright cover, some kind of novel.

"Yes?" she said, and he saw a little shock cross her face.

He had no idea what to say. Hadn't talked to women for years.

"Sorry," he said, "sorry to bother you, ma'am, and sorry to look so bad. My name's Swagger. Bob Lee. I knew your husband in the Marines. A finer young man there never was."

"You," she said. And then again, "You." A sudden

grimace as she bit off the word. He saw her tracking the details; his scrubby face, matted with dirt; his filthy shirt with the blood stain now faded almost rose-colored; the eyes bloodshot, the rank smell of a man beyond hygiene. She probably saw his absolute defenselessness, too. He knew he was simply throwing himself at her. He felt himself begin to wobble.

"My God, you look awful."

"Well, I got the whole damn government after me for something I never did. I've been driving for twenty-four straight hours. I came to you because—"

She looked at him some more, as if to say, Boy, this had better be good.

". . . because he said that he told you all about me in those letters. Well, that was the best I ever was, and if you believed what your husband said to you when he was in the middle of a war, maybe you'll believe me now, when I tell you that what they're saying about me isn't the truth, and that I need help in the worst possible way. Now that's my piece. You can let me in or you can call the police. One way or the other, at this point I'm not sure I could tell the difference."

She just stared at him.

"Will you help me, Mrs. Fenn? I haven't got another place to go, or I'd be there."

She eyed him up and down.

Finally she said, "You." She paused. "I knew you'd come. When I heard about it, I knew you'd come."

He went in and she led him to her bed, and threw back the cover and the sheets.

He collapsed.

"I'll move the car around back," she said and that was the last thing he remembered as he slid under.

Bob dreamed of Payne. He dreamed of that instant when he'd seen Solaratov fire and Payne had said his name and he'd turned and the gun muzzle exploded, the bright flame lighting the room, the noise enormous and the sensation of being kicked as the bullet drove through him. He dreamed of his knees buckling and the terrible rage he felt at his own impotence as he hit the floor.

It played over and over in his head: the flash of the shot, the fall, the sense of loss as he hit. He had the sensation of screaming.

Finally, he awoke.

It was morning, judging from the light. He was freshly bandaged, his arm in a tight sling against his chest. He was clean, too. Somebody had sponged him down. He was undressed. With his good hand, he pulled the blanket close about him, feeling even more vulnerable. He blinked, swallowed, realized suddenly how thirsty he was. His legs ached; his head ached; there was also a bandage on his arm, and some pain. Yes, he'd been hit there; almost forgot about it.

The details swam at him; the punctured holes of the acoustic ceiling, all neat and in rows; some curtains, and how the bright sun streamed through them from some sort of porthole. The room he was in was small and dark, except for the sunlight's beam. Next to him on a table was a pitcher filled with ice water.

He raised himself and poured a drink and swallowed it in one long gulp.

"How do you feel?"

She had slid into the doorway.

"Oh. Well, I feel like I might live a little bit. How long have I—"

"It's been three days."

"Jesus."

"You slept, you screamed, you cried, you begged. Who's Payne? You kept yelling about Payne."

"Payne. Oh, let's see. A fellow that pulled a trick on me."

"Why do I think there aren't too many men that have pulled tricks on you?"

"Maybe not. But he's one of them."

"The papers say you're a psychopathic killer, a crazy man with a rifle. They think if you're not in New Orleans, you're in Arkansas. Or dead. Some people think you're dead."

He didn't say anything. His head ached.

"I didn't kill the president."

"The president!"

"I wouldn't kill the pres—"

"It wasn't the president. Didn't you listen to the radio?"

"Ma'am, I've been in a swamp for a week, shooting one animal every two days to live. In the cars—hell, I just drove."

"Well, it wasn't the president. They say you aimed at the president but you hit some archbishop."

"I never missed what I aimed at in my life. Besides with that rifle—"

And then he stopped.

"That's what Donny said. And that's what I believe. But they have evidence. Fingerprints, the tests on the gun, that sort of thing."

"Well, maybe they aren't as smart as they think they are. Maybe I'm not so far up the tree as they say. A bishop?"

"My God, you really *don't* know. Either that or you're the best liar I've ever seen."

"I wouldn't shoot a priest. I wouldn't shoot anything. I haven't shot to kill in more than a decade."

Bob shook his head glumly.

Shooting a priest, he thought. And then he thought:

That's what it was all about. That's what it was always all about.

And then he thought: And they had me bird-dog it for them. Figure out the best way. Work it out for them. And then they used it against me. For some priest.

Then a thought came to him.

He took a deep breath.

"Say, was there anything in the papers about my dog?"

"Oh," she said. "You don't know?"

"They killed him?"

"They say you killed your dog."

"What they say and what happened are two different things," he said. But it hurt him that people could say such a thing of him.

He watched her watching him.

"The bastards. Kill a great old dog like that. Oh, the sons of bitches."

"It's amazing. You are the most hunted man in America. And your first question isn't about yourself but about a dog. And when he's dead—I can tell, you're really upset."

"That damned old dog loved me and I wish I'd been a better friend to him. He never cut out but stayed to do his job. He deserved more than he got."

"So does everybody. Look, you should get some rest. What you've been through, the physical stress, the blood loss. It would have killed most men. I know some Indians it wouldn't have killed, but I don't know too many white men who could have gotten through it."

He slept again, though this time without dreams. When he awoke, she was there too. He ate a little, then dozed off. And the third time he awoke, she was still there, just staring at him.

"What time is it?"

"Time? It's *Tuesday,* that's what time it is. You slept eighteen hours."

"I don't feel as if I'll ever walk again."

"Oh, I think you'll make it. You were very lucky. The bullet went right through you with very little damage. You were smart enough to plug that entrance wound with a clump of plastic wadding. That probably saved your life. I've been pumping you full of penicillin to preclude infection."

"What are they saying about me now?"

"Oh, they've gotten around to the psychiatrists and the psychologists, because they have no real news. There's a lot of theorizing going on about motive. Your anger at your father for dying, how that became your anger at the president. Your anger at not becoming a big hero like—do I have the name right?—Carl Hathco—"

"Hitchcock. Carl Hitchcock."

"Yes. Things like that."

"It's just a lot of talk. They don't know the first goddamn thing. My daddy was a great hero. And I never cared for medals. He didn't and I didn't. Talk's cheap."

"You're certainly right about that, Sergeant."

He stared off, bitterly. The mention of his father unsettled him. People had no right to bring his father into all this.

"You can't let it get to you," she said. "They've turned it into a circus. But they always do these days."

He looked back at her.

"I have to thank you. What you're doing, it's—"

"No, I don't need thanks. I knew in a split second you couldn't have shot at the president or that archbishop. If that was in you, Donny would have seen it all the years back; he would have sniffed it out."

Bob couldn't look at her. Hearing such judgments put baldly into language had the weird effect of shrinking him. He felt small and wan and self-conscious. He had to tell her the truth.

"If he told you I was some kind of hero, let me set you straight. I spent ten years drunk, and I used to beat on the only woman who ever loved me. But also I let myself slide into bitterness. That was maybe the worst. I let them get to me, and make me less a man."

A puzzled look came across her face.

"Who? Oh, you know who. They're always around: smart boys, have all the answers, always telling you what's wrong and why what you done, you should be ashamed of it.

"But worst of all, I was stupid. I let some smart boys come into my life and turn me around. Real smart boys. They knew all my weaknesses, got real deep inside where I thought nobody could. I don't know how they knew to get inside me like that. Turned me around, made me a fool. Christ, made me the most hated man in the country. Well, now, I seem to have survived all that. And so now it's my turn. I need to stay until I'm better and stronger and have figured out another move. I'm sorry to have brought all this trouble to your door. No other door was open to me. So I'm asking you, please: let me stay and mend. A few weeks, maybe a month. And let me study on my problems, figure what the next step is. I can't give you much but thanks. Will you consider it?"

She looked at him hard. Then her face lit up in a smile that just cracked him in two.

"Jesus," she said, "it's so nice to have a man around the house."

CHAPTER NINETEEN

Newly promoted Detective Sergeant Leon Timmons was drunk and he was high. He was sailing, he was floating. He felt so good.

"Hey, Payne, hey, damn, boy, we, we got it made, huh?"

Payne snorted. They were in Big Sam's, on Bourbon. Up on the stage a buxom woman shimmied. To Payne she looked like an animated piece of beef on a hook in a Jersey warehouse.

"Damn," Timmons said, "damn, boy, she all girl, eh, Payno?"

"She's all girl," said Payne. "She's a girl and a fuckin' half."

"Wooooo!" said Timmons, his eyes lighting up like headlamps.

Payne took a long swallow of Dixie beer. It was the only thing he liked about New Orleans and he was glad to be just about out of New Orleans.

Somebody put another beer in front of Timmons.

"Huh?" said Timmons.

"Leon, honey," said the waitress, "gintlemin over thar said thanks to the man what almost shot the man what almost shot the president."

Timmons raised the bottle in salute to his benefactors, who appeared to be a crowd of dentists from Dayton. They applauded in the red wash of light from the overheads, then went back to hooting at Bonnie Anne Clyde and her smoking .45's up there on the stage.

"You're quite a hero," said Payne.

"Damn betcha. You know, Payne, ain't yet heard whether old President what's-his-name gonna have me up at the White House. Hell, that old boy ought give me a ticket to the town with my name written all over it."

"That he should," said Payne. "You saved his life, man. You stopped Bob Lee Swagger from blowing him up and you almost nailed Bob the Nailer, the great sniper himself."

"That's right," said Timmons, who by now pretty much believed he'd actually fired the shot. He told Payne the story again in excruciating detail, with a few embellishments thrown in. Payne listened dully. Finally Timmons said, "You know, I might even be the NRA Police Officer of the Year."

"You ought to think about selling your story to the movies, bub."

"Ahead of you there, Payno. Got me a agent already, out in Hollywood. A very big guy. We gonna make a potful of money."

"You don't need no agent. You already got a potful of money."

"Cain't have too much money," said Payne. "Ain't no such thing as too much money."

"Ummm," said Payne.

Timmons's eyes went back to Bonnie Anne Clyde. He licked his lips; his face had the hard set of a man who'd seen what he liked and liked what he'd seen.

"I believe you could get yourself that girl," said Payne. "Seems to me she ought to be pleased to spend some time with the hero cop of New Orleans, who almost shot the man who almost shot the man who—well, you know."

"I believe you are right," said Timmons.

With a self-important twitch of his head, he beckoned the manager over. Quickly he told him what he wanted.

"Be right back," the guy said.

"Whooo, think I'm gone be in the hot spot tonight," said Timmons eagerly.

"Pussy-o-rama, Leon. Wall to wall and floor to ceiling," said Payne.

The manager came back after Bonnie left the stage, to be replaced by Miss Suzie Cue and her eight-balls.

"Okay, here's the deal," he said. "She says, yeah, sure, anything for Detective Sergeant Timmons. Only thing is, see, she has the boyfriend, mean nigger motherfucker. So, what she wants is, um, discretion. Quietude. Nothing to rile Ben, 'cause Ben whack her upside the haid he catch her with another man."

"Okay," said Timmons. "So how we work it?"

"Out back at midnight. He's a fireman, goes on duty at eleven-thirty. So you meet her out there, she takes you to her crib, you git your windshield wiper fluid changed but, like, good, my friend, Ben ain't the wiser, she done bagged a celebrity, and the old world just goes humpty-humping along."

"Oh, I lak thet," said Timmons greedily.

"You goan have a time," said the manager, a weaselly little rat-man with a pencil-thin mustache.

So Payne and Timmons sat through a couple of more sets, trying to put the Dixie Brewery out of business or at least get it to working nights, as if they were a pair of Navy bosun's mates on shore leave for the first time since the sixties. Timmons's elaborate hair, which bent in strange ways as it flowed off his ample, heroic brow, gleamed with mousse; he was set for a big night. Meanwhile Payne just sat there, sinking into himself further.

By the time it was nearly midnight, Timmons was extremely drunk. Payne got up, pointed to his watch, and Timmons lurched obediently to his feet, bulling his fat and sloppy way over.

"All set," he said hornily.

"Then let's go, big guy," said Payne, pulling him down the narrow aisle and out to Bourbon.

The street had filled. It looked like party time in Hell. College kids from Ole Miss, northern tourists, large groups of sailors, a few aristocratic types in blue blazers and khakis with their sallow, nearly fleshless women in tow, all seethed and bucked along the narrow concourse. There was smoke everywhere; up and down the street lines had formed, some to get into the strip joints or the transsexual shows, some to buy T-shirts in the dinky souvenir shops, some to get into the fancy restaurants like Antoine's or Arnaud's. A few disconsolate wallflowers peered down from the balconies overhanging the scene.

"Now which way we go?" asked Payne, surveying the turmoil. "I can't believe I'm skulking around to avoid riling some big nigger."

"Shoot," said Timmons, "no sense gittin' the boy upset when his old lady be handing out the sweets for free. Maybe you wanta little old taste after I finish?"

"How long you be? Maybe twenty seconds?"

"Haw! I can ride a mare like thet half the damn night!"

"Well, thanks, I'll pass. Number Two in the saddle ain't for me."

They ambled through the raucous crowd, were jostled by sailors. Payne hated sailors from the Army, where you were supposed to hate sailors. And he sort of felt like a fight. He wanted to drive one of his fat fists into the dumb, girlish face of some aviation candidate over from Pensacola, and watch the boy collapse, spitting blood and teeth. But he just pushed on. The night was blue. The moon was full, over the low pastel buildings of the quarter. It reminded him of a jungle city. Felt like Saigon. No gooks, though. Lots of niggers, lots of fatboys and pretty girls, lots of action; no gooks. He remembered the sense of war and doom and what-the-hell-we-die-tomorrow joy that he had so loved when he was a lean and dangerous young Forces sergeant in the 'Nam, floating on amphetamines, just back from a long crazed month or so in the fuckin' boonies, taking frontals.

Payne sighed, swept by melancholy. The whole world seemed to be here on Bourbon, coursing down the narrow street, all hot to trot, seething to get fucked, except for him. He stood apart. Jack Payne was different. He did the hard things.

Next to him, Timmons was aquiver with sexual tension. It was said that he could visit any brothel in New Orleans and have himself serviced mightily, so friendly and helpful was he to certain people, but there were always new experiences and sensations. So he was all hotted up.

"She a girl and a half," he said again.

"She sure is," said Payne. "Now where the hell we goin'?"

"Up here. Turn right, then behind the restaurant you

turn left and we head down the alley. She'll be in back, where the dancers park."

"You sure know this town."

"Know it well, that I do," said Timmons, almost singing with anticipation. He was a happy man.

The crowd thinned as they turned off Bourbon down Toulouse and then saw the alleyway, a small gap, just the width of a car, between the old brick buildings. They turned into it. It smelled of old garbage and piss.

Up ahead, however, there appeared to be something of an altercation. It was difficult to make out, but it looked as if a large black male was beating on a small white male.

"I do believe," said Jack Payne, "that that's a crime, isn't it?"

"Oh, shit," said Timmons. He reached under his jacket, and from the high-hip holster withdrew the famous Beretta and advanced at a coplike gait, yelling, "Halt, Police! Goddammit boy, y'all stop that."

Payne watched him go with something that wasn't quite sadness, for he truly detested Timmons, but out of some sense of camaraderie. The two had shared a lot, after all, and each had come to recognize the other as a man who walked the same side of the street.

"Goddamn, I say, *stop*!" shouted Timmons. He fired a shot into the air, and then rushed in harder, a little surprised that the black man hadn't cut and run, as was customary. He stopped short when he saw that the black man had a pistol of his own, which had come from nowhere.

"Now, wha—" Timmons began, when the first bullet hit him in the throat and the second, a split second later, under the left eye. They were only .25's, from some piece of junk that wouldn't shoot accurately over ten feet; the range was seven.

Timmons died clawing at the small hole in his face, which spurted blood like a broken pipe.

The black man ran by Jack Payne, pausing only to wink. It was Morgan State, as he was called, from the unit, Payne's second in command, a great shot, a cool hand with a lot of in-country time behind him, good man in a gunfight. Then he was gone.

The tourist was crying and bleeding from the beating but otherwise unhurt, as had been the plan, for an innocent witness was the fulcrum.

The sirens began howling, and in a few minutes the first cop car would be here.

Payne melted into the dark.

She had brought the magazines, all the newspapers, everything that she could find or acquire in Ajo without making a big fuss.

It was ten minutes into the reading that Bob found the mention of Mike's death. There it was in print. Somehow, that made it official.

Bob put the magazine down slowly, and stared out the window. He could see the bright desert light, the hot flat blue of the sky, an endless cruelty of needles spangling the low rills.

He just sat there most of the morning, mourning Mike and trying to figure who would kill him. Then of course he had it. To get his rifle from the trailer, of course, they'd have to shoot Mike. Mike wouldn't have let them in, he would have stayed on station come hell or high water; and if they drugged him, that would leave traces.

He read the sentence again.

"Evidently aware that after his deed he couldn't return to care for the dog, Swagger shot the animal once in the head with a 12-gauge shotgun and buried it in a shallow grave."

All right, he thought, *feel sorry for him later. You have some work to do.*

But the pain of it amazed him. He realized in a tiny part of his mind he'd been harboring some kind of illusion until now; he saw himself back at the place, and old Mike come up to nuzzle him, to press his sloppy jowl against him and gaze up with those dumb, adoring eyes.

All right, he thought, *you killed my dog. Now I got some work to do, so that I can settle up.*

He read slowly, without hurry, each article, from the earliest Julie had been able to find—which meant the most inaccurate—to the very latest. Nothing showed on his face. He sat on his bed and read it all, straight through. Then he read it again.

He saw himself laid bare, penetrated, turned inside out. He was fair game for them all; everybody had a theory, an idea, a notion. He realized he was no longer his own property; his private self had been taken from him forever.

They had it right—but wrong, too, terribly wrong. They were looking at him from such a twisted angle.

"Swagger's Navy Cross bespeaks his aggressive nature and his reckless will to kill and precurses the tragic events of March 1," *Time* said.

It was the second highest award his country could give him; and he'd saved a hundred lives those two days in the An Loc Valley. They made it seem like a crime.

"Violence is inbred in the Swagger clan. His father, Earl Swagger, destroyed three machine gun nests one morning on Iwo Jima and returned to violent encounters in law enforcement, climaxing in a bloody shootout where he killed two men but died himself off Highway 67 near Fort Smith."

They turned his old daddy, who only did his duty to country and state, into some kind of mentor in murder.

Nothing about the lives his dad had saved in giving up his own against Jimmy and Bub Pye that terrible evening.

There was a paragraph recounting his lawsuit against *Mercenary* magazine, which had put a picture of him on the cover and called him the most dangerous man in America. It told how sly old Sam Vincent had shaken thirty thousand dollars out of their pockets and warned all those gung-ho books to stay the hell away. But then *Time* dryly remarked, "It is doubtful that Swagger could win his case today."

He shook his head at all this, wondering what could twist people so. Where do these people come from? How do they learn things like this? Is there a school that teaches them? What gives them the damned right to just take over your life and bend it any which way they please?

They hadn't missed a damn thing. They'd pried everywhere. The inside of his trailer was photographed. His books were listed: the writers found it amusing that among the loading manuals and the classic works on rifles and shooting, such a violent man had poetry by Siegfried Sassoon, Wilfred Owen and Robert Graves, though it was noted that the works were "only bitter war poetry." There was his gun rack in loving detail, the weapons cataloged and judged by reporters who seemed disappointed to discover that he had no "assault rifles," as they called them. His rifle range was diagrammed. His two victories in the Arkansas State IPSC championships were probed. And he saw schematics of the shot he had supposedly taken in New Orleans from 415 St. Ann into Louis Armstrong Park. The madness of that second was broken down and analyzed, its physics and ballistics choreographed in infinite detail, its trajectories laid out in dotted lines to little X's that marked the strike of the bullet, all of it convincing, all of it wrong. He saw stills drawn from the videotape of what went on at the podium, the fall and twist of the man he'd supposedly "hit," the archbishop of whom he'd never even heard.

The completeness of it blew him away. They'd been so careful, they'd set it up so perfectly, and, worst of all, they'd known him so well.

Not these damn reporters who didn't know a thing, but them, the Agency boys, whoever they were. They'd known him perfectly. It was as if they'd lived his life or gotten in his brain.

"You look so hurt," she said.

"These people, they knew so much about me," he said. "It's scary how careful they were. Not that they took the time, but that they *knew* so much, they *knew* how my mind would work."

He thought back to the moment when he'd been truly hooked: when they came up with a trophy he couldn't say no to, the Russian sniper Solaratov, who he now realized probably didn't exist. It was so perfect. They knew how desperate he'd be.

Then he discovered, from *Newsweek*, that the guy he'd jumped coming out of the house on St. Ann Street was named Nick Memphis and he was from the FBI!

Now here was something that twisted in his imagination. Memphis, Memphis, where'd he heard that damn name before? It hung there, tantalizing him until he remembered after a bit. Memphis was the joker in Tulsa who'd missed and hit some woman. His was the archetypal botched shot, the sniper who fouled up. And he, Bob, back in Maryland, had re-created the whole thing in front of the fancy boys while they were gulling him along with their "Accutech" stuff.

He wondered if this Memphis were a part of it. Then he remembered the stunned surprise of the man, the slack, dumb look on the wide face, his squirming, the easy way the 10-mil came out of the holster when he reversed on him, and he doubted it. If he were one of what Bob thought now merely as "Them," he guessed that this Nick Memphis would have been ready and waiting. Besides, he wouldn't have left his car with the door open and the key in so helpfully there right outside on St. Ann Street.

There was a picture of the guy, a blurry thing snapped out front of the New Orleans FBI headquarters.

"Agent Memphis, who missed collar, hurries to car," the caption said.

It was the same man, equally disturbed, this time with a grave and somewhat embarrassed look to his face.

You screwed up, and now these people are going to nail you for it. You screwed up almost as big as I did, he thought.

Bob read on, looking for answers.

But there were only more questions.

CHAPTER TWENTY

Here I am, Nick thought, in Arkansas!

He was sitting around the temporary bull pen in the Mena, Arkansas, Holiday Motel, wading through the oceans of paperwork that attended the task force's relocation from New Orleans to Polk County, yet at the same time managing not to grieve too overwhelmingly for the passing of Leon Timmons, dropped by a mugger in a New Orleans alley two days or so ago. He wished it didn't please him so and he wished the publicity—HERO COP SLAIN IN FREAK CRIME—would go away, because his own incompetence was a part of the story.

"You sure you didn't smoke poor Leon there, Nick?" asked the ever mischievous Hap Fencl.

"You know, in blackface, with a little throw-down gun?"

The others had laughed; they couldn't mourn the braying Timmons either, who'd made the Bureau look so bad.

But Nick just smiled grimly and stayed on station as the operation's prime goat. Outside the window, the green and thunderous Ouachitas rippled away toward Oklahoma in the late afternoon sunlight. He returned to his document, a witness sighting report from the New Mexico State Police; a motorist claimed he'd seen Bob the Nailer, big as life, tooling down the highway in an '86 Merc. That was the common element in the sightings: as if Bob would be so *bold* to bull on through in broad daylight, sure his courage and his determination would get him through. These people were imprinting their own sense of Bob on ambiguous events and coming up with the strangest stuff.

The phone rang across the room and somebody else got it.

"Hey, Nick, it's for you."

Nick turned to the phone.

"Nick Memphis."

"Nick, it's Wally Deaver."

A little burst of excitement went off in Nick's chest.

"Wally, Christ, how are you? You got the pictures?"

"Yeah," said Wally and Nick didn't like the tone in his voice.

"It's not him?" he asked quickly. "That's not the guy you talked to in Cartagena? That's not Eduardo Lanzman of the Salvadoran National Police?"

"Shit, Nick. That's the terrible thing of it. I wish I could say one way or the other. I wish I could just *tell* you. But . . . I don't know. I was only with Eduardo during the meetings which lasted maybe a day or so. Two days max. And a bunch of us went out to dinner, had a few drinks. I can't say I *knew* him well. We exchanged cards, you know, the way cops do. Now these pictures—"

"Yeah."

"Nick, death doesn't do anybody any favors. Maybe this is the same guy. Maybe it isn't. It *could* be. It *might* be. Maybe it is. But . . . *maybe* it isn't. You didn't have the passport photo?"

"It didn't look a goddamned thing like him."

"What about any corroborating evidence?"

"Nothing. It all checked out, at least as near as we can tell. You know I can't get budget to go down there. And the Salvadorans, they say they don't know him at all, except that this is through our formal liaison with them which is run by the State Department, which means it's got to go through so many layers—"

"Yeah, that's why I bailed out, Nick. So many layers. Look, Nick, to be fair, it's a pretty dead horse without corroborating evidence. I mean, in good conscience, I couldn't go before a grand jury and—"

"Yeah, sure, I understand."

"Great."

"But tell me this. It *could* be. Just maybe, just somehow? At the outside."

"Okay, Nick. Yeah, yeah. It *could* be."

"Great, Wally."

"But Nick. Don't bet your career on it."

"Sure," said Nick. "I won't."

But he realized he already had.

She was rebandaging him.

"You must be a very tough guy, Sergeant Swagger. Looks to me like there isn't a weapon made they haven't tried out on your hide. You're a one-man proving ground."

"They had some fun with me, ma'am."

"I count—what, four gunshot wounds? *Old* gunshot wounds, that is. As opposed to the two *new* gunshot wounds, which resulted in *three* holes. The hole total comes out to—five? Six? You're a piece of Swiss cheese, Sergeant."

"I was only hit three times. Twice the first tour, none the second, then the bad one, the bullet in the hip that ended the third tour. They had to glue and wire the whole gizmo back together again. Don't know how they did such a thing. I thought I was set for the wheelchair my whole life. And that one old hole isn't a bullet."

"What is it?"

"You're not going to believe this. It's from a curtain rod."

"Oh, now *there's* a new weapon. Your wife, I presume, and I'll bet you gave her very good reason."

He laughed.

"My aunt. My mother's sister. A sweet woman. I was helping her in the farmhouse. 1954. I was eight. She lost her balance and the curtain rod she was hanging fell and she fell on top of it and it went through my side. It didn't hurt much. Bled a lot, didn't hurt much."

"I'll bet."

"That was before my daddy died. The year before. It was a happy year, I remember. Now let me ask you: How long before you think I'll be able to get out of here? The longer I'm here the more danger I'm putting you in."

"Another few weeks. Don't worry. The neighbors have seen men live here before. I've been around the block a few times myself."

He just nodded blankly. This didn't please him, though he didn't want to face it.

"How long has it been?" she said.

Since when? he wondered.

"You don't even know what it's called anymore? You know. With a woman. Wo-man. Female."

"Oh, that? I don't know."

"A month? A year? Ten years?"

"Not ten years. More than a year. I'm not sure."

"You could live without it that easily?"

"I had other things to keep me busy."

"I don't believe you."

He paused, considering it.

"I didn't want the complications. Someone said, 'Simplify, simplify.'"

"Ann Landers?"

"No," he said earnestly, "it was some old guy called Thoreau. He went and lived by himself, too, as I understand it. Anyway. I wanted to simplify. No wants, no needs, no hungers. Only rifles. Crazy as hell now that I think of it."

"So you went off and became Henry Thoreau of Walden, Arkansas?" Julie said.

"I was at my best with a rifle in my hand. I always loved rifles. So I decided to live in such a way that the rifle would be all I needed. And I succeeded."

"Were you happy up there in your trailer in the mountains without any people?"

"I didn't know it then. I suppose now that I was. I was raised and then trained not to think a lot about how I feel."

It was twilight of the third day since he'd been awake. The sun suffused the room with an orange glow. The quality of light was almost liquid and held everything it touched in perfect serenity. Her face had acquired a grave look in this fantastic light; and he loved the way she had of slyly making him see how ridiculous he could be. She seemed like some kind of angel to him, so radiant a savior that he could not hold her strong gaze and instead looked out the window, to where the mountains stood like a savage old bear's teeth on the rim of the earth. He remembered looking at her picture in the boonies. Donny always had it with him.

"Why is it men like you always have to be so alone?" she asked. "Why do you want to live by yourself and contrive situations under which you can go against *everybody* to prove how smart and tough and brave you are?"

Bob had no answer.

"You see, you make it so terrible for us," she said. "For the women. Because normal men want to be like you, they learn about you from movie versions of you, and they try for that same laconic spirit, that Hemingway stoicism. They manufacture themselves in your image but they don't have the guts or the power to bring it off. So they just exile themselves from us, *pretending* to be you and to have your power, and we can never reach them. Are you aware that Donny was scared every single day? He was so scared. He was no hero. He was a scared kid, but he believed in you."

"It doesn't matter if he was scared. He did his job; that made him a man. That made him as much man as there is."

"I'd rather have a little less man, who is alive now and could sleep with me, and be father to the children I never had and never will have. His being a 'man' didn't do me a hell of a lot of good. It's the same craziness that makes these poor Indian boys cut each other up on Saturday night. What do they get out of it, I wonder?"

"It can't be explained," he said. "It can be foolish as all get-out, yes, ma'am. It doesn't make much sense. But I was just taught to hurt no man except the man who hurt me and mine. I have no other star to steer by. That and to do my duty as I understand it. If I followed those two rules, I'd be okay."

It was so quiet you'd have thought it was the last second before a nuclear bomb was to go off, ending life on this earth. But instead, through the metal walls of the trailer, there came the shriek of a child.

Something came into her eyes and onto her face that he'd never seen before; it was pain.

"And I suppose the joke is, none of us care about that kind of man, the kind that you want to be. What we want is the kind that would stick around and be there the next morning. Mow the grass. Bring home a paycheck. That kind of man. And I see how funny that is now," she said, her anguish suddenly palpable. "You come in here, and I care for you, patch you up, and hide your car and get myself so deep into this I can never, ever get out, and never, ever have a normal life . . . and you don't care. You have to go off. And be a 'man.' "

After a time, he said, "I didn't just come here because I had to. I came because I wanted to. A long time ago in Vietnam when Donny Fenn showed me his young wife's picture, I had a moment where I hated him for having such a woman waiting for him. A part of me wanted him not to make it, and wanted to have you for me. But that passed when I saw what a damn fine boy he was, and how he deserved the very very best. And he had it, I see that now."

She touched him. A woman hadn't touched him in years, really *touched* him so that he could feel her wanting in it. Maybe no woman had ever touched him like that. It had been many years.

"What do you want from me, Sergeant?" she asked.

"I don't know," he said. "It makes going back to it hard. Truth is, I never ever stopped thinking about that picture and the fine woman Donny Fenn had waiting for him."

"That's why you kept writing?"

"I suppose it is. And you'd just send 'em back, unopened."

"I knew if I opened them, I was lost."

"Are you lost now?"

"No, I don't suppose so. I know where I'm headed. I can't stop it. Straight into catastrophe, and I don't even *want* to stop it."

He drew her to him. In the kiss there was an extraordinary sense of release. He felt himself sliding away, down a drain, surrounded by warm, urgent, healing liquids. He thought he'd slide until he died. He was also overwhelmed by smoothness. Everything about her was smooth; she was smooth everywhere, he'd never imagined that a person could be so smooth.

The explosion, so long in coming, seemed to build until it could not be held back, and bucked out of him in a series of emptying spasms. He was falling through floors toward solid earth, each one halting him for just a splinter of a second; and then he fell through to another one, and then another. He fell and fell and fell, stunned at the distance of the fall and how far it took him from himself.

"My God," he said.

"Oh, my God," she said.

The days passed. She was on the day shift and during it he stayed in the trailer and read what she had brought him from a trip to seven bookstores and every newsstand in Tucson. He told her to get everything. And she did. He read it all, the events of two weeks, then three weeks, then four weeks ago. He read about the Kennedy assassination, about other famous assassinations. He made copious notes and worked steadily, trying to find a line through the material.

When he learned that the hero policeman of New Orleans, Leon Timmons, had been killed in one of those stupid, pointless urban accidents, shot by a mugger during an attempt to prevent a crime, it didn't surprise him. He just breathed heavily. Timmons had been a link; of course he had to die. These boys were sealing themselves off, leaving no possible leads into their organization. They were pros. This bothered him but it also relieved him; it meant he didn't have to go back to New Orleans, for now there was nothing in New Orleans. But where would he go? He didn't yet know.

One night, NBC news did a special on it. He taped it on her VCR, taking notes. He watched it over and over, the diagrams, the interviews, the speculations. But particularly he watched that terrible moment when the bullet came shrieking out of nowhere and seemed to blow the president from his feet, while it had really just been the force of the other man, the archbishop Roberto Lopez, who had gone into him as the bullet opened in him and destroyed his brain.

Bob thought: It was a great shot.

Over twelve hundred yards from that damn church steeple, shooting into a very complicated sight picture, no matter how good his scope, shooting at a downward angle. Lots of problems to solve, and you solved them all.

Oh, my oh my, but you're a good boy, he thought.

Not but five, maybe six men in the world could hit a shot like that, or have the perfect confidence to risk everything on making it.

Bob realized the shooter was the key.

The whole plan, all the elaborate seduction of himself, the manipulations, the subterfuge, all of it rested only upon the fragile vessel of confidence that this shooter could make that shot.

Hell of a shot, Bob thought.

He thought of the man up there in that steeple behind the louvers just waiting, just gathering himself.

Could I have made that shot? Bob wondered.

He wasn't sure. It was right at the very edge of what

he could do with a rifle. Whoever he was, he was a shooter.

Bob remembered the superb neck-turned .308's he'd run through his rifle when they were gulling him on in that Accutech thing in Maryland. Those were precision-made rounds. Everything else about "Accutech" was a con, but the rounds were the real thing. Whoever made them knew how to sling a cartridge together for world-class long-range accuracy. It wasn't something many men knew: it took you into the realm of micromachining, of tolerances so fine most tools wouldn't register them, of actions worked like the inside of watches, of rifle barrels so polished and perfect they were jewels themselves almost; it was a rarefied part of the shooting world.

Again, only a few dozen men in the world knew it.

And the rifle itself. Where do you get a rifle so tight that you can count on it to send a 200-grain .30 caliber into, say, four inches, from twelve hundred yards? You're talking about .333 minute of angle at over half a mile. He knew a master gunsmith could build a rifle technically capable of such a thing, if a human could be found to get all that could be gotten out of it. Then he remembered the Model 70 he'd fired at the Accutech place, the last one, late in the day, when he'd fired the exercise that had more or less been the duplicate of Donny's death with a Model 70 he still yearned for; a rifle with a stock so dense and rigid it felt as if it was manufactured from plastic and an action so slick and a trigger so soft you could breathe on it to make it fire. He remembered: Number 100000. That was such a rifle. There couldn't be but one or two or three or four out of the millions of Model 70's that Winchester made that were that fine.

Who would own such a rifle? Then he remembered

that somebody told him a man had won a bunch of thousand-yard championships with that rifle.

And as he thought he began to puzzle the one aspect that had so far evaded him, the piece that was somehow wrong.

It was the bullet.

If they were going to hit the archbishop, they'd have to assume the police would recover the bullet. And that the bullet would have the imprint of the bore it had been fired down, as irrevocable as a fingerprint. They couldn't know the bullet would be mangled; that was a one in a thousand chance.

Why wouldn't this perturb them? It would screw up their entire plan. When the bullet didn't match the bore in Bob's rifle, the whole ruse would collapse. Somehow they'd figured a way to beat it. Somehow *he* had figured a way to beat it.

The bullet, he thought.

The mystery of the goddamn bullet, just as tantalizing in its way as the famous Kennedy assassination 6.5mm that had passed through one man's body, another man's chest and wrist, and yet was undamaged and unmistakably bore the imprint of Lee Harvey Oswald's bore.

It was as if the two mysteries were mirror opposites of one another, or different sides of one coin.

But they had bullets, he thought. They had bullets from my rifle.

He'd provided them with sixty-four bullets fired from the bore of his rifle, in Maryland.

He sat back.

"Bob?"

"Shhh."

"Bob, what are—"

He held up a hand to quiet her.

Then it was gone.

"Dammit."

"What?"

"Oh, I—"

Then he had it. It might be possible. He'd never heard of anyone doing it and there was no reason for anyone to do it, but . . . yes, it was possible.

You dig a fired .308 bullet out of the sand, scored with the imprint of a bore, but otherwise pristine and possessing the same ballistic integrity as a new bullet. You can reload that .308 bullet into a .300 H & H Magnum shell, a much longer shell with a much greater powder capacity and therefore a much longer range. You'd have to protect the bullet somehow, and this puzzled him, until he remembered an old technique called paper-patching, by which a fellow could wrap a bullet in wet paper before he loaded it on a shell; the paper would harden and form a sort of protective sheath. The trick was, you had to fire it down a slightly larger bore, maybe a .318. But even that was so simple: rebarrel the rifle with a custom bore, and refire Bob's bullet down the bore. The paper patching protects the ballistic signature; then burns off in the atmosphere; Bob's bullet, fired from this other rifle, arrives to do its terrible damage.

Oh, you were a smart boy, he thought.

But . . . if you were so smart, how come *I* had to bird-dog it out for you? I was your legs, wasn't I? That was part of it. I wasn't just there to be used as a dupe but I did the thinking, the seeing, the planning. Why? Why couldn't you do it? Why couldn't you go to the sites yourself and see what I saw?

One day he drove to Tucson, and concealed behind his new beard and sunglasses, stopped in a rummy old Gun and Pawn store in the Mexican section of the town. Didn't even look at the rifles that were on the wall, but went on and found in the back, as usually these places have, a big pile of old gun magazines. *Guns & Ammo* and *Shooting Times*, a long though tattered run of *The American Rifleman*. The mags were of little use to him, being far too full of pictures of new guns. But there was one that was useful: *Accuracy Shooting*, which was about benchrest shooting, those boring technocrats who worked on rifles so fine they could throw bullets in the same hole all day long. He himself had subscribed since the late seventies. But these were earlier, from the mid-sixties.

Benchresting was the R & D lab of all shooting; if you were at all serious about the game, you had to bank your time at the loading bench and the shooting bench; all other things stemmed from it. If his boy learned his stuff anywhere, he learned it in benchresting. The magazine, he learned, had begun as the newsletter of the first American benchrest shooter's club, which started up in the early fifties in upstate New York, following on the work of men like Warren Page, Harvey Donaldson and P. O. Ackley in the twenties and thirties. They were loaded with tabular matter, with long and dreary accounts of shooting matches of years ago, obscure names of great shooters and obsolete calibers like the .222½ and the 7 × 61 Sharpe and Hart.

He bought them all and that night he began to read them. When he'd read them all, he found more, and read them too. He haunted the secondhand shops, looking for old copies. When he found them, he read them, looking for something but what it was, he couldn't say.

I'll find you, you old bastard, he thought, for he assumed his quarry was old. Only old men could shoot like that, for it's a dying skill, not practiced by the young much; there was only one younger man who could have made that shot, but he was an illusion. Bob tried to put it out of his mind, because it spoiled things for him.

It's not T. Solaratov, he said to himself. It's not. It can't be.

In the evenings they made love. They made love for hours. Sometimes he felt like a piston that just kept on going.

And finally, several times, after he'd fallen through the last of his floors and lay there as if every atom in his body was at rest, he felt himself yielding to the fatigue. He couldn't move a thing.

"God," she said. "You must have saved up all that time at Walden Pond."

He snorted.

"I seem to be doing okay."

"I'll say," she said.

They lay there, breathing their way back to earth.

The terror of her was that she carried in her the seed of possibility. In her, he saw an alternate life. It occurred to him that he didn't have to live in solitude, hating the world, and that he didn't have to give himself to his rifles, like some kind of mad Jesuit. Didn't have to live in a little trailer off in the misty mountains, and face each visitor with mistrust.

The world was full of things that could be. He had a flash of them together somewhere, just enjoying each other, no complications. Somehow it had to do with water; he saw them at a beach, maybe Myrtle Beach, South Carolina, or maybe outside Biloxi or Galveston or some such; anyway, sand, water, sun, and nothing else in the world.

"What are you thinking of?" she asked. "You almost had a smile on your face. What was it?"

He knew if he told her he was lost. There would be no turning back from the softness. He lay there and the temptation to give in rose and rose in him. He wanted to let it swallow him up. He could feel himself disappearing in the wanting.

"Something from the Marines."

"That's a lie," she said.

"Sure. I was thinking how much I like this. It's a life I could love. But I have to tell you square-up: maybe it was a mistake. Maybe it costs me too much or gives me too much to hold on to. I have to be able to let go of things. It's like I'm bargaining; I have to be able to walk away from the deal at any time, elsewise I can never win. I have to be willing to die at any time, or I can't ever win. Any man in a war will tell you that; you must be willing to give up your life at any chance. If you're thinking about what's at home, you lose your edge."

She looked at him with those gray, calm eyes.

"I was right. I knew. Give me a taste. Then pull away. Go off on your crusade." She almost laughed. "I wish I could hate you, Bob. You are a true and deep son of a bitch. But hating you would be like hating the weather. No point to it at all."

"I'm sorry. There was never a better time. It was the best. It was special. Another time or two and I'd never leave."

"No. That's a lie. You'd leave. I know your type. You always leave."

"You're right," he said. "I'd leave. I have to."

She found this one a laugh.

"You *are* a bastard."

Bob nodded. Not much passed on his grave face.

"When?"

"I think it has to be tomorrow."

"So soon?"

"Yeah. It's time. I've got some ideas. I've got something of a plan, even."

"I just never thought it would be so soon."

"The sooner I leave, the sooner I come back."

"You're lying again, Bob. You're not coming back. You'll be dead in a week."

"More than likely," he said. "It's a shaky plan. But it's the only one I could come up with. But first, I've got a couple of things to do."

"And what're they?" she said, trying to show no pain.

"I've got to dig up my cache in the mountains where I've got thirty thousand dollars and some guns stashed, so I can pay my own way and defend myself. And then," he said, "I've got to bury my dog."

CHAPTER TWENTY-ONE

Shreck never walked through doors; he exploded through them like a grenade, blowing them nearly off their hinges as he blasted through, bent forward, his gait rock-steady and determined.

Dobbler looked up at the noise, and Shreck was already on him, having crossed the ten feet from threshold to desk front in about a half a second and no more than two paces.

"Colonel Shreck, I—"

Feeling rousted as if by a bull on a snap inspection, Dobbler made a clumsy attempt to rise but the stern man motioned him down impatiently.

"I'm running late, Dobbler. I just got in."

"My God, Colonel, are you all right?"

"Tired. Exhausted."

"Jet lag? You really should take your shoes off, and walk barefoot on the carpet and—"

"Doctor, I'd asked you to consider Swagger's disappearance. Can you summarize your thoughts for me?"

"Of course, of course," said Dobbler, nonplussed; Shreck had never crashed into his office before; almost always, he served at Shreck's summons.

Dobbler began to babble through his discovery of the strange florist's bill in Little Rock, his initial dead end when he learned that the florist kept no records, and his latest initiative, which was to ask one of the technonerds in Research to run a computer search through the memory of the FTD databank if he could get into the system, in hopes of locating that elusive destination to which Bob had dispatched his flowers. But halfway through he realized that Shreck wasn't focusing.

"That's very promising. But I want some feeling of what's going on in his head. What's he going to do?"

"Oh," said Dobbler, somewhat taken aback at being denied the compliment he expected. "Well, Payne says the FBI has now moved its base of operations to Arkansas. His home area. They believe he'll head there."

"What do you think?"

"Oh, he will," said Dobbler vaguely.

"Why do you believe that?"

"Because he has to do what we expect, and still beat us." Dobbler smiled. "That's really what's going on now. Bob's vanity. His desire not merely to survive but to triumph. To punish us for our delusion of superiority. He must now prove to us who is the alpha-male."

Shreck nodded, intently.

"Suppose the FBI takes him alive. What will he be able to tell them?"

"Ah, I doubt he will be taken alive. He's in a very

volatile state. The pressures on him are incredible. He—"

"But if he is?"

"If he is—it may make him insane. They won't believe him, of course, the trap is too tight, too well constructed. It may actually destroy his mind. I don't know if he can function under those circumstances."

Shreck followed this carefully. Then he said, "All right, good. That's very helpful."

"Why, thank you, Colonel Shreck," said Dobbler, pleased.

"It's good to have a Harvard man on the staff, Dr. Dobbler. Because I can count on you for consistency. You are full of shit. Always. Completely. That's a gift, Dobbler."

Dobbler was stunned.

"I—"

"You stupid asshole, don't you know a thing about how men's minds work? Or Swagger's kind of man? Don't you see the fucking joke in this? You see, we planned his death, but maybe we gave him his life. We have engaged him. He is back among the living, and he's got himself a war to fight, and all his skills and talents may be fully deployed. That's the terrible thing, the longer this goes on, the more he enjoys it, the stronger he gets. And he'll love it. He should pay us for it. We're giving him more fun than he's had since the war."

It was morning of the last day. She got up at four and made breakfast so that it was ready when he awoke at five. But he wanted to make love—so soon, after last night, and what she had thought would be the last time—so the breakfast waited. It tasted wonderful when they got to it.

Then he showered and she dressed his wounds.

"Jesus, but aren't you a stud-puppy?" she said. "I've never seen multiple trauma gunshot recovery so fast."

The arm wound was the ugliest, a raw welt at the outside of his left bicep about three inches above the elbow. But it was just bruised and burned meat that would eventually heal without complication.

The entrance and the exit wounds to the chest had resolved themselves into quarter-sized scabs that would ultimately pucker into scar tissue.

"It doesn't hurt?"

"I can handle it."

"I just bet you can."

Bob had let his beard stay. He was a tall, sunburned man with a thick shock of blond-brown hair and a powerful chest. His eyes were hard and small; his mouth was a jot of concentration. He was a man in blue; she'd gone into a Gap store in a mall in Tucson and bought, with cash, three pairs of blue jeans and three pairs of black jeans, waist 34, length 33, and ten blue denim work shirts, and had washed them all. She'd also gotten a pair of brown Nocona boots, size 11, double A width, and two dozen pair of white socks at the Pick-and-Save. It was all loaded in a duffel bag in the back of his stolen car.

"Bob . . ."

Bob took a last swig of coffee.

"You know, you could just *stay* here. In time, we'd move. We could always be a jump ahead of them."

A small smile came over his taut features.

"Sure. But I won't. You know, if I could walk in right now and say to them, hey, you've got the wrong boy, and they take a look at some things they've missed, and say, 'Damn, Swagger, you're right,' I still wouldn't do it. Because that just means I'm off the hook and that's not enough. I got some idea what it's like to live with debts to pay and no way to pay them. Well, this time, I do mean to pay them, in full."

He turned, looking at her obliquely, and she saw an odd and powerful light in his eyes. She saw, too, that he was no longer the man he'd been a month ago, that desperate, bloody, half-crazy fugitive who'd arrived on her doorstep.

She didn't know this man. This was the Bob that Donny had loved, so focused you felt his power even now, sitting in the bedroom as he buttoned up his shirt. Now he scared her a little.

"Julie, you listen here. When I'm gone, I want you to scrub down every surface in this house with ammonia, because it's the only thing that will take off fingerprint oils. Throw out all your dishes and glasses and silverware. Now, you know what you have to do?"

"Yes," she said.

"Run through it again. Tell me."

"In five days, I drive four hours in any direction to any pay phone I can find. Then I call long distance to—uh, the number is three-three-one, four-five-two, six-seven-eight-three and I do my Lurleen accent—low, trashy, the kind of girl Elvis used to pick up in Tupelo bars before the Ed Sullivan show—"

He smiled.

"Then I ask for Memphis. Agent Memphis."

"Yes."

"They'll test you. They'll ask you what the dog's name was, and it wasn't Pat like they put in the papers, it was Mike. I wasn't hit once, like they said, but twice. You'll have to tell them that."

"I know all that. Then I tell him what you told me."

"Yes."

"Then I hang up and drive away."

"How long on the phone?"

"No more than two minutes."

"Don't forget to stop and have lots of change for the phone. You should have at least ten dollars in quarters."

"All right."

"Then you drive back here. I can't begin to think there's a chance in hell they'd ever track you. You don't know about me, you never heard about me, I don't exist. Nobody will know."

"And then the fun part," she said bitterly, "you get killed. The FBI kills you in some little Arkansas roadhouse."

"Maybe. But I have a few cards up my sleeve."

"Oh, Bob."

The sun was coming over the eastern rim of the desert now, and it bled through the sky. For just a moment the room itself seemed soaked in blood—blood everywhere, red and glinting and wet and black. But blood most of all in the narrow eyes of Bob Lee Swagger.

She shuddered, and tried to think of other things.

"Nick!"

It was Howard, and he didn't sound pleased.

"Uh, yes, Howard?"

"Would you come in here, please?"

"Sure."

Nick left the bull pen and headed into the little office out of which Howard was running the operation.

"Nick—"

Howard did not ask him to sit down, not a good sign.

"Nick, just what *is* it you've been doing?"

"Ah, well, you know, mainly monitoring the reports on Bob's movements as they're routed here from Washington, and coordinating with the local officers and keeping contact with our surveillance teams sited in the area, and monitoring the readiness of our quick-react teams, you know, Howard, trying to stay alert and keep our readiness high and—"

"I've just had a very irate call from Ben Prine in D.C. The head of Cointelpro."

"Yes."

"He says a request originated from this office concerning access to Bureau files on a private security firm called RamDyne over my authorization. I didn't authorize *anything*. Do you know about this?"

Nick wasn't an adept liar. A tide of phlegm rose in his throat and he was stunned at his own sudden loss of confidence and clarity of thought.

"It was only to save you time, Howard. I know you've got your big picture to worry about, so I just routed the request through your office with your name . . . uh, it's just a kind of . . ."

He ran out of words.

Howard glowered at him.

"What do you think you're doing, Nick? What game are you playing?"

Nick bumbled into a confused account of his investigation of the Eduardo Lanzman affair, the source who'd told him Lanzman was Salvadoran, his idea that a high-tech electronic eavesdropping van may have been used, his clumsy discovery of the mysterious RamDyne firm that seemed to have a line on such expensive equipment. He rambled on semicoherently about the coincidence of a Salvadoran agent maybe being killed by the Salvadoran secret police only weeks immediately before the suspiciously "accidental" murder of a Salvadoran archbishop despised by certain elements of his own regime. But he saw that he wasn't making much progress with Howard.

"I tried all the usual channels and came up with nothing. Like, nothing. So I tried to show some *initiative* and . . ." He trailed off lamely.

"Nick," said Howard, a deep sadness coming over his

bland face, "I'm very disappointed in you. Why didn't you come to me with all this?"

"Well, Howard, actually, um, I *did* and you said—"

"Nick, we have an open-and-shut case on Bob Lee Swagger. We have means, motive and opportunity. We have some circumstantial ballistics evidence. We have witnesses, including, I might add, yourself. Nick, what on earth are you doing? Whose side are you on?"

"Howard, there's something I've been meaning to tell you about the ballistics. I'm wondering if it's technically possible to—"

"All right, Nick, this is how things fall apart. Junior agents running around on their own, not reporting to authority. Unauthorized leaks to the press. It's the beginning of the end of Bureau discipline, which is the beginning of the end of the Bureau."

"Howard, I—"

"RamDyne, you're right, is very connected. To our cousins in Langley, among half a dozen other secret agencies. They do a lot of things we can't afford to do officially. Sometimes these things don't look so good; sometimes they're ambiguous; sometimes they do little bad things to prevent big bad things. Their secrets are very closely held. If you pick at them, or uncover something out of context, it can lead you exactly where you shouldn't go, and cause all kinds of problems for all kinds of people. Do you understand that?"

"Yes, sir."

"Nick, you're not *supposed* to see the big picture. Other people do that. You're supposed to do the jobs we give and do them well. Let us connect the dots. You catch the crooks."

"Yes, sir."

"Nick, it pains me to do this. I'd thought perhaps after your screwups in the past, you'd turned over a new leaf, and I might have been tempted to forego your suspension. But you haven't. I'm removing you from this detail. You're to fly back to New Orleans immediately and begin your suspension. Sorry, it has to be this way. Some years ago you messed up. I thought you'd worked hard and overcome that mistake. But you keep messing up, Nick. You're a loose cannon. You're not a team player. You want too much, you want it too fast."

Nick realized he'd just gotten blindsided. It hit him with a force he hadn't felt since Myra died.

"All the way through, Nick, you insist on doing things your way. If you'd bumped Swagger up to the Alpha category, if you'd taken him prisoner, if—oh, Nick, you've done so *poorly*. We've tried so desperately to help you. And now you pull *this* on us."

"I'm sorry, Howard," blurted Nick, stunned. "I didn't know it was so serious. I was trying to do a thorough job and I—"

"Nick, that's all I have for you. I want you—"

"Nick?"

It was Hap Fencl leaning in.

"Excuse me, Howard," he said, "but I have a woman on the line who swears she knows where Bob Swagger is, and insists on talking to Nick."

"For Christ's sake, Fencl," blurted Howard, "she's probably just another—"

"She says he had an arm wound. We hadn't released that information."

There was a long pause.

Finally, disgustedly, Howard gestured to Nick to pick up the phone.

"It's line fourteen," said Hap.

"Nick Memphis, FBI, can I help you?"

"Mr. Memphis," came the voice like a bad country-western song, though somehow theatrical and a bit phony, "Mr. Memphis, Bob Lee was with me and he was my man fer a time, but he's gone now."

"Who is this?" Nick said.

"This ain't nobody," she said. "But I seen your pitcher in the magazine and if you're the johnny what's got to catch Bob Lee, then git yourself ready, 'cause he's a coming."

"When?"

"He left here today. Should be there in three days of hard driving. He's gone a little crazy, you know. I begged him not to go."

"How do I—"

"Because he said his dog's name was Mike, not Pat, like it said in the newspapers."

Another trap to weed out loony callers.

Nick took a deep breath, made a signal to Hap to indicate it was time to get going on the trace.

"He says he's coming home to bury his dog," said the woman. "Gonna bury his dog, don't care who he's got to kill to do it."

"I—"

"Don't hurt him, Mr. Memphis. He ain't hurt nobody."

Then she hung up.

The secure phone rang.

Shreck looked up at the men in his office.

"Get out," he said.

After they left, he picked it up.

"Shreck."

"Hello, Raymond," the old man's voice sang. "How are you today?"

"Mr. Meachum, you don't care how I am. What do you want?"

"I wanted you to be the first to hear the good news. I've heard from a friend that the Justice Department has just alerted the State Department to inform the Salvadorans that it has formally decided against reopening its inquiry into the Panther Battalion atrocity. The archbishop is gone, and there's nobody to pay any attention to it at all."

This did cheer Shreck.

"Well, that's something."

"Yes, it is. Of course General de Rujijo and his colleagues and peers will be delighted. Certain people in certain agencies in this town will breathe a good deal more easily. The past will be allowed to die; we can go on from here. It's the first day of the rest of our lives. You're to be congratulated once again, Colonel. You made the impossible happen. Extraordinary."

"Thank you, Mr. Meachum."

"Only that one loose end, and it's a very tiny one."

"We're on it, Mr. Meachum."

"Excellent," said the old man. "I knew I could count on you."

"Okay," said Howard, "now I want snipers on those two buildings, do you see. Put them on duty at four A.M. tonight. I want them there all day tomorrow, even if he's not supposed to be in till the day after. You can never tell."

"Yes, Howard," said Hap Fencl. "We'll put 'em up there, good boys. Nick? He's the best shot."

"No. Not Nick. Nick stays with me. Do you hear that, Nick?"

"Yes, I hear it," said Nick, still clinging to membership on the task force by his fingernails, his exile to New Orleans forestalled by the prospect of action.

They were standing in front of the new red-brick Polk County Health Complex, which contained the county morgue. The body of Mike the dog had been removed there and now rested inside.

It was a bright afternoon, and the green Ouachitas glared down at them. They were about a mile out of

Blue Eye, just off of Route 270 where it neared 71 and turned into Mena. Traffic hummed down the road.

"And I want shotgun teams on standby. Say, four-man units, ready to go, secured in the installation."

"Yes, Howard," said Hap. "Uh, what load? Do you want them carrying double-ought buck or deer slugs?"

"Hmm," said Howard.

"The boys like double-ought, because it doesn't kick so much and you don't have to make an exact shot placement. And, Howard, with those deer slugs, you got a .70 caliber chunk of lead moving at one thousand six hundred feet a second, and if you should happen to hit a civilian, Christ, the hoot from the newspapers."

"He's probably not going to be wearing body armor," said Howard. "All right, go with the double-ought."

"Howard, do you want to coordinate with the sheriff's office?" Hap asked. "Old Tell's getting pretty edgy as it is."

"No, I don't think so. This is our operation, this is a federal warrant, and we'll serve it. We'll alert the sheriff after we make the apprehension. Nick?"

"Yes, Howard," said Nick, standing there disconsolately next to Howard in the small knot of agents just outside the lobby.

"Nick, I want you to stay at the command post to handle the communications. Or do you want to ship out today?"

"No, Howard, I'll hang around until—"

But Howard had already turned away from Nick.

"I also want us to have people in the morgue and people on the floor and in the office. I want an observation post up near the snipers, ID-ing everybody who pulls into the lot."

"If we get a positive, will you green light?" asked Hap.

"Yes."

There was a quiet moment. Green light. Pull the trigger. Shoot to kill without warning. It was a rare operational condition.

"I want to take him here in the lot, not inside. We could get ourselves in some hostage situation or God knows what if he gets inside," said Howard. "This man is very dangerous. He could take down half a dozen men in the blink of an eye, and suddenly I'm looking at more dead than Miami."

"Howard," said Nick, knowing it was futile, "he had me dead to rights in New Orleans with my own pistol when the smart thing was to drill me, and he passed on it. He hasn't been found guilty of—"

"Nick, you are really disappointing me."

"Yeah, Nick," said Hap. "Howard's right. Gotta tag the guy if a clean chance shows."

Nick nodded bitterly. But what if he's innocent? Then he realized it didn't really matter anymore.

"All right, Hap, you get the men out and sited, very quietly. I don't want a lot of action on this. It's possible Bob has sympathizers in the community, and he'll be getting advance reports."

"Howard, he'll also scope out this place before he moves in," said Nick. "That's how he works. He's very careful. You'll want to be real careful how you hide these people. This guy can smell a trap a mile away."

"Nicky, we're pros too, remember," said Hap. "Hey, we'll do a real nice job. He won't know what hit him, Nicky. If he shows."

"Nick, you come with me," said Howdy Duty. "I want to see the administrator here and get all this cleared before we move in. I may need your diplomatic skills."

Nick and Howard went into the lobby waiting room, a bland, government-grim office that smelled of newness and plastic—the place was only a year or so old—

where beige furniture stood against beige walls and one bearded geezer was up at the desk, jawing in deep Arkansese with the girl there.

Howard led Nick to the counter and they waited politely in the otherwise empty office as the hillbilly or mountain man or whatever he was carried on 'bout the damned government or some such, and the girl listened with half an ear and half a brain, and kept saying, "But the papers aren't *ready* yet."

She was just letting him blow some steam and after a while he seemed to settle down and stepped aside, and Howard pushed his way to the counter, pulling his identification and announcing himself as Deputy Director Utey, Federal Bureau of Investigation.

It was only then that Nick looked up into the face of the man they'd rammed aside, and behind the blond beard and under the deep tan, realized he was looking into the gray eyes of Bob the Nailer.

CHAPTER TWENTY-TWO

Nick was fast; Bob was faster.

"Don't you do it, son," he said, the .45 Colt automatic a blue blur as it rose from nowhere and locked onto Nick's chest. Bob's voice was dead calm, dead serious.

Nick's hand had flashed to his own Smith, his fingers were wrapped around the shaft of the piece —a very good speed draw, in fact, by Bureau standards—but he was dead by a clean three-tenths of a second if Bob so chose.

Nick put his hands up.

"Hey, what—" Howard said.

"You boys just relax. Young lady, you relax too. I came only to get my old hound Mike, and no man should have to die for so silly a thing as a dog that's been dead a month or so, right, Memphis?"

There was a weirdly cheerful crackle in his voice.

The girl behind the counter sat back and her eyes got big as eggs. Howard, meanwhile, was still not quite with it.

"Who—"

"Howard, it's him, it's Swagger. He beat us here—no, he set us *up*. Isn't that right?"

"You, older guy, don't you do anything stupid, even if you do look stupid. Gun out, left hand reaching around, set it on the counter, just like the kid here."

"Mr. Swagger, there are federal agents all arou—"

"Just do it, old man, there's a good boy."

It stunned Nick how calm Bob was.

Howard's big Model 19 came out, went onto the countertop delicately.

"Young lady, pick each one up by the barrel and put 'em in that wastebasket over there."

She did as she was told, shaking all the way.

"Now, young lady, I want you to lie down on the floor over there by the wall and curl up, with your hands over your ears. You just stay there. If you hear shooting, you just stay there. You'll be fine if you just stay there."

The girl, a blonde with a murky face, did just that, sinking to the floor.

"Swagger," said Howard, "give it up. You won't make it out. If we don't get you today, we'll get you tomorrow. We have a thousand men on this."

"You just shut your mouth, sir," said Bob. "Now y'all come with me, smiling like we're old pals, you being just a touch ahead. Remember I can put the third of three bullets into each of you before you feel the first two. Now let's go. We're headed back past three halls, then turning to the right. Then you, Memphis, you're going to tell the man there, a Dr. Nivens I believe, how it's time to give up on the dog's body and send it on to Washington for further tests. You pick it up. Then we're going to walk out to my truck, and I'm going to drive off. And nobody has to get hurt over a damn dog. Fair enough?"

"Swagger, we have six eight-man reactive squads in the area. We can have a SWAT team here in three minutes. We have choppers and dogs. You'll never get it done. It's over. You shouldn't have come back."

"I came back to bury my old dog, and nobody's going to stop me. Now let's get going."

The three of them walked stiffly through the swinging doors.

"Now up here, to the left. You boys put him in the human morgue. That's proper, because he's a better man than most men, I'll tell you."

They reached the morgue.

"Here we are, Memphis. Don't fuck this up like you fucked up Tulsa. You hit the first time, Pork."

Nick blanched; his shame, yanked up out of the past on him. How had he known?

"Yes?"

It was Nivens, the county coroner, who'd done the autopsy on the dog.

"Uh, Dr. Nivens, my name's Nick Memphis, FBI," Nick said. Nick drew out his credentials and the three of them faced the runty little doctor.

"We've, uh, we've decided to send the dog's body on to Washington for further testing and—"

"Oh, God, Bob, Jesus, don't shoot—"

The doctor had recognized Bob even as Nick was talking. So Bob pulled the Colt out and said, "Now, don't do anything stupid, Doc, I just come to get my damned poor old dog. Give him to this young fool here."

But in the face of the pistol, the doctor simply surrendered; he was one of those natural victims eager to give up. He went to his knees and blubbered at Bob not to shoot him because he had three children, a mortgage, a sick wife.

"Where's the dog, dammit?" Bob asked.

The doctor mumbled something about Number 7, and Bob gave Nick a shove in the direction of the drawer marked 7. Nick ambled over to it. He had a Colt Agent .38 snub in a ballistic nylon holster strapped to his ankle, in accordance with the new Bureau reg that permitted backup guns in units with high-contact probability, but the problem with an ankle carry is its awkwardness. He'd never get to the piece, get it unstrapped, get it into his big hands and find a shooting position before Bob had shot him several dozen times. But he knew that Howard had a piece on his ankle also and he was afraid that Howard, now furiously ashamed to be taken so easily and caught up in the drama of a collapsing career, might lose it and go for the piece and get himself and probably everyone else in the room killed.

Nick slid open the drawer; it was cool inside. The dog, wrapped in a human body bag, was light enough. He hoisted it.

"Fine," said Bob, watching him, watching the doctor, watching poor Howard, "now bring him over here."

"Swagger, give it up," said Howard, "before somebody innocent gets hurt."

"Now, sir," said Bob, courtly as ever, "you just mind your own business and nothing sudden will happen to anybody. All's I want is to bury my dog."

Suddenly, they heard sirens.

"Colonel?" It was one of Payne's men, an ex-cop, and he'd just caught up with Shreck in the corridor.

"Yes?"

"It's Jack, in the Electrotek 5400 in Arkansas. He's just monitored an FBI report from outside Blue Eye to the effect that they've got Bob Lee Swagger caught in the Polk County Health Complex. They're just this second bringing in their SWAT teams and snipers, and the state cops and the local cops are pouring all kinds of stuff into the place."

Shreck's eyes acquired the color of ball bearings.

"I want you to get to Operations and bring it up off the shortwave on loudspeaker. I'll be there in a second. And clear the room. I want to hear this one without a lot of asshole chatter from the teams."

"Yes, sir."

"All right," said Shreck.

He felt nothing: no elation, no dizzying blast of happiness, no relief. He was a professional. But in the tunnel that was his mind, he had just a split second of pleasure. It was about to end.

He raced toward Operations.

"All right," said Bob, gesturing to Howard and the doctor. "Y'all lie down on the floor. Keep your heads down and don't try anything foolish. You, chubby, you're coming with me. Bring the dog."

Abruptly, they stepped through the swinging doors, leaving the stunned victims in the morgue.

"Hold it," Bob commanded.

He positioned himself next to the doors, and two seconds later they blew open to reveal Howard with his little .38 on a rampage, and Bob simply clipped him between the eyes with the hard butt of the .45, in a kind of insolent, backhanded swat, sending him down to the floor with a thump, his little revolver clattering away.

"Wasn't he the stupid one?" he said laconically to Nick, who watched the whole thing in astonishment.

"Now, this way," Bob directed with his .45, as the sirens grew louder outside.

"You got every SWAT team in six states on your ass," said Nick.

"Pork, you're here to carry the dog, so why not just keep that mouth buttoned up?"

Everywhere they ran through the building they encountered frightened people who melted away with shrieks or faints. But no officers; Howard hadn't gotten any men into the building yet and probably wouldn't until the evacuation was complete.

Nick felt his Colt Agent jostling in the ankle holster; but he still had no good shot at getting it out, not with the eerily aware Bob shoving him down the hallway toward God knew what.

"Where we headed?" he asked.

"Shut up, Pork," said Bob.

Suddenly the loudspeakers boomed through the hallways.

"Ladies and gentlemen, the FBI requests that you stay in your offices. There's evidently a felon loose in the complex."

"Jesus," Nick said, "they got you now."

A state police car whirled down Route 71 from Mena toward the health complex, siren blaring, blowing by the Electrotek van, which had been discreetly parked at a wayside stopover. Behind the police car came another and another. A helicopter churned overhead.

In the van, a scrawny ex-cop named Eddie Nicoletta and called Eddie Nickles, said, "His ass is grass."

But Jack Payne didn't say a thing. He just sat there listening to the orchestration of the law enforcement units over the radio intercept. Nothing showed on his mean little face.

The radio chattered on.

"Command, I got three State teams coming in."

"Okay, good, Victor Michael Five, I want you to work 'em around back and coordinate with our sniper post."

"Ten-four, Command. Are we green light?"

"That's a negative, Victor Michael Five, we have a federal officer as a hostage, I repeat, we have a federal officer as a hostage. I'll call the shot if it goes to it."

"But suppose we get him clean?"

"Ah, we'll have to get back to you, Victor Michael Five," said the command voice.

"Fuckin' feds," said Nicoletta, "they take over and then they don't know what the fuck their policy is. I remember this time, working narc, when—"

"Shut up, Nickles," said Payne. Then he turned to Pony, a Panther Battalion communications technician really named Pinto, and asked, "They getting this back at Dulles?"

"Loud and clear," the Salvadoran said. "I tell you, man, with this stuff you could start a radio station."

Another chopper roared down the road.

I want to be there, thought Jack Payne suddenly, a yearning going off in him like an inflating balloon.

But he sat tight.

"Don't touch that dial," he said.

Bob stopped to pull on the padlock of a door marked ENGINEERING ONLY. Magically, the lock popped open.

They stepped into a little closet. There was a grating on the floor and Bob bent to open it; beneath, Nick could see a metal ladder.

"That's our ticket out, Pork. Get your ass and a half down there and then go to prone, on your belly, legs and arms spread. You make a stupid move, I'll have to dump your bones here. Sad for a big boy like you to have to die over a dead dog."

Nick struggled down with the dog's corpse; he could

sense Bob above him, the yawning bore of the .45 always locked onto him. The man carried the gun lightly, easily, as if he'd been born with it.

At the bottom Nick looked up, and there was Bob, the gun on him. Obediently he went to the floor as Bob clambered down, pulling the grate shut after him.

"This way, now," he said.

Nick had to admit it; yes, he was impressed. Bob knew the layout of the place cold; he'd left the woman up front to call the cops because he wanted lots of commotion and chaos; he figured he could get out. But he couldn't make it with the dog, so he'd had to wait until a strong enough man showed up who could carry Mike while he, Bob, negotiated the obstacles.

Recon, remembered Nick. A good sniper always recons the area before he operates. He never goes in blind. He knows where everything is, he plans escape routes, evasion maneuvers, always has a plan.

At the end of the narrow tunnel they came to another ladder; this time Bob went up first, back against the rungs, the gun on Nick. Nick followed, covered the whole way, and had trouble lugging the dog's body up the ladder, but Bob didn't help him a bit. Finally, grunting heavily, he was up.

"Damn dog is *heavy*," he said.

"You ought to try humping a seventy-pound pack in the boonies in a-hundred-twenty-degree weather, Pork," said Bob. "Now shut up. This part might be tricky."

They were in another closet, close in the dark. Outside it, they could hear motion, the staticky crackle of a radio, the low murmuring of serious men.

"Hold on to that dog," whispered Bob.

Then he pressed open the door. They were in some sort of garage a good seventy yards from the main health complex building. Outside, Nick saw three state police cars set up to form a perimeter around the building. Cops were crouched behind their wheel wells, aiming shotguns or scoped rifles. But Bob and Nick were outside the perimeter.

"Now, we go out here, we walk, we don't run, about a hundred yards, to where you see a generating shack. Around back, there's a red pickup. That's where we're going. You make any sudden moves, son, and you know what's waiting for you."

"Yeah," said Nick.

"So let's do it."

They walked out into the bright sunlight and didn't look back. The damn dog was getting even heavier. Nick's arms ached. He watched as the generating shack wobbled closer, wondering when the hell Howard would shake the cobwebs from his skull and figure out what was going on and order his snipers to green light the two walking men. The bullets would sing out and since the guys didn't shoot worth a shit at any range over seven yards, he knew he'd get blasted. What made it worse was the sense of commotion rising behind them, two or three new choppers arriving, while all the sirens in the world seemed to be sounding, as if it were some kind of state police convention in Little Rock.

But they made it to the shed, and behind it found the red truck.

"Put the dog in back," said Bob, who had opened the cab and pulled out a short-barreled lever action carbine, an actual Winchester.

"Now, get in, Pork. You're driving, and I got this little rifle on your butt." He spat a leisurely gob into the dust.

"Jesus, now we're just going to drive on out of here? Like, nobody's going to notice? There's maybe five hundred men out there by now."

"We're going out the back way and up the hill."

"What back way? There is no back way."

"I think you're going to be surprised, son. Now get going. Key's in the ignition and I've got this damn poodle-shooter on you."

Suddenly there was a helicopter hovering overhead, whipping up a brisk curtain of dust and beating the trees back.

"You in the truck," came the loudspeakered voice, "out, or we'll fire."

"Shit," said Nick.

"Punch it," said Bob.

Feeling extremely mortal, Nick punched the truck. With a stunning leap, the vehicle took off, blowing up its own curtain of dust as it zoomed along the perimeter of the fence.

The shadow of the chopper stayed with them. Sirens rose; from around the sides of the building a fleet of squad cars emerged, plunging like a cavalry charge across the grounds at them.

"Now left, left," shrieked Bob.

But there was nothing left but Cyclone fence.

In Operations, the men sat quietly, faces grave. Nobody looked at anybody else. From the bank of communications equipment, they could hear the drama playing itself out.

"All units, all units, I have suspects in red pickup inside the wire perimeter, goddamn that's him, I swear, goddamn—"

"This is Command, this is Command, all units, stay in position, I want state police in pursuit, do you read, Victor Michael Five, get after him."

"Are we green light, are we green light?"

"Only if you get a clear shot, all units, suspect is armed and dangerous but he's got a federal hostage."

"Is hostage expendable?"

"You must not let suspect get away, that's imperative, all units."

"Jesus," said one of the Operations guys, "whoever's on command just said go ahead and drop their own guy if they have to. The feds want this boy bad."

Not as bad as I do, thought Shreck.

"*Left!*" screamed Bob, himself reaching over to shove the wheel. Nick felt the truck swerve and before it there was a steel fence post and he knew it would stop them and he'd end up wrapped around it. But the post went down like a snowman, yanking with it twenty feet of fence—Nick knew instantly it had already been cut through, that Bob had laid the whole thing out *hours* ago —and now they faced hill. Nick didn't need instructions. He pressed the gas and rocked backwards through the gears and the truck bucked and clawed its way up, through underbrush, until it felt like a rocket ship ascending toward gravity's release. It seemed almost vertical; he waited to slide back, felt the truck fighting and fighting and fighting.

Then, amazingly, they were over the crest of a ledge and on a dirt road.

"Go, go, you sonovabitch!" Swagger was yelling. "Wooo-eeee, left those old boys way back there."

Indeed the police cruisers and the FBI cars didn't have the gear ratios to make the incline. Nick could see one or two of them stuck halfway up and the others paralleling his course at ground level. But the choppers were everywhere, two, three, now four of them, darting like predatory birds.

"You won't shake the choppers," he yelled.

"You just drive, Pork. You let me worry about that," Bob commanded. He actually looked a little happy.

A shot tore into the hood of the truck with a clang.

"Oh, fuck, they're shooting," Nick said.

But Bob squirmed half out the window and brandished the carbine, and instantly the choppers fell back.

"Gutless bubbas," he said, sliding back in.

They tore down the high road at eighty, dogged at a distance by choppers. And behind them rose state police cars, their lights flashing. The squad cars gained.

"Go on, boy, hit it. Push this damn thing or I'll have to dump you at hundred miles per."

"It's pushed, dammit, I got the pedal on the floor, they're gonna get us!"

"Another mile or so, boy, that's all."

This distance narrowed appreciably over the next few seconds, as the state police cruisers rocketed down the road much faster than the truck could hit. In the rear-view mirror, Nick could see the offside man in the lead car slide a pump gun out the window and try to find enough of a sight picture to fire as the car drew nearer, but the road bucked too hard and the dust was too thick.

"Okay, boy, get ready!" shouted Bob, "she's coming up now."

Nick looked at him in horror and watched as his hand snaked out gleefully, seized the wheel, and gave it a hard yank to the right. Nick's foot reflexively shot to the brake but it was too late. The truck careened at sixty miles an hour off the edge of the road and back down the mountainside.

Through the windshield, the world tipped crazily, and turned to instant vegetation as branches and tufts of high grass whipped at the truck. It rocked savagely as it plummeted downward, now and then feeling about to launch itself in a gut-squeezing, heart-crushing thrust through the air. Then the wheels touched down again and the truck tore through the underbrush. Nick fought the wheel for some semblance of control; he saw trees again and heard himself screaming—and then he lost it.

The whole thing flipped; the windshield stretched and shivered and seemed to liquefy as it turned to silver webbing in the instant before it shattered, pouring a torrent of glass atop him. He felt himself careening and the smell of dust and gas filled his ears, amid bolts of pain as he banged his head hard against the door pillar. And then they were still.

It took Nick a second or two to realize he was alive. He heard the ticking of the truck and shook his head, touching it, tasting salt as blood ran into his mouth. His eyes shot open. He lay half in, half out of the vehicle, which had come to a twisted rest in a tangle of trees at the end of the long plunge down the mountain. Up top, he could see the police cars halted and a couple of troopers, guns in hands, edging down the steep slope. A chopper hovered above and then another one swooped low overhead, its roar deafening. Nick turned and watched as a whole cavalry charge of police cars roared across the flatland at them, still a good three minutes distant.

Where was Bob?

He blinked, shook his head, pulled himself free. His hand shot down to his ankle and he unlimbered the .38 Agent. Where was he?

Then he heard a grunt and looked back through the cab to see Bob lifting the body bag with Mike's corpse out of the truck bed. There was blood on his face too, and when he got the body to him, Nick saw him pause; there was a tenderness in him Nick would never have wired into his Bob Lee Swagger profile.

Then Bob spun and began to lurch away.

Nick had him.

"Stop!" He thrust out the .38, cupping it in two hands, as he thumbed back the hammer. He had its cylinder primed with Glaser safety slugs. At this range the bird-shot-loaded bluetips generated seventy-three percent one-shot stops.

"Goddammit, freeze!" Nick boomed again. He lurched forward, blinking blood from his eyes, and feeling himself begin to tremble like a child in the cold rain without a coat. He set himself against the canted hood of the truck, locking his elbows, sliding into a sight picture. It was a good hold; he had Bob, center mass, in the notch of the rear sight and the nub of the front.

Bob himself blinked away some blood as he studied on this new situation.

"Put the dog down and your hands behind your neck and get to your fucking knees, Swagger. You do some speed stuff on me and I swear to Christ I blow your spine out. These are Glasers."

"Hell, Pork," Bob said, "if you were going to shoot me, it'd be done by now."

Then the sonovabitch winked at him! And he turned and began to amble off, dog under one arm, Winchester carbine under the other.

Shoot him! Nick ordered himself. The trigger was a curse against his finger; he yearned to expel it, to end all his failures.

But shooting a man takes one of two things: an overwhelming fear of one's own death, which Nick did not have in the least; or conviction. It turned out he lacked this component as well.

He didn't miss vertically; he missed horizontally, Nick found himself thinking as he stood there, watching Bob run away.

Bob got to the field and shot across the meadow a hundred yards or so to what Nick now saw was your picture-postcard country cemetery under a tall stand of ancient trees, hard by a doddering wooden church. He watched as Bob vaulted the stone wall, and there among the teetering, blackened gravestones set the dog down in what must have been a perfectly sized hole already cut from the earth, and snatched up a shovel that must have been part of the master plan. With seven strong strokes, he heaped dirt upon it. In the next half-second, he'd scooped up the Winchester carbine and headed into the church.

Nick heard the cars closing in now, but they would not make it. Bob was inside the church and suddenly out the door skeedaddled a class of black children, running desperately, even as the first state cruiser arrived, and its occupants, Magnums and shotguns aimed and cocked, took cover behind it. Then came a second, a third and then ten more, then twenty; a whole caravan of lawmen was at the church in less than a minute, ready and waiting, when the last occupant emerged, a stooped black gentleman.

They got him, Nick thought.

Someone was screaming in his ear.

"You didn't shoot! You had him, goddammit," the voice said. He turned. It was a tough-looking state police sergeant. Behind him his buddy radiated contempt at Nick.

I'll have to pay for that one too.

"Goddamn," said another state policeman, holding aloft Bob's .45 as he found it in the cab. "It's fucking *empty*!"

Nick heard a bullhorn demanding surrender. There was just one second of silence. Then the sound of shots rose against the sky, and Nick turned in horror. The lawmen were shooting gas grenades into the church. He watched as the heavy shells sailed through and the cottony white fog began to steam through the broken windows. A tendril of smoke leaped out, and a flame, and then another from another window, and the church began to burn.

Jack Payne stood outside the van with his binoculars. Overhead a TV news helicopter zipped by and shortly a TV news van came screeching down the road toward the mass of flashing lightbars and the howl of sirens. Jack could hear the troopers over the radio intercept from inside the van.

"Shit, it's going up, that dry timber."

"Is he coming out?"

"Don't see a damned thing. I'm gonna—"

"That's a negative, Victor Michael Thirty-three, you stay put and keep those eyes open. Anybody seen the goddamned feds?"

"They're coming, Charlie."

At that moment four black cars raced by Jack, hell-bent for the church.

But it was too late. Jack watched the smoke, floating upward in a lazy column. Through the glass, he could see the flames.

"Wow."

It was Eddie Nickles, beside him.

"Shit, they burned him up. Man, he's all fucking toasty now."

"Shut up," said Jack. He didn't know why, he felt like hitting the younger man.

CHAPTER TWENTY-THREE

Shreck watched the church burn. When it was burned to the ground, he hit REWIND, and watched it burn again.

And each time, an earnest television correspondent repeated the news breathlessly.

"Behind me is the funeral pyre of the notorious attempted presidential assassin Bob Lee Swagger, whom Arkansas State Police officers and FBI agents pursued to this bucolic spot after his dramatic attempt to kidnap his dog's body. Despite the lawmen's requests that he come out, Swagger opened fire on the officers. A tear gas canister ignited the old structure into conflagration. The church has been burning for two hours now. In the morning, officials say, it will be cool enough to sift through the ashes for the body of Bob Lee Swagger."

Shreck saw holocaust. The flames gobbled the structure from the roof downward. They danced madly through it, issuing a lazy, smeary column of smoke.

He hit REWIND again.

It was dark in the room. Three or four of the men from Jack Payne's Operations unit were in the room, and Dobbler, making a rare appearance outside his cell-like little office, had slipped in, too.

"Play it again," said Shreck.

The TV people, in Blue Eye on rumors of federal activity and monitoring the police channels on the radio, had gotten there efficiently; they had it from a variety of angles. From a helicopter it looked like a funeral pyre: Shreck could see the church standing in the devotional ring of police vehicles a little to one side of the copse of trees and the old graveyard. It throbbed with flames.

"Nobody could get out of that alive," somebody said in the dark.

"Man, he's fried."

Then Shreck spoke.

"It's nothing until they find the body and issue a forensic report. Until then, it's nothing."

But he watched it again. The flames billowed orangely as they ate through the old building standing in a meadow in the lee of mountains on a bright and beautiful Arkansas day.

"I think it's over, sir," somebody said. "I think we can chalk it off."

"Then why would he do something so obviously stupid for a dog? This guy was a prick, but he wasn't stupid."

"But he was obsessional," said Dobbler, in the dark. "The dog *mattered* to him. It wasn't stupid to him. To us, yes. To Swagger, it mattered so much he was driven to come back."

"I'll buy it when they bring me his teeth," said Shreck.

His eyes went back to the television. He hit REWIND.

Hap found him the next day.

"Here, here he is, goddammit," he called after lifting the air filtration mask the men wore to protect their lungs from the clouds of ash. His words carried to the twenty agents and fifteen state policemen on hands and knees who sifted and pawed through the remains of Aurora Baptist, while a hundred yards away, like gawkers at a carnival midway, the reporters were kept in check by three more cops and a rope line.

The cops and agents gathered around. Nick pushed his way through the crowd. His head ached from the pounding he'd taken and he was afraid his stitches might not hold, but he had to see.

What was left of Bob Lee Swagger was not pretty. Bob's face had burned away and the hideous fleshlessness exposed his teeth, which had been blackened with the rest of him in the blaze. His spine had curled; it looked like an Apache bow, drawn, perhaps shrunken a little, much notched. The rest was loose body parts, black as sin, disconnected from each other.

One of the agents went away to be sick.

Nick, standing amid clouds of ashen dust in the hulk of the old church, pushed his mask off and saw what had happened. In extremis, his last moments of life on earth, as the incredible heat consumed him, Bob crawled to the altar. The fire consumed him, and spat out his bones. He had done his duty; he got that damned dog buried. It was so important to him, it was important enough to die for. Was that nobility or sheer craziness? Hard to read; and that was somehow pure-D

Bob Swagger. And that done, there was nothing left to do. What all his armed and dangerous enemies could not do, a single tear gas shell fired into the rafters of the church had done in seconds. Fitting? No. Too much pain. Death by fire wasn't transformation, it was as agonizing as crucifixion, with nails driven through every square centimeter of your skin.

"Hell of a way to die," someone said. "Creep or no creep, hell of a way to die."

"Who's going to body-bag him?"

"Not me," said Nick first and loudest. He had wanted to see the whole thing played out to the end, knowing his own end—or the end of his career—was near. There was nothing of the reliquary here for him; the bones of saints, being really just bones, made him queasy.

He stepped out of the ruins of the church. Nice to be on solid ground again, instead of shuffling through ash and fire-rotted splinters of wood.

He stood off to one side while others came to see, and wondered if this was how it was in 1934 when they got Dillinger, and everyone had to come and look and dip a finger or a handkerchief in the great gangster's blood.

The reporters sensed the discovery and became restive; Nick could see them surge forward and strain at the rope. It was Howard over there who quieted them with the news. Nick watched the network reporters cluster around him, then looked and saw that the photographers had finished, and now the guys from morgue had gotten what was left of Bob into a plastic sack. At least they had the decency to put him on a litter, rather than carrying him like a Halloween bag to the coroner's van.

Feeling suddenly wiped out, Nick thought how nice it would finally be to be done with it all. He had zero money because it had taken every cent he had to keep Myra taken care of, and soon he would have no job, but hey, he was alive, he was—

Then he saw something that made him sick.

He walked over to the graveyard.

"What the hell are you doing?"

Two black men were digging up the dog that Bob had buried, while two cameras blazed away and two TV reporters posed in front of them.

"I said, what the hell are you doing?"

The black men just looked at him foolishly.

"Do you have permission to dig here? This is state's evidence."

"Now, chief," said one of the reporters, coming over to him. "Nothing to get excited about. We're just doing our job. You're FBI, huh? So, what does it feel like now that Public Enemy Number One has—"

The microphone was pushed at him, and Nick saw the camera coming onto him. He also saw Howard rushing over to take command, a stricken look on his face.

"Nick," Howard was calling, "Nick, you aren't authorized to do press at this point. Mr. Baker, I'll have to ask you—"

Nick turned, the microphone was still there, big as a fist right at Nick's nose, and the reporter, who Nick now saw was wearing considerable makeup and whose hair was lacquered into frozen perfection, was asking him quite earnestly how it *felt* when he watched the church burn—

"Nick, no—"

He heard Howard as his fist traveled a short distance, maybe ten inches, and caught the talker square in his pretty mouth. Nothing had felt quite so good in months. The clown bumbled fearfully backward, spitting teeth, leaking blood, and the whole contingent of press guys quivered back, making room for him.

Now gone to complete savagery, Nick turned onto the digging men and screamed at them to get the hell out of there, and they scrambled away. So there he stood for just a second, all his enemies vanquished. Look at me, Ma, top of the world. Top of the world.

Then Howard had him, and several others pulled him back and were on him, including one state policeman who was handling him more roughly than was necessary.

"Yeah, you're tough with reporters," the officer spat, "but yesterday when it counted, you were pussy." And with that, he gave Nick an immensely powerful shove that sent him back a few feet, completely stripped of dignity.

It occurred to Nick for the first time how the cops must hate him. He hadn't worked it out, having spent the night in the hospital after various stitchings and X rays. But yes, he'd had a shot at Bob, and couldn't pull the trigger. Three minutes later it was state policemen who'd closed on Bob, fully armed and one of the most dangerous gunmen in the world. Had he wanted to, Bob could have filled Arkansas with state police widows even with that old-time cowboy carbine.

"Nick, goddamn, cool it, cool it," Hap was whispering in his ear, as he held him in a tender but firm embrace. "Damn, what has gotten into you, Jesus, you punch a reporter, you could get busted for *assault* and these Arkansas State boys ain't exactly your fan club, you know."

"Yeah, yeah," said Nick with phony surliness, as the cop slowly walked away, daring Nick to have a go at him. Meanwhile Howard had taken over with the reporters, trying to explain how Nick was "overextended."

He just felt totally whacked. Even breathing seemed too hard. If he could only sleep for a couple of centuries and then wake up and put the pieces together, it might make some sense.

Howard was back. Howard didn't have a vocabulary for anger, being by nature a conniver and a facilitator rather than a brute. But he was *mad.* Nick could see it in the tightness of his eyes and the straight, flat, hard line of his little mouth.

"Howard, I'm sorry. I hadn't really figured how stressed out I was. I really didn't—"

"Memphis, that's it. That's the end. I am formally relieving you of duties as of this second. You are off this case and off this team. Get back to the hotel and pack and shower. I'll have somebody drive you to the airport. You take a plane to God knows where—I don't give a damn. I'll have you formally notified when the review board will meet, but as of now you are officially suspended without pay pending the outcome of the board's decision."

"Howard, I want—"

"Memphis, shut up. Your involvement in the case has been a disaster. It's my biggest mistake. Now just get the hell out of here. I want you out of here."

"Sure, Howard. Sorry. I only wanted to be a good FBI agent. Sorry I blew it."

Nick turned and went to his car. He was feeling woozy. He thought he might be sick. Hap was standing there, too.

"Nick, let me drive you. I don't think you're in any shape to drive. I think it's a little postaction stress syndrome kicking in."

"I just got fired, Hap."

"I know, Nick. I'm real sorry."

"Can you get me to the airport? After I shower, I mean?"

"Sure. Nothing going on here but fine-combing the ruins. And waiting for the coroner's preliminary report."

They didn't talk much on the way back to the motel. Nick showered quickly, threw his clothes into a bag, and was ready to hit the drive to Little Rock in twenty minutes. He actually fell asleep on the way. As they were heading toward the airport entrance—there was a 5:45 to New Orleans—Hap awakened him.

He slept on the flight back too, and arrived around seven. The airport was almost deserted and there was no one, of course, to meet him. He walked down its empty corridors to the street and took a cab home. It cost him nineteen dollars.

There was nothing at home. He felt the emptiness without Myra keenly. He tried not to feel terribly sorry for himself, because he still had his youth, or at least a little of it, and he knew he was well liked and had it in him to be a good police officer, though possibly not at the federal level.

Just not cut out for the big leagues, he thought, morosely. He got himself a beer from the refrigerator and drank it while he watched CNN, but it didn't taste like much.

On the TV, it was the same stuff, and they even had the dog's body being removed from the grave by the two black men. There was a close-up of its body bag, half-deflated, that he had carried from the morgue to the truck that strange, mad day. Hard to believe it was only forty-eight hours ago. It seemed to belong to some other geological era.

"And now this," said the CNN anchorman, a stern, commanding black man who would have looked comfortable on the bridge of a destroyer. "FBI forensic technicians have confirmed from dental records the identity of the body found in the ruins of Aurora Baptist, near Blue Eye, Arkansas, as that of Bob Lee Swagger, the Marine hero who allegedly shot at the president of the United States and killed the archbishop of El

Salvador and has been for five weeks the most wanted man in America. The cause of death was a self-administered gunshot wound through the roof of the mouth and into the brain as the flames closed in."

So, Nick thought, you put the gun muzzle in your mouth and pulled the trigger.

It was fitting that no man had brought Bob the Nailer down but himself, by his own hand, sealing his secrets off forever.

"Well," Nick said to nobody in the empty room except the clock, the anchorman, and the can of beer, "we put him away. Hooray for us."

Julie Fenn held herself tight and somehow got through the day. There was still a wisp of a hope or a prayer or *something,* some little thing. She drove home through the fiery radiance of the Arizona twilight clinging to it. But that night came the evidence of the dental report, and that was the end. That was that.

And somehow she got through the next day, too. It wasn't easy but she was a strong woman and she had plenty of years of practice holding things in. But enough was enough. She called in the next day and said she was having family difficulties and would have to have a day or so off. Dr. Martin said that was fine, he understood, though under his voice there was a layer that said he didn't. She couldn't care. Dr. Martin was twenty-six; he needed Julie a lot more than Julie needed him. Who would run the clinic if she didn't?

So she sat in her trailer and tried to cry. She found she could not cry. In some way or other, she had moved beyond crying. She could not weep and she could not feel relief. It had always been possible, from that first second the knock on the door had come and she'd pulled it open to see a man who'd haunted her dreams, whom she'd loved and hated through twenty long years of nights, that her whole life could be pulled apart. She could have been arrested for being an accessory after the fact or something like that; at the very least there'd be that horrible kind of modern fame where every creep in the world thinks he owns you and has a right to your inner life, and you see the same bad picture of yourself in a thousand newspapers, and none of the people trying to talk to you or take your picture give a real damn about you. You're just that week's meat.

But to know that wouldn't happen now, that dead men tell nothing and indict no witnesses, offered no solace at all. She just wanted Bob, her Henry Thoreau with a rifle, the funny way he had said, "He went and lived by himself too." It had cracked her up, that little proud squeak of knowledge about a New England transcendentalist from the world's best manhunter.

So nice to have a man around the house.

She turned on the television, because the news was on. NBC. Tom Brokaw looked earnest and troubled tonight. He was telling Bob's story for the umpteenth time, the tragic story of the Marine hero who was the son of a Marine hero and had gone tragically astray in his bitterness, and yet who had died with such quixotic grandeur that a little part of everybody had to admire him. It was the dog angle that would propel Bob to incredible national celebrity, if he could be, in his current state as America's most wanted man, even more celebrated.

"And so," Brokaw concluded, the TV cheap irony tone coming into his syrupy voice, "a man of violence who allegedly killed a bishop has died to commit an innocent animal to a final act of dignity."

Other stories came on; dog lovers had gathered a petition to make certain the dog was buried where Bob had meant to bury it. There was an interview with some general in the Salvadoran army, taking pleasure that the archbishop's murderer had paid the ultimate price but somewhat upset that he was acquiring such a patina of sainthood for his kindness to a dead animal when he'd actually killed the animal himself and then the archbishop. He was asked about the Panther Battalion massacre and he said they were making good progress on that investigation.

Next, NBC flashed to Blue Eye and showed an interview with Sam Vincent, a lawyer, and he wondered why the FBI and the state police had to go and kill Bob, since no one had proved in a court of law that Bob was guilty. But the reporter kept wanting to get back to the dog, the dog, the dog, how much Bob had loved the dog.

"Oh," said Sam, finally, "yep, I s'pose he did, but Bob had a damn practical streak and if the dog were dead, I can't for the life of me figger out why he went and did such a fool thing."

The old man blinked into the camera.

"He weren't no fool," said Sam Vincent, "and you can put that in the damn bank." Then he spat into the dirt and walked away.

It puzzled her too, and she turned it over in her head that night, trying to make sense of it. It was a sleepless night. Once, she drifted off, and came awake an hour later in the dark with her head racing with memories.

"Bob? Bob Lee?" she called into the darkness. There was no response. She heard the ticking, the random noise, the sound of a car on the road, and far off in the desert, the cry of a coyote. But there was nothing else. Or was there? She felt something, a presence, or maybe just a sense of being watched. She shivered, and reached under the bed to the Smith & Wesson .32 camp gun, but nothing came of the feeling that night.

Nick sat in front of the tube the whole damned evening, drinking more and seeing nothing. Around eleven, not drunk but slightly blurry, he ambled to bed. That night he had a dream, involving Bob Lee Swagger and Myra and somehow also that terrifying crash down the mountainside, with the green branches beating at the windshield until the windshield went. Then he saw the door post as it came forward and hit him in the skull.

Myra! he screamed in his dream, Myra, I didn't mean it.

When he got out of the cab and reached for his little .38, he saw Bob Lee Swagger and Myra dancing on the green grass. Myra was barefoot and lively as a country tune. Her whole face radiated pleasure.

Stop or I'll shoot, he screamed, the little pistol tight in his big hand. Then he fired. In the dream he fired just as surely as in real life he had not, and Myra's back spurted black blood and she went down, crying, Nick, you killed my spine, you killed my spine. And Howdy Duty was there telling him what a terrible job he'd done, how he'd wrecked his career. And Bob was dancing away into the flames.

Nick sat up, blinking. He was covered with sweat. Someone was screaming. It was himself.

After that, he had trouble getting back to sleep, though he may have dozed some around dawn. He finally awakened for good about eight-thirty in the morning, dissociated and hung over. His head ached; he needed a shave. This was life after the Bureau. Another pointless day stretched before him. He had no will to go on, but he decided out of habit to shower and have a cup of coffee. Then he put on a summer-weight suit and a white shirt, just as if he were going to the office.

I will go to the office, he decided. He had a desk to clear out, farewells to be said, and there was some paperwork to be attended to. It was the one place that made him happy and though the happiness it gave him now was phony, he realized, he could not deny it. All right, I'll go, he thought. Have to anyway, sooner or later. Might as well be now.

Nick drove downtown and parked in the usual lot and went upstairs by the usual elevator. God, it was so familiar. He couldn't believe he'd never do this again. He walked in, through the foyer and the door marked GOV'T EMPLOYEES ONLY and down the corridor. In all the offices people were already busy. Clerks filed or worked at computer terminals, secretaries typed, special agents bustled about importantly. Nick knew the rhythms of the place, knew exactly what the men's room smelled like, and which of the three people who tended the coffee machine made the best coffee, and when the supervisory agent would be in and how long he took for lunch and what happened when he came in and what happened when he did not, and who was testifying in court that week and who was not. He knew the fastest way out; he knew where the rifles and the M-16's were stored for SWAT usage; he knew who was designated SWAT team leader on the Reactive Team that week (it was a rotating duty); he knew who was new to the office and who was due to be shuffled soon, and who was producing and who wasn't and—subtly different—who was thought to be producing but actually wasn't.

And he loved every damn bit of it.

He entered the big room where the agents sat at their desks. In a police station it would have been called a Squad Room, but here it was simply known as the bull pen. It was surprisingly empty today, because of course Howdy Duty had drawn primarily on New Orleans agents to staff the big stalk in Arkansas. Nick went to his desk, took his key out and opened it.

On a normal day, this was when he'd take off his

pistol and put it in the upper-right drawer. Today he had no pistol.

Instead, he opened the big central drawer. So little to show. A few files from cases he'd vetted for others, a few pencils, a few notepads. That was it. It was so empty.

Ahead of him, tacked on the burlap of the cubicle wall, was a picture of Myra, taken five years ago. It was an extreme close-up and she was smiling in the sunlight. You couldn't see her disability. She looked like a bright, pretty young woman who had her whole life ahead of her.

On the desk itself was the *Annotated Federal Code* and the huge green *Federal Bureau of Investigation Regulations and Procedures,* plus assorted carbonized forms for reporting incidents, for logging investigative reports, for filing for warrants, and a small pile of pink message slips, which, riffled through quickly, revealed nothing at all worth noting.

"Nick?"

He looked up. It was a guy named Fred Sandford, another special agent. Nick didn't know him well; he hadn't made the trip to Arkansas.

"Hi ya, Fred."

"Hey, just wanted to say, was real sorry to hear how it went down out there for you. I'm sure there was nothing you could do."

"I just did my best," he said, "and it didn't quite pan out."

"Wanted to tell you, my brother is a police chief in Red River, Idaho. You always were a good detective, Nick. I could give him a call. Maybe he's looking for someone."

"Ah, thanks. I'm not sure at this point I'm going to stick with law enforcement. Too much hassle for too little satisfaction and too little money."

"Sure. Got you. If you change your mind—"

"I appreciate it, Fred, really I do. I'm thinking about going back to school, getting my master's, and maybe taking up teaching. Something nice and quiet."

"Sure, whatever you say."

With that, he was alone again. He took the picture off the wall, retrieved his abortive LANZMAN file, hoping that one last scan might reveal a pattern where nothing else had. But it was another big zero. The reason why that poor guy was whacked in that motel room near the airport so horribly all that time ago would remain completely unknown, RamDyne or no RamDyne. Somebody else got away with it. Too bad. You were trying to reach me, and somebody put a big finger on you with about a million bucks worth of electronic gear, and it's just going to fall through the cracks, like seventy-one percent of the crimes in this country, and there isn't a damn thing I can do about it.

Hap's secretary, an officious woman named Doris Drabney, came by next. There was no sympathy in her eyes or face, but then there was no sanctimony either. There was simply nothing. "You've got some paperwork to sign," she said.

In spite of himself, Nick was slightly frightened by her.

"You mean about the, um—"

"The suspension, yes. Please stop by my desk on the way out." And she turned and left.

Nick watched her march off. There was something rigid and jointless in the way she moved. She was one of those people who'd just let the Bureau sink into her life until it filled her whole personality. Until it became her personality. She was a lifer in the worst possible way, so gone in the life no other was even possible.

Well, he thought, that won't happen to me. God knows what will, but that won't.

And suddenly he was out of things to do.

He looked down at his meager cardboard box of belongings. Then he looked around for a friend, a colleague, someone to embrace or to give him a look or to signify that he was still loved, or, hell, that he was still *alive.* But everywhere in the office the other agents seemed preoccupied. A kind of hush had fallen over them.

Yeah, sure, I get it, he thought.

He went to find Doris Drabney, sitting stiffly at her desk.

"Yes, yes, you've got, let's see, you've got to sign *this* and *this* and . . . oh, yes, *this.*"

Numbly he signed the forms. One had to do with his Government Credit Union account, one had to do with his GEICO insurance policy, which would cease to be in effect thirty days from today, and one required a formal acknowledgment that he was being placed on indefinite leave without pay pending a meeting of the review board in re his case blah blah blah.

"Is that it?"

"That's it. You'll be notified of the hearing."

I'm history, he thought.

"And your last paycheck is being held until you return the pistol."

"What?"

"Nick, that Smith & Wesson Model 1076 you lost during the incident of the speech. That was government property. Remember, you filed a lost-line-of-duty item report. And it was turned down? I sent the response to you in Arkansas. You're being billed for the pistol. It's four hundred fifty-five dollars."

He just looked at her.

It's probably an ingot mulched in with Bob Swagger's bones, he thought. Or somewhere in a soggy swamp, or in some ocean somewhere, wherever Bob had been before he died.

He turned to leave.

"Oh, and you're supposed to see Sally Ellion in Records, too."

Ach! Sally! She was a slight, pretty, very Southern girl with what people all called "personality"; she'd had a hundred boyfriends in her time, and was always dumping one for another and then the new one. He'd always liked her somehow, even if she scared him a little bit. What on earth could she want now?

"What for?"

"I haven't the slightest."

So, it came down to this last thing. He went to find the young woman, who of course was on break, and had to wait for half an hour feeling stupid and preposterous until she came back from the cafeteria. At last she hove into sight, beaming pep, with a small roll in her shoulders as she walked. She'd probably had a date every night in her life, Nick thought; her Saturday nights were one long festival. She probably dated quarterbacks and shortstops. Looking at her, he sank a bit deeper into his depression.

"Hi, uh, Sally, uh, someone said—"

"Nick, hi! Did I keep you waiting? Gosh, I'm sorry. Those fingerprint techs; they just wouldn't let me get out of the cafeteria."

Great. He'd been hung up here like a fish on a line, Howard's newest trophy, for the office to admire, while those lazy clowns were trying to make time with Sal.

"Well, anyway," she went on. "I have this thing for you. It just came in today. Where have you been? I called out to Arkansas yesterday and they said you'd gone, but you didn't check in last night."

"Uh, I sort of awarded myself a night off. You know, a little R and R, for a job well done."

"Shhhhh," she said. "Don't say that out loud. Someone might hear you and not realize you were joking."

"I'm beyond hurt at this point. Anyway, what's up, I really have to—"

"Well, it's only partially official. I wanted to say something to you. I just wanted to tell you how much I admired what you did with your wife. How you stuck with her. I think that's neat. Not many men would have done such a thing."

"Oh," said Nick, taken aback. "Oh, well, it seemed like the kind of thing you sort of had to do, that's all. You know, I don't like to quit on things. I like to stick with them. That's all. Stubborn. Stupid, but stubborn, just like a mule."

She laughed.

"Well," she said, "that's neat. Not many like that. Lots of people just quit on you."

"Ummm," Nick grunted, having run into a conversational brick wall and splatted against it. "Yeah. Ummm."

"*Anyhow,*" she said, after a minute when it became obvious first of all that she wanted him to say something like, "Gee, why don't we go out for lunch or a drink sometime?" and second of all that he didn't begin to possess the vocabulary for such a thing, "*anyhow,* I thought you might want to know, it came."

Her eyes were bright and sweet. She was so pretty. It angered him that she should be so pretty on the last day of his career and she was just prattling on about things he didn't understand.

Nick blinked.

"Huh?"

"You know. Don't you remember the last time I talked to you?"

He couldn't begin to put it together again in his head.

"You wanted that file from Washington, but they wouldn't send it because you weren't cleared."

He remembered asking her about it in the hallway at some point or other.

"Yeah?"

"Well, *I* put you in for the clearance."

"*You* put me in?" he asked, incredulously. "But that needs a supervisor's signature and, uh, I mean—"

"Oh, Mr. Utey signed it. He wasn't sure what it was, and anyway he was so busy I don't think he cared and you were his right-hand man and everything."

It suddenly occurred to him with a stupendous flash that Sally Ellion was so busy being the office's favorite girl that she hadn't caught on quite yet to the fact that he'd gotten the sack.

She smiled again.

"And you got it. The clearance."

"Uh huh," he said, not quite sure where this was going.

"And so they just authorized a printout. I just got it from the printing room."

She handed him a thick sheaf of computer-printed paper.

It was marked TOP SECRET/SENIOR SUPERVISORY PERSONNEL ONLY.

Nick looked at it.

It was the RamDyne file.

CHAPTER TWENTY-FOUR

Shreck, alone in his office now, was surprised how little elation he felt. It reminded him of the way it was when he came off a hill in Korea in 1953, when he was seventeen years old. Not relief, not guilt, just simple numbness. He knew it was classic postcombat stress syndrome; depletion, emotional and physical, and as you recharged you went into a kind of torpid state.

But it had only happened to him that one time in Korea, because he was so new to it. In all his other operations, as they wound into the triumph or bitterness but always survival, he'd felt incredibly lightened, charged, made whole again. This fucker Swagger had really gotten under his skin; a tough guy, a dangerous guy, just the sort of guy who could bring it all down.

When the phone call finally came, it was something of an anticlimax. Dobbler had managed to meet the Bureau contact without difficulty and was handed the actual forensic lab report, complete with X rays. From then on, Dobbler just babbled to Shreck, couldn't control himself, spoke too plainly, dithered and yammered too much. But the gist got through. The X rays checked. Everything was fine. Bob was dead. It was over.

Shreck felt some lightening of feeling, but not much. He was not a man of many pleasures; only duty and mission were pleasures. But this really was his finest triumph. He thought maybe he'd go shoot sporting clays this weekend. Maybe he'd buy a new car. But mainly he wanted to—

The secure phone rang.

He looked at it for a long second, before picking it up.

"Shreck."

It was Hugh Meachum.

"Colonel, we have a problem."

LANCER CLEARANCE NECESSARY

IF YOU ARE NOT LANCER CLEARED, IMMEDIATELY RETURN THIS FILE TO ITS JACKET, SECURE IT, AND RETURN IT TO ITS POINT OF ORIGIN. YOU MUST NOTIFY THE LANCER COMMITTEE IF YOU HAVE ENCOUNTERED THIS FILE IN AN UNAUTHORIZED METHOD.

Nick looked at it dumbly. In his years in the Bureau he'd bumped into a few strange commands, but he'd never hit this one before. He blinked, but the warning would not go away; there it was, big as life, all caps, booming out at him. He felt extremely guilty. Practically from birth, Nick had obeyed rules, signs, orders, directions, speed limits, legal technicalities, everything. Yet at the same time the illicit thrill of what he was about to do was giddy and sweet, even if it brought his breath from his lungs and made his head ache where he'd smashed it against the truck door.

He sat in his basement. It was well past nine, and after waiting all afternoon he'd at last come down the stairs, turned on the overhead light and settled into an old lawn chair. The air smelled of moisture and wood and oil. The bare bulb wobbled slightly. There was no other sound.

Lancer, he thought, taking one more deep breath.

Lancer? He knew that in their many years of uneasy operational coexistence, the Bureau and the Agency had many times bumbled into each other. And sometimes, under strict control (at least in theory) the Agency would do something that was technically in violation of the law; thus the Lancer Committee had to be that elite group in high Bureau quarters that was kept informed of these transgressions and made certain that no Bureau operatives moved forward aggressively to apprehend the perpetrator, thereby blowing an Agency scam or endangering Agency personnel.

That's what he guessed the Lancer Committee to be.

And as he looked at the early documents before him, he could see that the Lancer Committee had quite early on declared its power.

LANCER ADVISES NO FURTHER ACTION IN THIS MATTER. NATIONAL SECURITY INTERESTS ARE AT STAKE (REFER TO ANNEX B) was one of the first such decrees, dating from 1964, when agents in Los Angeles had uncovered a warehouse full of fifteen hundred Armalite rifles headed for the presidential guard of the then obscure country of South Vietnam. Perusing the material, Nick saw that the warehouse was owned by something called RamDyne Security, with an address in Miami. He whistled. He knew the Armalite was the early name for the rifle that was later called the M-16 when it was adopted by the United States Army and Marine Corps. Whoever could get Armalites in such numbers before they were officially adopted a) knew they were going to be adopted and b) put some big money up front. Who would that be? Only one answer.

So that meant RamDyne was CIA.

Or did it?

As he paged through the documents, LANCER ADVISES NO FURTHER ACTION IN THIS MATTER. NATIONAL SECURITY IS AT STAKE (REFER TO ANNEX B) suddenly began happening all over the place. RamDyne Security and Lancer Committee had a very busy time of it in the late sixties and early seventies; the imprimatur was showing up on Air America shipments from Bangkok to Manila—and not for envelopes, Nick guessed. RamDyne Security had a contract to import Swedish K's to something called the Special Operations Group—SOG—up near the Laotian border. RamDyne Security bought ten thousand surplus M-1 carbines from the Republic of Taiwan and shipped them to Phnom Penh, Cambodia, for unspecified use. RamDyne Security imported two thousand pairs of Hiatt's handcuffs to the Saigon police force. RamDyne Security shipped fifty obsolete T-28 trainers to the Cambodian Air Force. RamDyne grew and grew and prospered as the war expanded.

But by the mid to late seventies, the action had moved elsewhere. Riffling through the material, Nick was fascinated to see that RamDyne had connections in the Middle East. For example it served as a conduit for the shorty M-16's that showed up in the hands of Israeli commandos at Entebbe and for much of the sophisticated electronics that was the specialty of the Israeli air force.

Who are they? Nick wondered. Because he saw at a

glance that although just about everything that RamDyne did was conceived in such a way as to advance American interests, it also involved large sums of money for equipment, training or expertise in . . .

. . . in war?

Well, not exactly. What RamDyne sold was something that, although it was the essence of war, wasn't war itself, and it certainly wasn't standard military doctrine. No, it was something different, a purer distillation of a government's role on earth.

RamDyne sold force.

That was it: guns, torture, interrogation, police methods, financial transfers, avionics, whatever . . . always, force. The way in which an unpopular government stays in power or a shaky one consolidates its power or an isolated one fights off enemies several times its size. RamDyne had no neurosis about the use of force.

But who was RamDyne? It couldn't quite be the Agency. Too much money, too shady. Nick could see how RamDyne could help the Agency in its aims, without ever truly becoming the Agency; there would be a strange relationship between them. One would feed on the other. But who was RamDyne?

The only clue Lancer ever offered was tantalizing: RAMDYNE INFO CONTAINED IN ANNEX B, Lancer told one Bureau request, WHICH IS MOST TOP SECRET AND FOR DISPERSAL ON A NEEDTOKNOW BASIS ONLY.

Annex B again, thought Nick. Damn, would I like to get my hands on Annex B.

RamDyne began to move into Central America in the early eighties.

LANCER ADVISES NO FURTHER ACTION IN THIS MATTER. NATIONAL SECURITY IS AT STAKE (REFER TO ANNEX B). It appeared on a shipment of fléchette munitions on the way to Guatemala City, presumably for use by Contras in the war against the Sandinistas. A crate full of fléchette bombs had accidentally broken open at Kennedy Airport in New York. It was at that time illegal to export fléchette munitions, as they were one of the best-kept secrets of the war: the plastic darts didn't show up on X rays, so doctors couldn't operate to remove the shrapnel, so the wounded didn't heal, so the Sandinista medical infrastructure was theoretically stressed out. The box, under the guise of Medical Shipments, was being exported by RamDyne Security.

Next was a shipment of interrogation electrodes, cattle prods, whips, truncheons, and PR-24 batons for Pakistan; but Customs had intercepted the material in New York and alerted the Bureau.

LANCER ADVISES NO FURTHER ACTION IN THIS MATTER. NATIONAL SECURITY IS AT STAKE (REFER TO ANNEX B).

The shipment was being sent by RamDyne Security of St. Paul, Minnesota.

Nick Memphis turned the page. And then he came up against RamDyne at its classic and at last he understood.

It was RamDyne's involvement with the elite hunter battalion of the Salvadoran airborne rangers nicknamed *Los Gatos Negros.*

And so it was that Nick Memphis saw what RamDyne was selling. It was, he realized, something more than force; or if it had just been force in the beginning, it had transmuted into something else.

He read about Panther Battalion, and he began to cry.

It was a fine, gay day. Dobbler hadn't been out in ages, in decades. He'd been a hermit, a vampire living only on artificial light and information.

But now he was outside for the first time since the events in New Orleans, and the sky was filled with woolly clouds and an orange smear of sun settled toward the horizon. It was the magic hour, just before full twilight, when perfect clarity washes the world clean of its blemishes.

The doctor breathed deeply, enjoying the sweetness in the air. He let the sun caress him. He was walking along the lip of bank that flanks the Jefferson Memorial in Washington, D.C.; around him, like soldiers at parade rest, a thousand Japanese cherry trees stood heavy with leaf. The water was deep gray and calm; in the distance he could see the Lincoln Memorial, another temple to a dead president; and in another direction, the Washington Monument, that blank white spire.

But Dobbler was not thinking of dead presidents and their Roman temples or obelisks, nor of cherry trees. He was not thinking of the setting sun, or the pulsating traffic, or anything at all like that, though he enjoyed them all. He was thinking of teeth.

Glorious, glorious teeth. Teeth that never lie. That cannot lie. That are incapable of deceit.

For he had them now in his briefcase and would not let them go. He had survived.

The teeth were not actually in the briefcase, of course; what lay inside were Bob Swagger's dental X rays, taken from his dentist in Blue Eye, Arkansas, and forensic X rays of the blackened jaws found in the ashes of the Aurora Baptist Church, as taken by the sublimely gifted technicians of the Federal Bureau of Investigation crime lab in Washington, D.C., not a mile as the crow flew from where Dobbler now trod.

But neither the doctor nor Colonel Shreck had trusted the technicians. They had waited patiently until the right time and then the colonel made one of his magic phone calls to someone—Dobbler didn't even want to know who—and Dobbler went to Washington. He'd just gotten the two sets of X rays, and a more formal examination awaited them back at RamDyne. But he couldn't wait; he'd stolen into a public men's room, and pressed the two plastic membranes against the fluorescent lights. One by one he had chalked off the similarities. Yes, yes, there were three fillings on the left-hand side, in the second molar, the canine and the incisor. Yes, the first took the rough configuration of a star; the second was smaller, shaped roughly like an hourglass; and the third looked like the map of Sicily. Then there was the same slightly collapsed left lower jaw, where three teeth, for some unknown architectural reason, had sadly collapsed inward just a bit, with the middle one slightly twisted.

Those were the major parallels and he could see about a thousand minor ones. In fact, you could lay one X ray over the other, and though the scale was slightly off, it was obvious that the same mouth had been photographed.

That was it. A man may lie to his psychiatrist, his doctor, his wife, his employer, to God and to Mom, but his teeth tell all; they cannot lie. They yield all secrets. They confess. They are unambiguous.

So Dobbler had called Colonel Shreck, and then wandered across the mall and over to the tidal basin; it was time to enjoy life, which suddenly seemed mud-luscious with possibility. The whole world beckoned, offering its pleasures to Dr. Dobbler. He was purely, sheerly *happy*.

"Dr. Dobbler!"

Dobbler turned at his name, stunned that anyone knew him, and saw only a gray sedan, unremarkable, and in it a man who was also unremarkable but tough and coplike, whom he recognized from RamDyne.

"Dr. Dobbler. Colonel Shreck sent us. They need you."

"But—" Dobbler raised his briefcase as if to protest and ward them off. See, it's in here, he wanted to say, it's over, the evidence that it's over, finally, is in here.

"We got some big problems," said the man, and Dobbler read fear in his eyes.

It was technically the Fourth Battalion (Air-Ranger) of the First Brigade (Air-Ranger) of the elite Acatatl Division—but everybody called it Panther Battalion.

Nick read on. In April of 1991, the unit, some 250 men, a tough, blooded, jungle-warfare-center-trained elite of the Salvadoran Armed Forces, had been pulled from front-line antiguerrilla duty in the mountains for an intensive course in psychological warfare techniques. Because at the time the press was especially suspicious of the president's wild popularity in the wake of the Persian Gulf War, it was being extremely vigilant and cynical about American military aid to foreign countries; so the contract couldn't be taken on by certified American military or CIA special operations people. Through an elaborate scheme of diverted funds, this RamDyne outfit had gotten the contract. And for a month in an isolated jungle area, RamDyne operatives, veterans of some of the gaudiest special operations in history, had schooled the young Latinos in interrogation techniques, population control, intelligence gathering, ambush and counterambush, sniping and countersniping, a whole crash course in the dirty nitty-gritty of low-intensity warfare.

But there was a weird chemistry loose in that encampment.

"Unconfirmed reports insist," read the FBI investigation, which was forwarded to the Senate Intelligence Committee but never put on the record as being too sensitive, "that American trainers exhorted these young soldiers with voodoo rituals, thought-control processes and animal sacrifices that went well beyond the range of normal professional military training."

The file identified several of the trainers, and as Nick

gazed at the abstracted dossiers, he saw nothing that surprised him. The trainers were drawn from the various American elite units that had fought secret battles all around the world since the war in Vietnam. The honcho appeared to be an ex–Green Beret lieutenant colonel named Raymond Shreck, of Pottstown, Pennsylvania, a heavily decorated veteran of Korea, where he had been the youngest master sergeant in the United States Army at nineteen, an early Green Beret who'd helped train the Bay of Pigs volunteers in the early sixties when he was a young major, and a heavy-action three-tour 'Nam vet until, in 1968, he'd been court-martialed for torturing suspected Viet Cong agents. Somehow the Agency had taken care of him; he joined RamDyne the next year. His number-one man was Master Sergeant John D. ("Jack") ("Payne-O") Payne, of New York, New York, a former special forces noncommissioned officer, also with an extraordinary combat record in Vietnam. After the war, however, he had trouble readjusting to duties, was nabbed in an elaborate scheme to defraud the PX out of several thousand dollars, and, in lieu of a jail sentence and a dishonorable discharge, took an early retirement in 1978.

I'll bet you're a couple of tough pricks, thought Nick.

So maybe Payne and Shreck, pissed off the way their careers had gone belly-up, with their extraordinary records in combat and their flat-out willingness to go all the way were the true authors of what happened next. But there were other authors, as well. There was the increasingly hysterical right-wing fervor of the government of El Salvador; there was a stunning leftist victory, where a battalion of government troops had gone to sleep without putting out perimeter security and got badly shot up the next morning, losing twenty-eight men, all of them in front of American network news cameras; there was the pressure from Washington for results, results, results, something to show that American policy was working; and there was the anger, the fear, the bravado of Panther Battalion itself.

On June 8, 1991, Panther Battalion was airlifted from its secret mountain training camp into Ocalupo Valley, three hundred miles away, to conduct operations against a well-established guerrilla infrastructure. As the Panthers—so called because of their black and green striped jungle fatigues and their black berets—moved into the village of Cuembo, they came under sporadic sniper fire from a tree line flanking the village. The commander, Brigadier General Esteban Garcia de Rujijo, sent a reconnaissance squad into the village. Moving through the village square, the recon squad was caught in a clever crossfire. Two automatic weapons killed every single man. The guerrillas then mutilated the corpses and moved out.

It was the village of Cuembo that felt the full rage of Panther Battalion. Later (but unconfirmed) reports insisted that American training officers accompanied Panther Battalion into Cuembo but this was never proved. What is beyond dispute is that within the space of two hours on the afternoon of June 9, 1991, Panther Battalion killed over two hundred men, women and children. They were herded to the banks of the Sampul River, and there machine-gunned by the Panthers' automatic weapons. Dead children floated in the Sampul for days.

He made a face, and blinked, realizing that either out of rage or horror he'd begun to weep.

Shaking, he turned to the last page. No, it wasn't the famous Annex B, which was presumably locked up somewhere in the National Security Office or the Pentagon or FBI headquarters or out at Langley. But it was something quite interesting nevertheless.

It was an export order for an Electrotek AMSAT LC-L5400 series Directional Electronic Intercept Vehicle, on consignment to Salvadoran Military Intelligence, cleared by Customs, as delivered by RamDyne.

It was the kind of thing that could enable men in it to listen to a desperate man in a hotel room call FBI headquarters in New Orleans and ask for one Nick Memphis, and then go in and hack him to death with axes.

LANCER ADVISES NO FURTHER ACTION, said the stamp. NATIONAL SECURITY IS AT STAKE (REFER TO ANNEX B).

It was a war party.

Shreck, the hard-looking black man who was called Morgan State, and the serious Hatcher were waiting for him.

"Colonel Shreck, I—"

"Listen to me, Dobbler. I need a fast assessment. Try not to get this one wrong."

Shreck's face was hooded and taut; he looked like the statue of a violent medieval German knight in the armor room of the Metropolitan Museum of Art that had briefly fascinated Dobbler when he was a child.

"Just before Swagger was killed, he spent some time in that truck with an FBI agent. Now, what I have to know, would he have talked? As we break the incident down, they were not together more than four minutes, all of it highly stressed. Is it possible that during that period of time, Swagger could have told the agent something, convinced him of certain things?"

"Ah—" said Dobbler, stalling for time.

But then, "No. No, it's not probable. Swagger was a private, taciturn man, we saw it here. And he couldn't have trusted anyone and he couldn't have known who it was he'd have picked up. No, it's not likely."

"Possibly he passed him something," said Morgan State.

"But Colonel Shreck, there was no direct link to us.

We operated under dummy institutions, and left no trail. What could Swagger have known?"

The colonel nodded imperceptibly.

"May I ask what's happening?" Dobbler said.

"Tell him," Shreck said to Hatcher.

"We've learned from a friend that an FBI special agent named Nicholas Memphis—the agent Swagger kidnapped—has requested access to the FBI's RamDyne file. It's exactly the sort of thing that Lancer is supposed to protect us from. And somehow—stupidly, incredibly, by one of those bureaucratic screwups that happen, the transmission was authorized. He has the file. He knew Swagger and he has the file."

"Good lord," said Dobbler, a cold stab of fear coming into him. "Could he go to the press? Or to a politician? Or to—"

"It doesn't matter," said Shreck impatiently, turning to Morgan State. "Get Payne. Tell him we want this Memphis taken, interrogated, and all his secrets removed. Then Payne can kill him."

CHAPTER TWENTY-FIVE

The phone was ringing. Nick stopped drying his breakfast dishes and went to pick it up.

"Yeah."

"Nick?"

"Uh, yeah?" The voice, a female's, had a familiar lilt to it.

"Nick, it's Sally Ellion in Rec—"

"Sure, hi, what's up?"

"Nick, you've got me in so much trouble." She was whispering.

"Oh. The file."

"I didn't know you were on suspension."

"Ah. Yeah, yeah, it was crummy of me not to tell you. I'm very sorry. It wasn't honest behavior. I just had this damn case I was really hot to clear. I thought . . . oh, it was so stupid, I thought in my time off I'd just be able to concentrate on it."

"Nick, I've got a directive to return that file by special courier instantly."

"Oh, Jesus. I hope you're not in any trouble."

"I have to have that file back. You weren't even supposed to leave the building with it."

"Yeah, but since I couldn't stay in the building, I couldn't read it there, could I? Anyway, Sally, I'm very sorry to have disappointed you. I'm done with it, I'll leave in ten minutes and have it back to you in an hour. Okay? And could this be our little secret, I mean, the fact that I actually looked at it?"

"Oh, yes. It *has* to be. I can't tell them you left the building with it. Please hurry."

"I'm on my way."

Nick showered quickly, and put on a gray suit. In a strange way it pleased him to have some mission in life, even if it was only to deliver the file.

He'd been turning over what he'd learned in his head. He remembered the strange message the man who may have been the Salvadoran secret policeman Eduardo Lanzman had crawled into the bathroom to leave for him. ROM DO was the message in the blood, in the split second before it was obliterated. Possibly the beginnings of the words *Romeo Dog,* which was early-sixties Army radio code for the letters *R* and *D* and the Bay of Pigs invasion force call sign in 1962? *R* and *D*. Ram and Dyne. RamDyne . . .

It was almost something. But it was still nothing. Why didn't he write RA DY, why ROM DO, what was there about the radio codes of the Bay of Pigs? If it *was* from the Bay of Pigs?

He shook his head, feeling an ache begin in it somewhere. He now believed that he had an indication—but no legally constituted evidence, another matter entirely

—that this RamDyne was in some way involved in the murder of Eduardo Lanzman and possibly the murder, therefore, of Archbishop Jorge Roberto Lopez. He knew he'd ventured into very hazy areas, the vaunted wilderness of mirrors, where it was possible to lose your bearings in a second, and become so riddled with paranoia that nothing made sense anymore. Everything in him told him to back off, it was none of his business.

But the idea . . . those guys running around on their own special mission. Who watched them? Who paid them? Shreck, Payne, the others? To whom did they give their accounts? To some Lancer Committee. Who founded them? Where did they come from in the year 1964, suddenly rich and influential enough to get the deal going with fifteen hundred Armalite rifles. Who were they?

Annex B would tell him.

I've got to get Annex B, he told himself.

But what the fuck is Annex B?

"There he goes," said Tommy Montoya in the van, "that's my little Nicky."

Jack Payne, watching through the scope as Nick Memphis walked from his little suburban house to his Dodge, and climbed in, just grunted.

"Take him now, Payne-O?" asked Tommy.

"No. They're expecting him. Let him return the fucking file, then we'll nail him on the way out. What I want is someone in his house. He's got to have a piece in there. If it ain't a piece, he'll have a kitchen knife or a razor or something. I want it lifted. We'll use it when we chill his bones out after our little chat."

"Jack, man, it's no sweat, I can do the house," said one of the other team members.

"Yeah, Pony, that's fine, you do it. We'll wait on you."

"You don't want to tail him?" asked Mr. Ed, the driver.

"Nah. Let Pony get into the house and pick out a nice toy. No prints now, Pony, you got that?"

"Sí, Jack, sure, got it."

"Okay, go to it, son."

Pony stepped out of the back of the Electrotek 5400 surveillance van parked a discreet distance down from Memphis's house. Jack watched him go. He was dressed like a workman. He went to the house, knocked on the door, then blandly went around back.

"He'll get in," said Edwards, always called Mr. Ed. "I seen him do locks. He's like a fucking genius with locks."

"Great," said Jack.

It was true. Pony was back in thirty minutes. His trophy was a little Parkerized Colt Agent.

Payne, wearing plastic gloves, popped it open and gently plucked one round out.

"Ooooo," he said, "Glaser safeties," looking at the blue-tipped bullet nested in the brass case and imagining the clusters of lead suspended like bunches of grapes inside the jacket. "These nasty suckers make instant spaghetti," he said.

"Oh, Nicky," said Tommy Montoya. "You in the shit now, my friend."

"Hi, I—"

"Shhhhhh!" she whispered, her small pretty face knitting in anger. "Put it there," she commanded in the same conspiratorial whisper.

"Yeah, sure."

He set the box with the RamDyne file on her desk and backed away. She didn't look at it directly. He just stood there and could feel the sense of furious betrayal radiating off her neck, which was all he could see.

"Sally, I'm—"

And finally she looked up.

Her face was compressed with pain. She was trying to show him how much he'd hurt her. Hurt her? He didn't even know her! The abrupt envelope of intimacy somewhat befuddled him. It occurred to him suddenly that this pretty, idiotic girl conceived herself as being in love with him, one of those crush things, nurtured from afar down through the months. He could not have begun to engineer such a turn of events and now that it was here, it embarrassed him; he felt as if he'd trounced on a fragile secret thing of hers. He felt unworthy. But also irritated. Hey, I never knew I meant anything to you, do you see?

"Did you have any trouble?" she finally asked. "I mean, getting back into the building?"

"No. No, you know it's funny, even though I don't have an ID or anything, they just let me back in. You know, what's his name, Paul on security, he just waved mildly, like he has every day for the past four years. I guess some people didn't get the word."

"*I'll* say."

He let the silence sit between them for a while, trying to figure out how to deflate it.

"I'm sorry," he finally said. "I should have told you. This case was tantalizing me, though. It had nothing to do with my screwups of the last two months. I just hated to let the goddamn thing die, even if the career was shot. You handed me the damned file. I just didn't have the strength to walk away from it."

She swallowed.

"I'm sorry for what they're doing to you. I'm sure it's not your fault."

"Ahh, it is. I thought I was so smart, and I just kept blowing it. Look, I have to get out of here before I get you in any trouble. You'll be okay?"

"I think so. As long as I get it back to them by tomorrow. And I have to sign a form saying it never left the office."

"So you have to lie for me?"

"Yes."

"See, I'm great luck for women. Look, Sally, it was a crummy thing to do. I apologize. Could I—I don't know, make it up? Would you like me to buy you dinner or something?"

"I have a date tonight."

"Sure, I understand. Okay, I'm sorry again, now I'll get out of—"

"I don't have one tomorrow night."

"Oh. Uh, well, then. Um, can I pick you up in front of the building here at, say, six? Maybe we'll go down to the Quarter and get oysters before it fills up with tourists."

"Six," she said. "And don't worry about the lying. It's no problem."

"Thanks, Sal. Thanks a lot."

It was a glorious day out. Nick walked through the tall buildings of downtown New Orleans. He had nothing to do, and nothing but time to fill. So task-oriented all his life, he suddenly felt buoyant. Exhilarated, he thought he might walk on down to the Quarter now, have a nice lunch, then head on back to the house and take a nap. He felt cured of his depression. He had a date with an attractive girl, he was still young enough. He knew people. He'd be all right. Hey, maybe this wouldn't suck so bad after all. He had enough money to get through another couple of weeks or so.

Live a little, Nick. Don't have to be a Feeb grind your whole life. Maybe Sally would find him attractive, maybe she wouldn't. If it happened, it happened. But a world had just opened up. Amazing how good a woman's smile can make you feel.

It was at this moment in his ruminations—he was lost in the shadows of the tall commercial buildings and jostled by the anonymous lunchtime crowds—that he heard his name called.

"Nicky! Hey, Nicky, Nicky!"

He turned to see his old snitch Tommy Montoya, broadcasting Latino animal magnetism, his neck swimming in gold chain.

"Tommy!" he called. "Tommy, damn, I'm glad to see you. Hey, I was going to call you. Hey, you got a moment? I got some stuff I want to ask you."

"Sure, Nicky, no problem, man."

Nick stepped toward Tommy and in an instant three other men were on him, crushing inward roughly.

"Hey, what the—"

They went for his arms. He thrashed, thought he caught one with an elbow in the face, but as they crunched in upon him, all their huge weight just pressing against him, there came the prick of a needle through his suit coat into his lower back, and suddenly his legs lost their purchase on the earth, he lurched forward through swirls of light, and had the vaguest idea of sleep and surrender while he knew he was falling. He seemed to fall for quite a while and had only the vaguest impression of a van pulling up.

Nick awoke in darkness on the dirty floor of the van. He could hear the sawing of crickets and somehow he sensed a fetid, overhanging jungle atmosphere.

He tried to sit up but handcuffs had him manacled. His head felt as if someone had hydraulically pumped six tons of plastic waste in through his nostrils.

"Payne-O, he's come to."

"Oh, great. Hi ya, Nicky, how ya feel? Man, that sodium pentothal hits like a fucking truck, don't it?"

"Who the fuck are you?"

"Just working stiffs, sonny. Get him up."

"Right, Payne-O."

The name *Payne-O.* It was so familiar.

Rough pairs of hands lifted Nick. A flashlight beam hit him in the eyes. His head throbbed. He could make out the shadows of four men.

"You know what we've been talking about? How fast you'd see things our way and cooperate with us. I'm of the opinion that a good scout like you would see the error of his ways and come clean. Tommy here says you're going to be a stubborn motherfucker, giving us grief the whole night long. But you know what, Nick? It don't matter. We got plenty of time and no other place to be. And remember this: everybody always talks. Nobody's a hero."

"Tommy's a piece of shit."

"Nicky, I always liked you."

"You piece of shit!" Nick yelled.

"Oh, Nick's a tough boy, ain't he," said the heavyset, smaller man. Nick could see a tapestry of blue ink embossed on his thick arms.

He remembered the RamDyne file. *Payne-O.*

"You're Payne, right? The Green Beret. You were at the massacre on the Sampul River. Man, you must be real proud of yourself, you piece of shit."

"Oh, Nick, Nick, Nick. That was a wonderful job of work. We killed two hundred communists that day, so that fat assholes like you could rest in your fat little country, not a thought in their heads." He laughed an awful laugh. "Nick, that's what we do. You know, that's our job."

"Payne-O, you oughtn't to tell him—"

"Oh, we can trust Nick with all our secrets, can't we, Nick? Nick's one of the good scouts, right?"

"Fuck you, Payne," said Nick, liberated by the drunken freedom of the drug still in his system. "You let me out of these cuffs, man, I'll tear your fucking heart out. Your specialty is machine-gunning kids. I read the file. Let me tell you, motherfucker, I'd like to match you against an FBI SWAT team instead of women and kids in a river. We'd teach you something you didn't know about rock and roll, motherfucker." Nick was really screaming.

Payne laughed. Tommy laughed.

Nick looked beyond him and saw the darkness and the stillness of the Louisiana bayou. God knew where they were. Miles and miles beyond civilization. There was no help or mercy. He saw his own car parked just outside. He knew what that meant. It meant they would kill him in some way made to approximate a suicide and the car had to be there to explain how he'd gotten out there.

"Now, Nick, this can go hard or it can go easy. What's it going to be?"

"Either way it's fucking curtains for me, sucker."

"Not necessarily," said Tommy. "When we make you see how we're operating in National Security, you may even want to join us. We do what has to be done. You better be fucking glad somebody in this fucking country is. We're like the fucking Roman centurions, man. We keep the barbarians away. Isn't that right, Payne-O?"

"He's got that right."

"Shitasses like you always say you're doing something for the country. You're the barbarians, motherfucker."

Then Nick spat in Payne's face.

Something awesome and rhinolike flared in Payne; even in the darkness Nick could sense the surge of naked rage. At that second Payne wanted to rip his eyes out. But he regained his professional control, and wiped the phlegm off his forehead.

"Payne-O," said one of the other guys, "he ain't gonna volunteer any info."

Payne's eyes narrowed.

"Yeah, shit, you're right. That stretches it out. But it's fastest up front. So shoot him up."

Nick felt his jacket sleeve being shoved up.

"Oh, Nick, have we got a tongue loosener for you."

He felt the prick of a needle, its long slide into his vein, and the odd largeness as whatever was injected into him filled his veins.

"Okay, Nick, just relax, let it happen," Tommy said.

Nick tried to fight it.

"It's very sophisticated stuff. Phenobarbital-B, an advanced compound, state of the art for CIA interrogations. Go ahead, fight it. The more you fight, the more you talk."

Nick felt nothing. Then he felt everything. Lights were going on, then going off. He felt his will shredding. He felt it going away. In his weakness and terror, he yearned only to please.

"Now Nick," came the voice from very far away, "Nick, Nick, Nick. Tell us a story. Got the tape going, Pony?"

"It's on."

"Nick, how'd you first hear of RamDyne?"

Nick tried to find a way to resist, but the point of it seemed quite ridiculous. Why not give them what they wanted? Everybody did.

"I—I—"

"That's right. Go on."

"I was on surveillance with the Secret Service prior to Flashlight's visit. Um. One of their agents mentioned that RamDyne exported the big surveillance rigs to

Central American governments and I'd been looking for some way . . ."

And with that he was gone. He talked and talked and talked. He couldn't shut up. It just came out of him. It was like a purging. All the information he'd stored, all his doubts about Bob Lee Swagger's guilt, all his fears, his terror, worst of all, of his own inadequacy, it all came out of him. He talked for days, for years. In the end, he wore them out. He beat them by talking.

It was dawn. The crickets had shut up, even, he out-talked the crickets. Outside, the sun was rising, turning the day pale and green. Outside, Nick could see, everything was green. It was a wild driven craze of green, a dangerous green. They were near a river or a swamp; there were trees everywhere. The road was a dirt track. He was tired. He was so tired. Now all he wanted to do was rest.

But they had him up.

"I just want to sleep," he said.

"Nah. You want to go to the bathroom, right?" said Tommy.

"Nah, I wanna sleep."

"Shit. Walk him around, okay."

"You got it all, Payne-O?"

"Hey, can you think of anything I left out? This guy would sing the birdies out of the sky now."

"Ah, let me see. Let me check the list."

"It's all checked off. It's all on the list."

"Okay, you know the drill. Tommy, he's your buddy. You handle it. Pony, you stay with him. We'll leave you here. You wait till he pisses. Meanwhile, I gotta get the tape back ASAP."

"You got it, Payne-O."

Still crushed by the drug, Nick could at least put it together. He had no will and he had no pride.

"What are you gonna do to me?" he asked.

"What do you think, fuck?" said Payne. "You crossed the line. You been a-messin' where you shouldn't a been a-messin', and now the boots are gonna walk all over you. Someone's still got to do the hard thing, you little shit. You didn't have to find out about it. It was your choice. But now you're the hard thing, kid."

"National Security at Risk. Lancer Committee requests no further action be taken. Refer to Annex B," Nick quoted, but the irony was lost on them.

The two of them got into the surveillance van and drove away. Nick watched as the van disappeared down the dirt road, leaving a skirt of dust in the empty air.

Nick looked around. It was quite a beautiful place, actually. Completely deserted, but a kind of river basin, where the swamp momentarily yielded to a broad yellow-green meadow. A few hundred yards away the trees were dense and the land looked soupy. Here, in the fragrant morning, the land was solid. His car was parked over there, and another one.

Nick turned. Tommy and the other guy were eyeing him balefully. He twisted on his cuffs; they would not give. He could run, but to where? There was no place to run to.

"This is all wrong," he said. "I haven't done anything."

"It ain't about doing things wrong. It's about knowing too much. It's how these things work, man. It's how they always work," said Tommy. "You want a Coke or a cup of coffee? We have a thermos, Nicky."

"No."

"Nicky, I hate to tell you, you ain't no superman. You're gonna have to piss sooner or later. It's the nature of the beast."

"What's with the pissing?" he asked.

"You got too high a concentration of pheno-B in you.

You piss, it gets down to levels where it can't be spotted. See, that's why we got to wait. Sorry about it. Enjoy the morning. Just relax. It ain't gonna be nothing."

"Easy for you to say."

"Nicky, I seen a lot of guys check out. And my time will come soon enough. So let's just get through it as quickly and easily as possible. Don't cry or beg or nothing."

"Fuck you, I'm not going to cry or beg."

"Usually, they do," said Pony. "Usually they do."

Nick waited until his bladder betrayed him. It had to, finally. He fought it. But then Tommy said, "Hey, why put yourself through that? It ain't gonna matter much, really. I mean, is it?"

So finally he said it. "Have to go. Undo my hands."

"No can do, pard. You know that. Pony, undo his pants for him. Don't touch him. Let it be natural."

God, he hated them! It was the little touches of solicitousness, the softly remorseless way in which they did their job.

Pony, young and muscular and vaguely Latino, undid his pants. He was able to urinate himself dry, a last, long dying arc of life in the bright morning light in the blazing green of the swamp.

"Okay," he finally said. "Fuck you. Get it fucking over with."

They zipped and buttoned him up and led him down to the river. It lapped against the mud. A dragonfly flashed in the sun, big and prehistoric, like something liberated from a million or so years in amber. Nick was pushed to his knees.

He felt a belt being strapped around his waist. Then his left arm suddenly wore a new manacle, something attached to the belt. Jesus, they had *equipment* for this! That's how thought out it was, how perfect. They had a drill. They'd done it a thousand times!

Something was thrust into his hand; his fingers recognized the familiar contours of his Colt Agent. He tried to pull the trigger but it wouldn't budge; they had something wedged under it. He felt a binding of tape being wound about his knuckles, locking the small pistol in his grip.

"Hold his head back, Pony," Tommy said. Pony grabbed Nick by his hair, and pulled his head back. It fucking hurt.

"You motherfucking pricks," he screamed. "God, don't do this to me, don't do this to me. Tommy, Christ, please, I was your buddy."

"No, Nicky. You was just a fed, man. I can't cut you no slack. I got my job to do, man."

Nick heard a click behind him, and the first set of cuffs came away, freeing his right arm; but immediately it was ridden into submission by the full force and thrust of Tommy Montoya at his right.

"Okay, Nicky, don't fight me. Over in a second."

"Please don't do this," Nick begged.

"Okay, Nicky, up we go."

The man forced Nick's arm upward in an arc, curving the hand toward Nick's temple. His own hand was his enemy. Nick fought with all the strength he had, but the two men stood over him in postures that put the complete physics of leverage on their side. He saw his hand rise toward his head, guided by both muscular arms of his murderer. It was clear how it had to go; the arm would rise until the muzzle touched his temple; then Tommy would pull whatever he'd wedged behind the trigger—a RamDyne improvised suicide replication plug, part Number 4332 from the RamDyne Catalog, available to your friendly secret police force, no doubt—and crush Nick's trigger finger. The gun would blow Nick's brains out. He'd be found in the weeds by the river, his hand locked around his own pistol, his own car close at hand. There'd be no other physical evidence. They'd thought of everything. It was so fucking professional!

Nick strained against his own hand.

"Oh, Jesus, oh, Christ, don't do this."

"Just—ah, almost, there, don't fight it, goddammit, *don't* fight it!" And the gun rose and rose until at last Nick felt it touch the fragile shell of his temple. It felt like somebody pressing a penny against him. Through his strained peripheral vision he could see Tommy laboriously working on the gun, getting his own gloved finger half into the trigger guard, making ready to pull the plug.

"Watch yourself, Pony," Tommy said, warning his partner to steer clear of spatter, "I've almost got it, ah—"

Tommy Montoya's head exploded.

The sound of the report reached them.

Across the river a cloud of angry white birds rose as one in clattering agitation, rudely bumped from their perches by the rifle shot.

Nick, freed of half his constraint, turned to the other man, Pony, who stood still stupefied, not getting it.

But Nick got it.

"You're dead, motherfucker," he said, and at that precise instant the second bullet found Pony center chest, blowing through his heart. He pirouetted to the ground, the destroyed heart spurting blood as he fell.

The birds cawed and seethed in the air. The wind rose and whistled.

Nick sat back. His arm ached. He wanted to throw away the pistol, but couldn't, because it was taped to his hand. He figured the key would be somewhere on these two clowns.

He looked around and saw a man wading across the river. He was tall and rangy and tan, beardless now, in blue jeans and a tired blue denim shirt. He wore a baseball cap that said RAZORBACKS on it. He had harsh, gray, squirrel-shooter's eyes, unmirthful, focused, unafraid. His mouth was grim. He was quite tall.

He carried a fat-barreled Remington 700 rifle with about a yard of scope atop it. He carried it like a man who knew a little something about rifles.

He walked up to Nick.

"Mornin', Pork," said Bob the Nailer.

CHAPTER TWENTY-SIX

Nick looked at him with love-filled, moronic eyes.

"You're some sorry sight, sonny," said Bob. "Chained and trussed like a coon in a bag after a hunt. Those boys were about to have your patty-cake butt for breakfast." Nick watched him go over to each of the bodies, and search them for keys and papers.

He plucked two keys out of the late Tommy Montoya's pocket and came back over to take the cuffs off Nick.

"Goddamn," he said in disgust, "these boys even had a rig for phony suicide."

He stripped the tape from Nick's fist. Nick kept looking at him stupidly while he freed the little

Colt Agent. It fell to the earth. Swagger bent and picked it up.

"You're not going to shoot me with this little bitty gun, are you, Pork? I couldn't be sure the last time."

Dumbly, Nick shook his head.

"Here. Don't lose it. Now come on, boy, we've got to get these two pieces of human shit into the water, and more or less sanitize this area. You don't want the Louisiana State Police on your ass, do you? I sure don't, no sir. I've seen enough damn police to last me a century."

With that, he laid his rifle down on the hood of Nick's car and bent to one of the two bodies. As he bent, Nick saw that he had a Colt .45 automatic wedged cocked and locked into his jeans in a high hip-carry holster. The pistol was a custom job, with low mount sights and neoprene combat grips. It was the sort of pistol a man who has thought a lot about pistols might carry, as were the three spare magazines in Sparks mag holders on the other high hip.

Bob pulled each of the bodies to the lip of the river, and launched them with no ceremony at all. They sailed sluggishly out into the current, held afloat by the bladders of air trapped in their clothes; each man trailed a slick of blood.

"We're going to make some damn 'gators happy today, that's for sure," Bob said. "Now come on, boy, don't just sit there like a toad on a rock, get a move on!"

But Nick had lapsed into some kind of poststress letdown and was incapable of operating rationally. He just stared at Bob, eyes wide open, mouth agape, while Bob went to the men's station wagon. Finding nothing to interest him, he turned the key, gunned the engine, drove off the dirt road, aimed at the swamp, stepped out of the car and bent over, and with one hand gave the gas pedal a goose. The car took off with a squeal, blew through some weeds, sloshed into the river and disappeared under the surface in a commotion of bubbles and oil stains.

He turned.

"Now your car, sonny. Can't leave evidence. I'll buy you a new one some day, okay?"

Nick watched him repeat the ritual, and his little Dodge, once the pride of his life, disappeared in the black, quiet water.

"Okay, boy, take a last quick gander. Police up anything that doesn't belong. Come *on,* boy, just don't sit there like something's got a hold on your pecker, *do* something. Shit, you are some kind of lazy-ass yankee dead dick."

By this time, Nick could get himself up, but he didn't answer and he left it to Bob to do most of the checking.

"Okay. Time to take the freedom bird back to the world."

They walked a half mile down the road and found a white pickup pulled off under some trees. Nick, still silent, climbed in. Carefully, Bob drew a rifle case out from behind the backseat, wiped down and inserted his Remington, then climbed into the driver's seat. "Put your seat belt on, dammit," he said. "I'm not having you crash through the damned windshield."

Nick stared ahead, not registering anything as the swamp gave way to fields, to crops. On they drove through Louisiana in Bob's white rattling pickup, leaving the bayous and New Orleans miles and miles behind.

Finally Bob asked, "Hungry? There's a goddamned sandwich behind the seat and a thermos of coffee."

"I'm all right," said Nick. They were his first three words.

An hour later, just past the Arkansas line, they

stopped at a diner by the roadside in a town called Annalisle.

"Need a burger," said Bob. "Hungry."

He got out of the car and went in. Nick watched him walk. He never looked back, his eyes kept straight ahead, his shoulders gunnery-sergeant erect, his bearing precise. Nick stirred himself at last and followed. Bob was sitting in a booth at the far end by himself. A girl came, and they ordered a burger and coffee for Bob and scrambled eggs for Nick.

Nick spoke at last. "Thanks. That was fantastic shooting."

"I had to wait till the light was on them properly," Bob said. "I wanted to shoot out of the sun. I was afraid the damn birds would take off and tell them where I was. But it worked out."

"How do you throw a bolt so fast?"

"Practice, son. I've done some rifle shooting over the years."

"I saw you die. I saw the flames at the church. I was there when they found the body."

"Son, the closest I came to dying was when I walked away from you and you had that bitty little Colt. You were the only man that had me that day."

"I don't—"

"I'd been there over three days. The body you found belonged to a sad old boy named Bo Stark, dead by his own hand in a garage in Little Rock, and buried in the Aurora Redemption Baptist graveyard by myself and the Reverend Mr. Harris last year, a few months before all this started."

"But the dental rec—"

"Bo went to my same dentist, Doc LeMieux. Night before all that at the health complex, I broke in, and just switched his X rays with mine, easy as you please, because Doc LeMieux just has paste-on labels on the files. Old Bo finally did somebody some good in the world, even if it was a few months after he departed it."

"The flames. You were in—"

"I wasn't in anything, Memphis. As that church burned, I was twenty feet below it and a hundred feet to the west, in a limestone cave, drinking an RC Cola and eating a Moon Pie. There's a trapdoor under the altar, built back in the days when some people ran runaway slaves up North, until they were burned out by some bad old hill boys. Heard the stories myself, from my granddaddy. I knew the church would burn; I knew it would collapse; I knew Reverend Harris was raising funds to build a new church. Everybody's happy now. You boys especially: if you found a body, you'd not be likely to keep digging through the damned ruins."

"Jesus," said Nick.

"I am a very careful man, Pork."

"Jesus," said Nick, again.

"I had to have the freedom to do some looking into some matters. Being dead was the only way I could figure. And so I've been looking into things. And then I decided that I needed help. Only man I could trust was you, because you'd had a chance to kill me and didn't. So I was going to pay a visit on you at your house. Only, when I got there, I saw a fellow driving out in your car. He was one of the fellows I saw on a shooting range in Maryland some months back. Was Payne there?"

"Yes."

"Thought so," said Bob. "That boy gets around. Payne shot me in New Orleans. Payne shot my dog in Blue Eye. Sooner or later, time will come to settle up between the two of us."

The girl brought the food. Nick found he was ravenous.

"So who were they?" Bob asked. "Do you know?"

Nick took some pride in his answer. He thought if anything, this might impress Bob Lee Swagger.

"It's an outfit called RamDyne."

"An Agency front? I figured Agency. Only Agency works that professionally."

"No, they're not Agency. They're something else—but maybe invented by the Agency in the year 1964, certainly under the protection of the Agency, certainly useful to the Agency. But they've become something of their own, and they take pride in their professionalism and their ability to do the right thing, the hard thing. Motherfuckers, I'll tell you that. Been in some shit. While you were fighting, they were all over 'Nam selling torture instruments and guns to the secret police."

"You got any names for these boys?"

"You know Payne. Ex–Green Beret master sergeant. The head man is an ex–Green Beret colonel—"

"Tough-looking guy, fifties, hooded eyes, seen some shit in his time?"

"I've never seen him. His name's Shreck. Saw a lot of combat, but he was court-martialed in 1968 for torturing VC suspects."

"I can believe that. I've met him. Hard-core, the whole way."

"But RamDyne predates Shreck. He may run it now, but it was there before him. It's . . . it's somehow connected to other stuff. I don't quite know what they were up to. Do you?"

Bob laughed.

"I got some ideas."

"So tell me. Tell it to me all. You'll never have a better audience."

"All right," said Bob. "Let's get some coffee to go, and I'll tell you as we drive."

They paid for the food and coffee and went back to the truck. Bob pointed the vehicle north, and began to talk, beginning with the visit of the men from Accutech all those months ago. And Nick was right; he was a great audience. He was all ears.

Bob talked for more than an hour and a half. Now and then Nick would interrupt with a question.

"The ammunition in Maryland? It was accurate beyond factory standards?"

"Beyond *any* standards. Better than my own. Whoever loaded it knew a thing or two about precision reloading for accuracy."

"Do you know who it could be?"

"Oh, I have an idea or two." He moved on to other matters.

"Why didn't you know you were being set up in New Orleans? I mean, you *knew* there was some other game going on, that they weren't quite what they said they were."

"You're right. I was a goddamn fool. I think I wanted that Russian shooter, that T. Solaratov, so much it blinded me. I'd been thinking about him for so many years, not knowing who he was, only what he'd done, but just dreaming about going up against him. So I got careless and I got greedy. It's killed more than one man and it sure as hell nearly killed me."

"*Was* there a Solaratov? Does he really exist?"

"I sure don't know. What I do know is that these boys must have studied me like a bug on a pin for a long, long time. That's how smart they were. They knew how to get inside and turn me like a key. Burns my ass even now thinking how stupid I was and how those smart boys played; I feel like I've been raped from the inside out."

"They probably had a psychiatrist run a study on you. CIA is heavy into psychiatry now, it's doctrine. And there's a lot of CIA doctrine in this RamDyne."

On the subject of his recuperation, Bob would say nothing, other than that a friend had helped him. But Nick put it together; he knew it was a woman, the woman who'd called him. With that fake country-western accent.

About his ordeals, after the bloody escape from New Orleans, Bob was not eloquent.

"Yep," he said, "thought my hash was salted many a time. But somehow, I kept going."

Nick had a funny moment here, calculating how he and Bob had been weirdly circling each other through this whole damned mess, how many times they'd moved through each other's wakes. He shivered.

"I have to tell you if you ever get caught I can't be of much help. If these guys have been as professional as you say, they won't have made any mistakes. That setup in Maryland? It'll be—"

"It is," said Bob. "That was my first stop after I died. All those signs of that place are gone. The trailer that was their headquarters? Towed away. Turned out they just took out an option to buy an old shooting club property, put up twenty-five thousand dollars, then let it lapse. It's back for sale now. Didn't surprise me much."

"Yeah. And on the other hand, the forensic and ballistic evidence against you is overwhelming. I've read the Bureau lab report. They got your rifle with your fingerprints and your reloaded cartridge and . . . the bullet. They couldn't read the markings because the bullet was mangled and—"

"Yeah, I saw that in the papers. That's why they haven't done any shooting tests on the rifle."

"Yes. If they get to court, they don't want to say they tried but couldn't get a match. It makes them look bad in front of a jury."

"I get you."

"But they have a very sophisticated test that analyzes

the metallic residue left in the gun barrel. And it said positively that the bullet that hit the archbishop was consistent with the metallic residue. That's going to be hard to beat."

"I figured out how they did it, or how it *could* have been done." He explained the concept to Nick.

"Okay," said Nick, "yeah, I understand. Same bullet, slightly larger bore, paper-patching. But . . . you have to find some way to convince a *jury*. The jury won't be able to follow something that technical; they'll just look at the neutron analysis test—and Mr. Swagger, you are one screwed turkey."

Bob nodded.

"They did a very careful job on me. But just maybe nobody's quite as clear on all this as they think."

"Let me tell you right now," Nick said, "your best course is to hire a good lawyer. I can call the Bureau and we can work out some kind of deal. With my evidence and—"

But Bob was just looking at him.

"Son, I don't think you understand. These boys killed my *dog*."

"I'm telling you, this is the twentieth century. You just can't go to war on people, not in America. And that kind of attitude will—"

"Now, you listen here, Memphis. Even if I could walk out on this thing now as a free man, I wouldn't. Those boys would scatter and slip into new identities or whatever it is they do. We'd never catch them. They're too damned slick. They'd have gotten away with it. And in a year or so, when it was cool, they'd be back in business. What I mean to do is tether a goat and draw them in. They'll think they're hunting the goat, but the goat is hunting them. And who's the goat? I'm the damned goat. The only thing is, this goat has teeth. This goat bites. Now this is hard, hairy work, Memphis;

there's going to be some shooting and some people are going to die. It won't be pretty and we'll be all alone. It *is* a war. I didn't start it, but by Christ I mean to finish it. Now, Pork, tell me—are you in or are you out?"

Nick thought of the pig-gleam in Payne's eye; and this RamDyne with its willingness to do the hard thing; and he thought of how he'd been brutalized; and he thought of how confident and smooth and big these guys thought they were. And he thought about how they'd committed a war atrocity and gunned down women and kids.

And he thought about how he'd been dying to get back on a SWAT team.

"Okay," he said. "I'm in."

Something hard and metallic flickered in Bob's eye, like the shine of a brass cartridge as it catches a glint of light before the bolt locks vault-tight behind it.

"Now what?" asked Nick. "I've got some great ideas about Annex B. It seems to me—"

"Hold up there, Pork. First thing is, we're going to see a man about a rifle."

CHAPTER TWENTY-SEVEN

"Partial body found in bayou," proclaimed the cheerful headline.

"Go ahead," said Shreck, "read it."

Dobbler squinted.

Lafayette Parish

The partial body of a man was found floating yesterday near Spencerville, Lafayette Parish. Sheriff's deputies said the victim, who has been identified by fingerprints as Tomas Garcia Montoya, of McDonoughville, was evidently the subject of an alligator attack as his body, from the chest down, was missing.

Cause of death, however, was listed as a gunshot wound to head.

Montoya, a Cuban émigré, had listed his occupation as "consultant" but was known to police and other New Orleans law enforcement agencies as a paid informant. He was 54 years old.

Deputies speculated that he may have also been a victim of the escalating drug warfare in the state's rural parishes, in a struggle for control of the city's drug routes between old-line mob interests and newcomers representing the cocaine cartels of Central America.

Montoya was shot in the head by a heavy caliber rifle bullet.

"Only a large-caliber center fire rifle bullet does massive damage like that," said Lafayette Parish coroner Robert C. LaDoyne. "This man was shot, judging by the wound channel and tissue displacement, by a hollowpoint bullet of .30 caliber or more."

Parish deputies said it may represent the coming of a new kind of professional killer to the parish's drug wars.

"Mob boys favor the silenced .22 from close range," said Deputy Ed P. St. Etienne. "The Colombians like little machine pistols, and fire a hundred bullets into their victims. This boy is something entirely new."

"He's not new to us, is he, Dobbler?" said the colonel.

"No," said Dobbler, swallowing. "How on earth—? He's dead! We saw the—"

"Dobbler," snapped the colonel. "Look at me."

Dobbler looked into the colonel's forceful dark eyes and felt the full might of his wrath.

"Tommy Montoya was a free-lancer we used when

we operated in the South. He was with Nick Memphis. Now he's dead, sniper-dead. That means one thing and you'd better get used to it fast. All right? *Comprendez, amigo?*"

Dobbler swallowed miserably.

"Yes," he said. "I see."

"Swagger is alive. How, why, I don't know. I don't even give a fuck, because it doesn't matter. What matters is this new reality: he's teamed with the one man in America outside the proper circles who's seen our file. So right from the start, he knows more than anybody who's come after us before."

He looked hard at Dobbler.

"In case you don't get it, Doctor, we have a war on our hands. This motherfucker wants to track us down and blow us away. But what we're going to do is blow him away first. Are you listening, here, Dr. Harvard Psychiatrist? No bullshit; we have to get close, put the muzzle against his head and blast his brains all over the landscape. Or he'll do it to us."

The colonel's glare was unsettling; Dobbler swallowed.

"What do you want me to—"

"What I need from you is an idea how they'll operate. Their relationship—how's it going to play out? Will they get along? Will they fight? Do they make a good team?"

"Ah," said Dobbler, unprepared, "ah, Bob will be the strong one. He'll dominate the younger man. The younger man is no problem. Bureau trained, he'll be orthodox and plodding. No, Swagger is dangerous because of the unconventionality of his mind. He'll come at us out of instinct, brilliantly, improvising madly. He'll—"

"Where will they head?"

"Bob will head home. If he was in New Orleans to

meet or rescue Memphis, then he'll take him to the Ouachitas. It's where he'll feel safest. And the sense of safety is—"

"The chances of us making an interception are nil. Not in his territory. All right," said Shreck, leaning forward, "let me ask you a question. Have you ever hunted?"

"Hunted? Good God, no. I mean, it's so . . . *barbaric.*" A faint look of distaste came across Dobbler's face, unintended.

"Yes, well, you put all that aside now. You just became a hunter. It's your job to work out a way we can lure this tough old boy and his new pal into ambush. Hunt him, Dobbler. You don't have to kill him—we'll take care of that—but you have to hunt him."

Dobbler nodded apprehensively. And he noticed something he'd never quite seen before.

He swallowed.

Shreck is scared.

Some days later, Nick Memphis was in a contrary mood.

"Now what the hell is this?" he said. "Why are we—"

"I think I liked you better when you were Baby Googoo, and you just looked up at me with your mouth open. Now you won't shut up. Talk, talk, talk, like a woman. Now, don't say nothing here. You let me do the damned talking. Got that? I don't want you *explaining* something to this old coot and putting him into a coma."

There was no give in Bob's voice as he looked through the dust-spackled windshield at an extremely spacious ranch house on a spread just outside of Fort Supply, in western Oklahoma.

"You better—"

"You just smile, boy. This old man isn't going to want

to give up his information easy to strangers, but he knows more about what he knows about than any man alive. Come on, now."

Bob got out of the truck. He wore a straw Stetson and had found a gray jacket to go over his denim shirt; suddenly he looked strangely like some kind of cowboy royalty.

"I still don't—"

"Button it, Pork. You'll see."

An old lady sat in a rocker on the porch at the top of the stairs. She just watched them come, made no gesture of welcome. She fanned herself; it was hot and dusty out and the sun lurked over the hills behind a gassy spread of clouds.

"Howdy, ma'am," Bob sung out.

"Whachew want?" the old lady asked.

"See the colonel."

"Colonel don't see nobody these days."

"Hell, I have me a line on a pre-'64 70 in .270 once owned by a famous bad boy. Thought he might be interested."

"He's got enough guns."

"No such thing as enough guns, ma'am, I'll beg your pardon for saying so."

The woman eyed him suspiciously, then got her weary body up and yelled inside. "Rate? Rate, you in there? Fella out here says he gotta line on a 70."

"Well, shoo him in, then, honey," came the call from the dark interior.

Bob walked in and Nick followed.

The room was large. The man who owned it had at one time or other killed every creature large and dangerous that walked upon the earth, and now the heads of his victims looked down upon their slayer, who was a plump man in his seventies sitting in an Eames chair reading a copy of—Nick blinked, double-checked to make sure, but, yes—*The New York Review of Books.*

He didn't rise. The beasts stared from the walls. Most of the furniture was wooden and sleek and expensive, and Indian blankets and pottery were all over the place. And so were books, hundreds and hundreds of books. And rifles. Nick had never seen so many rifles and so many books in one place before.

"And who might you gentlemen be?" asked the fellow. He removed a blanket from his lap to reveal a six-shooter, high chromed, seven-and-a-half-inch barrel, and he had merry, clever eyes. There wasn't a morsel of fear in him anywhere. Nick had never seen a man who had less fear.

"Name's Bob Jennings, from over in Arkansas. Do some trading in fine firearms. This here's my associate, named Nick."

"Well, Mr. Jennings, I must say I know most of the fine gun dealers in this country, having spent much money in their abodes. Can't say I've heard much of you."

"I'm new to the business, sir," said Bob. "Just starting my reputation. But you know that fellow the FBI killed, that Bob Swagger?"

"That bad boy took that shot at our president and hit a poor cleric instead?"

"That old boy, yep."

"Heard of him."

"Well, he had a pre-'64 .270, rebarreled with a Douglas and restocked on a piece of English walnut by Loren Eccles of Chisholm, Wyoming. It was serial number 123453, which means it came off the line in about 1949. A fine rifle. He was a man who much loved fine rifles."

"I just believe he was. Some say if he'd have meant to shoot the president, he'd have hit the president."

"Well, who can say? Now, it so happens that his property will eventually come out of FBI impoundment and it so happens that his father, Earl, had a sister named Letitia who happened to be my mother. Bob Lee was my cousin, though I hadn't seen him in years. An ornery soul, if I recall from childhood. Now as his only living relative, it so happens his guns will therefore come into my possession and knowing how you treasure the Model 70, I might be persuaded to see it come your way."

The shrewd fellow looked Bob up and down and then lit out with a cackle and a yowl.

"I think I see a family resemblance," he said. "My, ain't life just full of surprises?"

"And since no man alive knows more about the Model 70, I can't think of a better man to receive that rifle, sir, than Colonel Rathford Marin O'Brien, author of *The Classic Rifle*, the premiere big game hunter of this country and our greatest living expert on the Model 70 rifle, Winchester's best."

"It sounds like a piece I'd be interested in. Lord knows, I've spent lots of foolish money on interesting rifles. If I didn't have so many damn oil wells, I might not be such a spendthrift, but I'm too old for women and I tired of killing some years back, so interesting rifles and the folly of New York intellectuals are my last remaining vices. And what would the price be?"

"Sir, I'll not insult you with talk of money," said Bob. "I'll trade you that damn rifle even up, for information. That's all I want. Some talk."

"They say a man who asks for little is always meaning to take a lot."

"Maybe they say that, sir, and maybe it's right. But I know Bob Lee Swagger thought you were a great American and he'd be pleased to have one of his rifles come to rest in your collection. And he'd consider it an even bargain and a good swap."

"All right, then, boy. Ask your damn questions. What I know that could be worth that much—properly authenticated, that gun would easily go fifteen thousand dollars at the big Las Vegas show—is mighty interesting to me."

"The Tenth Black King."

O'Brien looked at him, his hard eyes gleaming with sudden insight.

He glanced briefly at Nick, found him uninteresting, then returned to Bob.

What the hell was going on? Nick was thinking.

"Hell, boy," said Colonel O'Brien. "The Tenth Black King is a damned mystery."

Dobbler could no longer stand his office. The walls seemed to press down on him and his mind had ceased to operate. He had sat there for hours, trying to think of ways to get at Bob and he had come up with nothing.

So now he was wandering around the RamDyne complex, ducking now and then when a 747 would scream in on the flight path to Dulles. He knew that sometimes his unconscious could solve a problem if he did not let his conscious deal with it directly. It just happened, under the surface, so to speak. He prayed for such a leap in insight now. But he only saw blue sky, airplanes and crummy buildings.

He'd come at last to a large corrugated shed toward the rear of the complex. It bore the sign, OPERATIONS MOTOR POOL/NO ADMITTANCE TO UNAUTHORIZED PERSONNEL.

Why did he enter? Because it was there. No one stopped him as he slid in and in the darkness he blinked to adjust his eyes. He found himself in a garagelike structure of some size, in the center of which a number of men were bent over benches, working intently. The odor of gasoline, grease and some kind of chemical solvent filled the air like a vapor. He heard the click and snap of metal parts. He smiled at one of the workers, who just worked away contemptuously.

He saw then they were working on guns. Machine guns or assault rifles, complicated, dangerous-looking. They were snapping them, assembling them, greasing them, goofing around with them. And there were bullets too, crates of bullets, and some of the men were fitting the bullets into magazines. They all looked like barbarians. They were wild boys, yardbirds, the same breed of tough, scary trash that had frightened Dobbler into Russell Isandhlwana's comforting ministrations. Some had crew cuts, some ponytails, all had tattoos and bad teeth. And the guns: he could tell. They loved the damned guns.

There was so much electricity between the men and their weapons. It was like nothing he'd ever seen. How they adored them!

The guns, Dobbler thought.

"Well," said Colonel O'Brien, "I'd guess you think you might find that damned rifle and make yourself a half a million dollars. Friend, I'd bet you're chasing a mirage. I think it's buried in some unknown hole with its poor last owner."

Bob couldn't tell him he'd fired the damn thing in Maryland last January.

"Now you know that the Ten Black Kings were ten extra-fine Model 70 target rifles in the model known as the Bull Gun, with a heavy, extra-long barrel that the company planned to put out as Presentation Rifles in the year 1950. These ten rifles—serial number 99991 through 100000—were stocked from a trunk of black American walnut from a tree that had been felled in Salem, Oregon. For some odd reason, the wood in the tree really *was* black; that is, it was so old and dense it was almost like ebony. The completed rifles were so lovely that someone came up with the name 'Black Kings' to describe them. I've handled several. They are beautiful rifles, believe me.

"The rifles were then presented to the usual great men and now rest in various museums around the world. Except for the last one—serial number 100000, in the thousand-yard caliber—"

".300 H & H Magnum," said Bob.

"You have it, son. This one was presented to an employee, Art Scott, who'd for many years been Winchester's expert marksman. Art was a wonderful rifle shot. He'd won the Wimbledon cup and won the thousand-yard match at Bisley, in England, and won the nationals at Camp Perry, and had been the NRA shooter of the year several times. He may have been the best shot this country ever produced, until that man in Vietnam came along."

"You must mean Carl Hitchcock?" said Bob.

"That's the boy."

"Go on, Colonel," Bob said. "What happened to the Tenth Black King? You didn't say in your book. You said, 'Someday the tragic story of the Tenth Black King will come out, but for now, as it is unfinished, I will not begin it.' "

"Well, it's a sad story. The Tenth Black King was the only one of the ten that was regularly used in competition; its action had even been specially milled from a new Swedish steel so that it was mighty strong and could stand up to the heavy powder loads the thousand-yard shooters burn up. It was used not only by Art, who was in his sixties by that time, and had lost a bit of his edge, but by his son Lon. Lon Scott was a lovely young man, handsome and fair, a Yale graduate, a shooter's shooter. He had his whole life before him; he'd been accepted at Harvard Law School in 1954; he had everything, including the Tenth Black King and his father's inherited fund of shooting knowledge, learned from growing up in a shooting family. A father-son thing, quite holy in certain precincts. Do you shoot, young man?"

"Now and then," said Bob.

"It's not as simple as point and pull the trigger, you know?"

"So I hear," said Bob.

"Well, anyway, in 1954, Lon Scott finished fourth in the National Thousand Yard Rifle Championships at Camp Perry. The season was over. He had a few of his loads left, and he and his dad went out one afternoon to shoot them up. But you know the curse of the rifle. When you think you've mastered it, it'll punish you for your vanity, reach out and destroy everything you've ever earned or made in your life. A rifle can be a cruel and vengeful slut. One of those stupid accidents, where the basic law of safety—treat every gun as if it's loaded —was violated. A target-grade trigger, very delicate, one of them putting the rifle in the case, the safety not off but not quite on either. Art Scott accidentally shot his son in the spine, paralyzing him forever from the mid-chest down. Sentencing him to a lifetime in a wheelchair.

"The boy was in the hospital and in physical therapy for two years. All that he'd wanted for himself and that Art had wanted for him was gone. A week after the shooting, Art used the same rifle on himself. Blew his own brains out in the family cabin in Vermont. The boy lost everything in that second's carelessness: his legs, his life, his father."

"What happened to him?"

"When he recovered, he didn't destroy the rifle. You'd think he would, wouldn't you? But he didn't, because he believed that the firearm was simply a tool, and it had no guilt. But he wasn't untouched. If anything, he set out to master it. For about five years in the mid-fifties he gave himself up entirely to the discipline of the rifle and became one of the premiere thousand-yard shooters because he could still fire from the prone, of course. Won the championship in 1956 and 1957. He was a great benchrest shooter, too. But I wonder? What can it do to a vital young person to have his life twisted so terribly by a bullet?"

Nick, silent all the time they had been there, finally spoke up.

"I think I know. I was married to a woman accidentally paralyzed in a shooting. If you were a good person, like my Myra, you become a better one. But if you were bad—fundamentally bad—it can turn you black and horrible. I used to talk to the doctors when I took Myra in for therapy once a week. They once told me that there was nobody more bitter than a strong, firm man exiled into a metal chair forever."

Bob said, "Is that what happened to Lon Scott?"

"Oh, I wouldn't want to say," said the colonel. "That's between himself and God."

"What did happen?"

"He gave up. He disappeared. No one knows where he went. But he was a genius, all right. He was one of the first to enter the world of micro-accuracy. He was the first, for example, to see the importance of neck-turning for precision reloading, to get maximum accuracy. In 1963, his last year of competitive shooting, at the National Bench Rest Championships at Lake Erie, Ohio, he shot a three-hundred-yard group that measured .289 minute of angle; it's been surpassed in the last few years now that the equipment has gotten so refined, but it stood for over thirteen years, the longest single accuracy record in American history. And that was the last time anybody ever saw him."

"There must have been rumors," said Bob.

"Oh, the usual nonsense. That he was this or that. More likely, he just went off and got on with the rest of his life. Nothing dramatic. That's all. But that rifle today—hell, it would be worth a half a million dollars, I'd bet."

"You said Lon Scott was a genius?"

"I suppose he might have been. He knew how to get the most out of a rifle, I'll say that. He, Warren Page, P. O. Ackley, Pop Eimer, a few others."

"Well, Colonel O'Brien, I thank you. You've done me right well. I'll see you get Bob the Nailer's rifle, you can bet on that."

"Now that old Bob the Nailer, he's another interesting case. Can't figure how a boy like that would go so wrong."

"Maybe he was used by bad people."

"Well, I'd like to believe that. Hate to see a hero brought low. Ever read *Othello,* gentlemen?"

"Don't read plays," said Bob.

"I read it in high school," Nick added lamely.

"Well, old Bob reminds me of Othello. A great soldier, a good man. Twisted, played with, used by an Iago for some dreadful purpose. That play was a tragedy, one of Mr. Shakespeare's finest. Just like poor Bob's life—an American tragedy."

"Well," said Bob, "don't believe Mr. Shakespeare had much use for happy endings, but the Bob Lee Swagger I knew all those years back, he may have been as stubborn as a goddamned mule, but he wasn't a fool either. So maybe somehow it'll work out for him. Goodbye, Colonel."

"Well, I hope so, boys," said the colonel, with just a hint of glee in his voice. "Because I'm too old for tragedy. I like a nice happy ending too."

As they drove away, Nick found himself increasingly agitated. Finally, he let it all spill out.

"What the hell was that all about? Why did we drive three days to—"

"I'd read in the records of five great shooters in the late fifties. Lon Scott just happened to be one of them. I had to tie one of them to that damned black rifle. I figured if anybody could give us a line, it'd be that old man."

"But what did we—"

"Don't you get it yet, boy? These boys, they didn't just want me to use as a dupe. No sir. I had to go to all the shooting sites and bird-dog them out. I had to read the angles, I had to figure the positions, I had to test the winds. I had to set it up for them. Now why? The real shooter would want to do that himself . . . unless he couldn't. The sleep I've lost thinking this one through! Why couldn't he? He couldn't because he's in a wheelchair, remember? I was his damn legs."

Nick bolted upward. Of course!

"We just learned the name of the man who shot Roberto Lopez in New Orleans. Don't you see, dammit, everything these birds have done has turned on one damned thing. And that is that they had at their disposal a world-class shot. They wouldn't have set up the operation they set up if they didn't have a man who could hit a standing target at twelve hundred yards, like he did in New Orleans. That's fantastic shooting. Aren't but seven, maybe eight men in the world who'd have the confidence to take that shot."

"But none of this is worth a damn in a court of law," Nick protested. "And we have no leads on where this Lon Scott is! If he's even alive! Nothing. That old man couldn't tell us a damned thing about where this crippled sniper was! We ought to be looking for Annex B. That's where—"

"You are the most contrary man I ever met. If someone handed you a glass of free beer that was nine-tenths full, you'd cry over the missing tenth. Listen, if I have a name, I can dog him out. Shooters will know of him. It's a small world, the shooting world. He'll have left tracks, you'll see. And when we find him, we find them."

They drove away, down the bumpy road.

CHAPTER TWENTY-EIGHT

Dr. Dobbler's fingers were black with newsprint. He sat alone in his office late at night, turning the pages, concentrating. He was surrounded by piles of magazines, some slick and gaudy, some amazingly primitive. But he had, after much investigation, settled on this document as his road map to Bob Lee Swagger.

It was cheaply printed, on newsprint, and its ink soaked into his fingertips. The words were often semiliterate, almost always utilitarian, the type packed together inelegantly, without reference to any modern theory of layout, as if the men responsible were just trying to crush as much information in as possible, the pictures often murky and sometimes indecipherable. It could have come from a different universe.

Dobbler turned one of the flimsy pages, feeling as if he were sinking deeper and deeper into strangeness.

Tokarev Military TU-90. Free Ammo. $119 each.

Banger's Distribution, America's Best Colt Distributor, Offers You the Colt Gold Cup Ten—$669.99 each/2 or more $649.99 ea.

Subscribe Now to *Machine Gun News*—Special Introductory Price.

Paragon Makes It Easy to Buy Ammo.

Maryland/Howard County Weapons Fair, November 10–11.

The Gun Cellar—Prices Are Lower in the Cellar.

Machine Gun Conversion Videos.

And on and on it went, for 195 pages. The publication was called *The Shotgun News,* though shotguns were only a small part of the news. If it shot or related to shooting or documented shooting, you could find it in *The Shotgun News,* the urtext of the subculture.

Dobbler was fascinated. Guns everywhere, of every shape and form and description, for every taste and wallet. They could be so cheap and so expensive, so demure and so awesome, so ridiculous and so sublime.

He wondered about the men who worshiped them with such ardency, whose lives were bounded by their complexities or liberated by their possibilities.

What was there to see in all this?

Well, passion for order for one thing. So much of gun culture was about parts, units, systems, things fitting together. There were whole institutions that existed merely to sell parts of obsolete weapons. So there was a puzzle aspect to it, a sense of bringing order to chaos.

Power? The damned things were so absolute in their meaning that yes, there had to be the lure of power. But beauty also. Some of them, he was stunned to discover, were strangely beautiful. He especially liked one called a Luger and another called a New Frontier single action.

And freedom, or at least the illusion of it, by the narrowest of definitions. To Dobbler, freedom was essentially intellectual, but he supposed that to someone in a more primal world, it was physical—freedom of movement, freedom from harassment, freedom from being messed around with. Outdoor freedom. And a man who holds a gun in his hand must feel it passionately. No government can rule you absolutely. Yours is always the last option.

And masculinity. Nothing soft and feminine about guns: they were too direct, too brutal. The phallic business so provocative to Freudians didn't seem to him to be very helpful; if these guns *were* penises, their purchasers were too self-oblivious to know or care.

And then again: data. To him a gun was just a gun, but to some of these people it was obviously an endless font of information—a history, a set of specifications, an involvement with a company, usually a corporate entity, a connection to certain traditions, a whole hierarchy of meanings that yielded yet more meanings and had to be deciphered like some runic code. To shoot wasn't enough: there was something almost Borgesian about the labyrinths the damned things conjured in the imagination.

The clock ticked away and the pages fled by and after a bit, he ceased looking at the display ads from the gun wholesale places, but instead, fascinated, looked to smaller fry: the columns and columns of classifieds, where more oblique needs were addressed. It was like *The New York Review of Books* personal ads, only for guns and their affiliated phenomena, not sex.

REMINTON 25, Rifle in mint. cond, 25–20, 99% original blue, mint bore, wood perfict, SN 26827, 100% unaltered, these little pumps are a joy, only $895

Pre-64, M70 220 SWIFT, Super grade, 98% overall, nice dark wood, factory jeweled bolt body and extractor, exc. bore, $1,595.

LUGER list and price guide, 200 + quality collectors Lugers and accessories for sale on each bi-monthly list. Send $1 for sample or $5 for year subscription.

MILITARY RIFLES OF JAPAN, 1989 Third Edition, $37. Postpaid! SASE for discriptive flyers. At your dealer or Fred Honeycutt, 6731 Pilgrim Way, Palm Frond Village, FLA 33411.

DISCOUNT GUN BOOKS: ALL SHIPPED FREE. Great New Book, Winchester, An American Legend, Wilson, $58.50. Colt Encyclopedia II, Cochran, $58.50. Discount Gun Books, P.O. Box 762, Nescopeck, PA 18635.

It was somewhere in here, lost amid the lists of old guns, new books and reloading components and magazines for pistols that hadn't been manufactured since World War I that something began to tick in his mind.

They hid deep in the timber, after disappearing down many remote lumber roads. It was a small, one-room hunting cabin, built years ago, a rustic place of logs and wooden roof. Bob swiftly shot three squirrels with a Mini-14, then set about to skin them for the stewpot.

"Is there anything I should be doing?" asked Nick.

"Just don't get in the way," said Bob.

"Now I think we should—"

"Memphis, don't *explain* anything to me. All right?"

Nick, fuming and pissed at himself and at Bob, had never known anybody so used to silence and so uninterested in conversation, so hidden behind an impassive face. But it wasn't the impassivity of relaxation—that was a complete illusion, Nick now saw, like some kind of mask to keep the world away while its owner shrewdly calculated moves two jumps down the line.

"Where are we?" asked Nick.

"Ouachitas," said Bob. "Nobody's going to find us here, unless we want them to."

"Ah," said Nick. "Um, what are your thoughts on what we do next?"

Bob just went on skinning the squirrels.

"I haven't figured yet."

"Well, I've been thinking," said Nick.

"Uh-oh," said Bob.

"I still think the damned key is Annex B. Now, where is Annex B? Well, it's got to be in Washington. In fact, *everything's* in Washington. I think that's where we ought to go. We can do some nosing around, maybe get a line on it. Then . . ."

He had nothing to say after the *then*.

"Now, don't you think they might figure that out?" Bob asked.

"Well . . ." said Nick.

"One thing I know. In a war, you don't go where they expect you. That earns you a body bag."

"Well, then . . . what?"

"We lay up here a few more days, till the buzz dies

down. We both need sleep; I'll kill a deer tomorrow so we'll eat good. Then I'll figure something."

"Look, I have to tell you as a professional criminal investigator of twelve years' experience, we just aren't—"

"Young Mr. Pork Memphis, I am not a fancy government man. I only studied at the University of Vietnam. I don't know anything about investigating anything. But I do know the key to this damn thing is a rare rifle that has been used at least once in mortal circumstances. And I know its owner is one of the best shots in America and one of the great ballistic technicians, as well as having spent almost forty years in a wheelchair. And I have a funny feeling that he works for this RamDyne. That's the only card I got, so it's the card I'm going to play. Now let me think on it. Go for a walk or something. But don't get lost. I don't have time to go looking for you."

Well, maybe I'll do some thinking too, thought Nick, consigning himself to be the only one to press against the mysteries of Annex B.

Dr. Dobbler licked his lips nervously, swallowed a time or two, and then knocked on the door.

"Yes?"

"Colonel Shreck?"

"Yes, come in, Doctor."

Dobbler stepped into Shreck's office, to find Payne and the colonel bent in conversation.

"What is it, Doctor?"

"Ah, I have a—a *plan*."

The colonel looked at Dobbler. Russell Isandhlwana used to look at him like that, more with pity than anything else. In some ways Russell and the colonel were the same man. They just took what they wanted. And

Dobbler knew that he desperately wanted to please them both.

"All right," said Shreck, waiting for more.

"Bob is too sharp and suspicious to be taken as we had hoped. He's always watching. We must beat him on his strength, which is patience. We must put something before him so subtly that not a man in a thousand would notice it. But we must put it there and let him sniff at it and go away, sniff again and go away, reconnoiter and re-reconnoiter, until he has at last satisfied himself that the way is clear. We must nurse him in slowly, never being greedy, draw him in with utmost care and discipline, being as ready as he is to disengage if conditions do not favor us. We must be more patient. Then and only then—"

Shreck was impatient.

"That's wonderful. Now tell me how."

"Yes sir," said Dobbler. "All right. Here it is. Am I not certain that somewhere in the secret files of this organization there is access to a man who does the shooting? Really. There has to be a shooter. An excellent shooter. After all, *somebody* took that shot in New Orleans."

Shreck thought about it, but didn't commit himself. Then he said, "Go on."

"This shooter, I guarantee you, would interest Bob. He would fascinate Bob. Bob is probably already theoretically aware of his existence and attempting to puzzle out a name for the man, and a location. And certainly Bob noted the rifle such a man used. After all, didn't he use it in Maryland during the recruitment stage?"

"Yes."

"My thought is that in the subtlest possible way, we put the shooter's name before Bob."

"And what way would that be?"

"There's a publication called *The Shotgun News* that

comes out three times a month. Thousands of custom or rare rifles are advertised through classified ads in each issue, as well as other items—reloading stuff, parts, surplus clothes, ammunition . . . and books. This was a surprise to me. But it's true. These men who love guns, somehow are driven to record and document their love. They've created a whole other literature, a parallel literature. And just as mainstream culture is riven by ideological differences between left and right, so is gun culture, though it isn't really left and right so much as traditionalist and progressive. Anyway, a common thread is guerrilla publishing—self-publishing, if you will. I was fascinated to see a book on Japanese military rifles being sold for thirty-seven dollars through the mail! Imagine that. Someone so fascinated by Japanese rifles that he goes to the trouble to write a book—a catalog, more, I suspect—anyway, he goes to all that *trouble* and then there are actually people out there mad enough to send thirty-seven dollars through the mail for—"

"Get to the point, goddammit!"

"Yes, I'm sorry. Why not—a book? A self-published book on the history of that particular rifle Bob used in Maryland. Published by some obscure researcher–devotee in some small town. As advertised in a small item in *The Shotgun News*. Bob would see it. I guarantee you. And he would think, Hmmmmm. Here's somebody who knows about this rifle and its background. Maybe in his researches, he came across a clue that will lead me to the next step. And so he would approach this obscure researcher–devotee. He will have to. And in that way we lure him to a remote place and—"

"A mountaintop," Payne spoke up for the first time. "You want to drive him up a mountain, so there's a point where he can't get any further. Hit him with a lot of men."

"Yes. Drive him up, then hit him with a lot of men. More men than he can handle."

"So where we going get a lot of new boys?" said Payne.

"Let me work on that," said Shreck.

They were sitting outside the cabin well after dark. It was as if Bob had flown off into the ether. Nick realized he'd never quite known the meaning of the word *concentration* before; there was no concentration like the concentration of the sniper. Nick was afraid almost to speak to him.

Bob sat by the fire, simply staring into it. The fire crackled and blazed, sending small flares out into the night, its light playing across his taut, lean face. His eyes were steady, lost in the middle distance.

Meanwhile, in his solitude, Nick tried to zero on Annex B. How do you get at something deep in the FBI files, especially when you have been suspended by the Bureau and your only source into its computer system has been compromised. But he was convinced that if he could just find some orderly, logical methodology, it could be done. Perhaps some computer hacker could penetrate, some damned high school kid. They were getting into things all the time. Or maybe if he went to someone like Hap Fencl, laid all this out in a nice orderly fashion, maybe Hap would bypass the dreaded Howard D. Utey and go to even higher-ups and that way . . . but even as he was conjuring the bubble of this fantasy, it burst on him. Hap wasn't as bad as Howard, but he was Howard in a way: old Bureau, inflexibly wedded to the ways of the bureaucracy, however individually decent completely unable to get his mind to consider violating its mandates. You couldn't go to Hap *unless* you had Annex B already.

Nick snorted suddenly. That used to be me. Now

look at me: camping in the woods, locked in a private war against a shadowy spook agency that was half official, half not. Annex B: that's where the answers lay. He was sure of that. Annex B would give him the answer.

Somewhere in the dark an animal skittered and howled. The fire had burned low, and across from it, Bob still sat hunkered and remote, lost in his own head.

He wished he had Myra to talk to. She'd have an idea or at least be willing to hear him out. He missed her. Goddamn, he missed her a lot.

"Memphis?"

He looked over. Bob was staring at him harshly.

"Huh? Yeah?"

"Memphis, you willing to do some hard work? I mean hard, dirty, boring crap work? The kind nobody likes to do anymore? Can you give me a week of it, twelve, eighteen hours a day?"

Nick gulped. That was his specialty, his only talent. To lean against something not with great brainpower but with sheer dogged will, until he or it broke apart.

"Yeah, sure."

Then Nick saw something he'd never seen, not at all, not in all their hours together, not in the aftermath of the swamp shooting, not in the long talks on RamDyne and the world they lived in.

In the firelight, Bob the Nailer smiled.

"Then I got him," he said, his war eyes totally focused. "He's mine. The boy who pulled the trigger. I own his ass."

The martyred president sat in marble wisdom on his throne, surrounded by Doric pillars and the rubbery thumps of two hundred pairs of athletic shoes on the floor. Shouts and screams bounced off the cavernous arch of the dome. An eighth-grade class was visiting the Lincoln Memorial.

Any semblance of order had long since broken down, and there had never been a semblance of respect. The youngsters tore about.

"Barbarians," said Hugh Meachum from around the stem of his pipe, amid a haze of smoke. "They have no sense of decorum at all, do they?"

The old man was miffed. Shreck said nothing.

"There should be a way to surgically remove and store children's tongues as soon as they learn to speak," said Hugh. "Then, when they've graduated from college and distinguished themselves in the workplace, they could file a petition to have their tongues reattached."

"I don't think that's feasible, Mr. Meachum," said Shreck.

"Dammit, Colonel, don't humor me. I hate it when I am being humored. Now. You called this meeting. I take it the news is not good. People won't be pleased, Colonel. I'm telling you frankly, they won't be pleased. Now what is it?"

A teacher sped by, harassed and exhausted, in pursuit of a knot of seething kids.

"An end we thought was tied off," said Shreck. "It just untied itself."

"Meaning?" said Hugh, taking another deep draw from his pipe. The aroma of gin hung over him.

"Meaning that Bob Lee Swagger is not dead. He's very much alive. And he's hunting us. That means he's hunting all of us."

Hugh shook his head, reached into his pocket and came out with a flask.

"Drink, Colonel?"

"No, sir."

Hugh took a quick tot. It seemed to do him some good.

"All right. You must find him and kill him. Surely you understand that?"

"We've got a plan. It's clever, it looks promising."

"Yes, yes."

"But I have two problems."

"Only two?"

"One is easy. The other . . ."

He let it trail off.

"All right. Number One?"

"Number One is manpower. I don't want to take any chances. I want a lot of men; he can kill twenty or fifty and I want fifty more there to take him down. I can't recruit anew; there isn't enough time."

"God, Colonel, you can't expect us to provide you with men. Good heavens, the risk is—"

"No, no. I have men. They're just not here. I need approval at a high level to fly a Hercules in from down south, and land without Customs interference. That can be arranged, can't it? Surely your associates can prevail on something so minor. They'll fly in, do the job, and fly out. They'll be in-country for no more than a week, I swear. No one will see them."

Hugh considered.

"I suppose it could be arranged. And who are you bringing in, Colonel Shreck?"

"I need good, hard men, men who've been in battle, Mr. Meachum. The only place I can get men of that quality fast enough and in sufficient quantity is from El Salvador."

Hugh looked at him.

"That's right," said Shreck. "I'm bringing in the counterinsurgency company from Panther Battalion, the one we trained. It's their mess we're still cleaning up. Let them go up the mountain after Bob Lee Swagger."

"God," said Meachum. "All right. I suppose it can be

arranged. You'll get me the details at the right time. And what's Number Two?"

Shreck paused, swallowed. This was the one he didn't like. He knew he sailed into dangerous waters here.

"Go on, go on," said Hugh, impatiently.

"My people never saw him," said Shreck. "We have no idea who he is or what he did. We only know that he can shoot better than any man on this earth. And we know he isn't mobile, because he had to work from Bob's report and couldn't handle it himself. And we had the sense that he was once famous, in a way, or at least public. So there has to be history there. And we examined his rifle. We know that it was used to win championships."

Hugh's eyes flashed over at Shreck.

"Among other things it was used for," he said. "The security was important, indeed crucial. There are things you don't need to know. I told you I would handle that part of it. That it didn't involve you or your people. Didn't I? Now what on earth can this be about, Colonel?"

"Our plan needs bait. This Swagger is a difficult antagonist, but he has weaknesses. He had a weakness for a Soviet sniper he thought shot and killed his best friend. My staff psychiatrist, Dobbler, put that together; and it worked, Mr. Meachum. It got us Swagger on a platter. But we couldn't keep him there."

"Obviously."

"Now Dobbler thinks that Swagger will have somehow *sensed* the other shooter. And will find him as provocative as he found the Russian. I want to put him before Swagger. It needn't be complicated, but it must be authentic. I want a sense of him, I want his cooperation."

"As bait?"

"Yes. Well, not physically. But we'll need name, history, background, accomplishments, that sort of—"

"Well, for your information, he and I go way back. We went to school together, in fact. His life has been . . . remarkable. Colonel, his identity is the one secret I hold most precious."

"If we don't get Swagger, he'll blow us away, Mr. Meachum."

Hugh considered.

"I'll have to ask him," he said. "I couldn't think of doing it without his agreement."

CHAPTER TWENTY-NINE

They pulled up outside the house. It was a quiet twilight in Syracuse, New York. Nick wore a suit, a white shirt, a tie, all recently purchased from Bob's cache of nearly thirty thousand dollars that he wore in a moneybelt. Bob had bought a suit and tie, too —he looked almost civilized.

Nick turned and faced the house, and took a swallow.

"Oh, my," Nick suddenly said. "We are finally here."

This was the hardest thing, and it had placed a large ball of ice in his stomach.

Bob just chewed on a toothpick, looked ahead through the windshield of the rented Buick.

"Got to do it, Memphis."

Nick exhaled four or six lungsful of air, just kept blowing the stuff off as the melancholy crept through him.

"I cross this line, I may never get back."

"You don't cross this line, they may kill you on the wrong side of it."

"Doesn't help much," said Nick. "Not the way I was raised."

The line was the felony line. It had haunted him since Bob had laid the plan before him; but it was the only way.

"This is it?"

"Yeah, 'fraid so. No other way to get what we want and get it fast. Look at it this way. These bad boys from this RamDyne outfit probably going to blow you out of your socks in a day or two anyway, what difference does it make then?"

Bob smiled at him again.

"Okay," said Nick. He knew that so far in his adventures he'd done nothing illegal, though he'd stretched the elasticity of the law considerably. This was different. He was about to represent himself as a Federal agent, when he no longer was one. It violated Federal Code 28–02.4, and it carried three to five, though if he ever went over on it, he knew he'd be out in six months maximum, unless somebody was really mad at him. But he also knew he'd never work his side of the street again.

"Okay," said Nick again. "Let's do it. And to hell with Howdy Duty."

"This *is* your duty," said Bob.

They knocked on the door and a little girl answered. Nick took out his identification.

"Hi," he said. "My name is Nicholas Memphis and I'm a special agent of the Federal Bureau of Investigation. May I see your daddy, please, honey?"

She ducked in and in a few seconds a grave, thin man in a cardigan appeared.

"Yes?" he asked, running a hand through his hair.

"Mr. Porter, I'm Nicholas Memphis, special agent of the Federal Bureau of Investigation. My associate, Special Agent Fencl."

"Sir," nodded Bob.

"Have I—"

"No, no, sir," said Nick fast. "But if our information is correct, it's from this address that you edit and collate and send out *Accuracy Shooting*, the newsletter of benchrest shooting?"

Porter swallowed.

"Uh, yes, that's correct. I'm an insurance executive but I've been benchresting fifteen years. I inherited the editorship ten years ago. A labor of love, really. I lose time and money on it. But I've gotten some good friends out of it and had lots of fun."

"Yes, sir. We understand."

"Mr. Porter," said Bob, "we're looking for a man who may be involved in several shootings."

"Oh, God—" said Porter.

"And our information suggests that he was at one time one of the leading benchresters in the country."

"Oh, no," said Porter. "Benchresters aren't like that. We're not talking about, you know, survivalists, AK-47's, that sort of thing. These are just tinkerers who love to play with their completely useless rifles and loads and shoot tiny groups. Gosh, they just sit there and shoot and cuss, that's all. It's the most boring thing you ever saw. It's enormously challenging to do, but to watch it it's—"

"Our information is pretty good, Mr. Porter. You know, there's always one or two in any group who can give it a bad name."

"God, it's so *harmless*," Porter said. "I'd hate to have

the damn newspapers to get ahold of something like this and say, you know, that benchresting was training for sniping or some such—"

"Mr. Porter, the last thing we'd ever do is talk to the press, you can be sure of that. What we'd like to do is examine your subscription list. This is an older man, he was active in benchrest shooting back in the late fifties, and we believe that if he's a subscriber, he'd almost certainly have been one for a long time. As we understand it, the publication began as a shooting club newsletter right back in the early sixties?"

"That's right. You're looking for a name?"

"No, sir, almost certainly he's living under a pseudonym. But we have several other characteristics, and if we get a set of names from you, we can compare them to other lists and look for correspondences. We can assure you your information will be held in strictest confidence."

"And I suppose if I said no, you'd get a subpoena."

"Mr. Porter," said Nick, "this is a friendly visit, not a hostile one. If you'd like to call a family lawyer and have him come over and advise you, that would be fine. We can wait."

"No, no," said Porter. "No, come on in. Would you guys like some coffee?"

"Thank you, no, sir," said Nick.

Porter led them through pleasant rooms until at last they reached his study, where an IBM PC and an Epson printer stood on the desk. The room was heavily lined with shelves, and Nick recognized many standard texts of ballistics, many reloading manuals, but also *Crime and Punishment*, *Portnoy's Complaint* and *The Great War and Modern Memory*, all books he'd planned on reading sometime. On one wall hung a series of the typescript covers of *Accuracy Shooting*.

"I went to the computer two years ago," Porter said.

"It was getting to be too damn much with the paste-up. I can do each issue in one operation now. And I've got loads of volunteer help. And my wife helps with the typing. It's great fun, we've loved every second of it."

"Yes, sir," said Nick. Bob hung back, letting Nick do the talking. Great, Nick thought, I'm in so deep now there's no way of ever getting out.

"Now, I have twenty-seven-thousand-five-hundred-odd subscribers, Mr. Memphis. Do you want me to print out a whole list or something?"

"Sir, is there any way you can break it down by chronology? That is, early subscribers, that sort of thing. First subscribers. We're quite convinced that our man would have found out about you early and been one of the first subscribers."

"Hmmm," said Porter. "You know, I don't think I could run a program to shake it out that way; I've set the whole thing up to run alphabetically. Whenever I get a new subscriber, I add him to the list and the thing just inserts it where it should be."

"I see."

"How did you get your subscribers, Mr. Porter?" asked Bob.

"Well, I've taken out classified ads in *SGN* and in the slick gun mags. And of course there's a subscription form in every copy of the magazine."

"No, I mean *originally*. When it was first started. That first year, what was that, 1964? How'd they start it off?"

"Well, as I understand it, it was started informally as a newsletter of match results. And now and then a small technical article. The men were all driven to communicate what they were working on. And people who were just interested in the sport or the experiments or what have you began to ask to get on the mailing list. And I think they first started selling subscriptions, yes, it was 1964, after the newsletter became an actual magazine."

"Those first subscription requests. Say, the first thousand. Any idea what became of them?"

"Oh, Lord. Did I throw them away? I got all that stuff from old Milt Omahundro who used to put it out. God, I—No, I think I've got some old cartons out in the garage."

"Could we see them?"

"Sure. This way."

And he led them out into the garage, where against one wall a pile of cardboard boxes stood.

"Oh, Lord, I just don't—"

"Mr. Porter," said Bob. "Tell you what. If you get me some coffee like you offered before this young man said no, I'd be happy to go through those boxes for you. And I'll make damn sure it's as neat when we leave as it is now. Fair enough?"

"Well, that's the best offer I've had in weeks," said Porter.

Bob and Nick got busy, and it was Bob who worked the hardest. Taking off his coat and folding it neatly, he threw himself against the task with that same thorough intensity that always numbed Nick. He'd pause to take a sip of the coffee now and then, but mainly he just plunged ahead.

He'd make a good cop, thought Nick, who had never been outworked before.

It was in the last box and it was Bob who found them: the first thousand or so subscription forms to *Accuracy Shooting*, now yellowed with age. Many were simply letters that had had checks enclosed and still bore the imprint of a paper clip or the punctures of a staple; some were index cards or postcards. Only a few were forms. It was a box of old memories crumbling into dust. Hard to look at it and think that something so utterly banal—a box of forgotten letters and forms—might hold a key to something so monstrous as the shooting of Archbishop Roberto Lopez in New Orleans.

"I'll be," said Porter. "That takes me back awhile. I'd forgotten all about those. Didn't even know I still had them."

"Sir," said Nick, "what we'd like to do is write you out a receipt for this material, then return it to you when we've completed our investigation."

"Oh, I don't know. If I'd have found them, I might have thrown them out myself. Why don't you just take the damned things and if you lose them, so much the better."

"Yes, sir, but I'd be happy to write out the receipt."

"No, you just go on and go. I've got work to do."

The next day, Shreck drove alone down through Virginia and into North Carolina, following complicated directions. There, in the shadows of the Blue Ridge Mountains, just over the state line, he turned down a private road for perhaps a mile until he came to an electronic gate. He got out of the car and pressed the buzzer on an intercom system.

"Yes?" came the voice.

"My name is Shreck," he said.

"All right," came the voice.

The door slid open, and Shreck got in and drove for another two hundred yards. Sitting in the shadow of a six-hundred-foot hill was a handsome ranch house, rambling, bright, and open. Shreck had always lived in apartments, almost monastically: but he had a moment of awe when he saw the spread—it was beautiful, and if he ever had a place, this is the sort of place he'd have. Whoever this guy was, he had money. He parked and got out. A cement ramp led up to double doors. The house had no steps.

Shreck walked up the ramp, found the door open.

"I'm in the shop," came the call over the loud-speaker.

Shreck walked through the house, through its wide doors, past the sun deck. Out back he could see the rifle range, the white targets lodged against the base of the hill.

At last he reached the rear of the house, and stepped through another wide door. A man who looked ten years older than he was sat curled in a wheelchair and was very carefully turning a single brass shell in his hand as he worked it with some kind of metalworking tool, a keylike handle that embraced a brass cartridge case locked in a vise.

"Hello, Colonel Shreck."

"Hello, Mr. Scott."

Lon Scott wore his gray hair short and neat above the long face and aquiline profile of a blue blood. His eyes were dark and ropes of veins showed along the muscled ridges of his forearms and hands. But his body was horribly twisted, the spine bent like a bow, his dead legs awkwardly spindled beneath him. He couldn't exercise his body, so it had acquired a packing of fat, and his stomach bulged under his belt. Once beautiful, he was now grotesque.

Shreck tried to let nothing show on his face, but he knew a trace of horror had crept into his eyes; and he knew Scott noticed.

"Not very pretty, is it? That's what a bullet in the spine can do to a healthy growing boy, Colonel. Turn him into a geranium."

"I'm sorry, sir. I just—"

"Don't worry. I can handle it. Now, my friend Hugh Meachum said you had some bad news for me. Let's have it, Colonel. You don't look like the sort of man who pulls his punches."

"Yes, sir," said Shreck. "It's a loose end. A detail that

won't go away. New Orleans. The man we were using as our asset."

"The Marine?"

"Yes. He was supposed to be dealt with; by some freak he survived a point-blank chest shot. Must have missed his heart by a hair. And now he's back, teamed up with an FBI agent."

"This Marine. A good man?"

"The very best."

"As good as you are? I understand you're quite the warrior."

"Better."

"But you have a plan?"

"That's correct. It's our feeling that he'd be unusually responsive to something from shooting culture. For example, he may have identified the rifle of yours that he used in Maryland. It's our idea to put an ad in *The Shotgun News* for a book of some sort, a privately printed volume as is common in the culture, on famous target rifles or shooters or some such, and if he sees it, he'd want to approach the author. And we nail him."

"Why do you need my permission?"

"Well, sir, in this business, we find that as close as we can come to the authentic when we fabricate, the better off we are. We can't just make stuff up. We've got to build a legend that he can verify himself from other sources. This is a very careful man. And that's why we need . . . well, information as well as permission."

Lon Scott nodded.

"My past? My family? That sort of thing?"

"Yes, sir."

Scott seemed to have a funny moment here; it was an odd shiver, something between a shudder and a snort. As if he almost laughed or almost choked.

"My father," he finally said. "My poor old father."

"Yes, sir."

"I see," said Scott, following intently.

"There are alternatives," said the colonel, who had now, with much effort, mastered the blank look in the face of Lon's infirmity. "We can hope to ride this out while Swagger and this FBI agent peck away at us. Our tracks have been hidden well, but . . . but they've consistently surprised us. Eventually, they just might stumble onto something, and possibly by that time it would be too late. My theory of war has always been aggressive offensive operations. I was once called a meat grinder. But I believe you ultimately spare lives by responding aggressively."

Lon listened raptly, only stopping momentarily to hawk up a wad of brackish phlegm from somewhere in his throat to dribble it into a spittoon that the colonel had not until then noticed.

"There are risks, of course. The first is that we must feed him your name. I understand your privacy is important to you."

"My name has not been in public print since I stopped bench resting in the early sixties. I'm sure I'm forgotten now. It frightens me, of course. It's such a small thing . . . but of course it opens up the faint possibility of inquiries that might lead to associations and linkages . . . well, who knows? Pandora's box. These things take on a life of their own."

"Yes, sir. It's just that I feel there's no other way. Swagger would see through everything else. He'd nibble us to death for years. We'd be stuck. We must eliminate him, or everything will be gone."

Scott sighed. Melancholy seemed to overtake him, too.

"My, my, my," he finally said. "After all these years."

"Yes, sir."

"And I suppose if this man isn't stopped, he puts Hugh at risk as well."

"Yes, sir," said Colonel Shreck.

"Well, I owe Hugh a considerable debt, Colonel Shreck. He's a great man. How long have you known him?"

"Since 1961, sir, when we were training the Bay of Pigs invasion force in Guatemala. He's watched over my career ever since."

"That's Hugh. He takes responsibility. He *cares.* He lets you become what your talents allow. Without him, I'd have lost myself in my bitterness. I made a deal with Hugh Meachum and it's paid dividends to both of us. I'm with you. Whatever you say, whatever you require. I'm yours."

"Yes, sir. Thank you, sir. As I say, Mr. Scott, your name, your family, his—"

"Well, you know, you've certainly hit the jackpot there. My father was a famous man, a celebrity back in the thirties. The story of what he accomplished with the Tenth Black King and what it led to . . . well, it *would* make a great American book. And in the shooting world, his name even to this day is instantly recognizable. Yes, I'll get you some things that you'll find helpful."

"Thank you."

"But I want something from you in return."

"Yes, sir?"

"I want in all the way. If I'm bait, then let him come to me. To me here. We'll go all the way. I'll do my part. This place is perfect; remote, access to a mountain, everything you need. Your boys can drive him up Bone Hill." He gestured over his shoulder and Shreck could see the Blue Ridge foothill out back, its flanks covered in scrubby vegetation, its knob bald. "That's where he'll die, atop Bone Hill."

This was exactly what Shreck had been playing for. Once again, the great Lon Scott had hit the bull's-eye.

"That'll make it much easier, sir," Shreck said.

"Now what?" asked Nick. "We've got over a thousand names here. One of them may be phony, the pseudonym of a man who disappeared himself close to thirty years ago. How are the two of us going to winnow them down?"

"He can change a name, Memphis. He can change an address, an appearance, a way of talking. One thing he can't fake. He can't fake legs."

Memphis looked at him. Bob crouched in the half-dark of the motel room, his face lost in shadow.

Nick had to admit it; yes, it was very neatly thought out, elegant perhaps. But he had to take it a further step.

"Is there some kind of register of handicapped persons I don't know about? I mean, we can't call a thousand men whose addresses from thirty years ago we have and ask them if they're paralyzed?"

"There is. We break it down by state, get a list for each state. Then you call each state's Department of Motor Vehicles. You call and you find out who on the list has a handicapped license plate. State computers ought to be able to shake it out real fast."

"*Damn!*" shouted Nick. "Goddamn right, yes, yes. Then, in fifty phone calls we've winnowed the thousand down to just a few. How many can there be? And we *can* check them out."

"That's it, Pork. I'd bet a dollar against tomorrow one of those men will be Lon Scott. Be nice to find out how come he's been hiding all these years, and how it was his famous rifle ended up in the hands of an outfit that kills important people for a living."

Nick began calling the next morning in a rented loft space in downtown Syracuse, near the university, as soon as the phone company got the phones hooked up. Using his federal identification code number, which authenticated him to the supervisory personnel, he was able to begin the computer searches in six states in a couple of hours. But it was exhausting, excruciating work and Nick was astonished to find in himself something he'd never allowed before—dreaminess.

He saw himself on the road, he saw himself somewhat like Bob: free, beholden to nobody. It occurred to him: Could I invent my own life instead of allowing the Bureau to invent it for me? He'd been a man of many masters and eager to do their bidding; now he considered that he could be his own master.

Meanwhile Bob took the calls that came back on the other line.

"Agent Fencl, FBI," he'd say, trying to subdue his Arkansas twang. "Yes, sir, but Agent Memphis is on another line. May I take your information please? I'll see that it reaches him. Yes, ma'am. Yes, could you spell that please? Yes, and is there an address? Thank you very much, you've been very helpful."

It took three days. In the end, they had seven names—that is, seven men who were among the first thousand subscribers to *Accuracy Shooting* and who had been issued handicapped license plates by their state department of motor vehicles sometime between 1964 and today.

"Wow," said Nick. "All that work for seven names. Now, if I were in the damned Bureau, all's I'd have to do is call up the offices in the states of these guys, and have them check them all out. I'd get reports back in thirty minutes. But I suppose our next move is to individually check these seven guys out?"

"Yep. Of course I don't know what the original Lon Scott looked like. But I do know that he dropped out of sight in 1963 and hasn't been heard from since. So seems to me, one thing we ought to find out is how old these boys are, and we can reject anybody who wasn't at least in his twenties in 1962; and we can reject anybody who wasn't already crippled in 1962. Maybe that'll get it down some."

"No, wait a minute," said Nick. "No, we're going at this wrong. Look, think about it this way. The guy we're looking for, the real Lon Scott, has one distinguishing characteristic—that is, he has a new identity. Now, the classical way in which you build a new identity is to take over the identity of a child who was born on or about the same time you were but who died in the next few years. See, nobody ever correlates birth certificates with death certificates. So you get the name of a child who died a few years after he was born from a graveyard or an old newspaper obituary; then you write to the state department of birth registration and say you're him and you get a copy of his birth certificate. Then you use that as the basis of the new identity. Right?"

It was right. Bob nodded, for the first time looking almost as if impressed.

"Go on," he finally said.

"So we call the counties in which the seven names reside, we call the death certificate registries, and we find which of the seven has died. And if we find one of those to be the case, then we know that somebody's resurrected the name to use as the basis for the new identity. And wouldn't that be our man?"

Bob looked at him long and hard.

Then he said, "You finally said something worth listening to, though you *explained* half to death. Now get busy."

"The ad runs today," said Dobbler, "in the 'Books and Magazines' section of *The Shotgun News,* just a few lines. Here's the copy."

He handed it to Shreck.

ART SCOTT: AMERICAN SHOOTER. The true story of the fabled marksman of the thirties who won the National Thousand Yard Match four times in the thirties and forties and twice more in the fifties with his famous TENTH BLACK KING Model 70 .300 H & H Magnum. Complete with pictures drawn from family archives and load data. Postpaid, $49.50, or order from James Thomas Albright, P.O. Box 511, Newtsville, N.C. 28777, 704-555-0967; Visa, MasterCard.

"It doesn't even mention Lon Scott," said Shreck.

"It can't. Too obvious. It has to be subtle! If it's obvious, he'll smell a trap and never come close. He's made the connection to the Tenth Black King, I guarantee you! You can't *force* these things!"

He almost shouted, forgetting to whom he was talking.

Shreck just took a pace back.

"How do we know he'll spot it?" he asked.

"We *trust* him. He might not find it right away. But as he travels he'll talk to people who will have seen it. He *will* find it, that I guarantee you. And he'll obey the instructions in the ad."

The phone number reached, through several blind linkages, an answering machine in RamDyne headquarters.

"The message they hear simply tells them to leave Visa or MasterCard numbers, and to give their addresses," said Dobbler. "So they leave their voices on the tape. Now this is very important. You see, we have the taped interrogations of both Memphis and Swagger, Memphis recorded in the interrogation in the swamp and Swagger during your discussions with him back in Maryland. So we've made a voice scan and reduced their voices to an electronic signature, which is in turn coded into a computer. Every call we get is automatically filtered through the computer and it is instantaneously checked against the vocal signatures. When we get a match, it lets us know."

"And then . . ."

"And then we reel him in. Slowly. Ever so slowly, trusting our instincts and our reading of Swagger's character. We reel him in and destroy him. It's like hunting a predator with bait. The bait is the research . . . or it's his illusion that he can get out of this and somehow clear himself."

Shreck nodded.

"It *is* clever," he conceded.

Dobbler looked at Shreck and realized that for the first time, he wasn't frightened of him.

For almost a week there were so many times they were close that it made them almost half-crazy. They spent the days on the phone in the Syracuse loft, and after the close of business hours in the last of the western states, they'd come out and go for a walk, get something to eat, just stretch and decompress. They made an odd couple: the tall, thin middle-aged man who had a way of holding himself in; the thicker, friendlier younger man, hair blond and thatchy, eyes brown and warm, whose gentle bulk hid considerable strength. They almost never talked as they walked and ate. They seemed comfortable in the silence.

Then one night, Bob asked about the chair.

"What's it do to a person? The chair."

At first Nick thought he was asking about the *electric* chair, and thought somehow in his FBI career Nick had seen an execution or two. But then he realized Bob meant to touch on something he'd said at Colonel O'Brien's. Chair. Wheelchair.

"Ah. It sucks. I think I hated it more than she did. Because it was my damn failure, my damn guilt. Sometimes at night, I'd lie there listening to her breathe. You could see the damn thing in the moonlight. It was like it was laughing at you."

"Suppose you were in it? Suppose your own daddy had put you there, and then blown the top of his head off in grief. What would that do to you?"

"I don't know," said Nick.

"Well, dammit, think about it. Give me an answer. I have to know why this bird did what he did."

"Hell, bitterness, I suppose. It could cripple you so bad you'd hate the world. That didn't happen to her, of course; she was too special and decent. But to someone else? I suppose it could easily lead you to guns, to feel the power in them that your body was deprived of. The gun could complete a paraplegic. It could make him very, very dangerous. But there are so many killers in this world who aren't crippled. What's so special about one that is?"

Bob just looked at him, rather sadly.

"You still don't get it, do you, Pork?"

"Get what?"

"Come on, we'd best be heading back. More phone calls tomorrow."

But as the time passed, the chance of the great breakthrough seemed to recede. All the calls had been made, sometimes two and three times. In ever widening circles, they'd tried to match death certificates against the seven names, patiently hunting through counties and then states. Somehow, however, the connection seemed to evaporate as they drew near to it.

"Suppose we'll just have to drive out and find each of these damn guys and eyeball 'em and go from there," Bob said. He was looking at the current issue of *The Shotgun News*, which he'd just picked up on a newsstand, as he did every other week, irritating Nick no end. It was such a dirty little rag, full of close print and murky black and white pictures of surplus guns. "The rag," Bob called it with a snort of joyful contempt. It didn't even have stories—just pages and pages of gun deals.

"You know, I'm really beginning to wonder if pursuing Annex B might not be a more reasonable course at this point. Working with Sally Ellion, there still might be a way to get into the Bureau's computer bank. She's very smart. She likes me. I think—"

"You just want to nail that nice young gal, Pork, why don't you admit it?"

"No, she's a *nice* girl, I just—"

The phone rang.

"Agent Memphis."

"Mr. Memphis. I'm Susan Jeremiah, in the Clark County, North Carolina, registrar's office?"

"Oh, yes, right, I remember. I talked to you some days ago. About the seven names—"

"That's right."

"And you couldn't help?"

"No sir. But I got to thinking on it. One of those names on that list was a James Thomas Albright. And there was no James Thomas Albright on my list of deaths for the years 1935 through 1945."

"No. That's what you told me—"

"But I got to thinking there *was* an Albright. A Robert Parrish Albright, who died when he was two in 1938, right here in Clark County."

"I see," said Nick.

"The names being so similar. I just got curious and couldn't stop thinking about it. So I went and checked our names registration. You know, with a valid birth certificate, you can petition the court to change your name legally."

"Of course."

"And I was stunned to discover that in June of 1963,

a Robert Parrish Albright of this county petitioned the court to change his name to James Thomas Albright. The request was granted, and nobody had ever bothered to check the changed name against the death certificates. No one knew that the real Robert Parrish Albright had died in 1938."

Nick swallowed. He felt as if he'd just looked behind a veil someone had very carefully put in place years back. For him it was one of those queer, powerful moments when an investigation, out of so many loose threads and blind paths and false leads, suddenly connected into something. A small, powerful jolt blasted through him.

"Thank you, Mrs. Jeremiah. Thank you so much." And then he turned to Bob, trying to seem laconic.

"I found him," he said.

"Oh, yeah," said Bob, yawning. "James T. Albright of North Carolina. Hey, I found him too." He held up *The Shotgun News*. "The dumb bastard wrote a book!"

The suspense was murderous: all those phone calls from all over the United States. It shouldn't have amazed Dobbler that there were so many of them but it did.

"Hello, my name is Walter Murbach of Sherman Oaks, California. I am very interested in the book about the Tenth Black King. My Visa card number is . . ."

There were dozens like that, and in a week or two the dozens permutated into hundreds. Over 350 calls were received, all of them earnest, none of them, according to vocal signature, Bob or Nick Memphis.

"I don't think it's working," said Shreck.

"It will work," said Dobbler. "I know Bob. Bob has been my project for close to a year. I know him. This is the only way."

Shreck grunted, displeased.

And so they waited. And so another day passed and

another, and Dobbler was at home in his apartment, paging through back issues of *The American Rifleman*, when the phone call came.

"Dobbler."

"Dr. Dobbler, it's the phone watch operations officer. We think we've got a positive ID on a phone call we received approximately seven minutes ago. The computer analysis makes it an almost perfect match to Memphis."

"What name did he leave?"

"Ah . . . he left the name Special Agent Nicholas Memphis, Federal Bureau of Investigation."

Yes, this is Special Agent Nicholas Memphis, Federal Bureau of Investigation, calling for Mr. Albright. We have reason to seek an interview with Lon Scott, who was the son of Art Scott, and wonder if Mr. Albright has any information pertaining to his whereabouts. The number is four-four-two, three-one-two, three-oh-eight-oh. I should add that refusal to cooperate could be actionable under federal statute.

Nick's voice spun itself out of the tape recorder.

"Congratulations," said Shreck. "Now give me some sense of how we play it."

"Thank you, Colonel," Dobbler said, secretly very pleased. "Now, um, as to operating principles. There's only one, and I can't press it too forcefully. At no point until the ultimate moment must we seem aggressive. Bob is abnormally attuned to aggression; he lives in Condition Yellow, never completely at rest, always scanning the horizon for clues. His radar never goes down. And when he senses threat, it sets his bells off; nothing must be forced. No one must stare. Nothing must be elongated. No hints of trap must be given. We must operate totally without self-consciousness. Now. Who's going to call him?"

"You are," said Shreck.

The phone rang.

"Oh, my," said Nick.

"Answer it," said Bob.

"Oh, my," said Nick again. It had been almost a week since they'd made the initial call.

"Go on," said Bob.

"Agent Memphis," Nick said, picking up the phone.

"Yes, this is James Albright. I was told to call you in a phone message last week. I only played the tape today. I— What's this all about?"

"Yes, thank you for getting back to me," said Nick as officiously as possible. "It's come to our attention that you've published a book about Art Scott, the target shooter?"

"Yes. I knew Art years back. I saw him shoot one of his last championships. He was a wonderful—"

"We have reason to suspect that a rifle owned by Mr. Scott's son Lon may have been used in a serious Federal crime—"

"The Tenth Black King? Do you know where it is?"

"Ah," said Nick, a little taken aback, "no, no, we hoped *you* might know where it is?"

"I wish I did. That rifle would be worth tens of thousands of dollars today."

"Well, we're trying to locate Lon Scott, who seems to have vanished thirty years ago."

"Now there's a mystery for you. Wish I could help you."

"Hmmm. Yes. Your ad says you have some of Art Scott's personal effects—"

"I have all his shooter's notebooks, his notes on reloading, the results of his experiments, many of his medals and ribbons. But nothing personal—well, a couple of diaries which I never paid much attention to."

"I see. Mr. Albright, it's imperative that we locate

either Lon Scott or his remains. It's my thought that in his father's effects there might be information useful to us. Perhaps I could send a team down and examine the materials."

"That's all you want? Hell, why didn't you say so. Sure, come on down. Be happy to let you see the stuff."

"Thank you very much."

The man on the other end gave him directions and Nick said he'd see him in two days, Thursday, at nine-thirty. Mr. Albright said that was okay by him, he wasn't going anywhere.

"Not bad," said the Colonel.

"Did I slather on the old-boy business too heavily?" Dobbler wanted to know.

"No," said the Colonel, his shrewd eyes narrowed in concentration. "You brought the family in, then backed out of it. You established your distance from 'Lon Scott.' What they think they're getting is another step in the link, and not the final step. Now all we have to do is wait. They're coming in."

The waiting was hardest on Payne, man of action. Thus, without orders, he seconded himself to central Virginia and the RamDyne training facility. The men of Panther Battalion, his old compadres under arms, had arrived on its thousands of acres to prepare their assault on Fortress Bob.

There he watched as the lean young troopers worked on the assault plan. He watched them deploy, having moved off their mock helicopters, move up the hill that was a close duplicate of Bone Hill under heavy automatic weapons suppressive fire, and assault its summit, where Bob would be alone with no weapon other than the Colt automatic he was known to favor.

Even Brigadier General de Rujijo had come along on this mission.

"Is it not too much, *Sergento*?" he asked Payne. "This is one man, no?"

It was a logical question. With a base of full automatic suppressive fire, plus the fire and movement elements pouring out lead as they progressed upwards, Payne had calculated that over ten thousand bullets would be hurled at the summit in less than two minutes. For one man?

"He must be *el grande hombre*," said de Rujijo.

"He ain't that big a deal," Payne said. "My boys could smoke him." But still, he took great pleasure in the display. The bullets, soaring raucously upwards and blasting against the summit, had literally torn it to shreds. There was no place to hide or survive on that mean ground; it was the land of the sucking chest wound and the exit hole six times as large as the entrance.

The plan was simple. Three platoons from the counterinsurgency company of Panther Battalion—close to 120 men, all heavily armed with Israeli Galil assault rifles in 5.56mm—were to be deployed at a small deserted airfield some two miles from Lon Scott's house, their presence completely unknown to the target, and no hints of it allowed to surface. When Bob made his approach, whosoever was playing Lon—not yet determined—would activate a signal simply by removing his hand from the wheelchair grip and thereby allowing a photocell to be stimulated by the light, no buttons to push, no anything. The four choppers with eight men apiece would be airborne in seconds and deploy for the assault within two minutes; four minutes later the choppers would return with the second load of men, then repeat until all 120 men were on site. The debarked troops, as well as the men from RamDyne's own Action

Unit, would converge on the house frontally. Bob, upon seeing the extent of the trap, would almost certainly depart the back, by the pool and the rifle range and discover only Bone Hill, six hundred feet of scrubby pine, gulches, washouts and switchbacks, up top of which was a bare knob. The sniper would almost certainly choose to climb it. Up he'd go, until there was no place to go.

CHAPTER THIRTY

Lon insisted. And Lon could be stubborn and willful and infuriatingly impossible to budge.

"Mr. Scott, I can't have it," Shreck said. "We have extremely competent people for this sort of thing. It's not for you. It's far too dangerous."

"It's my house. I'm the bait," he said. "So I'll be the one."

"The second he sees you in that wheelchair, he'll know who you are."

"Fine. It makes no difference."

"Suppose he shoots you?"

"Then I've had a full life. Considering my limitations, I've had a wonderful life. If it happens, it'll happen. But it won't happen."

"Why not?"

"This Marine. He's not like that. He couldn't pull his pistol and execute a man in a wheelchair no matter what crimes the man in the wheelchair has committed and no matter that he himself, when he hears the helicopters landing, will understand that he's a dead man. He still won't do it. I know him. I knew his type among the Southern shooters before I lost my legs. My father was a lot like him. No, he won't do it. He's sick with honor."

Shreck had to concede that Scott was probably right. No less a Bob Lee Swagger expert than Dobbler had given his acquiescence to Scott's decision.

But Shreck himself was curious about it.

He looked at the misshapen man, whose handsome skull now lolled idiotically to the left, as its owner had momentarily lost control of it.

"Why? What do you gain from it?"

Lon smiled from his wheelchair and Shreck shuddered. Lon's even, distant, icy gaze bore into him. Outside he could hear the hammers and crowbars pounding and ripping as a work detail from Tiger Battalion tore down the wheelchair ramp into the house.

Finally, Lon Scott answered.

"I want the chance to look him in the eye. I want to share the moment with him. I want him to see me and know who I am and what I've done with what I was handed. I want some eye contact with him and see what electricity transfers between us in those last seconds when he knows he's doomed. The great Bob Lee Swagger, who's killed so many times. We should have this moment together, Bob and I. We are at the top of our profession."

Shreck thought it would be quite a meeting; a summit of professional world-class killers, each strangely courageous.

"All right, Mr. Scott, but don't do anything foolish. Don't get cute with him. You let him come in, you remove your hand from the light cell, and you hide. Panther Battalion will be here in seconds; and we waste his ass. That's all it's about: killing him, before he kills us."

"Fine."

The surveillance was extremely soft, men without radios who had been instructed to stare at nothing, to make no eye contact, but just to hope that what they'd been sent to see would arrive. They were established at various roads into the area, at coffee shops, across from shopping malls, at restaurants.

And it did happen, late that night. A rented red Chevy pulled into the parking area outside the Danville Sheraton, and from the darkness on the roof of the Big Boy across the street a RamDyne spotter watched as a tall lanky man got out, stretched in the bright pool of the fluorescent light, then went into the motel office. He came out in a bit and moved the car. Then he and another man, husky and blond, walked up the outside stairs leading to the second-floor balcony that ran the full length of the building and into two adjacent rooms. The spotter watched as they came back out to the car, and was able to follow its passage a quarter of a mile to the Pizza Hut; then he called headquarters.

Within ten minutes, the Electrotek 5400 surveillance van pulled up discreetly across the street.

"You want me to try and get a tap into their rooms?" asked Eddie Nickles.

"Nah," said Payne, not quite believing it was happening. "Nah, we don't even know if it's them."

But it was. The Chevy pulled up and parked, and Payne watched as Bob Lee Swagger, big as life, got out of the car two hundred yards away. He'd recognize that lanky walk anywhere, with its faint hitch in one leg from the wound so long ago; he'd studied it for weeks, and dreamed about it for months.

Jesus, if he had a rifle with a good night scope. With infrared, he could do Bob right here as he ambled with his buddy toward the stairway up to the second-floor balcony, place the dot in the center of the back and squeeze. Blow his spine out. It would be over in the space of time it took the bullet to eat up the yardage.

But the only thing he had was his Remington sawed-off in the custom rig running down his left side, under his fatigue jacket.

"It's him?" asked Eddie Nicoletta.

"Yes, goddammit," Payne said sharply.

"Shit, man, they look like they don't suspect a thing. Man, we could do it, Payne-O, you, me, the guys. Hit him hard and fast. Kick in the fuckin' door, you let fly with your double-ought, I empty a clip, then it's over, man. We're fuckin' home free, plus we're heroes."

"You think he don't sleep with a piece cocked and locked? One tenth of a second after you're through that door, you're dead. The guy's a fuckin' champ, and you know it. Now shut up and let me think."

He turned to the Electrotek technician.

"Can you put the directional microphone beam on their room?"

"No problem," said the man. "If there's not a lot of white noise in the air, we'll get 'em big as day."

Suddenly, the door to the young one's room opened and he went running down the balcony and began banging excitedly on Swagger's door.

"Fuckin' guy's excited, Payne-O."

"Hurry up," Payne said to the technician.

Swinging the long foam-covered boom, the technician sighted in, twisted knobs.

"Bring it up," said Payne. "And get the tapes going."

Two voices began to crystallize over the babble as the man worked his digitized control panel.

"—more promising, really. I'm telling you."

Yes, it was Memphis, emerging out of the background noise.

"I don't know."

Swagger now. The voice was bell-clear, its drawly Arkansas rhythms stretching it out.

"Look, listen to me on this just once, okay?"

Bob was silent.

"She said she'd brief me on the organization of the computerized files and the code word structure. That's a start, at least. It's better than chasing this wild-goose hope that there's some information buried in diaries thirty years old."

"Memphis, I don't like going in without a backup gun around."

"Listen to me, Bob, please, just this once. If we can get Annex B it gives us names. Not names like 'Payne' and 'Shreck.' Those are the up-front guys. Annex B gives us the real powers—the people who don't carry the guns but figure it all out and give the orders. *Names.* Addresses. It's the only way we'll take these guys down. Otherwise we lose. Bob, I have to go to her and try and get her working with us again."

There was something that sounded like a transmission breakup but then it came to Payne that Swagger was sighing.

"I hate going into any place blind," he finally said.

"It's an old man who wrote a book about a shooter who died in the fifties. You don't need backup. What you need is a little patience. You're going to have to sit there all afternoon and read those diaries. Maybe you'll come up with something, maybe you won't. But that was your idea, not mine. Meanwhile, I'll get down to

New Orleans, and meet with her and we'll have some idea of what we're up against. Then . . . then we can go to the Bureau. With the evidence, we can get indictments. We can bring them down, we can save our own lives. We can bring it off."

But Bob just repeated, "Hate to go into any place blind, no backup."

"He's a cautious bastard, isn't he," said Nickles. "Scary son of a bitch."

"That's why he don't make mistakes," said Payne.

"I called," Nick was saying. "I can get a cab to drive me to the Richmond airport. I can get an eight A.M. flight to New Orleans and get there by ten."

The conversation trailed off.

Finally, Bob said, "Shit. Meet me back here at noon day after tomorrow. And be careful, dammit. Be careful. You won't have any backup either."

"I'm just going to New Orleans," said Memphis, radiant with delight, sounding like a man in love.

"Christ," said Eddie Nickles. "Do we follow him?"

Payne studied on it. Then he said, "We ain't got enough guys. We can always nail this fucking weenie kid. No. Swagger's the one. We'll stick with Swagger and nail him tomorrow."

Dobbler was alone in his office. It was late, past eleven, and he thought maybe he'd try to scrunch up on the sofa instead of going home. Then, tomorrow . . .

Well, tomorrow would take care of tomorrow. Bob would go up the mountain. Panther Battalion would go up the mountain.

But Dobbler knew he was too excited to sleep. His mind was abuzz with possibility. He looked at his watch again. Only seven minutes had passed since. Time was crawling.

He decided to work. He sat at his desk, looked at the

Bob Swagger folders before him, one for RELATIONSHIPS and another for SOUTHERN HERITAGE and another for PARENTS and still another on SHOOTING. Yet he could not bring himself to open them. What was there to be learned at this late date?

Then he looked at his in-basket. Funny, he hadn't noticed it before, a brown interoffice envelope. What could it possibly mean? He hated interoffice mail; it always equaled trouble. He had an impulse to throw the thing in the wastebasket.

Sighing, he opened it anyway. It was a good thing he did.

In the command tent by the deserted airfield seven miles from Lon Scott's place, Shreck was almost asleep when the call came. It took him a while to quite understand what Dobbler was raving about. But then it came through.

"Yes. They tried for weeks and weeks to get into the FTD computer network and finally they did! Anyway, they ran a program to dredge out all the FTD shipments—"

"What are you talking about, Dobbler?"

"Flowers. Flowers! Bob has sent flowers to someone once a year for ten years. Anyway, a guy in Computer Services, they got into the FTD system at last. We thought it was a dead end, but he kept trying, he got into the system, he managed to break the code for the Little Rock florists, he called out all their orders, he broke it down by dates, and every December eleventh for the past ten years, a shipment has gone to a woman in Ajo, Arizona. Roses."

"I—"

"Colonel Shreck, there *is* a woman in Swagger's life. It's the only woman he knows. It's the woman he loves.

Her name is Julie Fenn. It's his great friend Donny Fenn's widow!"

"Ajo, Arizona?" Shreck repeated, thinking. Finally he said, "Good work, Dobbler."

Then he called an aide. "Go get Payne," he said.

CHAPTER THIRTY-ONE

Payne left before dawn, having booked a 10:30 A.M. flight from Richmond to Tucson by two. The whole thing struck him as pretty fucked up. Bob would probably be finished well before that time. What was the point? The woman was irrelevant by then. But he would not question Colonel Shreck.

As he drove off, the men of Panther Battalion were up and making ready for the day. Payne knew this part of the ritual, the preparation for battle. He'd done it himself perhaps a thousand times in the last twenty years. He could feel the tension in the soldiers and also their coarse energy and eagerness to get started. In the darkness, men cursed and jostled tightly, or laughed. Cigarettes glowed, a few men coughed, a few shivered.

But it secretly pleased him to be leaving. As no man ever had except the gook who got inside the wire with his rusted rifle and bayonet, Bob had scared him. He'd shot the fucker in the chest, seen the blood fly, watched him go down. And then he'd gotten up. He'd tracked them. He'd dusted two boys in the swamp. He was a major massacre waiting to happen. It frightened Payne, knowing that he was not capable of what Bob had done.

As the camp disappeared behind him, Payne discovered a sense of release. Let these tough kids go against Bob Lee Swagger. They'd get him, because they had no respect and did not know who he was or care what he had done. To them he was just another gringo. That was what it would take to finally get Bob Lee Swagger: stupidity and overwhelming firepower superiority.

But he knew Swagger would get more than a couple of them.

Bob awakened at around nine-thirty and showered slowly, taking his own sweet time. The men in the surveillance van kept the directional boom aimed on his room, and heard only the sounds of the shower, the easy noises of a man preparing to encounter a relatively benevolent world for the first time. There was no sense of urgency or despair, no track of fear.

He left the room at ten-fifteen, checked out of the motel, threw his bag into the trunk of the rental car, then moseyed into the Howard Johnson's and had a nice breakfast. Two eggs, scrambled, three pieces of bacon, toast and jelly. He bought the Danville *Courier*, and read it at a leisurely pace. The directional boom, in the van discreetly parked two hundred yards away behind the Pizza Hut, stayed on him the whole time.

"Ma'am, could I have another cup of coffee?"

"Why, sure. Nice day."

"Sure is."

"Now let me think, did you take cream and sugar with that?"

"No, ma'am. Black is how I like it."

It took him close to forty minutes to eat. Then he stepped out in the bright sun, a tall, powerful man in jeans and a denim workshirt with a corduroy sport jacket with pearl buttons, put on his sunglasses, and climbed in to be off.

"Bravo Six, this is Bravo Four, the package is on the way," said the observation team leader into his radio. "The package is on the way."

Sitting in the operations shack next to the Millersville Airport where four black-painted Huey helicopters waited, Shreck received the message grimly.

"General de Rujijo! Have your sergeants get the first four squads onloaded the slicks," he said.

The Latino officer grinned, his white teeth glowing.

He turned, and barked in Spanish. Men began to deploy to their ships in seconds, heavily armed, faces blackened with paint, rifles at the high port, festooned in gaudy belts of ammunition for the heavy automatic weapons, black berets at a rakish tilt. With a shrieking whine, the choppers coughed to life and the rhythmic beating of their engines and the roar of the dust their rotors sucked from the earth became a part of the drama.

"It is a good day for a battle, I think," said de Rujijo. "My men are very anxious. They will make me proud, I know. And now we have this thing finished."

Shreck nodded, but said nothing. He looked at his watch.

It would take Bob about a half an hour to drive the last thirty miles to Skytop.

He picked up the phone and dialed Lon Scott.

"Hello."

"Mr. Scott, he's on his way. Half an hour."

"All right."

"How do you feel?"

"I feel fine. Are we set?"

"I guarantee it. The report says he's expecting nothing except some old papers."

"Good," said Lon Scott. "I'm curious to meet him."

"Don't be curious, sir. Just help us kill him. When he comes in the door, you take your hand off the photocell; in two minutes we'll have the first four squads, that's twenty-four heavily armed men there. In ten minutes there'll be more than 150 troopers ringing the hill. Don't mess with him. Let him run clear."

"Oh, I understand," said Lon.

Headquarters had never been so deserted. Dobbler felt as if he were alone in the building. Nearly everyone else was so caught up in the drama they were either down there in North Carolina with Colonel Shreck and Panther Battalion or had gone home. Dobbler also had the odd sense that people were peeling off, slipping away to new lives. Rats deserting a ship, that sort of thing.

Dobbler was finished typing. He was afraid that in the excitement of finally getting Bob, his own contributions to the project would be overlooked. So he'd sat down and typed a long nine-page memo detailing, as modestly as possible, his own role in the Bob Lee Swagger episode. After all, it had been considerable—he had designed the mechanism by which Bob had been initially trapped, he had designed the mechanism by which Bob's "second life" had been terminated, and he had found the woman to whom Bob turned.

He was doing so well here! It was wonderful! And now it was only a matter of waiting. He checked his watch, saw that it was mid-morning and knew even as he stood there that Bob had to be on his way into the trap.

He decided the report was too important to leave to RamDyne's indifferent internal mail system. He walked through the deserted corridors and crossed into Shreck's building. He tried his office door; it was locked. Damn!

"Dr. Dobbler?"

"What! Oh, you surprised me!"

It was one of the security guards.

"Uh, I have to leave this report in Colonel Shreck's office. Do you have a master key?"

"Dr. Dobbler, he don't like nobody in his office."

"The colonel himself just called. He *needs* the report."

Dobbler was amazed at his own assertiveness. He knew his confidence was growing but he hadn't been this assertive since before the arrest. The man's weak eyes blurred in confusion; he could not meet Dobbler's authoritative glare. In seconds, the security man had yielded, opened the room, and allowed him in.

"I'll wait out here till you leave," the guard said.

"No, I'll close up. I have to get some papers too."

"Yes, sir," said the man, in some confusion.

Dobbler went in. In a strange way, he didn't dare turn on the light. He also felt strangely excited. He was violating Shreck's space, albeit harmlessly, but the experience felt titillating.

But the room was as unimpressive as always. It seemed to have no personality whatsoever; the colonel kept his eccentricities, if he had any at all, under the tightest of discipline. There were no pictures on the walls, the desk was bare, there were no loose papers about. The place had the scrubbed, nearly antiseptic sense of the professional military to it; in the dim light, Dobbler could see the whorls the buffer left in the wax on the linoleum floor; those sweeping circles, catching and reflecting the light, were the only evidence of spontaneity in the place.

Dobbler set the report down on Shreck's barren desk. The colonel could not miss it. It was time to leave, but he didn't want the experience to end. He hadn't felt this powerful in years. His eyes hooked on the old wall safe behind the colonel's desk; he had a massive stab of curiosity and mischievousness. The safe was exactly the same as the one in his office, which he rarely bothered to lock. He wondered about the combination—could it be the same, too?

Looking around for just a second to make certain of his isolation, he walked to the safe, and spun the dial. He pulled. Nothing happened.

He laughed.

Of course not. How stupid.

He turned. And turned back, and gave the handle another tug.

It popped open.

The observation post was concealed on a hilltop a mile away from the entrance to Skytop. Young Eddie Nicoletta had drawn the duty because he'd been with Payne on the observation mission in Blue Eye and had eyeballed him through a scope. He was sitting in a hole about four feet deep and looking out a small viewer's slot in some ersatz bushes just inside a ridge line. Before him was a Celestron 8, an eight-inch surveillance telescope, state of the art, forty-three pounds of Schmidt-Cassegrain optics that could be dialed up to 480×, which is where he had it now.

It was tiring peering through the aperture of the lens, which was seated at right angles to the tube itself, a huge fat wad of curved steel atop a squat tripod. Nickles's head hurt and his neck ached.

The Celestron 8 was trained on the road running into

the place called Skytop, and a bit of the ribbon of macadam of the two-lane highway that ran by it. Now and then a truck or a car would materialize out of the wobbling, foreshortened perspective, seem to assemble itself out of pure bolts of light, and purr through his range of focus. Jesus, a mile away and you could see *faces*! It was said you could read a newspaper at a hundred yards with one of these things and Nickles believed it.

But every once in a while, he just had to look up to keep from losing his mind. What he saw then was the half-mile dirt road up to the house itself, though he couldn't see much of the rambling, one-story building beneath the trees. It was enough to tell that it was good-sized, the house of a man who was well off or better. Behind it was a swimming pool, some cement walkways to what appeared to be a shooting range (why cement? Nickles wondered) and beyond that, dominating the property, what they called Bone Hill.

Bone Hill was heavily forested about halfway up its three hundred feet or so of bulk, but then it gave way, as it steepened, to coarse grass and scrawny trees. Its top was bare except for the grass and a few stones strewn about.

That's where he'll go, Eddie Nickles told himself. When the first chopper arrives and the greasers with their combat gear come crashing out, that's where he'll go. He'll go up. He'll run up, and he'll run and run and pretty soon there'll be no place to go.

Nickles got to see it all happen. That pleased him.

"Bravo Four! Bravo Four, you there, goddammit?"

It was Shreck.

"Ah, sorry, Colonel. Yeah, I'm here, nothing much going on."

"Keep your goddamn eyes open, Nicoletta. He ought to be here any minute now."

"Yes, sir," said Nickles.

He put his eye back to the eyepiece, and watched as a Coca-Cola truck lumbered down the road out of the bright nothingness. Then the road was quiet. Minutes passed.

He saw the roof first, emerging over a crest, just a flash. Then it was clear, heading down the road, just as they said, the red Chevy they'd been driving last night, with a single looming, steady silhouette cut off behind the glare of the windshield.

His tension growing, Nickles watched as the face assembled itself from flecks of light as the car moved into the focus zone, a pair of hard-set eyes, a taut jawline, a sense of steadiness.

At a mile away, Bob the Nailer still scared him.

"He's here," Nickles shrieked into the hands-free mike, forgetting all radio procedure. "Bob the Nailer's here."

Bob stopped at the turnoff to Skytop and got out of his car. He took a look around. What he saw was miles and miles of lush North Carolina landscape, rolling hills, a few rills of hard rock, a universe of green. It had been a hot, dry fall and although it was October, the leaves hadn't begun to turn yet.

He took a deep breath as he looked around and his trained eyes probed and saw nothing. The sky was an intense blue, untainted with cloud. The sun was high. It seemed as if the day had stalled somehow, calm and guileless.

Bob took another deep breath, climbed back into his car and went down the road between a double line of swaying poplars to the house. He pulled up on the gravel patch that awaited visitors.

He went up the stairs and knocked on the door.

"It's open," came a call from deep inside. "Come on in, Agent Memphis."

"Thanks," said Bob, walking into the wide hall, and into a sunny beauty of a room lined on one wall with floor-to-ceiling books. The open sliding glass door at the rear gave way to a small jewel of a swimming pool—he could smell the chlorination in the air—and beyond he saw the slope of a large green hunk of hill.

"Mr. Albright?" he called.

What he heard next was an electric purring. Then a man in a motorized chair emerged.

"My name isn't Memphis," said Bob.

"I don't believe it is. I believe it's Bob Lee Swagger."

Bob's eyes beheld the man calmly. He saw the powerful shoulders, the long arms, and the deformed body, soft and twisted and mulched and locked in its chair; and the legs, spindly and bizarre.

"And I believe you'd be Lon Scott."

"Yes, I am."

Bob's hand slipped back into his jeans; without hurry he had the .45 out, thumb snicking off the oversize safety. It was now cocked and unlocked, two pounds of trigger pressure away from the shot that would be the end of Lon Scott. But Scott was still, evidently unarmed.

"You won't shoot me. No matter what we've done to you, I still don't believe you're the kind of man who could shoot a cripple in a chair."

"Cripple? For a cripple, that was a right smart shot you hit in New Orleans, mister. You dropped that bishop at fifteen hundred yards."

"It was fourteen fifty-one. I rebarreled the Black King to .318 and saboted one of the rounds you pumped into the bank in Maryland behind 59 grains of IMR-4895."

Bob raised the pistol and put the front sight on the middle of Lon Scott's swollen belly. He wondered if he shot whether pus would come out. It was like aiming at a tumor or a larva or something. He took about a half a pound out of the trigger.

But Scott didn't scare. It was as if he really didn't give a fuck if Bob pulled the trigger or not.

"It's over. When I saw your face, I took my hand off the chair here and uncovered a photoelectric cell. That sent a signal. Even as we talk they're on their way. Lots of them. Pulling that trigger doesn't mean a thing. You want to take me hostage? Go ahead. They'll shoot right through me into you."

Bob put the pistol down.

He heard the roar of the helicopters. Outside, leaves began to shake under the pulsing of the rotors and vibrations filled the air as the birds swooped in to offload the first squads of killers. It reminded him of the 'Nam; the swift arrival of the choppers, the deployment of the men, the merciless closing in upon the prey. It was the classic air-assault tactic.

"Bob," said Lon Scott, over the noise, "they'll be here in seconds and once those Latino cowboys show up with their assault rifles, there's no stopping them. Let me save you. Let me give you a new life. We're the same man."

Bob flicked the safety back on the Colt, slid it back into his jeans, then smiled.

"Don't kid yourself, wormboy. I'm a soldier. You're only a murderer. And because of what you've done, every man who ever loved a rifle is a suspect in his own house. I know who you are. And you ain't seen nothin' yet."

Then he turned and raced out the door.

Dobbler looked inside the safe. Its contents were prosaic. He saw a handgun, some kind of automatic. There was a wad of bills, and a passport and driver's license, both fake. The colonel had made plans for a fast getaway, prudent enough preparation for a man in his line of work.

And that was it. No family jewels, no dark secrets, nothing remotely incriminating. Dobbler was somewhat disappointed. He'd expected a bit more. He replaced the passport and the license, and felt his fingers bump against something. He withdrew it. It was only a black plastic videotape cassette, unmarked.

Dobbler stood in the darkened office. He could hear each tick and sigh in the building, but no human activity. He stared at the cassette, tempted, a bit afraid. He looked over and yes, the big Sony TV was still at the table on one side of the room, a VCR underneath it on the shelf.

He walked over and inserted the cassette.

His finger trembled as he pushed PLAY.

Bob dashed through the open door to the pool and saw three of them. They had just come around the side of the house at a hell-bent pace, safeties off, fingers cupping and tensing their Galil triggers. They saw him.

They were fast. The rifles came up . . . Bob fired three Silvertips in what seemed a burst but was really three aimed shots unleashed in three tenths of a second, the gun flicking from recoil to sight picture to recoil to sight picture at a speed too quick to measure. He killed two instantly with center-chest hits, dead before their knees gave and they toppled; the third, hit in the throat, began to bleed out spectacularly all over the cement. Then Bob, hardly having paused to fire, cleared the deck of the pool, fell into the deep underbrush and began to thrash his way toward the hill.

When he reached the incline, he paused just long enough to shuck his jacket, hit a fast combat reload on the Colt. He climbed through loblolly and stunted pines, clawing his way over ground cover and tufts of dried grass. The trees were not tall here, and now and then he'd run a dangerous trek over open ground. Behind him, he could hear the choppers ferrying in more troops. This was a big operation. They were throwing everything at him. Now and then a shot would come arching toward him, and one hit close by, lofting a cloud of dust and fragments. He winced but kept climbing.

At one point, he paused for a quick recon. They were searching for him with binoculars but he knew they would wait until they had all the men there, could ring the damned thing, before they'd move up the hill in coordinated maneuver. That's how he'd do it, at any rate, and he knew these cowboys were pros. He looked and thought he could see movement, the troops assembling into their squads under the cover of the trees. The house was visible below and Lon Scott in his electric wheelchair was talking to somebody in jungle fatigues by the pool. They were pointing up the hill. Bob could not make out the other man's face. But he guessed he knew who it was.

He turned. The hill was steep here and he was almost out of cover. Then there was a last hundred feet up the bare ground to the summit. He slid the Colt back into the holster. The summit was a bare knob standing out against that blue, pure sky. Sweat raced down his face into his eyes; he blinked.

Now he had to move. This was the worst part, the open part. Would they have snipers? Would they have a guy with a good rifle, a steady hand, who could down a running man at six hundred feet? Time to find out.

Bob touched the green grass and took a deep breath and began the last pull over the bare ground to the hilltop, thinking, Lots of men have died on hilltops.

———

"There he goes," said Lon, whose eyesight, like Bob's, was still extraordinary.

Shreck picked him up in the next second, a man running desperately up the scruffy hilltop. He brought the binoculars to bear and through their magnifying lenses saw a tall angular figure racing agilely up the last few feet to the top of the hill.

"I could have hit him," said Lon.

"It doesn't matter," said Shreck. "He's finished now. It's all over now."

A few shots rang out from lower down the hill as various Panther Battalion troopers, having a view of Bob, threw their rifles to their shoulders and squeezed off rounds. The bullets struck near him and at one point they thought they saw him falter, but he regathered his strength and launched himself over the edge, out of sight.

"General de Rujijo!" Shreck barked.

De Rujijo, who had been standing next to his RTO and two junior officers, came over smartly.

"What's your situation?"

"*Colonel*, we have all one hundred twenty men on the ground now. I'm only waiting for a confirmation from my second platoon, on the other side of the objective, that they are in position. Then I'll move my assault troops up in two elements, and in a few minutes I'll bring enfilading fire to bear, move my final assault team up, and bring you this man's head."

"I just want his corpse," said Shreck.

He turned back to Scott.

"We've got his ass now."

"I wonder what he's thinking about," said Scott. "It would be very interesting to know what such a man thinks about at such a moment."

Shreck said, "I was once on a hill waiting to die. You don't think about much. You think about how you wish you could get another day, that's all. But this son of a bitch is probably thinking about how many of us he can take out before we nail him. Well, I have one last thing for him to think about."

General de Rujijo was suddenly waving at him.

"*Colonel* Shreck, the ring is complete. Shall we move out?"

"One second," said Shreck. He turned to Scott. "I want to send this bastard to hell knowing all the bad news."

"Colonel Shreck," said Scott. "You shouldn't let it get personal. Hugh wouldn't want it to become personal."

"Fuck Hugh," said Shreck, "it's always personal."

He raised the bullhorn.

Bob lay atop the hill. He was extremely winded. Below, about four hundred yards or so, he could see the house, Scott in his chair and some officers and several junior officers standing around the pool. Men moved through the trees below.

Suddenly, there came a voice vibrating through the air.

"*Bob Lee Swagger. Bob Lee Swagger. You know who I am. Swagger, I wanted you to know before I send the troops up to get you that we found your woman in Ajo, Arizona.*"

Shit, Bob thought.

"*I sent Payne. Payne will kill her. She may be already dead.*"

Swagger sat back from the rocks.

He heard whistles as the troops began to move out.

Payne had no trouble at all. It went so easily, the flight to Tucson, the rental car, the hour or so drive to Ajo. He found the trailer without difficulty. He parked, and went up to the door and knocked.

When she answered he said, "Nurse Fenn?"

"Yes?" She was the kind of woman that Payne had never had. He'd had whores all the world over, listless women with shriveled tits, or young and stupid and poor and desperate. Having sex with them was nothing. It was like doing yourself and in time Payne lost interest in either, unless he was drunk.

This one was classy, somehow. It enraged him that Bob had once had such a fine woman and he'd had nothing like her.

"Aren't you the one who was with him?" he asked.

"I'm not sure I—"

"You know, *him*. Bob Lee Swagger. Tried to kill the president in New Orleans."

Her face lost its color; she was not a liar.

"I— Are you with the police?"

"No such fuckin' luck, lady," he said, and pulled out the Remington cut-down as he stepped inside. Standing, he felt his force overpower her. He advanced, driving her to the wall, and stood against her, squashing her, the huge 12-gauge muzzle against the flesh of her cheek.

"What is—"

"Just shut up and listen. Your goddamned boyfriend is alive, in case you don't know, but now he's dead, I mean really *dead*. Now you just sit down and cool it, or goddammit, I'll kill you myself. Just shut your mouth and do what I tell you."

"I don't—"

"Shut up. Now, we're gonna hang tight for a time. Don't you try nothing. Believe me, I ain't like any guy you ever met, and if I have to, I will shoot you in the head and walk away from it without looking back."

"I understand," she said.

"Swagger can't help you now," he said. "Some boys

got him on a fuckin' hilltop and they ain't got no mercy in their hearts."

She looked him in the eyes. Then she said, "He's been on hilltops before, you fool. Don't you understand it yet? He *loves* hilltops. It's where he belongs."

The images were grainy, hard to make out. Soldiers, burning huts, people running every which way, all of it caught in the jumpy, ill-framed haste of the inexperienced cameraman.

Dobbler swallowed.

Then he saw Colonel Shreck and Jack Payne and a third man, a Latino officer, in a black beret with mirror sunglasses. All wore exotic camouflage uniforms and were heavily armed.

They were conferring over a map.

Dobbler hit FAST FORWARD.

The images hurtled by at warp-speed, made ridiculous, like vaudeville. The soldiers were burning the huts and it looked like the pictures he'd seen taken in the Ukraine in 1943, where the SS men had burned the villages as they retreated. But it was so different, because these soldiers were young and strong and having so much fun.

As the tape rushed along, the troops left the village and seemed to head down a slope. The camera panned and he could see what had drawn them. The village people had escaped to the water. They stood in the torrent of the river, but were blocked at both ends by small knots of soldiers with machine guns. They stood, shivering in the water. He could see that they were mostly women and children.

Dobbler watched as the hard young men walked to the water's edge. His finger went off FAST FORWARD.

In real time, he saw Shreck and the powerful Latino officer in discussion.

He heard Shreck say, "Tell them to get it over with. Then let's chopper the fuck out of here. No rapes. Just finish the job and let's evac the hell out of here, General."

The general gave an order and the camera shifted back to the water.

"No," Dobbler screamed in the office, "no!"

But it did no good.

The machine gun bullets from *Los Gatos Negros* tore into the people in the water, kicking up foam and blood, knocking them down.

"No," Dobbler repeated over and over, "no, no, no."

Bob heard a voice.

"I didn't think you were going to make it up that damn hill, old man," Nick Memphis said.

Bob swiveled on his belly and saw him slithering toward him.

"Pork, I have a spry step or two left in these old bones," said Swagger. "Now where's my—"

Memphis, in his black FBI SWAT uniform with the Mini-14 slung over his back, pushed a long canvas satchel over at Bob. Swagger unzipped it, reached in, then with a flick of the wrist sent the guncase scuttling through the dust as he unsheathed the Remington 700V with its Leupold 12× scope.

His finger snicked off the safety as he drew the rifle to him, knowing it contained five M852 7.62mm match cartridges, each sporting a 168-grain Sierra boattailed hollowpoint.

"Time to hunt," he said.

CHAPTER THIRTY-TWO

Shreck was listening to General de Rujijo.

"I have all my men placed now, *Colonel* Shreck, and I'm going to give the signal to move out."

"Good," said Shreck. "Let's do it."

De Rujijo turned to his RTO and reached for the telephone mike to bark orders. He was a vivid, powerful man, in slime-and-mud dappled jungle fatigues, face lean and leathery, eyes sealed off behind the reflective surface of his sunglasses, black beret pulled low, Uzi slung rakishly across the front of his camouflage tunic, bright black star on his collar.

Shreck saw what happened next very clearly. The general was speaking decisively in Spanish when the bullet hit him, eviscerating the lower rear of his skull just above his spine and tunneling through to blow his jaw off.

The spray flumed across Shreck's face. Shreck blinked as the jawless apparition with the blank eyes toppled forward just three feet in front of him. He felt a stab of shock and in less than a second crushed it to death by sheer force of will and experience. He understood that the next bullet off the mountain was aimed for him. He dropped and pivoted, executing a neat half gainer off the pool deck, badly spraining a wrist, but getting himself out of the line of fire.

The second bullet instead struck de Rujijo's aide-de-camp, a young major, in the center chest. The third bullet tracked the now fleeing RTO man, hit the radio, ripped through it, destroying it, and carried into the soldier himself, pulling him down to die of shock and blood loss.

Lon Scott saw the three soldiers die in less than two seconds and he watched Shreck's swift exit from the kill zone. He fell into spastic panic so intense it almost killed him there on the spot. In a split second, he had recovered, hit the toggle on his wheelchair and spun quickly. Too quickly, because he was leaning forward from the shoulders and he realized he'd blown by the center of gravity; he jerked back, but it was too late. The chair spilled, pitching him on the cement of the pool deck, anchored by the deadweight of the useless lower half of his body.

He was helpless. He heard the shots mounting. The fear in him went berserk.

"*Aghhhhhhhhhh!*" he screamed.

Bob lay in the classic prone. Smoothly sliding the rifle around on a hard, flat sandbag that Nick had lugged up to the hilltop, along with the rifle and lots of ammunition, he brought it to bear on the glade of trees where most of the Panther Battalion troops had assembled and were momentarily confused by the sound of the shots. He laid his cross hair upon another officer talking into a radio mike, and tagged him in the chest. He swung the rifle just a millimeter as he rocketed through a bolt throw, and shot another man. He cocked, fired, cocked, fired, cocked, fired. He killed five men in seven seconds, then, pulling the bolt open, grabbed five brass shells from the case six inches from his rifle, and rolled them into the breach, slammed the bolt home.

In the perfect O of the scope, he became the crucifier. He laid the cross wire of the lens on the forms cowering before him, twelve times their normal size, twelve times more confused and frightened, twelve times more desperate for leadership, and he began to destroy them. They seemed so innocent; it was so easy; they died without protest or awareness that he had come to nail them. But he didn't care.

He hunted yelling men—sergeants and platoon leaders, heroes—and blew them away. He shot for center body, and in the jump of the recoil, he could still see that instant deflation that signified a hit. If he saw a man, he hit him. If he only had a head to see, he shot that and when he hit a head it snapped back brokenly, leaking and wrecked.

He shot fast to break the charge. He knew if they did he was history. That was their only hope—to move up the slope aggressively, under the doctrine of maneuver and fire, taking casualties in the dozens but closing for the ultimate kill. But not today; these boys had lost their stomach for carnage in the first few seconds, when his bullets unerringly picked and took out their heroes.

A brave corporal slithered lizardlike to a fallen RTO, and Bob broke his spine. An automatic weapons team tried to maneuver to the left to set up a suppressive fire; Bob gutshot the gunner and when the loader tried to pull the weapon from his stricken hands, Bob shot him low in the abdomen. A private stood to shame his comrades into the advance; Bob rewarded him with 168 grains of hollowpoint delivered at two thousand feet per second.

"Come on, you fuckers," he yelled hoarsely, as his system loaded itself to the hairline with adrenaline. It was the An Loc all over again, a valleyful of NVA and he was there on his lonesome to take them out. In the circular universe of the scope some men quit; they just settled back and waited in the trees for him to find them; others fled, racing across the road, their rifles abandoned. A few tried to move up toward the cover of enfilades or arroyos, but by now his eyesight was verging on the supernatural; he was into the zone, the rifle so a part of him that it felt organic; he could not remember, ever, not having the rifle, not having a world of targets. He slipped into craziness, the sniper's twisted identification with an angry God and he shot faster and better still. He shot through the heat and the mirage and when now and then a ragged volley of shots rose toward him, he was incapable of caring. Let them come. Let them all come.

Lon Scott lay with his mouth on the cement, listening to the relentless cracks of the rifle, dry and far away. It was astonishing with what speed the man could fire. In the trees, now and then, Lon would hear a scream or see the thrashing of someone mortally hit. He knew it was only a matter of seconds before there'd be a lull in the shooting, and Bob would swing on back to pot him. With his strong arms he tried to pull himself along, hating the mutilated thing that was his body, hating his father for doing this to him all those years ago, hating his life for the strange paths it had taken. He began to cry. He had thought he was ready to die, but he wasn't. He was terrified.

"Help me," he screamed. But no one helped him.

Oh, please don't let me die, he prayed.

Suddenly he heard footsteps. Some fool ran across the naked cement, bent to him, and with incredible strength hoisted him over his shoulder. The man ran, Lon bouncing and clinging, the two of them vulnerable to Bob's whimsy for what seemed an eternity. But they made it, and with an animal leap, the man jumped from the edge of the deck to the cover in its lee. Lon banged against the bony shoulders and rolled off.

"Oh, Christ," he said to his savior, "oh, Christ, that was the bravest thing I ever saw in my life."

Colonel Shreck merely said, "No," and pointed to the top of the hill. "*That's* bravery, that sonovabitch."

Then they heard the sound of a helicopter.

When the helicopter arose from behind the tree line, its hatch door bristling with guns, and began to swoop toward him like a hawk homing on some prey, Bob simply pulled himself from his belly to his knees and found the braced offhand position, his right or strong-side elbow held above the level of the scope as if his arm were a guy wire to brace the rifle. He saw the pilot's white face blurred behind the windscreen in a split second when the bird pulled from pitched forward, to shield the canopy by the whirring of its rotor, to pitched upward, to shield the fliers by virtue of the armor of the nose cupping them from beneath.

He fired. Fuck you, he thought. Fuck you all.

The bullet hit low in the Plexiglas windscreen; through the scope he saw the sudden quicksilver of fracture smearing the glass and behind it the mortal squirm of a man hit badly and slipping into shock. Bob threw himself down, reset the rifle on its bag, and began to engage targets downhill, where a group of men who'd broken to the right as he was attending to the helicopter were skipping around the base of the hill, and he took them down like skeet, one, two, three, and four, coming dry on the fifth. He was rolling five new cartridges into the Remington when the pilotless chopper slid back into the trees, gnashed violently as it fought them, then gave up as it whirred to the earth. In another second, it had detonated, throwing a fountain of oily flame high into the sky.

The brilliance of the flash momentarily drained the color from the day, and the bright green trees; Bob didn't notice. He was looking for targets.

Come on, he was thinking. Come on, fight me. I want to fight some more.

Shreck sat with his back to the action, beneath the deck level of the pool in a niche by the walkway out of the house, breathing hard from his run with Scott. Scott wheezed noisily and might even be weeping, but he took no notice.

Seven feet of reinforced concrete protected him from the fire. He was safe. He breathed hard, trying to work it out. From the shooting, and then the explosion of the helicopter, he read the course of battle. He understood now that Bob had been a step ahead of Dobbler and had somehow found Lon Scott on his own. He'd let them think they were luring him in when he was luring them in. He tricked them into the killing ground where the odds were to his advantage: high ground, protected shooting, and a world of skittish, leaderless targets before him.

The shooting was dying down now.

On the other side of the summit, Nick watched them move out of the trees. They were a good three hundred yards out. Without a scope on the Mini-14, that was quite a shot for a .223. But if he had to defend an entire horizon against an infantry company with a single semi-automatic rifle, he knew that he'd do better to hit them early than to let them get too close where they could carry the crest in a single rush. He could hear Bob still firing on the other side. Now it was his turn.

He was also in the classic prone, aiming through a tuft of ragged bushes that he had artlessly pulled and thrown together into something like a shooting blind. He was breathing hard but he felt surprisingly calm. He could still hear Bob laying down fire but he had no idea what was going on over there.

Carefully, he drew the rifle to him, found what he took to be a spot-weld, let his bones hold the weight of the piece, and squinted through the peep sight until it no longer existed. He saw only the body of the leader, behind the wedge of the front sight. He hoped he'd hit something this time.

Front sight, front sight, he told himself, ordering his pupil to contract until it was as clear as a dollar bill and behind it, the target was a blur. Why this worked he didn't know, but it was the essence of shooting.

He willed the trigger to break and somehow it did.

The gun bucked; the sight picture was gone, an empty shell popped away. And when he returned again to see what could be seen, what could be seen was nothing.

"Goddammit, gimme that gun, you missed again, you jerk," Bob yelled in his ear, and yanked the Mini-14 from Nick's grasp. He threw it to his shoulder and cracked off the rest of the magazine, all twenty-nine shots. The shells popcorned from the breech, a bright cascade of sunlit brass. Below them, on the far side of the trees, they could see the survivors of Panther Battalion running raggedly for the far crest line.

"They're way out of range for that gun," said Nick.

"Oh, yeah? Well, not for this one."

He retrieved his Remington, threw the bolt, and rammed it home.

Bob was breathing heavily. His face looked crazy with fury, his eyes shrunk to hard, glaring kernels. He was blinking a bit strangely. His face was smeared with greasy smudges from all the gunsmoke he'd breathed, and his hands and shirt were almost black. He kept blinking crazily.

"Jesus," said Nick again. "Let 'em go. They're running. They're broken. What's it prove?"

"He ain't broken," said Bob, gesturing savagely to a hill a mile away. "There's a goddamn spotter over there, Donny. Seen the flash of his lens. He's been glassing us all along. You know your ballistic tables?"

"No."

"Well, a goddamn .308 drops about eighteen feet at a thousand yards. Wind's about five miles an hour. I'm gonna hold eighteen feet high and a mite to the left for the wind drift."

He dropped to prone, found his spot-weld and his shooting position. Then he cranked off five shots in four seconds, flicking the bolt and ejecting a shell each time.

"That ought to fix him. Now come on, Donny."

Nick gaped at him.

"Huh? Are you all right?"

"Come on, Donny. I want to see what we bagged. I have to find out what they did with my woman."

"Bob, my name is—"

"Come on, boy. We've done enough for today. Time to get out of the zone."

And with that the sniper headed off the mountain, his rifle in his blistered hands, to the copse a mile away where they'd stashed Bob's truck two days earlier.

Nick went running after.

Eddie Nickles thought he'd bleed to death. His Celestron 8 was shattered, a bullet having drilled it through its wide lens and rattled through its insides. It was nothing but a tube full of broken shards.

He himself had been hit twice, once high in the head—a glancing shot, without penetration, he thought—and in the leg, a ricochet as he cowered shitting and weeping in the split second after he saw the tall man through the scope suddenly spin to zero on him.

He knew he'd never get out. He'd be gone before help arrived. There simply wasn't much help left. He'd watched Bob shoot, the motherfucker, and shoot and shoot. He knew what that meant.

"Hey, asshole."

He looked up to see the man himself. He was attended by a Beach Boy with a crew cut.

"You killed me," he blurted.

"I doubt that, sonny. From the looks, you'll recover, that is if you've half a heart."

"Don't shoot me. I just sat here and watched."

"Was Payne here?"

"No. No, they sent Payne somewhere. They sent him to get your girl."

"God*damm*it," Bob said.

"They'll do her, Swagger. These guys, they'll do anybody. This guy Shreck, runs the outfit, he can do stuff like that."

Bob seemed to think this over.

"Was Shreck here?"

"Yes."

"If he isn't dead, and I don't think he is, you tell him to leave the woman alone. If he wants me, I'll tell him where he can find me. But he's to leave the woman alone, or so help me Christ what's gone before will seem like Sunday school."

"I'll tell him."

"Good. You tell him to look for me in the Ouachitas, because that's where I'm going. If he's man enough to come alone, that's where he'll find me."

"He won't come alone."

"I know it. But you tell him anyways. Tell him to bring the woman and Payne. Tell him to come Sunday morning, nine A.M., the town square, Blue Eye, two weeks from now. That's the first Sunday in November. We'll set it up."

Then he was gone.

CHAPTER THIRTY-THREE

The call came at seven-thirty that evening.

"Go on," said Payne. "Get it."

She picked up the phone and listened.

"Are you Payne?" she asked.

He took the phone.

"Payne?"

"Yes."

"It's bad. We didn't get him. He led us in."

Payne listened numbly to the details.

"Yeah," he said finally. "In two hours. No sweat."

He put the phone down.

"Your unlucky day, honey," he said, watching her face. "My orders were to kill you if they got Swagger. I was just going to walk away and say I did. But they didn't get him. He got them. Your boyfriend killed forty-four men today, honey. And that means you and I got bad trouble."

Payne had to laugh. Swagger wasn't good, he was beyond good. He was so fucking good it was scary. He could hear the fear in Shreck's voice. Forty-four men dead, including nine of his best guys who'd climbed aboard a chopper in an attempt to get some firepower on Bob from a new angle, and had been rewarded with a flaming death. Then, dozens wounded, Panther Battalion spread all over North Carolina, all kinds of cops hanging around, drawn by the smoke from the burning chopper, the whole thing a complete fuckup.

"Let's go."

"Where are we going?"

"East. Your boyfriend's gonna wanna meet you. We need you for that. You got a job to do for us."

"And if I don't?"

"Then I cap you here. You want that? You just drive with me in the desert. Chopper picks us up, ferries us to an airfield, where a private jet has us in a few hours. No sweat."

"I'm the bait, that's it? You think you'll get Bob because you have me, is that it?"

"Lady, I don't think the stuff up. I just follow orders."

"Bob will eat you alive. Bob will chew you up and spit you out. You're dead, you know that?"

Payne laughed. The bitch had some edge.

"There's lots of blood between him and me, honey. Lots of it, and more to come. But I got one thing he wants, and that makes me a god to him."

She looked at him.

"I got you, bitch."

Deputy Director Howard D. Utey of the FBI was known far and wide in his own organization and several others in the federal security sector as the man who "got" Bob Lee Swagger.

This reputation had not done his career any harm; in fact, his recent promotion to the DD level and the fine corner office he now occupied on the fifth floor of the J. Edgar Hoover Building on Pennsylvania Avenue in Washington, D.C., was largely a result of the successful manhunt. Moreover, the image of the burning church, ingrained in the national subconscious, was a lesson to those who would trifle with the security of the president of the United States, a lesson provided by the Federal Bureau of Investigation and not the Secret Service, which had provided no lessons.

Everywhere he looked, all was serenity. He had nurtured contacts carefully over the course of his career, worked diligently, extracted maximum performance from those beneath him, formed relationships with powerful men, shed himself quickly of those who couldn't perform and, most important, knew the difference, instantly, between those who could and those who couldn't. He was careful to have men under him who were not quite as bright as he, and he particularly understood the dangers of talent, which was that while it was capable of producing spectacular results, it was just as apt to go off by itself to nurse obscure grudges or lick psychic wounds after gross expenditures of energy. Talent wasn't consistent or loyal or pliant enough to be trusted; Howard deeply hated talent, and made certain that none of the men who worked for him ever had any talent. He'd driven seven talented men out of the Bureau and only one had stood against him, the idiot Nick Memphis, once so bright and brimming with enthusiasms, carefully betrayed at each step of the way, and yet stubborn in his refusal to leave the Bureau.

But now he had Nick at last. It was the hearing. Suspended agents are given two months off without pay and then are asked to present themselves at a certain time and place to defend their records. Most understand that their careers are over, and quietly turn in resignations, in exchange for good recommendations. Some fight the inevitable at the hearing, but Howard had always prevailed.

But nobody had ever done what Nick had just done. Nobody simply *ignored* the suspension hearing, simply didn't show. Added to everything else—even subtracted from everything else—it alone was cause for dismissal.

Howard didn't hate Nick. He looked on him as a young man who just never learned the lessons of the team. In Tulsa, Nick had blown his shot all those years ago by refusing to acknowledge Howard's control. And look at how it had cost him and that poor young woman he ended up marrying.

Then in New Orleans, Nick had screwed up and screwed up again. It was as if he'd learned nothing from the hold that had been put on his career. He still thought he could do it his way, by his instincts, his talents and his guts. A supervisor cannot run a well-oiled, professionally disciplined unit under such circumstances.

Now Howard looked at the separation order before him. He had merely to sign it, as had three supervisors on the hearing board that Nick had ignored, and Nick was gone.

He never enjoyed this part. He was not a cruel man who relished his power. What he relished was the system itself and his own mastery of it. He believed that what was in his best interest was also in the Bureau's best interest. Nick's greatest sin was that he couldn't be a team player. He couldn't get with the program. Poor Nick. Doomed to be an outsider, a loser, his whole life.

Howard's pen poised over the document. He paused, just a second, then—

"Ah, Mr. Utey?"

He looked up. It was his assistant.

"Yes, Robert."

"Ah—" Robert was distinctly uncomfortable, which was strange, for what had recommended Robert was his complete passivity. Robert had no personality whatsoever. Howard liked that in a man.

"Go on, Robert."

"You'll recall that strange shootout in North Carolina yesterday?"

"Yes." Who could not recall it? Some drug war thing, forty-odd men killed, wounded Latinos babbling of ambush and slaughter, a DEA task force down there trying to shake it all out.

"Well, sir, they found over fifty-five 7.62mm shells atop that mountain."

"Yes?"

"We just got the lab report. Latent prints got seven good completes and four partials. The computer spat them out a few minutes ago. Sir, I thought you should know immediately."

Howard still didn't see where this was headed. At his level, he was no longer responsible for on-site investigations. Wasn't that Bob Mattingly over on the Bureau/DEA liaison committee?

"Sir. Uh, the prints check out positively."

"Check out *how*?"

"Yes, sir. They're Bob Lee Swagger's."

Howard looked at him. He let nothing show on his face. He felt a little something rise in his stomach.

"There must be some mistake. Swagger is dead and buried, we ID'd the corpse through forensics, everything was all—"

"Sir, I'm only telling you what the computer said."

"I see."

"And sir, there was a rental automobile recovered at the site."

"Yes?"

More bad news?

"Go on."

"It was rented by Nick Memphis."

Oh, Christ, thought Howard.

Nick came awake in the cab of the truck when Bob nudged him. He'd been dreaming about Sally Ellion, of all things. Sally was laughing at a joke he'd told her. There was something about Sally he really liked. It was—

But he blinked awake, somewhat chilly, aware of the jounce of the truck, the gray air of dawn. He wasn't even sure when he'd fallen asleep.

"Time to get up, Nick," said Bob.

"Yeah," he said. "You want me to drive. No sweat."

"No," said Bob. "We're almost there and it's almost time."

Nick looked around. He saw that they were headed up the access road toward an airport terminal. In the gray distance, a small jet was getting ready to take off.

"What—"

"You got a job to do."

"What are—"

"In twenty minutes you'll be on a United flight to New Orleans. Be in by seven-thirty."

"What the hell are you talking about?"

"Annex B. You been *explaining* it to me for a month and a half. Now it's time to find the goddamn thing."

"But—"

"But nothing. These birds have someone. A woman who helped me once. Goddamned wonderful woman, the best. They got her and there's nothing I can do but stew and they know it and they like it. It gives them all the goddamned leverage. But when it comes to meeting time, I got to have some leverage or she's dead. They'll use her to get at me and they'll blow me away and then they'll blow her away and then they go on with the rest of their lives, happy as pigs in a bath of shit. You got to get me some leverage, Nick. That's all there is to it."

Nick swallowed.

"I— I don't know if— It's hard. Maybe it's there or maybe it's in Washington or maybe it's—"

"Nick, you've been explaining to me how I was doing this all wrong. I'm man enough to say you're right, I was a fool, all I managed to do was get some people killed. Now it's time to let a professional work. I'll step aside. You go get this Annex B."

Nick looked at him.

He tried to think.

"But it's probably in Washington. It's buried in some computer file in Washington that only people on Lancer Committee can get to with special performance and—"

He stopped himself.

The words ROM DO formed in his mind.

It all came back to ROM DO. The message that Eduardo Lanzman had left him all those months ago, on the day that his wife died.

Eduardo Lanzman had come to see him.

But think about it, he told himself. He wouldn't have just *come.* That's what's been haunting me. He wouldn't have just come with some crazy story. He was a pro, pro enough to know he'd been made, pro enough to try and protect himself from electronic eavesdropping as per the latest Agency hot tips. And pro enough to know he'd have to bring something along, something I could use to go to higher people and stop the assassination.

He must have— I don't know, but we didn't find anything on his body.

Maybe his killers took it.

No. Why'd they chop him? To get him to talk. But he was a tough bastard, who believed in one thing, Nick Memphis of the FBI. Whatever he had, he hid it. Between the plane and the motel room, he hid it. And he told me where—he left me a message. ROM DO—Romeo Dog. R-D. RamDyne.

"Nick?"

"Huh?"

"Nick, we're here."

The truck had stopped. He looked and yes, they were there.

"Remember," said Bob. "You be back by the first Sunday in November. You meet me at the cabin in the mountains. The day before hunting season."

The most absurd document in the world, Shreck thought.

He looked at Dobbler's report on his desk. A glance had told him that it was self-serving bullshit. Dobbler was hopeless.

Shreck was waiting for the doctor to show up. There was work to do and not much time left. His session with Hugh had not gone well. Hugh was capable of being extremely uncivil and in this episode he hadn't disappointed Shreck. He was a vindictive, bitter old man, who raved about legacy, about heritage, about responsibility. He was enraged that the colonel had endangered poor Lon, after all Lon had suffered. And now Lon had to give up so much. When the colonel told him that Lon seemed happy, even excited about the whole thing and was treating it like some mad adventure, and was quite happily nailing silhouette targets at a thousand yards in central Virginia, it still didn't sit well with Hugh.

You two Yale boys certainly go back a long way, the colonel had thought. I wonder to what?

Hugh finally wondered, frankly, if he could do a damned thing for the colonel anymore.

Shreck had told him he didn't want anything, the situation had resolved itself to a three- or four-man play in Arkansas some two weeks hence, and that he would prevail or die, and that would be the end of it.

Nothing would come out. There'd be no embarrassment. Lon Scott could go back to obscurity. The colonel held the trump card, the woman; with the woman, he'd be able to manipulate Bob in ways previously impossible. They could chopper Lon Scott into any point in the mountain range and set him up to handle any long-distance shooting chores, and Payne, probably the best small unit man the Special Forces ever turned out, would be along for the close stuff. He himself had two wars' worth of taking frontals, as well as twenty years running outfit ops and hits. Then they had the devious Dobbler masterminding things; he'd proven his worth. They needed only one thing—first-class topographic surveys of the Ouachitas, satellite-quality layout of the mountains.

Hugh fumed, but in the end, he saw how little of him was required and how protected he still was. When he realized he knew just who to call, he relented.

Now there was little to do except wait. Lon would be prepping the shot he'd have to take, Payne watching the girl, and he and Dobbler working on the tactical and psychological maneuvers. It was just a period of waiting, staying calm, bringing it off.

"Colonel Shreck?" came the voice over the intercom, one of the Operations people who hadn't died in the chopper crash.

"Yeah?" said Shreck.

"I can't get any answer from Dr. Dobbler. And I've called three times. No one has seen him since he logged out two nights ago at midnight."

"Thank you."

Shreck looked at the document before him. It was some time before it occurred to him that it meant that Dobbler had been in his office, but only thirty seconds after that when he discovered that the videotape was missing from his safe.

"Now what have we got?" Utey asked his assembled people.

Getting himself appointed the head of the Bob Lee Swagger Task Force had not been an easy job, but somehow, demanding returns on favors granted and offering still more favors, uncounted favors, in the future, and working fast off the tip, he'd managed it, and gotten his old team in place and was now staffing the first meeting in New Orleans.

"Sir," said Hap Fencl, "here's how it shakes down. They found fifteen discarded cartons of Lake City M852 7.62mm Match ammunition atop that mountain, Lot 543-101B. They managed to track it by that number to a surplus outfit called Survival, Inc., in Tuscaloosa, Alabama, August fifteenth. I went over there myself yesterday morning. They sold a thousand-round case of the stuff to two men. Tall, rangy guy, mid-forties, very quiet. And heavyset blond guy, crew cut, who did all the talking. They couldn't positively ID Bob but the salesman gave me an absolute total yes on Nick Memphis."

"Nick, Nick, Nick," said Utey.

"Howard," said Hap, "is there any possibility Nick is working very deep cover for someone on a higher level? I can't believe Nick would go renegade on us. Nick's a good Bureau guy, Bureau to his bones and even deeper."

Howard considered carefully.

"You never can tell," he said. "He loved it more than

it could love him, based on his performance. And that's where the trouble starts. Love can turn to hate, just like that."

"I can't believe anything bad about old Nick. He was true blue, a square shooter."

This disturbed Howard. Couldn't have men on the team who'd made an emotional connection to the quarry.

"Go ahead, Mr. Fencl," he said stonily.

"These shot-up Salvadorans, they tell a strange goddamned story. It was guys from this Panther Battalion outfit, you remember, all that stuff about that atrocity last year that the CIA denied any knowledge of. But they say this time they were working CIA, going after a big communist agent for the CIA. And they ran into Superman, or Rambo, or whatever. They got their booties kicked. And that's all they say, and brother, is the Agency keeping mum on this one."

"Umm," said Howard.

"Was CIA involved with Panther Battalion?" somebody asked.

"Hard to say," another agent said. "Our files indicate it was a contract thing with an outfit called RamDyne, which handles a lot of Agency funny business without involving the Agency directly. But there's not much about RamDyne. You ask and all you get is a reference to Lancer Committee, which is our liaison committee with CIA. You can't tell about some of these outfits who pick up and deliver the Agency's garbage for them. Sometimes they get so far out there they lose their bearings. Or maybe they never had any bearings to begin with."

"So anyway," said Hap, "we got these Central American commandos thinking they're after some commie and running into Bob the Nailer at the top of his game on somebody named James Thomas Albright's farm and nobody has seen hide nor hair of James Albright and there is zero, I mean like, no paper on Albright. No records, no nothing. Guy was handicapped, too. DEA swears there isn't a direct drug connection. But boy, it sounds druggie to me. So what's Bob doing making war on a bunch of greasers? Or what are they doing making war on him? Who told them he was a commie? Who wants Bob dead? Who knew he was alive? We sure didn't. The Agency? Could the Agency have been—"

"Gentlemen," said Howard, working swiftly to cut off the apostasy, "I don't think pursuing the Central Intelligence Agency or its affiliates is going to get us anywhere. Our first priority is the capture of Bob Lee Swagger before the news gets out that he's alive. It would be humiliating to us if this became widely known; *when* we take him, that's when we can go public with it. Is that understood?"

"Howard, if the Agency—" began Hap.

"Mr. Fencl, please," said Howard.

Some murmurs, noddings, grumbles.

"Now, suggestions?"

"Sir," one of the men said, "the last time Bob was in a jam, he went back to Blue Eye and the Ouachitas. Most men would have the sense not to try it a second time. But this guy, he believes in things. He believes in home and knowing the territory. If he's going to play a game, don't you think he'd play it on his territory?"

"Yes," said Utey. "He would."

He paused.

"All right," he said, "I'm ordering the relocation of Task Force Swagger to Mena, Arkansas. We'll set it up as before. Mr. Fencl, I want you to handle liaisons with Sheriff Tell of Polk County and the Arkansas State Police. Mr. Bryson, you establish contact with Milt Sillito over at DEA because we'll need all the information from their loop. And Mr. Nelson, I want you to supervise the SWAT equipment and locate air support through the forestry department."

"Poor Nick," said Hap. "I hope he hasn't bitten off more than he can chew. The only thing he ever wanted to be was an FBI agent."

CHAPTER THIRTY-FOUR

Nick sat at Gate 24 in the New Orleans International Airport at 10:38 A.M. on a Tuesday. Delta Flight 554 was arriving from Mexico City. As the passengers began to emerge and disperse into the terminal, he stood up and joined them, trying to see with another man's eyes.

What would he think? What would he notice? How would his mind work?

Eduardo Lanzman, if you were Eduardo Lanzman, you got off this flight six months ago. You saw what I am seeing now. You were a pro, your eyes scanned left and right, up the hall and down the hall. You were scared, you had something in your possession that could kill you, and you knew you were being hunted.

This was it. This was your break for freedom and your desperate attempt to save the life of Archbishop Jorge Roberto Lopez. And why? Even if you are a secret policeman, you were raised a Catholic. This killing of an archbishop, is it going too far? Or perhaps you lost somebody on the Sampul River that day, cut down by Panther Battalion in the red-running water.

No matter. What would you see?

Nick walked with the passengers through the terminal. Then another question hit him.

Why wouldn't you call me from here? Why wait until you get to that motel?

As he thought about it, an answer formed. Because Lanzman thought he was safe. He hadn't been made. He was all right. He read the crowd and he read the signs, and he thought everything was fine, it was a straight shot, it was no problem.

Nick let his imaginary trip through the head of Eduardo Lanzman carry him across the main concourse and out to the taxi stand by the street. It was not particularly busy.

You want to get this over with. You'll just take a cab straight into the Federal Building, right? You'll ask to see me. If you have to wait, you'll have to wait, that's all.

Nick hailed a cab.

"Yeah?"

"Uh, you know where the Federal Building is? Seven-oh-one Loyola Street, downtown."

"Sure, man. Hop in."

Nick climbed in, the cab sped away.

"New to the Big Easy?" the guy asked.

"No," said Nick, trying to concentrate.

He watched as they left the airport, sped along the access road toward I-10, the big strip of federal highway that transects the shelf of land between the big river and Lake Pontchartrain upon which the city is built.

Along the road there was nothing. It was featureless, nondescript, a little parcel of anonymous America.

As they took the ramp and began to sweep toward a merge on the rush of I-10, Nick could see the gaudy parade of motels over on the right, down Veterans Memorial Boulevard.

"Stop!" he hollered.

"Huh?"

"Stop, dammit! I said pull over."

"What the—" The cabby, a bald black guy with a gold tooth, fumed, but he obeyed. His name, Nick could tell from the hack license pinned to the right sunshade, was JERRY NILES.

"Now what?"

"Just shut up for a second."

Nick sat there. The cab had slewed onto the shoulder and cars whirled by toward the city ahead.

No, he thought. He didn't get this far. Because if he's going to the Palm Court Motel, you can't get there once you get onto I-70. You've got to make your mind up before you take the ramp.

"Buddy?"

"Shut up," said Nick.

What does that tell you?

That tells you he made his pursuers on the access road, was afraid they'd nail him on the road, and made a snap decision to hunker down before they could do so.

It also meant he knew exactly how desperate they were—that they would be willing to risk some kind of terrible public scene to stop him. Pros prefer to work in private; they only go public with wet business if they have no other choice, unless they're Colombian drug scum.

"Back up and head down Veterans Boulevard."

"Hey, mister, I can't back up and—"

"There's a fifty in it for you."

"Okay, but if a cop comes—"

"I am a cop," said Nick, reflexively, then wished it were still true.

The driver backed up the ramp, executed a Kamikaze-like 240 and managed to get them, after some honking and screeching, headed down Veterans. The Palm Court was the third motel past the turnoff.

"Pull in here," said Nick.

The driver obeyed.

"You want me to—"

"Just wait a minute."

Nick sat, thinking.

He's been made. He knows they're close. Whatever he's got—documents, a microchip, photos, whatever—he's got to dump in some place that he can recover.

Dump it. Go into the motel before they spot him. Get a room near the Coke machines in case they've got electronic penetration capacity, call Nick Memphis, and then wait.

He doesn't know they've got an Electrotek 5400. He doesn't know they'll hear his call. He doesn't know that when the knock on the door comes, and he says who's there, and the answer comes "Nick Memphis," he's letting his own death squad in.

No matter, Nick thought.

The key thing is, he's got to hide his package.

Something else came to Nick.

Eduardo, you've been hit now, you've been whacked by guys with axes, they've cut your fucking heart out. But somehow—Jesus, man, you had a set of balls on you—somehow you crawl into the bathroom and on the linoleum you write a message in your own blood. No, not the name of your killers, but something else.

You write—ROM DO.

What's it mean? What's the message?

ROM DO.

"I want you to go back to the airport where you picked me up, and then repeat this journey."

"You kidding?"

"I am not."

"Okay, pal. Hope you got a big expense account."

The cabby swirled the vehicle around and returned to the terminal.

"Don't stop. Just follow the same route."

Nick watched the scenery roll by.

Along here you were made, he thought. You looked up, you saw a car following you that wasn't a taxi, you hit the panic button. You saw them, maybe reading their profiles through the windshield or maybe recognizing the vehicle. But it had to be here, along this dull, limited access road, with no escape, no place to hide, not even a place to stop.

They reached the parking lot of the motel again.

"Okay, pal?"

"Shut up," said Nick.

He sat there, trying to think.

ROM DO.

ROM DO.

He looked around for ROM DO. But the only words he could see from the parking lot were inside the cab. JERRY NILES, it read, in caps, up there on the sun visor.

Dobbler felt absurd. Here he was among country types in the very small and rude town of Blue Eye, Arkansas, a few hours west of Hot Springs. There was nothing friendly about the place. What had happened to the famous American small-town hospitality? People looked at him sullenly. It was one of those one-horse places, a scabby, peeling town square around a Confederate monument. A banner floated above the main street, proclaiming to all the world THE BUCKS ARE STOPPED HERE. Hunting. Dobbler shivered. He felt trapped in this godforsaken nightmare, sealed in by the mountains everywhere he looked, towering claustrophobically over the town.

The mountains scared him. Heavily encrusted with pines and on this rainy morning shrouded in mist, they looked as if they could kill you. He didn't want to go up there but he had to. That's where Bob would be.

Dobbler really had no idea what to do. With the cassette in his briefcase, he knew the only safety lay here. That is, if he could find Bob Lee Swagger. No one else could stop them. That was the irony. In America, with its FBI and its hundreds of police forces, no one could stop them except Bob Lee Swagger, the man with the rifle.

If these people knew anything they weren't talking, especially to an outsider like him, in his lumpy suit, with his eastern beard. They probably thought he was gay. He'd better watch himself. High school boys might beat him to death with shovels or festoon him in a dress and drag him behind a pickup truck through town to the boundary of Polk County. But he had to have a plan. There had to be a plan.

He had thought he might go back to the now-notorious Bob sites, the burned church, Bob's own still-sealed-off trailer eight miles out of town or the Polk County Health Complex, where Bob had so flummoxed the FBI—and RamDyne. But when he'd visited all these places that morning, he'd found them returned to banality, their brush with glory and the national media completely over.

Maybe guns were the hook. He had gone to a gun store on the edge of town and tried to start up a conversation. This was a big mistake. The owner looked at him as if he were from Mars, and asked him rudely if he wanted to see something or what.

"That one," he said nervously.

The man took a large rifle off the rack, opened the bolt, and handed it over.

It was very heavy.

"Is this like the one Bob Lee Swagger used?" Dobbler asked.

The old man's eyes narrowed. Then he allowed, "Sir, in these parts some folks don't think Bob done what they all say he done. They say if Bob had taken a shot at the president, we'd be havin' ourselves a new president. Now that rifle's a Savage 110 in thirty-ought-six. Are you serious about buying or do you just want to cuddle on up to it and pretend you're Bob Lee Swagger?"

This hostility had frightened Dobbler; he handed the rifle back and fumbled his way out of the shop. Now it was three hours later and all he'd done since was to wander around foolishly, wishing to hell he knew what to do.

I know he's here, he thought. *This is where he'd go, he'd have to go.*

Dobbler looked up into the mountains. They all looked the same to him, menacing. It reminded him of his first glance into the yard at Norfolk State, the terror and vulnerability he felt. He resolved to develop some steel. He resolved to be courageous. He determined to go up to the mountains, yes, to go up there and somehow face the man he had to face. Tomorrow.

Dobbler got into his rented car and drove back to the motel, feeling utterly beaten. He went to his room, realizing he'd wasted his first day entirely and that it wouldn't take Shreck and his goons long to figure out where he'd run to. He had no place else to go.

He got out of the car and walked to his room. He fumbled with the lock and stepped into darkness. He wished he had stopped to buy something to eat, feeling suddenly feeble.

He turned on the light.

"Hello, little buddy," said Bob the Nailer. "Believe you and I have some talking to do."

He was afraid she'd have a date or a car pool arrangement, or something. But Nick was lucky as he sat parked just across the street from the Federal Building on Loyola at 5:35 P.M. Sally came out of the building alone, crossed the street, went into the Payless Parking Garage, and emerged three minutes later in a gold Honda Civic.

He followed her into the traffic, trying to remember where she lived, or if she'd ever said. He simply latched on behind as she headed out I-10, east, until she reached the lakeside, then followed the sign that pointed the way to Gentilly Woods. He watched as she stopped at a Fill-a-Sack. When she came out a few minutes later with two plastic bags, he decided it was time to move.

"Sally! Hey, Sally!"

He dashed across the parking lot to her, but when she heard his voice and he saw suspicion flee across her pretty face, he knew in a second he had no chance at all of pretending he'd just bumped into her.

"Nick! Are you trying to get me fired! What are you doing here? You followed me. You *followed* me!"

"All right. Yeah, I did."

"Well, you're lucky I didn't have a date."

"I know that. You're the most popular woman in New Orleans, I keep forgetting."

"Nick, you're in a lot of trouble. You could get me in a lot of trouble."

"You haven't told anyone I've been talking to you on the phone?"

"Hold it right there. You haven't exactly been *talking* to me on the phone. When you *want* something, like a top secret government report, then you talk to me on the phone. When you don't want anything, then you don't have the decency to give me the time of day. And why do I think you're here now? To tell me how much you like my dress?"

"It's very pretty."

"To tell me how much you like my new cologne?"

"Hey, it smells great."

"To tell me how you've missed me?"

"I've missed you a lot."

"What do you want, Nick? You always *want* something. And it's not even me. You don't want to kiss me or sleep with me or anything. You just want some favor that's going to cost me my job."

"It's real easy. It's *so* easy. It'll take you two minutes. I know you can do it."

"What is it? Steal Mr. Utey's billfold? Sneak an M-16 out of the armory?"

"Run some numbers for me. You can do it. You're tied into the municipal numbers, I know you are."

"I knew it. Boy, if you aren't the predictable one. Nick, I just can't—"

"Do you think I'd do this if it weren't important?"

"It's always important. It's always just one more little thing. Why don't you just go to Hap Fencl and explain. He *likes* you. Everybody *likes* you."

"Ah . . . it just wouldn't work out. Trust me. Sally, I need you to get into the New Orleans Municipal Motor Vehicles Registry. I need a name or a number or . . . well, I don't know."

"What are you talking about?"

"Oh. Taxis. Didn't I say that? *Taxis*. I'm looking for . . . well, I don't quite know what."

"When?"

"When?"

"When! When do you need it by?"

"I was hoping . . . I was hoping you'd let me take you out to dinner. Then I was hoping you'd let me drive you back downtown. Then I was hoping you'd run upstairs. And run the numbers tonight."

"God, Nick, you deserve some sort of award for shamelessness. I mean, this sets a new record even by your standards."

"Sally . . . I can't even tell you what this is about or what I've been up to or who I've been with. But—please, trust me. This is *so* important."

"Oh, Christ, Nick. Do you have a quarter?"

"A quarter?"

"A quarter."

"Yes."

"Give it here, then."

"Sure. What—"

"I *do* have a date. I'll go break it."

"Oh, um—hey, with *who?*"

"Norm Fesper."

"*That* guy? He's a defense lawyer, for Christ's sake. Oh, come on, you can do better than that!"

"I just did," she said, walking away to make the call.

They kept her locked in a room in a Quonset hut. The room smelled of rust and old paint, but it was warm and dry. She had a television. They brought her food three times a day, bland, nutritious institutional stuff. They brought her magazines, and someone changed the linen every third day. Between eleven and twelve and then again between three and four, they took her for long walks across the empty, rolling fields. She could see mountains in the distance.

She had two guards. Both were dour Latino men who avoided direct eye contact and treated her with what might be called gentle firmness. She was a practical woman: she understood that hating them was pointless.

"Where are we?" she asked. "Are we in Virginia or Maryland? I know it's somewhere in the East."

They would not answer. But she knew it was the East, because it was turning cold. She had forgotten the cold, living all those years in the desert. But now the cold insinuated itself into her life, crawling down the black wool sweater they'd given her to wear over a jumpsuit, or into the bed when she slept. There was frost on the window when she awoke, and the days were hard and crisp, the sky aching blue.

Finally, she was brought before a man. There was no mercy in his eyes; he looked like a deputy sheriff she'd once known who'd shot three men over his career. Here at last, she understood, was someone worthy of her anger.

"Where am I? Why are you doing this to me?"

"We're not doing this to you, Ms. Fenn. Your friend Bob Lee Swagger is doing this."

"That's bullshit. This is bullshit. It's all bullshit. Bob Lee wouldn't do anything to hurt me."

"I'm not here to argue with you about that. Bob Lee Swagger is a traitor and a murderer. We have to apprehend him. He is a danger to his country."

"More bullshit. Bob Lee Swagger would never do anything to hurt his country. He fought and bled for it for three long tours in Vietnam. He was wounded terribly for his country. He was in a hospital for over a year for his country. He loves his country."

The man waited patiently for her to finish.

"He became an assassin and a spy, bent on destruction. He must be stopped. We'll use you to stop him. It's our duty to this country."

"I don't know who you are, or why you think you can do this to me, but when I hear the words 'duty' and 'this country' in your mouth, I want to puke. I think you're just a mob of gangsters and what you're trying to save isn't the country but your own asses."

"You're here to help us stop him. That's all we care about at this point. I'm telling you this on good faith, because I don't want you to hate me. I want you to be willing to cooperate with me and with your country."

"You're not my country."

"I am your country," he said. "I'm the part of your country that's willing to stand up for what must be done, for what is necessary."

"Mister, if you think you can get the best of Bob Lee Swagger, then you're just another fool who'll end up in the ground."

It was sheer bravado, of course, and even as she said it, she wished it were true and prayed that it were true and knew that it couldn't be. There were so many of them: this horrible leader, the little creep Payne, with his tattoos and beady, scary eyes, and all the robotlike Latinos, and some white trash, all with guns, all with attitudes. It was a mob, a manhunt, a posse. Who was Bob Lee Swagger to stand up to all this anger? He was just a man, she knew, and she knew what happened to men.

They were going to take him from her.

"How did you—"

"I still have some friends in this place, mister. They told me some Eastern cookie-boy was asking questions." Then he lapsed into barren silence.

They drove for what seemed hours. Bob pushed the white pickup far into the mountains. They drove ruthlessly up dirt roads, slithered through puddles and blew through fog banks, and crawled along the edges of cliffs. Now and then they passed a run-down old trailer or some dilapidated cabin. Once a shaft of sunlight pierced the gloom and Dobbler had a sense of vista: he looked, and saw a roiling green wilderness of mountain, forest, and ravine. He shivered. A terrible place.

Dobbler at last said, "You—you killed a lot of men a few days ago."

"Well, they were fixing to do the same to me."

"I know all about you. I've been studying you for months."

"I remember you," Bob suddenly said, "from that scene in Maryland. You just looked at me, mister. I could tell what a specimen you thought I was. You thought I was some kind of special wild bear or something."

"You are an amazing man. You've been pursued by one of the most ruthlessly efficient intelligence organizations in the world, comprised mainly of ex-CIA people and ex-military. You've destroyed them. They may kill you yet, but effectively, you've already won. And they know it, too. You've beaten them."

Bob spat out the window.

"Mister," he said, "it's not over till I put your Colonel Shreck in a goddamned body bag and his pal Payne, too. And get my girl back. And clear my name. Now why the hell are *you* here?"

"Two reasons, really. Because they have to be stopped. And because you're the only one who can stop them."

"You been cashing their checks for a mighty long time. A little late to come up on the right side of the game."

Dobbler held out his briefcase.

"What I've got in here is a tape that shows what they do. I didn't know what it was. I thought it was all spy plots, greater good calculations, trying to work to save the country. And I guess I was into denial. Do you know what that is?"

"I know more than you think."

"Yes, you do. Of course you do. And yes, you would know denial. Anyway, I— I looked at the tape. That was the end of the denial."

"What's on the tape?"

The doctor paused.

"Auschwitz in the jungle."

At 10:12 she said the dinner part was over.

"You're really trying, I'll give you that. And it was a very nice dinner. You're a very decent guy. I always knew that. But you want your numbers, don't you? You'll make me pay for a couple of hours with you. I've got to do you the favor, right."

"Ah—have I been pushing it? I mean, did I bring it up?"

"Well, we got through your year of law school and my broken engagement to Jack Fellows and why I quit the Kappa house at Ole Miss the same week I broke up with Jack, and how long it's been since you've been out with a girl—we got through all that just fine. But about six minutes ago—I think it was my crush on Sam Hawks, the high school fullback?"

"Yeah—"

"That's when the meter was up and you had paid me all the attention you were going to pay me. Now it's AB Nick, All Business Nick, that's what the women call you. All those years with a crippled wife and you never even *looked* at any of us. Men like you don't grow on trees, I'll tell you that. Now let's go and get your numbers, all right, AB Nick?"

"Sure."

He paid the check and they drove down to the Federal Building.

"Now, what is it I'm looking for?"

"Okay. I want you to run municipal taxi drivers' licenses two ways. First, by numbers. I'm looking for numbers with a sequence of R, O, one, one, one, space, D, O, something like that . . ."

"Wow, that's not much."

"Okay, and then I want names. From the licenses. I want all the names that start with either ROM or DO and all the names that start DO and end ROM. And variations on ROMDO or DOROM?"

"Nick?"

"What?"

"Nick, what on earth—?"

"I think a guy trying to reach me with something left me a clue. I first thought it was the name of an organization. But now I see that's all wrong. He was trying to tell me how he hid what he hid for me. And the only place he could have stashed it was in the cab that brought him to his death. So he either memorized the driver's name from the hack license over the right half of the windshield on the visor, or the license plate number as the cab drove away. See, he had to have a way to ID the cab. So I—"

"Okay. Okay. I'll try. I can't promise anything."

She leaned over abruptly and gave him a kiss on the cheek.

"What was that for?" he said.

"For being a pain in the ass," she said. Then she got out and went into the building.

Nick waited and waited. Twice, a cop car prowled along the street and flashed a beam onto him, but his bland white face and coat and tie spoke the Esperanto of class to the cops, and they let him be. The streets were otherwise deserted. He knew up there in the office the skeleton crew was on—the FBI never sleeps, all that stuff—and he could visualize her hunched at her terminal, the low buzz of the office at quarter-staff, the sense of restfulness and ease that comes on the graveyard shift. He'd worked it himself his first year in the office and was aware how lulling it could be.

At last, she emerged but he could tell by the tentativeness in her body language that her luck hadn't been good.

"No home runs?" he said when she got in.

"Nick, I tried and tried. There's not much to go on."

"Yeah. Well, you're right. Did you get anything?"

"Well, first off, the license number idea doesn't pan out at all. It seems that cab plates are all numerical—there aren't any letters in them. Don't ask me why. So there aren't any license numbers beginning with an *R*."

"Dammit, that's right! I think I even knew that once."

"Maybe it was an *8*, or a *5*, and the number sort of fell apart, but—"

She trailed off.

"Okay. One down. What about names? Did you get any names?"

She sighed, and handed him the printout. He opened the door just a bit to bring on the dome light.

"It's not great. It's not even promising. There are two first names and one last name that begin with ROM, in which the other name has a DO in it."

"Shit," said Nick, stricken, feeling like an idiot.

"Nick, don't take it so hard."

"Ah, Christ, I just—"

But he couldn't finish. He looked up the deserted street. He looked down the deserted street. Another failure.

He looked at the names.

The list read:

ROMNEY DONAHUE
ROMAN DOHENY
D'ORLY ROBARDS

And that was it.

"Oh, Jesus," said Nick, in despair.

"It's no good?"

He groped.

"You got me exactly what I asked for. But . . . why would he only write down *part* of the first name and *part* of the last name? I just don't—"

He trailed off. The connection to Lanzman's dying message, ROM DO, suddenly seemed vaporous.

Well, he thought. It was an extremely long shot, but he still ought to look them up, check out their cabs and—

"What are these other names?"

"Well, just to be on the safe side, I got all the cabbies whose first names begin with either *R* or *D* and whose last names begin with *R* or *D*. That was my first field of discrimination. Just in case your copy was wrong or—"

"It wasn't. I saw it. I saw it. Sally, the guy wrote it in his own blood as he was dying on a linoleum floor. I saw it in the linoleum, on the tiles, and then watched as it disappeared when—"

Nick stopped talking.

He stared at the list.

"Nick? Nick, are you all right? Nick, what's going—"

"Jesus Christ," he said.

He pointed to a name on the list.

"Suppose the blood ran together in some spots. It connected letters that shouldn't be connected. And suppose he died before he finished."

"I don't—"

"Look, Sally. Look. He was writing a name but the last two letters joined together at the top. The blood ran across a crack in the tile and bridged two letters. And he didn't finish."

Nick had one of those weird sensations you get once or twice in a career, when it all comes together.

"An *N* and an *I* at the end of the first name; they ran together and it formed an *M*. And he wrote the middle initial. And then he couldn't quite finish the last name. But here it is."

He pointed to it, on the list.

Roni D. Ovitz, it said. Sun Cab Co., 5508 St. Charles Avenue.

It was a magnificent workup, Shreck acknowledged. The Defense Cartographic Agency had created a masterpiece. Represented in multicolored Plasticine topography were the many heights and levels of the Ouachita range, the gaps, the valleys, the enfilades. It stretched for twenty feet, almost six feet wide. On the relief map, dappled in green for forestation exactly as the satellite had recorded it, the mountain range had been resolved into a maze of elevations. They were all there: Black Thorn, Winding Stair, Poteau, Mount Bayonet, Hard Bargain Valley . . .

"What do you see, Mr. Scott?" Shreck asked.

The man in the wheelchair hunched forward, his keen shooter's eyes devouring the landform represented before him.

"Space," he said. "I want space. Lots of space."

"It'll turn on some sort of transfer. We have the woman; they'll have Dobbler's treasure. They'll want to trade; we'll want to trade. We'll use the girl. We'll draw them to us with the girl."

"Don't worry about it," said Lon. "Give me the shot, and I guarantee you I will make it."

"Mr. Scott," said the Colonel, "pardon me for not being polite but being polite isn't my business. You're about to go against a combat sniper. You don't have any mobility. Shit, you don't have any *legs*. You may have to take fire, to return fire under fire. And . . . your disability. He can move, if it comes to that, and you can't.

And what happens if we're hit or have to retreat? There you are, out there, paralyzed, on the ground, with no help. Nobody will come for you. There's nothing for you except death."

Scott met his stare for what seemed the longest time. The handsome head and shoulders on the collapsed body and the dead legs: even now Shreck hadn't quite grown accustomed to it.

"Do you know, Colonel Shreck, you've given a cripple a chance that no cripple ever had." He smiled, almost ruefully. "You've given me a chance to go to war. And to test myself against the very best. You've given me the chance to be complete, if only for a few seconds."

Shreck said, "I don't know who you are, Mr. Scott, or what the hell you've done. But I'll say this for you, you've got a set of balls on you."

At Sun Cab, it turned swiftly to anticlimax. First came the news that Roni D. Ovitz, an Israeli émigré, had been shot in a robbery two months ago and though only suffering a flesh wound had quit the taxi business and was working as a counterman at his brother-in-law's TCBY franchise in a suburban mall. But his cab was still the property of Sun Cab and a quick check of the records located it, now on the road with another driver.

The dispatcher, faced with two people with earnest faces and FBI identifications, didn't hesitate an instant. He ordered the cab in, and it dropped its fare in the French Quarter, and got to the garage in about ten minutes.

"So what's the beef, Charlie?"

"Fed beef. These two FBI agents. They—"

"Hey, I didn't do a damned thing, I—"

"That's okay, pal," said Nick, in his calming voice. "This isn't about you. It's about the cab."

"That buggy is bad luck. Somebody shot Roni Ovitz through the neck and before that a guy named Tim Ryan was fuckin' killed and—"

But Nick wasn't listening.

Okay, he thought. *You're in the backseat of the cab. You know you've been made. You've just got a few seconds. What do you do? The trunk? How can you get to the trunk? You can't get to the trunk.*

Under the front seat? No. The driver would see you, and whatever you stashed, he'd dig it out a few seconds later.

Nick said "Excuse me" to Sally, then went and climbed into the automobile, a 1987 Ford Fairlane. He sat there, his eyes closed, smelling the odor of the old and sodden upholstery, the stench of a hundred thousand other, unremarkable passengers, the tang of gasoline and oil, and, he supposed, one other coppery whiff in the air, the whiff of fear. Roni Ovitz's fear. Tim Ryan's fear. And, for surely by the time they reached the motel, Lanzman knew he was quite probably doomed, Lanzman's fear.

Oh, you were a cool one, Nick thought. You held together to the very end. Whatever it was that motivated you—patriotism, faith, machismo—whatever it was, it was strong and beautiful stuff. Oh, you were a man, my friend. An *hombre.* Oh, yes you were.

His fingers had of their own accord fallen to the seat where, blindly, they probed and pushed at the juncture between cushion and back. There was a gap there, when the yielding cushioning was peeled back; you could slide a document through.

Nick got out of the car, turned, leaned in and pushed his hand through. He gave a mighty tug and yanked, and the seat lurched forward on hinges. Underneath it lay a tapestry of Western civilization and its contents: candy wrappers, cigarette packs, combs, pens, quarters and tokens, two playing cards, a business card and a rolled wad of some kind of heavy paper.

"Nick," said Sally at his shoulder, pointing. "Is that it?"

Nick picked it up.

He unrolled it carefully. He saw immediately that it was on some sort of light-sensitive paper that made it impervious to photocopying. And even as he unscrolled it, he thought he watched the type dilute in clarity; an hour in the sun and this baby was history. No one could duplicate it, except maybe the geniuses at the Bureau's legendary Forensic Documents Division.

The cover letter was written in Spanish, addressed to somebody named General Esteban Garcia de Rujijo of the Fourth Battalion (Air-Ranger), First Brigade, First Division ("Acatatl"), Salvadoran Army. It was signed by a Hugh Meachum, no affiliation given. It said, as best as Nick's clumsy Spanish could understand, that the mission as outlined orally in their last meeting was being undertaken by the extremely efficient organization with which the writer was certain the general was familiar, and that it was to everybody's best interest that the business be completed as quickly as possible. The writer also took the liberty of enclosing some background material—highly sensitive! most secret!—so that the general could rest assured the very best professional people were handling the job, and that therefore he was not to make any attempts himself, as that would completely undermine the cause in whose service they all labored so diligently.

Nick lifted the cover letter to examine the document itself.

It was Annex B.

CHAPTER THIRTY-FIVE

When he wasn't shooting, Lon was studying.

He began with rote memory; he divided the map into one foot squares and attempted to commit each to the files deep in his brain. He worked everything out, slowly, one step at a time, with plodding thoroughness. He sat there in the field headquarters hut in Virginia in his wheelchair and just stared and stared at the miniaturized plastic mountain range spread out on the table before him, rocking back and forth on the fulcrum of his belly.

After memorizing the material so perfectly that he could see it in his dreams, he began to look for firing lines. He needed a certain distance, height, a good vantage point, the light behind him, no cross breezes, plenty of camouflage. One by one, he tested sites against his cluster of requirements, finding and discarding possibilities.

When he worked, no emotion showed on his face. It was a wintry Yankee face, iron as New England, the face of a man who knew death because he was himself mostly corpse.

Finally, days into the study, he beckoned to Colonel Shreck.

"Here," he said. "I found it."

His finger touched a valley deep in the vastness of the Ouachitas, far, far from the town of Blue Eye.

Shreck bent to read the inscription where the blunt finger marked it.

HARD BARGAIN VALLEY, it said.

Dobbler was astounded at how banal Bob found him. He had presumed, with no small amount of vanity, that Bob would find him fascinating, would ply him with questions, would in some way admire him.

Using Bob as others had used him, Dobbler had unburdened himself in one epic purge, like a mega-couch-session, letting it all pour out, his sins, his fears, his weaknesses, his guilts. He even blubbered as he confessed, while secretly admiring his own performance.

But Bob had just looked at him all squinty-eyed.

"What do you want?" Dobbler demanded when he was done. "Tell me, and I'll give it to you."

Bob regarded him without much interest.

"Don't you trust me?" Dobbler wanted to know.

"It doesn't matter a lot."

"Why don't you ask me more questions?"

"You've talked enough. You've talked too much."

"Don't you want to know how Shreck's mind works? About the relationship between him and Payne? Don't you want—"

"Can you tell me how to kill him?"

"Uh—no."

"Then you don't know a thing that interests me."

"But there's so much more—"

"You think what you told me is so important. But it doesn't matter a spoon of grease to me, unless it can give me an advantage in a week or so. Meanwhile, you save it for Memphis; he'll listen to you. I just want you to stay here and don't wander off, you hear? You're just another problem I have to solve."

That was the beginning. Then Bob went out with his rifle for several hours, leaving Dobbler cabin-bound. Bob didn't have to tell him that to wander off was to die in these remote regions.

In the cabin, Dobbler was always cold. He shivered from dawn till dusk, threw wood on the fire—"If you don't stop using up that goddamn wood, I'm going to make you chop it your own damn self," Bob had said testily—and sat there, sinking into misery, unmoved by the showy blaze of autumn that was exploding like napalm bursts all around. He hated the filth of it also, the lack of a toilet and toilet paper, the same socks and underwear day in and day out. He hated his own smell and wondered why he just got dirtier and Bob somehow seemed always immaculate.

Then one night, late, the door burst open.

Dobbler bolted up in sheer terror, sure they'd been discovered by one of the colonel's raiding parties. But it was a large, angry young man with a thatch of blond hair and a rumpled business suit who seemed to be wearing four guns under his coat. This would be Memphis, the doctor surmised, and indeed it was. He smiled, anticipating someone more in his world than Bob.

"Who's this sorry sack of shit?" Nick wanted to know.

"Says he's one of Shreck's men. He's come over to

our side because he didn't realize these boys were Nazis. He has a tape over there with the massacre on it."

"Who the hell are you, mister? Are you working for Shreck?"

"My name is David Dobbler. I'm a graduate of Brandeis University and Harvard Medical School. I'm a practicing psychiatrist—although some years ago the board removed my certification."

"He was the smart boy who looked at me like a bug on a pin back in Maryland, Pork."

"Jesus Christ!"

"As I told Mr. Swagger, I recently discovered that the acts of RamDyne were not, as I had been informed, in the national interest but rather the adventurings of a rogue unit. Naturally, I felt—"

"That's all shit, mister," said Memphis, who had the policeman's gift for locating weaknesses swiftly and exploiting them greedily. "You must have found something out that you thought Shreck would kill you over. And he probably would."

"Yes, he would. I have—evidence. Of a massacre."

"Evidence," snorted Nick. "The world is full of evidence."

"Visual evidence. On tape."

Bob pointed to the cassette, which lay haphazardly on the mantel.

"He says they filmed it."

"Terrible things," Dobbler said. "Women, children, in the water. The machine guns, the laughing soldiers, the commanders. The Americans."

"You have this Shreck? On *tape*?" Nick said, astounded.

"Yes. And little Jack Payne as well. Giving the orders, guiding a Salvadoran general. It's all—"

Nick turned to Bob.

"Jesus, just maybe that would do it. It would certainly suggest a motive for killing the archbishop, and with a motive we could get the investigation reopened and other things might come out."

Bob thought on this for a second.

Then he said, "Hear him out. See what he's got. I'm getting out of here for a time. You two geniuses of education jawing away like piglets in the slop could give me a serious pain in the eyes."

It took time but Nick and Dobbler, fierce adversaries at first, soon enough found their common ground. Bob himself disappeared with his rifle and as the two of them were talking there came the far-off sound of shots. When he returned, he regarded them without enthusiasm. Nick rose and came at him.

"Now what have you got cooked up, Memphis?" Bob asked.

"It's all here," Nick finally said. "With what he's got and what I've got, we can put them away. We can clear you."

But Bob just went to the cabinet where he stored his cleaning rod and equipment, and began the laborious, greasy job of scrubbing down the bore of the rifle.

In his remoteness, it wasn't so much that he offered a counterargument, but that he communicated his displeasure by his stoicism and the hard look on his face. Nick pressed on, bringing a trophy out for all to see.

"Annex B. This is it." He lifted the green bag of documents he'd found under the cab seat in New Orleans. "It turns out that Annex B is simply the Bureau abstract of the Agency file on its contract outfit, RamDyne, except that all the names and dates and pertinent memoranda are included. The facts are what we knew from the Bureau file itself. It was started in 1962, right after Bay of Pigs. Who started it? My bet is that it was founded by somebody who was formerly with CIA who was actively involved in planning the invasion, but who got the ax when the invasion failed. Does that add up?"

Dobbler said, "Yes. Bay of Pigs was weakness, failure, lack of nerve. They hated weakness."

"Of course," said Nick.

"Neurotically. And I can see how to them the Bay of Pigs was the beginning of American weakness—of committing to something, then changing your mind, beginning to equivocate, beginning to undercut, and finally dooming your operation to failure by your own doubts. RamDyne was about following through. About seeing the course."

"The name even comes from Bay of Pigs," said Nick. "*RamDyne*, large *R*, large *D:* it has no meaning except *R* and *D*, which a guy I used to know said computed out in Army lingo, sixty-two-style, to Romeo Dog, which was the call sign for the Second Battalion of Twenty-twenty-six Brigade at Red Beach, the force that got cut off, chopped up and captured. So calling it RamDyne, maybe that's somebody's way of commemorating the past and setting course for the future. That sound right to you, doc?"

"They were zealots," Dobbler said. "They were true believers. They had a sense of building from the ruins, like Hitler, I suppose. It guided them. To God knows what."

Bob just sat there, listening to the pitch, running the rod, with its bright crown of bronze bristle and its dank lubrication of Shooter's Choice, through the bore guide and up and down the rifle barrel.

"Bob, we can put them away. In a jail. There can be a happy ending. There can be justice."

"He's right, Mr. Swagger. Terrible wrongs were done. But the world can be restored to order. And some of us in this room—there's a provisional salvation for us, too. You can be at peace."

Bob looked at them harshly.

"It's just words," he said. "In Vietnam we had a saying. 'Don't mean a thing.' That's what this is. It don't mean a thing."

He put the rod down, removed the Delrin bore guide from the action, and began to scrub at the insides of the chamber and the receiver with a blackened toothbrush, giving the weapon his full attention.

"It's all here!" Nick exploded. "Or most of it. I don't quite know what mission first got them together in the early sixties. That's lost to history. And the early stuff is mundane, when they worked for the Agency as a cover organization for shipping illegal cargos to various hot spots in the world. It gets interesting in sixty-nine when this nutcase Shreck was recruited after the Army sacked him, with the mission of building an operational and training arm. He seems to have created a kind of Green-Beret-for-Hire unit. These boys saw some action, no shit. Africa in the early seventies. Lots of time in the Mideast in the late seventies and eighties, and, lately, lots of time in Central America. Whenever some tin-pot country had a job that needed doing but not the capacity, RamDyne could field an operations nasty-ass team. But never so nasty as with Panther Battalion on the Sampul River last year. They talk about that much, Doctor?"

"Nothing. They had perfect professional discipline. I didn't know until I saw the tape. And the job on the bishop—they said he was a secret guerrilla and that he was working to sabotage the peace process. He had to be stopped so that peace could be achieved. He was an enemy of peace."

Nick leaned toward Bob.

"This is the key part. Two hundred civilians, most of

them women and kids, all wiped out. But it wasn't a mistake. That's the secret of the Sampul River. It's what this thing has always been about. They did it on purpose."

He had Bob's attention now.

"Here's the killer," Nick said. "Here's the only thing in Annex B that's worth a damn. It's what puts Shreck, Payne, and all the RamDyne yo-yos in the chamber when they drop the little pill."

He handed it over to the doctor.

"It's a note from Shreck to—name obliterated, notice how the big guys protect themselves—dated 2 May '91, sent through U.S. diplomatic pouch from the embassy in El Salvador. Read it to us, Doctor."

Dobbler cleared his throat.

> Eyes Only: xxxxxxxxxxxxx
>
> Washington, D.C.
>
> Re: Panther Bn. training operations, Ocalupo, Salvador.
>
> General de Rujijo agrees that punitive measures must be taken against the peasant population but finds that his soldiers, drawn from the same population, are reluctant on the scale we have conceptualized. My training cadre has isolated two platoons of Panther Battalion and we seem to be making real progress in bringing them to the proper level of willingness. Will be moving onto Sampul River district in June and commencing counterinsurgency ops that area. Anticipate sanitation program to commence that date.
>
> Signed,
>
> *Raymond F. Shreck*

There was a moment of silence.

"You see," said Nick, "some genius in an office

somewhere wants to get the guerrillas to the peace talks. But there's no pressure on them. Nothing's happening. They've made some kind of deal with the rural population. So he dreams up this idea: send in some crack troops, line up the peasants and blow 'em away. It was a massacre ordered up out of a catalogue. Atrocity, one each, OD, Summer Issue, Number 5554442. Murder-R-Us. The point being to scare the peasants so fucking bad they'll *never* help the guerrillas again. The guerrillas have to come in and make powwow. And here's the worst part: it worked. He's probably even proud of himself. He did the hard thing. He made the world a better place, and it only cost two hundred or so women and kids. That's RamDyne, isn't it, Doctor? I mean, that's classic RamDyne."

"The hard thing," said Dobbler. "Yes, they could have done that. Yes, that's what the tape shows."

"Anyway," said Nick, "with the tape and Annex B, Shreck's dead. The whole fucking program is blown out of the water. And anybody who sailed on the ship—that includes the Bureau's Lancer Committee, who bought the National Interest bullshit hook, line and sinker—goes down with her. Down to the bottom."

Bob just nodded grimly.

"There's only one problem," said Nick. "This file was sent to the general prior to the operation against the archbishop. It was meant to keep him from going hog-wild. And boy, the stink it's going to make when it gets out. Man, it'll make Watergate and Iran–Contra look like tea parties. But maybe it'll get you off the hook. And maybe it won't."

Bob was done with the action. He took an aerosol can of Gun Scrubber and began to blow compressed-air-driven solvent into the trigger mechanism with a sharp, wet hiss.

"It doesn't matter," said Bob.

"Here's the plan," said Shreck. "Very simple. It's how we bring Bob into Scott's kill zone. Scott says he can deliver the one-shot kill at ranges no man, not even Bob, can guarantee. He'll take it at between fifteen hundred and seventeen hundred yards. A mile, perhaps. He's operating at the very edge of the envelope, where not even Bob has been before. And that's our advantage. This is how we do it."

Payne leaned forward to listen.

"Scott goes in independently about a day in advance of our arrival. He'll never hit Blue Eye, so nobody will see him or even know he's there, and no one will believe that a man with his infirmity could penetrate so deep in the wilderness. He'll go in by 'chute, a HALO job, high altitude, low opening, the night before, landing in Hard Bargain Valley. Nicoletta goes in with him and we'll drop an ATV. Nicoletta will be his legs and get him up to the ridge and dig him a spider hole.

"Meanwhile, our end of the operation takes the form of a barter. We have the girl. Bob has the cassette. The woman will mean more to him than the cassette to us. We make contact with him, just as he said, in Blue Eye. We'll offer him the woman for the cassette."

Payne wanted the woman, too.

"We'll offer him the woman and a fresh start," the colonel continued. "We'll tell him that we can set it up so that he's no longer a marked man. He can have his life back, he can have the woman. He'll seem to accept, but of course it'll be a lie. He'll make the exchange, then count on his skills to double around and kill us from afar. But he can't do it until the woman is safe. That's the key. We have to preempt him."

"How do we set up a swap?" Payne asked.

"We tell him that we're worried about his ability to pick us off at long range. We can't give him that opportunity. We tell him that at 1000 hours on November third, we'll fire a flare in the sky, a red flare. He makes a compass fix on it and has one hour to make it to the site. When he's there, he finds a flare pistol. *He* fires an answering flare so we know he's in position. We fire another answering flare. Again he has an hour to reach the spot. Again he finds a flare, and lets us know he's arrived. In that way we bounce him through the mountains. He never has time to get set up because he's got to stay on the move to get to the site so that he can fire the pistol so that *we* fire our flare pistol. We maneuver him into Hard Bargain Valley. He should be exhausted and desperate. In the middle of the valley we wait for him. He'll feel safe there, because the closest shooting range is well over fifteen hundred yards, and he knows nobody can hit at that range. *He* can't hit at that range. Plus, how could we get poor old crippled Lon in to even attempt such a thing? At one hundred yards distance, he sends over Memphis with the cassette, we send over you with the woman. When I see the cassette is all right, I simply press a button on my watch that emits a high pitch of noise that Lon's radio can pick up. Hearing the signal, Lon takes Bob down from fifteen hundred yards; you and I shoot Memphis. It's over."

"The woman?"

"Payne, that's a stupid question."

"Yeah," said Payne.

Nick looked at him for just a moment; the way he processed information somehow got fouled up and then he realized that indeed Bob had said what Bob had said.

"It doesn't matter?" he exploded. "Are you kidding? It *does* matter. You're innocent! This whole thing has been about your innocence! Not because it's you but because that's how the system works: the innocent go free, the guilty go to jail. That's America. That's what's at stake—"

Bob put down the cleaning implements.

"Pork, this here thing isn't about getting me off a hook. It's about something else. I got a woman who did me good who is now Payne's playtoy. I got a dog that stuck by me when no one else would and ended up in the ground. I got a country that thinks anybody who fought in Vietnam is some kind of crazy sniper who shoots at the president and any man who owns a gun is a crazy man. Those are debts that have to be paid first off. And then there's the goddamn tape and that letter. I don't want that goddamn thing playing on the TV like a movie, and all those reporters getting rich and writing books off that letter for years to come. No, sir, not by me, not if I have breath to stop it."

"You have to let the cards fall where they—"

"The cards fall where I put them. And here's where I put them. Plain and simple, we're going to zip the bag on those boys, and save that woman and then I'll deal with the other thing. Agree with me or get out of here. Julie first, Shreck and Payne second, and nothing third. Got that?"

Nick looked at Bob sitting there, stolid as a rock. He felt like Geraldo Rivera interviewing Wyatt Earp and Wild Bill Hickok at the same time. There was no bend in Bob's furious rectitude, his nutty conviction that he would do what he had to do.

"Jesus, you are a stubborn bastard, Bob," he said. "Your only way out is with this letter and the tape and—"

"Play it my way or don't play it. That's all. Got that? If I don't believe you're on my program, I'll ship you out of here. You can go back to New Orleans and that little girl and let me take care of the men's work."

Nick didn't have to think a second. He was in. Always had been. Had to see how it would finish. He'd given himself to this strange bird, and so he elected to stay the course, not that he had a real choice.

"Sure," he finally said. "It's fine. We'll do it your way."

"I haven't told you everything," said Dobbler. "And now I will."

They both turned to look at him.

"What makes Shreck such a powerful antagonist. One of my duties at RamDyne was to interpret tests. He had once been tested, when he went to work there. The psychologist then was an idiot and didn't understand. But the results are clear. Shreck is more than a sociopath, he's one of those rare men who is simply not afraid to die. Who, in fact, wants to die. Payne is the same way. You see, that's why they are so frightening. Most men care about life. In the end, most men always act out of self-preservation. But these two don't care and won't act that way. It's a function of self-hatred so passionately held that it's off the charts."

Another pause. Then Bob said, "You know, doctor-man, you must come from some pretty soft places to find that so remarkable. You could be describing one half of the world's professional soldiers and both halves of its professional criminals. Truth is, I used to be one of those boys. Didn't give two hairs about surviving. Now I have something to live for. Now I'm scared to hell I'll die. Will it cost me my edge?"

He almost smiled, one of the few times Nick had ever seen anything so gentle play across the strong, hard features of his face.

"Sure is going to be damned entertaining to find out, isn't it?" Bob said.

CHAPTER THIRTY-SIX

Nick said he'd do it.

Bob was stern. "No funny business. No heroics. You play hero, you kill us all. Do you understand?"

"Yeah, I understand. I can handle this."

"I know you can. I'm just telling you. Whatever they say, you agree. You listen hard, and you agree."

Nick climbed into the pickup and drove down the mountain in the dark. It was a wet, shaggy pre-dawn and tendrils of fog clung to the hollows and valleys. For Nick, it was like driving through some half-remembered land from his childhood, as if dragons lurked in the tall pines and the deep caves.

Many switchbacks and crossovers later, he came to flatland, farmland and a highway, passed the burned church, and then drove on in to the town of Blue Eye itself, which even in the rain looked festive. The sun was up as he arrived. THE BUCKS ARE STOPPED HERE, the sign still said, fluttering over the town square. Bright shiny pickups and Rec-Vs lined the street, rifles visible hanging in the racks in their back windows. Everywhere Nick could see men proud in their blaze-orange camouflage. Tomorrow was the first day of deer season.

Nick parked and pushed his way through the crowd, which seemed to have been drawn to some epic pancake feed put on by the Kiwanis or Jaycees. The boys were talking rifles and loads, hunting techniques, telling stories of giant animals who'd soaked up bullet after bullet and then walked away. There was a common anticipation and a sporting crowd's fever in the air. All agreed that, what with a moist and succulent summer, the Arkansas whitetails were everywhere. It would be, everybody said, a great year for a venison harvest.

But Nick, melancholy as always with the approach of action, ignored all this, went to the square, and sat himself down on a bench near a statue of some ancient Confederate hee-row in pigeon-shit-green copper. There he slumped, a glowering figure in jeans and a rough workman's coat, his Beretta in a speed holster upside down under his left arm, not three inches from where his right hand just happened to fall.

He sat and he sat, and in time—he had no sense of it at all—a man came and sat with him. It was very smoothly done, but then everything these birds did they did smoothly. They were professionals.

"Memphis?"

"Yes."

"Good. There," said the man. "Can you see her?"

"No," said Nick.

"See, the Plymouth Voyager van. The back door is open. She's sitting there. Can you see her?"

He could. She was a lean middle-aged woman, handsome and composed, dressed in a sweater and jeans, and with a grave look on her face. There was something stiff in the way she sat.

Sitting next to her was Payne. He remembered Payne from the swamp, and the jaunty, relishing way he had interrogated Nick and got him ready to die. And he remembered Payne from Annex B: Payne, of the Sampul River.

"Yeah, I see them."

"Do you want to talk to her?"

"No."

"You have the cassette?"

"The cassette, you bet. But we've got more than that. I also managed to dig Annex B up."

"Oh," said Shreck.

"There's enough to send you and Payne to the electric chair three times. Man, they'll deep-fat fry you to a crisp."

Shreck laughed.

"Not this time, sonny. Now you know how this has to happen. We need that cassette. Swagger thinks the woman is important. And we both know Bob has a stubborn, romantic streak, don't we?"

Nick turned. He looked at Raymond F. Shreck for the first time. He wasn't disappointed. He thought of the word *tough* and imagined it carried out to some science fiction degree. Short-haired, steady and strong, the colonel looked like a .45 hardball round in flesh. He was all blunt force, hard eyes, sitting ramrod straight, not a tremor or a line of doubt anywhere about him.

"You know if it were up to me, and I was still with the Bureau, I'd bust your ass so fast you'd leave your teeth in the street."

Shreck smiled.

"Sonny, people have been trying to kill me for nearly forty years. They're all dead and buried and I'm still here. So don't try to scare me. It's a little late in the day for that."

He was wearing a Trebark camouflage suit and a blaze-orange baseball cap that said in gold sans serif across the front, AMERICAN HUNTER AND DAMN PROUD OF IT. His eyes met and held Nick's as forcefully as an assault, and it was Nick who finally looked away.

"Tell Swagger if he crosses me, I kill the woman. Kill her dead. Cut her throat, watch her die, walk away. I've got tons of money and a thousand new identities I can slip into. I'm home free at any second if I want to be."

"But you want that cassette. And those documents."

"Frankly, I don't really give a shit about the documents. But the cassette does have my face on it; it's the only absolute record of my appearance. Life could be difficult if it got out. But the people I work for will be excited about the documents. So bring them too, or I kill the woman. Now this is how we play it."

Nick listened intently as the colonel laid out the plan. At the conclusion, Shreck handed over a map, a geodesic survey of the high Ouachitas, with the start point laid out, and a 40mm brass flare pistol.

"We don't want the Nailer nailing us. We have to see him moving so we know he isn't setting up somewhere above us to take us down from eight hundred yards."

"Maybe you'll have a guy to nail him," Nick said.

"No way. We can't nail him because he may not have the cassette and Annex B with him. He's got insurance, I've got insurance. Mutual deterrence. It kept the world alive for fifty years. I'll set it up so the final exchange is in the wide-open spaces, way beyond any rifle range."

"Uh-huh."

"And when the exchange is made, we walk away. It's

over. We're out of business, but so is he. He has his woman and his freedom. The Feds think he's dead. He can have his whole life back if he lets it lie. He's had a hell of a war, but the war is over now. It's time for him to go someplace in Montana, where beaucoup deer and antelope roam, and just shoot and fuck all day long."

Toward late afternoon of that same day, a banal van left a motel and drove to a civilian hangar at a small airport twenty miles south of Little Rock. It contained three men: one of them was Eddie Nickles and another was a dour figure with the head and shoulders of a Greek god and a broken body, who sat alone with his rifle in a wheelchair in the back. He spoke to no one. It made Eddie Nickles nervous.

If Bob scared him, this guy scared him too, especially in that he wasn't even whole. He had the aura of death to him, that was for sure; he was like a butcher or an embalmer.

"Guy fuckin' scares the shit out of me," Nickles said to his companion, one of the morose survivors of Panther Battalion's assault on Bone Hill, another lad who'd lost his sand.

At the hangar, they pulled up next to a DC-3, glistening silver. ARKANSAS CENTRAL AIRLINES it said in green art deco print under the windows. A double cargo door had been opened two thirds down the fuselage toward the tail.

Nickles got out, went over and conferred briefly with the pilot. Then he leaned into the open cargo bay and saw the ATV, a three-wheeled Honda with soft fat studded tires for gobbling up the rough land and steep inclines of the wilderness; it had been staked to a board with heavy yellow rope; a bulky pack that he knew was a cargo parachute was lashed to it.

"Everything okay, chief?" he called to the cargo master still checking the rigging.

"Thumbs up, Bud," said the man.

Nickles went back to the van.

"Sir, I'm going to load you now," he said.

"Don't touch me. Get the ramp down and stand aside."

"Yes, sir."

Nickles pulled the ramp out of the van. He stepped back and watched as the man leaned over and took the blocks out from under his wheelchair tires. Then he forcefully rocketed himself to the edge, shot down the ramp and headed to the plane.

The man wore a black baseball cap and had smeared his face with black and green paint. He wore black boots and a black and green camouflage tunic. The rifle, encased in a plastic sheath against the damp weather, lay in his lap; he had a Browning Hi-Power pistol in a black shoulder holster.

"Okay," Nickles yelled up to the cargo master. "We need the winch now."

The crewman swung out the device and with an electric purr, the wire descended from its pulley, bearing a hook.

"I have this harness for you, sir," said Nickles.

The man looked at him and Nickles recognized with a stab the fury and humiliation in him; to be that helpless among all these robust men! But, uncomplainingly, the man slipped it on and cinched it tight. His jaw trim, his eyes set, he adjusted himself to the indignity of being loaded aboard the plane like a haunch of beef.

Lon was free. He fell in darkness feeling the wind pounding at him. For just a second he was a boy again, stalking the hills of Connecticut twenty miles west of

New Haven with his father. The sun was a bronze smear; the earth leaped toward him.

Then with a thud, his chute opened, rustling in the wind like a sail. He remembered sailing when he was a boy on the Sound. His father had taught him to sail. Those had been wonderful times.

Hard Bargain Valley hit him with a bang. He lay in the grass. He struggled with the harness, and the chute fell away. He sat upright. He could see the ATV a few hundred feet away, its chute plump in the breeze that coursed along the valley floor. But no sign of Nickles.

He looked at his watch. It was almost five. And suppose Nickles had killed himself in the jump; his parachute hadn't opened, he'd hit the ground at eight hundred feet per second?

Lon laughed. After all the planning he'd gone through in his life, wouldn't that be a final joke?

He looked around, alone on the floor of the valley. To the east he saw the ridge, sweeping and grass covered; to the west a line of trees as the elevation fell away toward the forest below. He saw other mountains, too. It was completely quiet except for the popping and snapping of the chute on the ATV.

"Sir?"

He turned; Nickles was approaching him from the south, with the rifle in a sling over his arm.

"Where the hell have you been?"

"My chute opened early and I carried about a half mile away."

Lon realized the boy had panicked, not trusting the altimeter device rigged to blow the chute out at six hundred feet, and had pulled the emergency ripcord. But it didn't matter now.

"Okay. Get the ATV rigged, collect the chutes and let's get the hell up the ridge."

"Yes, sir."

Payne woke Julie Fenn early in the back of the van, around four, yet when they drove through the dark town, the streets were crawling with men.

On the first day of deer season, the animals would be stupidest and least wary, and the hunters were moving into the woods to be in position by sunup for that first shot.

"You just keep your mouth shut," Payne told her. "You got another day. Then it's all over for you and you get to go home."

But he was lying. She'd seen the other man's face. She knew that doomed her. There was something secretly savage in his eyes; he could look at her and talk to her and plan to kill her all at once.

But she had difficulty concentrating these days. She wasn't sure what the drug was: she guessed it to be something in the Amobarbital-B range, a powerful barbiturate that had the additional effect of eroding the will. They'd been gradually increasing the dosages, too, until on some days she couldn't remember who she was or why this was happening. Always so tired, all she longed for was to go back to sleep and wake up back in Arizona. Very occasionally, she wished she had something to fight them with. But they had taken her only weapons.

They sat her in the seat behind them and drove the van up high mountain ridges, down dusty roads, passing hordes of other four-wheel-drive vehicles, watching as men clambered out in the glare of the headlamps, snorting plumes of hot breath in the night air, their rifles glinting and jingling as they headed out for their stands.

And after a while, the hunters thinned, and then ceased altogether. They drove on endlessly. She looked up dreamily, her head resting on the cool pane of the window: the stars above were bright like pinwheels of fire, the air brisk and magical. She could lose herself in them totally; she felt herself drifting through them and only the sudden sharp bounce of the tire on a rut in the road jerked her back to the present.

With effort, she fought her way toward a consideration of her circumstances. She wanted to kill them; she wanted to see them die, smashed into the earth. But it hurt to hold that thought in the front of her mind for very long; she felt the idea break loose from her brain and begin to drift away until it could no longer be grasped or recognized.

But just as it seemed to disappear forever, she had one last instant of clarity: *I hope you're there, Bob,* she thought. *I hope you make them pay.*

"We're here," said Payne. "This is as close as we can get by vehicle to the first checkpoint. It's about two miles and we've got a few hours yet. No sweat."

"No sweat," said Shreck. "Now let's suit up."

The two men got out of the van and Payne slid the cargo door open. Inside the woman sat passively while Payne bent to the floor, where two Kevlar Second-Chance ballistic vests lay. He retrieved one and handed it to the colonel.

"Thanks," said Shreck.

They slipped their coats off and pulled the heavy vests on, securing the snaps.

"Heavy as shit," said Payne.

"But it'll stop goddamn near anything, including a .308 rifle bullet," said Shreck. He fastened the last snap and said, "Get the woman."

Payne stepped back inside. Julie sat there limply, a vacant look on that beautiful face.

"Come on, sweetie. Time to play with the big boys."

Pulling her by the arm, he was again amazed at how light she seemed. And compliant now, after the spirit she'd shown in Arizona. She seemed to be in another gravity or something; you could launch her in a direction, and she'd sail on out in that direction until she was stopped or bumped into something. God, if Bob the Nailer knew what Shreck had done to her. But Bob wouldn't be knowing anything after a few hours.

"Okay," he said. "All set."

"Fine," said Shreck. Shreck had his rifle out; it was a bland little Marlin lever gun with a scope. He had on his baseball cap and an expensive camouflage outfit and he looked for all the world like a prosperous hunter, in case they should run into forest rangers or park service personnel, though that was highly unlikely. They didn't like to come into the forest on the first day of deer season unless they had to.

Shreck led. Though the vests were heavy and the ground was rough and they were climbing, it wasn't hard and they pushed the woman along when she dragged behind. Eventually, the sky turned orange and the sun rose. It looked to be a clear day, with one of those high, piercing skies, sweet blue, the wind brisk and moist and pure.

First day of deer season, thought Payne. A good day for killing.

A shot rang out far away, a crisp rolling echo. Somebody had drawn blood. It was a good omen.

"All right," said Bob. "Last chance for questions? Any questions? We did it all a hundred times yesterday. You forget it all yet?"

Dobbler and Memphis looked at him. Nick was grave, stiff, but determined; Bob saw that Marine look, that Donny Fenn look, that said, Hey, I don't want to be here, but I don't see anyone else. He'd be all right.

Dobbler was something else. He was on the edge of panic. Bob could see him lick his lips, stroke his chin, his eyes shifting nervously. This was all new to him. He was cherry. Would he hang tough or bug out? Bob didn't know and he didn't like the gamble. But he had to play with the cards he had.

"Dr. Dobbler?"

"No."

"Memphis?"

"This is so *chancy*. I still—"

"That it is. You have a better idea?"

"You should be on the rifle. Not—"

"Don't you worry, Nick."

"Bob, you know what I did the last time."

"I know what you'll do this time."

"The whole thing turns on my—"

"You're the man who found Annex B. You're a goddamned FBI agent, one of the best. You can do it."

"You're the war hero, not me."

"No such thing as a hero. You forget heroes, Nick. This is about doing the job and coming home. You do your job and you come home, I swear it."

"But you—"

"Don't you worry about me. None of your business about me. I got what I signed up for. Okay?"

"Okay," Nick said sullenly.

The doctor tried to say something, but the words caught in his throat.

"Hey, Doc," said Bob, "in three tours in Vietnam, I've been in some scrapes. It's okay to be scared shitless."

Dobbler cracked a wretched smile.

"If Russell Isandhlwana could see me now!" he finally said.

"I don't know who he is, but he'd crap in his pants, that I guarantee you," said Bob.

He winked, actually happy, and they set off.

"Okay," said Shreck. "1000 hours. Set, Payne?"

"Let's do it, sir."

"It's going to be a long day. Fire the first flare."

Payne lifted the flare pistol, pulled the trigger, felt the crispest pop, and watched as a red arc of intense light soared overhead, caught on its own parachute, then began to drift flutteringly to earth. In twenty seconds it was out; in thirty seconds it was down.

They walked to the little silk chute and the blackened, sulfurous husk of the burned-out illumination round.

"Leave a round there," said Shreck. "A green one."

Payne threw a brass flare round into the furls of the parachute.

"Now, we move to our next position. They've got a long hard climb to make this one, and we don't have very far at all. In fact we should be able to watch them come."

They pushed the woman along, and walked the crest of the ridge. It was easy moving, because the ground was clear and stony and the air bright. They covered a mile in fifteen minutes, then plunged downhill for a swift half mile. There, nestling in a grove, was a canoe that Payne had planted days ago. He righted it, plunged it into a stream, and the three climbed in. Propelled by Payne's powerful strokes, they made three miles in the remaining time. Then, hiding the canoe, they came to another ridge. Payne bent into the underbrush, pulled out a lank rope, and yanked it tight so that it coiled and slithered under his tension, like an awakening snake. It extended halfway up the ridge to where it had been pinioned into the stone. At that point, Payne had dangled another rope from still higher on the ridge.

"All right, Mrs. Fenn. You just pull yourself up as you climb. You'll find it's much, much easier than climbing unsupported."

At each stage, Payne coiled the rope and hid it.

When they reached the crest, none of them were even breathing hard.

"The telescope," said Shreck. "They'll be on the ridge soon enough."

Payne pulled a case out of his pack and unlimbered a Redfield Regal VI spotting scope with a 20×–60× zoom lens, mounted it to its tripod and bent to its angled eyepiece, jacked the magnification up to maximum, and found a clear view of the ridge across the way.

"All set, Colonel Shreck."

"Well, they're late. This early in the game and they're late. They're losing it."

"They had a long pull. They had four miles, over two ridge lines, with a stream to ford. They'd only just now be making it."

Finally, with three minutes gone over the hour deadline, the green flare rose and floated down.

"All right, fire quickly. Don't give them any time to rest."

Payne fired a blue flare into the air and in the last moment of its arc, he saw a figure come straggling over the surface to take a fast compass reading.

Just barely made it, bubba, he thought.

A few minutes later three figures were visible on the crest line two miles away. Magnified sixty times, they were still ants, but recognizable ants.

And it became immediately obvious what the difficulty was.

It must have been Bob out front. He looked as if he could go for another ten years.

Too bad they don't make a two-mile rifle, motherfucker, Payne thought. I'd have a snipe at you myself.

The middle one would be the younger guy, Memphis. He remembered Memphis. Memphis wore an FBI raid jacket, and its initials almost yielded their individual meanings before collapsing back into blaze-yellow blur. Memphis's face was lost behind a mask of camouflage paint but his body language looked stolid and determined.

The problem was the third one.

Jesus, it was Dobbler. Face painted like a commando or not, he was still recognizable by his pansy body and that prissy lack of strength in his flapping limbs.

"It's Dobbler!" Payne yelled. "Colonel Shreck, for Christ's sakes, they brought Dobbler along and he don't look happy."

Dobbler had gone to his knees and his mouth was open—Payne imagined he could hear the ruckus even two miles away.

"I can see he's yelling. Jesus, I can just hear him: 'I can't make it, I can't go on, why did I ever do this,' that kind of candy-ass shit."

"Let me see," said Shreck.

Payne moved to let Shreck at the scope.

"Swagger, you fool," said Shreck, with a contemptuous snort as he watched. "You should have shot him."

Eventually, they saw the other two get the abject figure to his feet.

"I wonder how long he'll last," said Shreck.

Payne would shoot Dobbler, just as he knew Shreck would. If you ain't up to the field, you die. That was all. That was the rule. He himself had shot a captain once who'd fucked up so bad in an A-camp fight and was weeping piteously in the bunker. He'd bet Shreck had done it too.

But not Bob. Bob was a secret pussy. He didn't have what Shreck had and what Payne had: he couldn't do the final thing. He couldn't get it done. That's why now, at the end, when it came down to balls and nothing else, he'd lose.

Dobbler finally gave up around one o'clock. It was

surprising that he lasted that long. They saw it happen, having extended their lead and now sited themselves on another ridge for a checkup.

"Look, Colonel Shreck, look!"

Shreck bent to the scope and saw what Payne had seen: a mile and a half away, Dobbler had quit. He lay in the high grass, clearly begging for mercy. Memphis appeared to be the angry one. They saw him try and pick Dobbler up but Dobbler simply collapsed. Dobbler would not rise.

And giving up had its dire implications. Who would come back for him? Shreck knew these two wouldn't; in two hours they'd be under the gun of Lon Scott. Dobbler would perish in these mountains, though he couldn't know this now. He'd wander, winding down further each day. Maybe he'd be lucky and run into a party of hunters, but they were so deep in the fastness of the Ouachitas now, that prospect seemed unlikely.

"If he stays, he's dead," said Shreck.

"And if he goes, he's dead," said Payne.

Bob appeared to have disengaged. He stood away from them, unmoving, as Memphis did all the screaming. Finally, Shreck could just barely make out through the scope that he was saying something; then he turned and walked away. Shreck watched Memphis bend quickly to Dobbler, the yellow letters of his FBI raid jacket flashing as he opened it to peel his own canteen from his belt, and hand it to the man. Then he turned to run after Bob.

Shreck, Payne and the woman had achieved Hard Bargain Valley from the southwest, coming across a screen of trees and over a little creek. They were more than an hour ahead of Swagger and Memphis, though in the hours since dumping poor Dr. Dobbler, the two pursuers had closed the gap considerably.

It had not been an easy approach, for no roads lead to the valley and it must be earned by several hours of desperately difficult hiking over rills and hills and gulches, up stony mountainsides, through dense trees.

And then a splurge of yellow openness. A mile wide at its most open, it is one of the largest, flattest geological phenomena in all of Arkansas, a virtual tabletop in the middle of the mountains.

At one side is the ridge that could be said to overlook it, although it's not high, and it doesn't afford much in the way of observation. On the other side is just a forest, which leads downhill eventually to a valley and then to another mountain. Not even the deer will roam on the flatness of Hard Bargain Valley, because they are creatures of the forest, and feel vulnerable in the open. So it is predominantly the kingdom of the crows, who wheel overhead on the breeze like bad omens.

"I want us to be on that side," said Shreck. "We'll have the meet in the dead center, fifteen hundred yards from the nearest shootable elevation."

"Where is *he*?" asked Payne. Snipers made Payne a little nervous. Even snipers on his own side.

"Oh, he's up there. You can count on it," Shreck said tersely.

Lon's mood had darkened. He sat alone in his spider hole, fifteen hundred yards from the flat yellow center of Hard Bargain Valley on its western rim. He suddenly felt cursed.

It had begun as a lovely day. But a few hours ago, a huge red buck had pranced down the ridge in front of him. He remembered the deer hunts of his boyhood, before his father shot him. It filled him with a kind of joy. On impulse he brought the rifle to bear on the buck. The animal was about 250 paces out, gigantic in the magnification of the Unertl 36×. Lon put his cross hairs on the creature and felt a thrill as he played with the notion of making the creature's beauty his own by extinguishing it forever.

The animal, a bearded old geezer with two stubs where his antlers had been sheared off in some freak accident, paused as the scope settled upon him. It turned its magnificent head and fixed two bold, calm eyes upon Lon. It appeared not to fear him at all; worse, it had no respect for him. This enraged him in some strange way. He felt his finger take three ounces of slack out of the six-ounce trigger, until the animal lived only on the stretch of the thinnest of hairs. The buck stared at him insolently, as if daring him to go ahead and shoot. He knew this was impossible: the animal could not have seen him. But haughtily, nevertheless, the old creature cast its evil eye on him, until he became aware of the pressure in his trigger finger and the beads of sweat in his hairline. He slackened off the trigger.

The animal spluttered, threw his beautiful red-hazed old head in the sunlight, then trotted away with an aristocratic saunter as if to snub him, and make him feel unworthy.

Yet he was strangely agitated.

Be still, he told himself. *It's nothing.* But he could not get it out of his mind.

The hours had passed. Now, moodily, he scanned the far ridge of trees in search of human motion. He had glanced at his watch for the thousandth time; it was well past three and time for the action to begin.

Ah! There! *There!*

He made them through the spotting scope as they came out of the trees and began their slow trek across the open space to the far side. Though at this range it was impossible to make out details or faces, he could read them from their body types. The tall one was

Shreck; the stumpy one, hunched and dangerous, was the little soldier Payne. And third was the woman, the tethered bait.

He watched them walk across the field, and set up below him; now their faces were distinct, but they could not see him. Then, suddenly, commotion: the two men both stood and looked and pointed.

Yes, there it was, just as Colonel Shreck had promised, though a bit late: a yellow flare, barely distinguishable in the bright sunlight, floating down behind the ridge line.

He saw Payne fire an answering flare, letting the pursuers know their next move, and upon what field the game would be played.

Lon flexed his fingers and tried to will his body to alertness as he slid in behind the rifle once again.

He touched the radio receiver that would receive the bolt of sound that meant Shreck was green-lighting the shot. He touched, as if to draw on their magic, the .300 H & H Magnums laid out before him, tapering brass tubes close to four inches long, glinting, their heavy, cratered noses stolid and somehow faintly greasy.

Now it was merely a matter of waiting.

The buck was forgotten at last; he thought only of the hellacious long shot he had to make, that no man had a right to make, that he knew he *could* make. He'd made them before.

"All right, Payne," said Shreck as they languished on the far side of Hard Bargain Valley. "This is the easy part. Get her ready."

"Yes, sir," said Payne.

He turned to Julie.

"Okay, honey," he said. "Just this one last little thing."

She looked at him with drug-dumb eyes. There

wasn't a flicker of will or resistance in their glassy depthlessness. A stupid half-smile played across her mouth.

Payne shucked his pack and reached into it. There he removed his cut-down Remington 1100 semiautomatic shotgun. It held six 12-gauge shells in double-ought buckshot, each of which contained nine .32 caliber pellets. It was possibly the most devastating close-quarters weapon ever devised. In less than two seconds it could blow out fifty-four man-killing balls of lead with an effective range of fifteen yards.

He walked around behind the woman.

"You just relax now," he said. "This is nothing. Don't worry about it."

She looked as if she'd never worried about anything in her life.

Setting the shotgun down momentarily, he plucked a roll of black electrician's tape from his pocket. With swift and sure motions, he unstripped the end of the tape, planted it squarely in the middle of her forehead, and began to run loops of the tape around her skull, drawing them tight.

She whimpered as the greasy stuff was yanked tight about her head, cutting against her eyes so that the vision was destroyed, between her lips so that her voice was stifled and across her nose so that the breathing was impaired and around her hair, where its adhesive quickly matted to her skull, but he said, "There, there, it's nothing, baby, it's nothing."

Having constructed a snare of tape, he then brought the little shotgun up and began to unspool yet more tape, wrapping it crudely about the barrel and fore end of the piece, entwining the woman's head and the gun in the same seven-yard-long constriction, until both were joined. Then he cut the tape.

He reached down with his left hand and engaged the

pistol grip of the weapon, inserting his finger in the trigger guard. He felt the tension in the trigger.

"Colonel Shreck?"

Shreck took the spool and continued the ritual of the binding, until Payne's hand was almost one with the shotgun's pistol grip and trigger in a solid, gummy nest of tape. Shreck bent and jacked the shotgun's bolt, and both men felt the shiver as the bolt slid back, lofted a shell into the chamber, then plunged forward to lock the shell in.

"You know what to do?"

"Yes, sir," said Payne. In case of trouble, he was to blow the woman's head off; then swing the short-barreled weapon and blow away whoever stood against them. At the same time, he was untouchable: no bullet could penetrate his vest and a head shot would produce either by spasm or by the weight of his fall the blast that would destroy the woman. Nobody was going to play hero with Payne booby-trapped to the woman like this.

It wasn't going well. These Arkansas types were close-mouthed, clannish and not terribly interested in helping.

Still, the reports that reached the headquarters of Task Force Swagger, now in the basement of the Sheriff's Office, were persistent, if vague. Two hunters off on a preseason scouting hike had watched through binoculars as a stocky man had laid and moored coils of rope to a ridge deep in the Ouachitas. They didn't move any closer because through the glass the guy had looked as tough as a commando. And no, they probably couldn't find the place again anyway.

"Maybe just some other hunter," said Hap. "Laying in ropes to get up that ridge in the dark on the first day of the hunting season."

"Ummm," was all that Howdy Duty would commit himself too.

Then someone swore he'd seen a lean blond man talking to Sam Vincent, the lawyer who had sued the magazine on Bob's behalf. He was Bob's oldest friend, demi-daddy and hunting buddy of years gone by. The man could have been Bob the Nailer, and the talk took place on a high road miles off a main highway that the observer, a postman, had just happened to breeze by.

But Sam Vincent was a wily, tough old bird and he knew the law as well as any man alive.

"Now, sir," the old lizard had said to Utey, leaning forward and fixing him with what was known as the "chair-eye" (for Sam, as a state prosecutor in the fifties and sixties had sent thirteen men to the electric chair), "you know a damned sight better than I do that I cain't be compelled to cooperate unless I want to, and no subpoena and no threat of government harassment's going to change that. I'm too old to scare and too stubborn to budge. If I seen Bob Lee Swagger and ain't told you, I've committed a federal felony. So essentially"—and here his shrewd old eyes knitted up—"you're asking me to testify agin' myself. Against the Constitution, young feller. And against Arkansas state law, Code D-547.1, see *Conyers* v. *Mercantile Trust.* You got that?"

Howard got it indeed, but assigned a tail on Sam. No such luck; within the hour an injunction arrived from the Third District Court of Arkansas, the Hon. Justice Buford M. Roubelieux presiding, requiring the government to show cause for assigning surveillance upon a distinguished eighty-one-year-old citizen like Sam Vincent and issuing, until such compliance could be met (the next available court date was July 1998), a cease and desist order, under penalty of law.

That had been the low point.

There hadn't been any high points.

Until today, just now, when the phone rang.

Hap answered it, spoke for two minutes, then said, "I'll call you right back."

Howard looked up; two of the other men watched as Hap shot over to Howard. They gathered round.

"Maybe this is nothing, I don't know," said Hap. "But I just got a call from a guy in the National Forest Service. Says three hunters, at three different times this morning, saw military flares being shot into the air deep in the Ouachitas."

"Somebody in trouble?" asked an agent.

"More like a signal," somebody else said.

"But no fires started," said Hap. "The service ordered up a couple of flybys out of their spotter planes, but there were no fires. And the flares seem to be coming from different locations, spread over about a twenty-mile-square area."

Howard concentrated on this. Who would use flares in daylight? Who would even see a flare in daylight, unless they were looking for it? It had to be a kind of signal.

"Did they get a location?" he asked.

"Well, they've had several, but the Forest Service guy says his people plotted it out on a big map they've got, and the direction is largely trending north by northwest."

"Okay," said Howard. "Toward what? Toward anything?"

"There's a big flat, nearly inaccessible valley way up there they call Hard Bargain Valley," said Hap. "It's way the hell off the mainstream. The Forest Service says hardly any hunters go up there because the deer much prefer the lower forest land. It's flat and barren and almost a mile across."

Howard thought.

Hard Bargain Valley?

"Okay," he said. "Let's saddle up. Full SWAT gear. Call the field. I want the chopper to pick us up in ten minutes. Hap, call the Forest Service back and tell them we need a guide to get us to Hard Bargain Valley."

"There," said Payne, seeing them first.

The two figures had emerged from the trees across the wide valley.

Shreck looked at them through his binoculars but they were too far off for details. Their faces were green, like commandos.

He snorted.

"He thinks he's going to a war," he said to Payne.

Payne stood up, and gingerly drew the woman up off her haunches.

"Now, honey," he said. "You walk real slow. Don't you trip or stumble, or you'll be history."

She moaned, then made a noise through the tape.

"Shut up, Mrs. Fenn," said Shreck. "Damn, she's come out of it. You should give her another injection."

"I can't," said Payne. "Not taped up like this."

"Look, lady," said Shreck, "I want you to know this is the end, you've only got another few minutes. We make the swap, and off you go with your boyfriend. That's a security arrangement; the gun isn't even loaded."

Under the bonds of the tape, her eyes tightened in terror.

He ignored her and signaled to Payne to get her moving. Haltingly, the three of them began to walk across the wide field. It had turned into a lovely, sunny fall day, about fifty-five, crisp and clean. Around them, like waves, were the ragged ridges and crests of the Ouachitas, now brilliantly ablaze in color.

The sniper's breath came in soft spurts. He was trying to keep himself calm for what lay ahead. It was time to shut down. It was time to get into the zone.

He felt his body complying. He had known it would; he trusted it. He watched his target, exactly where it was supposed to be, in the most obvious place. It wasn't even an ant, but a speck, the dot over an *i*. He'd never hit at this range before but he wasn't scared. This was a shot he'd owed himself for a long time; it was time to get it right.

His eyes were dilating, his ears sealing off, his breathing going softer. He was sliding into tunnel vision, where the concentration was so intense that all other cues in the world dropped away and respiration bled to a hum.

He pulled the rifle to him. No time now to think of it: he could not allow himself to be aware of the instrument because he had to be beyond the instrument. His will was the instrument.

Now he slid behind the scope, finding the spot-weld, where cheek and gun joined while his fingers discovered their place by slow degree. That was the secret; to make everything the same. Simplify, simplify. To make of oneself nothingness; to slide into the great numbness beyond want and hope; to simply be.

He was beyond computation. He knew the range, he knew the angle, he knew the wind, he knew the bullet's trajectory and velocity, he knew its drop and how it would leak energy as it sped along. He had accounted for all this and he now engaged his target through the bright circle of the scope.

Even magnified, the man was a small, a very small object, hardly recognizable as human. Just a squirming dot. He watched the tremble in the reticle as he willed himself through minute subverbal corrections, not thinking so much as feeling. It was very, very close now.

Don't blow it, he ordered himself. *Not this time!*

Nick breathed out a little. Lon Scott was just where Bob had said he would be, beneath the crest line where the osage had been crushed by an all-terrain vehicle as it delivered him. He was in a spider hole, only his painted face and the rifle barrel visible.

At a hundred yards, Shreck put up his hands.

"No guns," he shouted. "No guns or the woman is dead. You got that?"

Each of the two men raised his hands, pirouetted slowly to show that he wore no visible weapons, then let his hands stay high.

"You got the cassette and Annex B?"

Bob raised the knapsack he was carrying.

"Right here," he yelled back.

"Okay. You bring the stuff. When I authenticate it, we'll release the girl. You see how we've got her? You make a funny move, you look funny, you do anything stupid, you get unlucky and trip, anything, *anything,* my friends, and she's fucked. Payne'll do it, you know he will. Only chance she's got is our rules."

"You're calling the shots," Bob said. "Now just take it easy with that damned shotgun, Payne."

Slowly and warily, the two men approached, hands held high and stiff.

At last Shreck faced Bob the Nailer, big as life, who stood but six feet away and he looked him in the eyes. He looked as calm as a pond on a summer day.

"Hello, Colonel," came a familiar voice.

Shreck looked to the other man, the young FBI agent. Only it wasn't the young FBI agent, even though he wore a black FBI raid jacket and baseball cap and greenish paint on his face. It was Dr. Dobbler.

Shreck looked back to Bob, realized in a flash the game had changed. He pressed the button on a unit on his belt, sending a shriek of radio noise that would signal Scott to fire.

There came the sound, from far away, of a rifle shot.

The shrillness of the beep somewhat surprised Lon and he saw the cross hairs dance a tiny jig and come off Bob.

So soon? he thought.

He exhaled half a lungful of air and gently as a lover squeezed the reticle back onto Bob, center chest, and began to draw the slack from the trigger and—

Nick fired and in the split second the rifle jumped and the scope-picture blurred, he called it a hit. He looked back quickly in recovery. The bullet had struck Lon Scott in the head. It was the brain shot. Blood seemed to have been flung everywhere by the impact. Lon sagged back and slid into his spider hole. Only the rifle was left to show.

Nick, in his own spider hole in the vastness of Hard Bargain Valley, threw the bolt and tried to bring Bob's Remington to bear on the party of five in the open. A sudden wave of weakness thundered over him.

Jesus, he thought, *you just hit a thousand-yard shot!*

He started to tremble.

The woman screamed, but Payne pulled her down, twisted her to brandish the shotgun, and didn't panic.

Bob said to the colonel, "My boy just tagged your boy. You're all alone."

The colonel was calm. Maybe a half-smile played across his mouth. At some not so secret level he was a happy man.

"It doesn't mean a thing, Swagger," he said, thinking quickly. "Now let me tell you what's going to happen. Nothing's changed. Only thing we want now is out. We're going on a nice slow walk out of here with the woman and with the cassette and the documents. You follow, she's wasted. So don't you try a goddamn thing. You put the gun down. You got that?"

"I'll kill this fucking woman," said Payne. "You know I will. I got the gun taped to her head. I swear, I'll blow her away. Now you back off."

Bob dropped the knapsack. Only his hand wasn't empty. It held a Remington 1100 semiautomatic shotgun, cut down to pistol grip and sawed-off barrel.

Nick's second mandate was Shreck. He disengaged the rifle from Lon's spider hole and brought it to bear on the five figures five hundred yards to his left.

Goddamn!

He could only see the tops of heads. The action had come to play in one of the subtle folds in the earth that ran across the valley floor and his targets were beneath his line of vision.

Which one was Shreck?

He couldn't tell.

Oh, Christ, Bob, he thought.

He looked around desperately, seeking a tree he could climb to get some elevation into the fold, but there was nothing. He put the rifle down, drew his Beretta, feeling helpless rage.

"Put the gun down," said Payne. "I'll blow her fuckin' brains out."

"He will, you know," said the colonel.

So here we are, Bob thought. *Come a long way for this party. Let's see who's got the stones for close work.*

Bob leveled the short, mean semiautomatic shotgun at Payne. Payne could see the yawing bore peeping out from the forestock.

"He isn't going to shoot," said the colonel forcefully. "Payne, he's bluffing, he doesn't have a shot."

"I'm not going to shoot," said Bob. "Here's the damn deal. I put the gun down, you cut the girl free. Everybody walks. Okay?"

Dobbler backed away nervously.

"Done," said the colonel. "The smart move."

"Okay," said Bob. "I'm going to count to three, then I'm putting the gun down. Nobody get excited here."

"Do it slow, Swagger," said Payne.

"One," said Bob, and then "Two," and then he fired.

Payne was astounded that it happened like this, the crazy fucking fuck, the moron, he actually fired, and in the explosion he fired too, sending the woman to hell, fuck them all, fuck all who fucked with Jack Payne, soldier and killer of men.

And he felt the gun buck and knew the woman's head was gone, except that it wasn't, for she fell backwards somehow, screaming in terror but intact and he fired again, felt the impulse to squeeze run from his brain down through his arm to his finger, felt it squeeze, waited for the gun to go off.

Only then did he realize he was squeezing a phantom finger on a phantom hand.

Swagger had blown a charge of double-ought clean through his elbow from a range of two feet, literally severing it. The hand still grasped the shotgun bound in tape to her skull; it simply was no longer attached to him.

In horror, Payne held his stump high, and watched jets of bright blood pulse out into the clear fall air. In that second the incredible agony of it hit him.

"You fucker," he screamed. "*You fucker!*"

Bob put the muzzle of the Remington against Payne's stout little chest, and sent a deer slug through the Kevlar vest that tunneled to his spine. Payne disappeared as he collapsed.

In the same attenuated microsecond, Shreck broke

through the shards of disbelief that clotted his actions and yanked the Marlin up to put a shot into Bob, but he was not quite fast enough. Bob, pivoting through a short arc to his new target, beat him by a clean tenth-second and double-tapped a pair of deer slugs through Shreck's vest so swiftly the blasts seemed like a single sound. Their roar hit the mountains and rolled back across the valley and still vibrated in the air as the colonel's legs went and he toppled backwards.

Shreck felt no pain. He lay on his back in the yellow grass. He thought of landing zones, frontals, good men dead in far places, K-rations and C-4, and that bitch duty whom he'd never once betrayed, always doing the hard thing.

Bob stood over him. Shreck blinked and felt his fingers turn to feathers. He had no legs, he had no body. He was very thirsty and confused. Then he realized: it had finally happened.

"I deal in lead, friend," Bob said, and fired another deer slug into him. It blew out his heart.

In an instant, Bob ran to Julie.

"Okay, okay, honey, it's all right," he said to her, taking her in his hands. "Don't move, don't jerk, just be calm, we're almost home free, Dobbler, *Dobbler, goddammit, come here*!"

He tried to get her to lie still, terrified that a sudden motion might somehow trip the trigger. She was blinded by the tape and making mewling noises, but now he got his arms around her, squeezing her tight, just to hold her steady against his own strength.

"Now, just relax, baby girl, please, just relax."

He reached into his boot and drew out his razor-sharp Randall Survivor. Looking at the knotted strands of black tape he was at first unsure where to cut, afraid that if he cut too savagely, the vibration on some unseen strand of the stuff might fire the gun. Very carefully, he began to slice through the strands around her face until he'd freed it and peeled the strands away. One by one they broke, but the gun did not budge.

"Okay, okay, we're almost there, nothing's going to happen to you, we're almost home free."

Gently he rotated her trembling head and inserted the blade in a knot of tape right under the muzzle and began to saw. The edge devoured the tape, one by one popping the individual links. But the gun remained jammed against her and seemed a living thing, a snake almost, with its fangs sunk crazily into her skull. He didn't want to touch it; he could see that the safety was off and that the weight of Payne's dead finger still lay across the trigger.

He sliced another strand of tape and the gun seemed to loosen and slide. The breath came so hard to him he thought he'd pass out and someone seemed to be pounding a kettledrum against his ears. Then another strand went, and the gun dropped and Bob had the thing, free and clear.

He looked at it. Soaked in blood, one of Payne's tattoos remained visible. AIRBORNE ALL THE WAY, it said. You got that right, son, he thought and heaved the goddamn thing as far as he could. It landed in the grass fifty feet away, and did not go off.

"Oh, Jesus," she was saying as he pulled the tape from her face.

"You're okay, you're okay, you're fine, we made it." He hugged her, held her very tight.

Dobbler was crouching beside them. He lifted one of her eyelids, looked into her pupil, read her pulse.

"What did they give you?" he asked.

"I don't know," she said.

"Well, you're stable. Bob, give her your coat. The

danger is shock. If we keep her warm, there should be no problem."

She lay back, clutching the coat.

"It's all over. We're home free, I swear to you. Nobody can hurt you now or ever again."

He set her down on the grass, where she settled in, though she did not want to let go of his hand. But he had some other business still.

He drew the doctor away from her until they confronted the bodies in the grass. Dobbler stopped and stared.

"G-god," said Dobbler. "I can't believe we—"

Bob silenced him.

Four feet apart, Payne and the colonel lay in the yellow grass. The colonel's eyes were open, Payne's were closed. Payne's grotesque stump still gushed a magenta delta into the yellow grass. The vests, however, constricted the blood from the chest wounds in both men; only the burned puckers where the slugs had blasted through signified the cause of their deaths.

"Look at them," Dobbler said, half in shock. "I can't believe—"

"They're men. Shoot 'em, they die, that's all," said Bob. "Listen here, we don't have much time. I've thought this out carefully." He reached into his shirt and pulled something out. Dobbler saw that it was a money belt.

"There's seven thousand dollars in here. It's all I have left from my magazine money. You take it."

"I—"

"Now just listen. I want you out of here and gone before that damned boy shows up with his badge and remembers what he does for a living. You see that white pine at the far end of the valley?"

He pointed to the tree.

Dobbler nodded.

"At the tree, you'll find a creek bed. You follow it about seven miles, mostly downhill, to a river. You can follow the river either way, it doesn't matter. If you walk hard you'll come out of the forest around three tomorrow on U.S. Route two-seventy. Flag down the Greyhound that makes the four P.M. run to Oklahoma City. Take the money. Disappear. Start a new life."

Dobbler looked at him in shock.

"But—You need a witness. You need someone to testify. You—"

"Don't you worry about me, Doc. You did your part. It doesn't matter what came before. You go on that stand and you'll be in a mess that'll destroy you forever. I know. I've been there. Take your freedom and go."

"But—"

"But nothing," said Bob. "Now get out of here before that damned kid shows up." He pushed the doctor along and then watched as the man, confused at first, but then with more spirit in his step, made a beeline for the white tree. Soon, he had disappeared.

Bob returned to Julie. She lay quietly in the grass, breathing softly.

He knelt. Her hand came up and touched his. He bent and kissed her on the lips.

"We're going to have plenty of time together," he whispered. "I guarantee it. Now I have just one little thing to do."

He went to the knapsack, still lying in the grass.

He opened it and removed the green plastic bag that held Annex B and the cover letter. He ripped it open, took out the paper. He couldn't wait for the sun. He pulled out a Zippo lighter that said USMC and beneath that SEMPER FI, a souvenir of the days when he smoked. He ignited it, held the bright, small flame against the corner of one of the pages, watched the flame begin to spread. In seconds, Annex B was engulfed. He held it until he could hold it no longer, then tossed it. It burned to ash.

"Stop it! Stop it!"

It was Nick, yelling at him from two hundred yards away. He began to race toward him. "What are you doing? Jesus Christ!"

But Bob now grabbed the video cassette. He placed it on the ground and drove his boot into it, smashing the plastic. He pulled the tape out into a loose jumble, leaned over and lit it. It went like a flash and was gone in seconds.

"Jesus fucking A, what are you doing?"

Nick stood over him, dark with anger.

"That's evidence! That's the goddamn *evidence* that can get you off the goddamn hook! What the fuck are you doing?"

"You know what I'm doing," Bob said.

"Bob, I—"

"Now you shut up, boy, and you listen. It's over. These boys are in the goddamn body bags now and what they did is going in there with them. And that's where it'll stay. There's nothing left to tell elsewise now."

"You'll go to—"

"Nick, you saved my ass with that shot. We're even up now, and you have to be your own man and make your own decisions. You're free of me, do you get it?"

Nick looked at him, openmouthed.

Then they heard the helicopter and turned to see a Huey hurtling low over the far end of the valley.

Oh, Christ, thought Nick. It's Howdy Duty time.

CHAPTER THIRTY-SEVEN

It amazed Nick that they worked so hard when he was so willing to tell the entire truth from the start; he even waived his right to legal counsel without giving it a second thought.

"Hey, I don't need it. You'll see. I don't need it."

But they insisted on working hard; it was the Bureau way.

They had removed him to a safe house outside New Orleans, an estate out in Lafayette Parish, not far from a swamp; and there they set to their labors for close to a month. Their first go-round was the friendly approach, with his old buddy Hap Fencl and his ex-partner Mickey Sontag.

For a time it was like the good old days in the New Orleans district office bull pen on Loyola

Street, the three of them just swapping yarns and laughing it up and having a great time. But underneath there was serious business, and Nick let it all come out. He told everything from his procurement of the Bureau RamDyne file (though he overplayed his pressure on Sally to spare her what trouble he could) to his abduction by Jack Payne and his henchmen, his near fake-suicide in the swamp, and the private war he'd fought with Bob Lee Swagger against the agents of RamDyne.

"You ought to see this damned guy in a fight, Hap," he heard himself saying in awe. "This is the best gunfighter this country ever produced. He doesn't miss, he doesn't panic, he doesn't quit thinking and he never gives up. He's fantastic."

He got to the embarrassing part, too.

"Look, I may as well be up-front with you guys. I did represent myself as a federal officer when I was officially on suspension. I did it over the phone at least two or three dozen times and in person at least three times. So are you going to bust me? Hell, I broke the New Orleans thing for you, gave you the biggest scoop you'll ever have."

They laughed and wrote it all down, asking gentle questions, coming back the next day with other questions.

But they wouldn't tell him anything else, either.

"So where's Bob? What's become of him?"

"Nick, I think they have him in a safe house too, going through the same kind of debriefing. Truth is, I don't really know. Would you mind if we got back to you, Nick?"

"No, sure, no problem."

This went on for two weeks.

Then, suddenly, Hap and Mickey were gone. Instead, along came two hard-eyed guys from what Nick assumed was the crack counterintelligence squad called

Cointelpro, expert interrogators. They were very, very smart, much smarter than Hap and Mickey. And, naturally, distant; not hostile so much as remote, utterly professional. They were like sharks; they ate him alive and seemed to know the material as well as he did. They pored through it—and him—for minor inconsistencies, for small glitches, as if they wanted the lint of the operation and not the truth.

But he cooperated, again offering eagerness as his only defense, holding nothing back, telling everything, everything.

"Now the bills he used to finance the operation—"

"It wasn't an *operation.* We just made it up as we went along. Anyway, he'd evidently cached quite a bit of cash from that lawsuit plus some guns in the mountains and when he got back to them before we ran into him at the health complex, he must have dug it up. He always had cash, he always paid cash."

"You can't trace cash, not old, small bills. He had plenty of old small bills."

"Cash isn't a crime. At least it didn't used to be. What have you got him on? A few minor car theft charges for which there's really no proof, and no prosecutor would bring to court. The rest was self-defense. He never shot a man who wasn't trying to kill him or someone else. He was green light all the way."

"New Orleans."

"New *Orleans*! I told you, it was a professional setup! They used a different rifle to shoot a bullet that had been already fired out of his rifle. They had a great shot, Lon Scott, in the steeple. It's possible, you know it's possible."

"Okay, Memphis, this isn't the time to argue. Now could we go back to—"

Then, finally, there were the scientific gentlemen. Nick took three polygraph tests, and volunteered to undergo both hypnosis and sodium pentothal treatment. He was probed, drugged, pricked, psyched, drained and squeezed. He got through it all with only moderate testiness: old Nick, everybody's helper, friend to all men, duty hound, stalwart and chum.

One day, late in the process, he was told he had a visitor. Blinking, he went outside to the porch, there to discover the nervous Sally Ellion awaiting him.

"Hi! God, Sally, hi, how are you, Jesus, you're looking great!"

And Sally was looking great.

"Hi, Nick. How are you?" She still had that soft Southern accent, as if the Mississippi itself poured through her words.

"Oh, I'm okay, you know. I'm fine. I'm sorry I haven't called you. They've got me pretty busy and I don't think they're going to spring me soon."

"You're not in any trouble, are you?"

"Nah. Nah, I'm fine. I want to work with the guys and get this all straightened out. It'll be fine, you'll see. I'm hoping that when this is over, we can go out to dinner again. That was great fun. How are you?"

She looked terrific to him.

"I'm okay. Nick, they came to me and wanted—"

"I know, I know. Just tell them the truth. You didn't do anything wrong. Remember, you didn't know I'd been suspended when you gave me that file. You're okay, don't worry."

"I'm not worried about myself, Nick. I'm worried about you. He said you might have broken some laws. He was very upset about what might happen to you."

"Um. Howard?"

"Yes. Mr. Utey."

"Yeah, I smell him all over this thing. Don't worry. Howard's an old pal. He'll look out for me. What's going on in the outside world?"

"Oh, the television and papers have made a big thing about Bob Lee Swagger. I think the government wants to settle it quickly. Get it off the front page."

"What have they done with Bob?"

"He's in a holding facility in—"

"A *prison*?"

"Yes. He's got a lawyer. But there's so much publicity that I think they're going to do something soon."

This shook Nick greatly.

"He shouldn't be in a prison. He's a hero. He did great things for—"

But he saw a hurt look on her face and realized he'd begun to sound deranged.

"Well, anyway. Sally, I hope this hasn't been hard on you."

"No. It was a little scary at first, all the questions. But I think I'm out of it."

"Great. I've tried to make them see it's all my fault. I'm to blame, that's all. I'm sure they'll understand."

"I'm sure they will. Nick, are you sure you're going to call me when all this is over? I'd like to see you."

"Sure, of course."

"Because if you don't, I'm going to call you."

"I'll call you. I swear. You know, old AB Nick. I want to hear more about the time when you ditched that quarterback. Tom, Terry—?"

"Ted." She laughed. "God, what a horrible guy. I can't believe I was engaged to him."

The memory brought a smile to her face, a little one; then it was time for her to go.

They pretty much left Nick alone for a week after Sally's visit, with only two incurious bodyguards who let him go for walks. They let him watch TV and he caught up on the events of the last month and the controversy surrounding Bob Lee Swagger, amazed to see what a huge national story it had become, with all the networks camped outside the Louisiana State Reformatory where Bob was being kept in isolation, with visits only from his lawyer, a doughty-looking, sly old boy—operative word *old*—named Sam Vincent. Meanwhile a grand jury investigated the matter and all the Louisiana state prosecutors were lined up, waiting their turn.

"Looks like a carnival," Nick said, and nobody answered.

Then finally, inevitably, Howard arrived, with a sharp young man along, who had Ambitious Federal Prosecutor written all over his feral little features. And an older man, twinkly, with an almost academic air about him, as he sucked on a pipe.

"Nick, Nick, Nick," said Howard, expansive and embracing. "Nick, I want you to meet Phil Kelso, who works on a lot of cases with us. Phil's a damned fine prosecutor, Nick. The best."

"Um," said Nick.

"And this is Hugh Meachum, of the State Department. Nick, he's here to advise us on national security implications of the situation. The Salvadorans are very interested in the way this turns out."

Nick shot a quick look at Hugh, smelled gin, felt his blood begin to roar in his head.

"We hear you've been extremely cooperative," said Kelso. "That's wonderful. That's a big plus on your behalf. Right now, Nick, we're in the zone of attitude. Attitude is everything, Nick. We need great attitude from you."

"Well, I always try and do my best," said Nick, swallowing hard, somehow not wanting to look at Meachum.

"That's Nick," said Howard. "Nick tries real hard. Nick's a worker, a plugger, a scrapper. You could see it seven years ago in Tulsa and you can see it now."

"An extraordinary young man," said the elderly gentleman.

"Now, Nick, guess what day this is? Can you guess?"

Howard was effusive and charismatic today; Nick only saw him like this when he wanted something big.

"No, Howard."

"Nick, it's the first day of the rest of your life. Nick, it's your lucky day. You can walk out of here in an hour. In ten minutes, a free man, Nick. No questions asked. Nick, the only thing you have to do is your duty, that's all."

But Nick was hardly listening. He could only think of Meachum on the cover letter that sent Annex B to the general and set the whole thing in motion.

He kept trying to keep his eyes off the old man, but he could not control himself. He saw some sort of benevolence on the pink face, pleasurable anticipation that Nick was turning into such a team player, such a smashing young man.

"Nick, you can have more than your life back," Howard was saying when Nick tuned back in. "You can have it *all.* You can have your career. Nick, what do you want? Do you want Cointelpro? I don't mind telling you, you impressed Dave and Tom. They thought you were a plenty sharp operator, and they are the best, Nick. You know Cointelpro is the elite squad. You can have it. Or do you want a Hostage Rescue Unit? We could get you on HRU in Miami or Dallas, Nick, a hot city where you'd see a lot of action. Those HRU boys pick up the medals and they get on the fast track to Washington, Nick. Nick, we may be starting up a squad to extradite suspects from foreign countries. Now that'll be fast, exciting work, and some top people are coming aboard, Nick. I think that's what I'd pick, if I were you and had my whole career ahead of me. But it's up to you, Nick. You can have anything. No more dumpy little Taco Circuit cities for you, Nick. No Tulsas or Buttes or Boises. You name it—San Francisco, New York and organized crime, Philadelphia, Washington, Chicago, Chicago's a great town, Nick."

Nick just watched Howard.

"Okay," he finally said. "What's the deal?"

Nick caught Kelso firing a little what-the-fuck? glance at Howard.

Howard sailed on.

"Nick, listen to me. It can play one of two ways. *Only* one of two ways. It's to everybody's benefit—yours, mine, most particularly the Bureau's and the country's—if it plays a certain way. Okay?"

"Sure," said Nick. "What way?"

Now Kelso and Howard exchanged glances. They took a pause, then both looked back to Hugh, who smiled, his pale blue eyes aglitter.

Finally, Kelso spoke.

"Nick, it's Murder One on Bob Lee Swagger. We're going for the chair."

"Are you all right?" Bob asked her.

"I'm fine."

"You just answer their questions. You just tell the truth, that's all."

Behind the glass wall of the visiting room, he looked sallow and grim. His voice was reedy through the distorting sound of the telephone. She put her hand on the glass, aware that before her thousands of women had put their hands on the glass, and left a residue of wanting and sorrow as they peered at their men.

"Bob," Julie said, "that's just it. They haven't asked me *any* questions. I was kidnapped. I was drugged and held at gunpoint for close to a month. I can't get them to care about it. I even called the sheriff of Ajo County and he said, 'Julie, there's no proof. We have to let the federal government decide what to do.' "

"Julie, he gave you good advice. We don't have a thing to worry about. This is just some sort of preliminary investigation, and they can't have me running around. It doesn't matter. This is the FBI. They're going to be fair."

"Bob, I—"

"Once Sam gets it all explained to them, I'll be out of here in seconds. All our troubles are over. I'm hoping we can get back to Arizona. I liked the feeling of that desert. Arkansas is getting too crowded. Think I'd like to settle down out there in the Southwest."

"Bob, I—"

But he winked at her, still looking imposing in prison denims. He was manacled to the chair.

"Honey," he said. "We don't have a thing to worry about. We can trust the U.S. government."

Nick swallowed. He had a little difficulty understanding.

"I—I—I don't—"

"Nick, for one reason and one reason only. Nick, he's guilty," said Howard. "Nick, he took the shot that nailed Archbishop Jorge Roberto Lopez. He's got to pay. He—"

"No!" said Nick. "Listen, I *explained* that, Howard, didn't you read the interrogation reports? It was RamDyne. RamDyne set him up, Shreck, Payne, Dobbler, Lon Scott. They set him up. Lon Scott fired the bullet. It was a bullet that had already been through Bob's gun so it was supposed to have Bob's rifling on it. He was shooting from the St. Louis Cathedral, he—"

"Nick, the cathedral is fourteen hundred yards away. Fourteen hundred fifty-one yards, we measured," said

Howard. "Nobody can hit a target at fourteen hundred yards with a .308."

"It wasn't a .308! It was a 200-grain Sierra bullet that Bob had already fired. They loaded it into a Holland and Holland .300 Magnum case with a ton of powder, saboted it in plastic or paper, and blew it down a barrel that had been bored out to .318 or so! Check! Check with the experts! You'll see it's possible. Also, I bet you could find that special barrel at Lon Scott's house. Did you think of that? Did you check that?"

"Lon Scott died in 1965; we have his death certificate. That dead man on that mountain ridge was named James Thomas Albright, born Robert Parrish Albright."

"No, we traced it back. The real Robert Parrish Albright died in 1939, when he was a child. That was—"

"Nick," said Hugh Meachum calmly, "it's not unusual for a young man who is interested in heroes to bond to an older man, particularly a man of Bob Swagger's courage and cunning. But Nick, the bottom line is that Bob Lee Swagger took that shot. What happened later—well, maybe he was extraordinarily heroic in this war against RamDyne. Still, it was a war among gangsters. Bob took the shot, then Leon Timmons shot *him*. He escaped. That's all. RamDyne no longer exists. The Agency won't comment on any relationships it may have had with it and you'll never get them into a court of law because of national interest. Colonel Raymond Shreck was a difficult, complex, charismatic man. Like Bob he was a great hero once; like Bob, he was seduced by the power of the guns he loved. He may have been involved in narcotics at the end of his life, as his empire collapsed and he needed to raise money to sustain his life-style."

"He had millions—"

"Not that we can find," said Howard. "What we find is a disgraced war hero who had a great run with Agency contracts in the seventies who had lost his way and was facing financial ruin. That's all. It was a narcotics war or something. The official explanation will be that he died in a hunting accident on the first day of deer season. It doesn't concern us. What concerns us is the immediate: Bob Lee Swagger took that shot from four hundred yards at the president of the United States from the house on St. Ann Street in the Quarter outside Louis Armstrong Park. He missed and hit Archbishop Jorge Roberto Lopez, a great man who only wanted justice for the atrocities in his native country, and was mourned the world over. It's Murder One for Swagger. It's the chair. That's all."

"No," said Nick, desperate in his urgency to explain the obvious to these idiots, "no, you see—"

"Nick, the evidence is simply overwhelming. His rifle, identifiable fragments of his bullet, his prints, his empty shell. He was there, he had motive, he had opportunity, he had—"

"That's the frame-up. They *framed* him. The cassette. Dobbler had a cassette of atrocities. I had Annex B! I—"

"Nick, this Dobbler's disappeared. We've had a nationwide alert out for him, and we haven't come up with anything. He probably wandered off in the deep woods and died. Nick, we can't even prove he was in the woods with you. There's simply no proof. Only bizarre conspiracy theories."

"No," said Nick, "listen, just listen. It was a frame-up and Bob burned the Annex and the tape because he didn't want the press twisting them. He's a goddamned hero. He took out guys who killed kids in this country's name and now he's hanging himself rather than—"

"Nick, let's get back to reality, okay?" said the prosecutor, Kelso. "We've got a real deal for you. It's more than I would have offered, but your boss here and Mr.

Meachum insisted. Now you listen to it. It's very generous, very forgiving. It's a wonderful deal."

"Nick, Bob is gone. Bob will never see the outside world again. He knows it and his lawyer knows it. There's nothing you can do except save yourself," counseled Howard.

"I can't—"

"Earth to Nick," said Kelso. "Bob Lee Swagger is history. He's finished. Only a moron couldn't get a conviction off this overwhelming body of evidence. I've got a forty-six-page report from the FBI ballistics lab. I've got his threatening letter to the president; I've got the late Leon Timmons's sworn testimony that he shot Bob Lee Swagger in the attic of a house on St. Ann's street in New Orleans after discovering him in the act of firing the shot; and I've got you to testify that Bob leapt out of that building, overwhelmed you, stole your gun and your car. I've got him. He's gone."

"I—"

"Nick, damn it, listen to me," said Howard. "It can go two ways. One way you win; one way you lose. Those are the only possibilities. In either event, Bob is lost. Are you listening?"

Nick finally nodded.

"Number one. You are called to the stand as a cooperating witness. You are, after all, the hero of the hour. You are, after all, the FBI agent who penetrated the Bob Lee Swagger conspiracy and went underground with him—"

"I—"

"Shut up and listen, Nick," said Howard. "—who went underground with him on his trek through America, under the deception that he had been killed, which we established as a fiction after the shoot-out at the Baptist church in Blue Eye. You gained his confidence and you shared his danger, as you made certain there was no larger conspiracy. It's one of the most brilliant undercover operations the Bureau has ever brought off, by the way, Nick. It's your triumph—and it's mine. Credit where credit is due. The spoils go to the victor. Then, when you were certain, you called us in, and we apprehended him. As a consequence, we closed down Raymond Shreck's narcotics smuggling ring and eliminated close to fifty Latin gunmen, veterans of the infamous 'Panther Battalion Massacre.' It was quite an operation, Nick. It'll make stars out of all of us."

Nick just looked at him.

The "stars" line, and Howard's transparent greed hung in the air for just a second. Then the old man, Hugh Meachum, leaned forward.

"Excuse me, Howard. I wonder if I might say one thing to Nick?"

"Of course, Hugh," said Howard.

"Now Nick," said Hugh. "I know how complicated all this has been for you but I'm afraid there's yet another level of complexity that I have to put before you. I know you'll be able to handle it."

He smiled in a grandfatherly way that made Nick almost want to punch his old teeth out.

"Nick, I know you think you've seen Annex B. I know what you're thinking: that I'm involved somehow. Perhaps you think I'm the architect of all this, that I orchestrated this whole thing, the destruction of Cuembo, the murder of the archbishop, the frame-up of Bob. Nick, it's so dangerous where you are. You're in the famous Wildnerness of Mirrors that is counterintelligence. I've seen that document. A Cuban double agent tried to peddle it to the *New York Times* a couple of months ago. A translated version actually saw print in a Syrian newspaper. The Japanese news agency Torakata paid thirty-five thousand dollars for a copy, then never printed it. Nick, it's a plant. Cuban military intelligence, very crafty, very clever. That's why it's so dangerous when young men like you wander into these regions. This poor Lanzman who tried to reach you: he may actually have believed it or he may simply have thought that you'd believe it. Nick, it's mischief."

Nick looked at him.

"Mister, you're full of—"

"Nick, if it helps, go ahead and hate me. It doesn't matter if you hate me. It's allowed. But Nick, let me tell you something that isn't allowed. You actually have an opportunity to save lives. Thousands of lives. To really make a difference in the world. It's not allowed to stay on the sidelines and watch it happen.

"Now, you know that a Salvadoran Army unit called Panther Battalion was involved in a terrible atrocity on the Sampul River. Several hundred innocent villagers, many of them women and children, were killed. I shouldn't tell you this, but it appears there was some American involvement in the episode. Yes, your Colonel Shreck, working for General de Rujijo. Annex B had just enough truth in it to seem convincing. But the American government *had nothing* to do with it. And that's why this is a precious secret, Nick. It's precious because it's dangerous. If the usual enemies—the press, certain members of Congress, others on the mischievous left, sympathizers, fellow travelers, the like—Nick, if they should get ahold of that information and publicize it, they could sabotage for another five years any chances at peace in that country. Nick, think of the children who'll die if *that* happens. Nick, we have a peace now. We can't risk it." Nick swallowed, hating the confusion in his head.

"Now the second possibility is distinctly less pleasant than the first," said Howard. "You are subpoenaed as a hostile witness, a disgraced federal officer, now on suspension awaiting termination. You are asked very strict, limited questions about your participation in the events of March 1, 1992, in New Orleans: where you were, what you saw, how you messed up. Then you are dismissed. If Bob's lawyer tries to cross-examine you, we'll object to every single thing that doesn't refer to March first and we'll be sustained. The minute after you are done testifying, you are indicted on three counts of impersonating a federal officer. Mr. Kelso himself will prosecute, and we will bring witnesses who will absolutely nail you, Nick. You'll do at least seven years hard time. And you won't have done Bob a damned bit of good. You will have just thrown your life away for nothing."

Howard sat back.

Nick then said, "Is that all?"

"No, of course it's not all," said Kelso. "The same day you are indicted for impersonating a federal officer, Sally Ellion is indicted for espionage—delivering classified government files to a private citizen."

"Howard, goddammit—"

"Shut up, Nick," said Howard.

"Nick," said Kelso, "I'll prosecute that one, too. It happens to be a much more serious charge than the charge against you. You'll be out in seven years, five with good behavior. She won't be out for twenty."

Nick looked at the three men.

"Howard, she didn't do anything. She didn't do *anything.* You can't do this—"

"You're the one that's doing this, Nick. Just like you put Myra in a wheelchair for the rest of her life and doomed her, now you're going to doom Sally. Is that what you want, Nick? I had a long talk with her when she confessed everything. We have it on tape before witnesses. On top of that, the silly girl thinks she's in love with you; you're going to pay her for her innocence by sending her up?"

"Nick, you've got to make a decision. You've got to do what's best for you, for Sally, and for the Bureau."

"And for your country," said Hugh Meachum.

"And for you, isn't that right, Howard? And you, Hugh?"

"Nick, you'd better—"

Nick sat back, no longer listening. He wished he could shut them up, wished he knew what to do.

You have to be your own man, make your own decisions, Bob said.

He seemed to be having a little trouble breathing. Nothing was in focus.

"Nick," said Meachum. "We have to have a commitment from you."

Save yourself, Nick thought.

He decided to sell Bob out. He couldn't help him. Bob was gone. It was a pity, but that's the way it goes. Hardball world. No prisoners. That's life.

"Think of the Bureau, Nick," said Howard. "Think of saving the Bureau."

Save yourself, Nick thought.

But when he opened his mouth, what came out was, "Howard, you don't give a shit about the Bureau. You're not the Bureau. You're just one scuzzy little asskisser trying to make it to the top, and you'll fuck anybody who gets in your way, the way you fucked me in Tulsa seven years ago. I didn't put Myra in that chair, you did, because you were so fucking scared you wouldn't shut up on the radio. And I didn't have the guts to stop you."

He took a deep breath.

"And I see the last thing, too, Howard, you just bet I do. *You're* on Lancer Committee! Right? Yeah, it's exactly the kind of swank connection a political suck-up like you would go for. And for years now you've been slip-streaming for the Agency's use of RamDyne, and that's how you meet a piece of smooth-talking scum like Old Hugh over here, who authorized his pal Ray Shreck to wipe out a village and then to hit the one man in the world with the guts to stand up to it. And then framed a great American hero because it was convenient, it tied up a lot of loose ends and protected his own precious ass! And if that ever gets out, you and everybody on the Lancer Committee, you're all finished."

Nick stared at them. He didn't feel particularly serene but he knew what he was going to do now. He took a deep breath, smiled and then spoke his answer.

"Well, this is where it ends. This is where you're stopped. But let me tell you something, boys. You're going up against the best. And many's the time slick operators have thought they had Bob Lee Swagger nailed. And just as they moved in for the kill, he blew 'em away. He's going to do that to you, too, and I'm going to watch it happen, and then Sally and I are going to walk out of there. Howard, here's the bad news, buddy. You're history. You're the fucking past. It's payback time. You answer for Myra and you answer for Sally and you answer for Lancer and you answer for the Sampul River and whatever the hell else you've done. I'm going to watch it happen. Now get the fuck out of here."

After they left, he noticed that he couldn't stop shaking.

Two federal marshals delivered Nick's subpoena that afternoon, requiring him to appear at the New Orleans District Federal Courthouse two days hence for the Preliminary Hearing for Case Number 44–481, the *Government* v. *Bob Lee Swagger*. A sternly worded note appended to the sheet warned him that he was subject to arrest if he failed to appear. Half an hour later, he got a call from the U.S. Attorney's office informing him that he wasn't to leave the city as he was about to be indicted on three charges of impersonating a federal officer, and that he'd better get himself legal representation. And before the day was out, to bring off the hat trick, he received official notification that, for failing to show up at the suspension hearing on August 8, 1992, he was formally terminated from service in the Federal Bureau of Investigation, and was under legal obligation to therefore return any and all Bureau property before next Friday or face indictment on charges of grand theft of government property.

For some reason, that was the one that hurt most. There was no return. Howard was cutting off all the exits, preventing all possibilities. Howard was tightening the screws.

Nick returned to his little house in Metairie, mowed the lawn—which needed it badly—paid what bills he could afford, contemplated his desperate financial straits—he hadn't drawn salary for close to three months—and contemplated his woe.

There were moments at his lowest point when he felt like calling Howard. It would be so easy and it was so tempting.

"Uh, Howard, look, I think I sort of blew it a few days ago, do you think—"

But then he thought of Howard triumphant, Howard bleating, Howard beaming, Howard's biggest moment. No, he couldn't do it. He simply couldn't make himself do it.

He knew he had to do one thing, however. He had to call Sally.

"Hello."

"Hi. It's me."

"Nick—" She was crying. "Oh, Nick, they're telling me they're going to charge me with espionage. Oh,

God, Nick, what should I do? I didn't *do* anything. How can they—"

"Honey, listen to me, they're bluffing. They're trying to bump me into doing something that'll make them look good. Howard's probably under a lot of pressure to deliver on this thing and to protect his ass, so he's playing it hardball. But don't worry. I swear to you, you don't have to worry. Trust me. They haven't got a thing."

Even as he said it, he cursed himself for not having the guts to tell her the truth; that they had *everything,* and they were going to sweep Bob and himself and her and anybody who'd ever done anything for Bob Lee Swagger away.

"What should I do?" she asked.

"Nothing, for now. Let's see what happens at that preliminary hearing tomorrow. It's the deal where the defense can require that the government establish that it does have a reasonable case, so that a trial date can be set. Once that's out of the way, we'll see where we stand."

"Nick—"

"Honey, I know it's hard. But it just goes on a little longer. Do you want to come to court tomorrow? I'd be happy to take you. It's not much of a date, but—"

"Yes. Yes, I'd like that very much."

That night was Nick's worst. Worst ever. Worst since the night after Myra died. He couldn't get to sleep until nearly three, and kept thinking of poor Sally in some federal shithole for the next twenty years, of poor Bob being strapped into a chair and blitzed away, of goddamned Howard and his pet prosecutor Kelso and that hoary old fraud Meachum riding the publicity of their triumph on to better and better things.

Senator Howard D. Utey, the man who nailed Bob the Nailer!

It put Nick into dark rage and when he finally got to sleep, his memories were haunted by Howard's laughing little face, his smug confidence. God, Howard, you've dogged me ever since Tulsa.

Why didn't you shut up on that goddamned radio?

Why didn't I hit that shot?

Poor Myra. Poor Sally. Poor women who made the mistake of falling for Nick Memphis.

The alarm went off at seven; Nick limped grimly into the bathroom and faced his own grave self, a sallow, scrawny, melancholiac. His crew cut had grown out and the pouchiness of his face had vanished. He was thin as death, and maybe just as hard.

He showered, dressed slowly, putting on a suit for the first time in months, had a cup of coffee and then went to pick up Sally. He had $11 in his pocket and $236 in his checking account and over $4,000 in bills. Today he would be indicted on three counts of a federal felony.

Again, the impulse flew at him to call Howard.

It probably wasn't too late.

He tried to imagine life after selling out: how nice it would be.

But then he remembered the time Tommy Montoya was forcing the gun barrel of his Colt Agent toward his head and he was a second from his own death, when Bob's shot had come from nowhere and saved him.

Howard never saved shit. Howard only took.

Hugh Meachum only took.

Okay, Bob the Nailer, thought Nick. In for a penny, in for a pound, going to heaven, going to hell, I'm along for the ride, my friend. Here's hoping you've got it today.

CHAPTER THIRTY-EIGHT

"All rise, all rise, the Fifth United States Circuit Court is now in session, the Honorable Roland O. Hughes presiding."

Nick and Sally stood up, with two hundred others, including dozens of reporters, about half the New Orleans FBI office and Howard and his prosecuting angel, Kelso, at the prosecution table, which happened by absurd coincidence to be near Nick and Sally's seats in the front row of the courtroom. Hugh Meachum sat behind the prosecutor's table, in a three-piece gray herringbone suit. He had a little red bow tie on and Nick decided he looked three hundred years old.

Sam Vincent also stood. He was a slouchy grandpop with a face like a bowl of walnut shells, and not much hair on his head. He wore a string tie and a pair of bottle-bottom glasses; his fingers were long and gnarly and dirty from the pipe he was continually stuffing when he wasn't in court, and the thick lenses inflated his pale blue eyes when they fixed on you, so they were as large as shark's eyes. He was nearly eighty and had won the Silver Star in the Battle of the Bulge in World War II.

"You may be seated," said Judge Hughes, a stern black man in his fifties. "Now ladies and gentlemen, first I want to warn you that although today's case has national implications, it is first and foremost a case of law and it will be treated as such. I warn spectators, particularly those of you with the press, to conduct yourself with the proper decorum or I will clear this courtroom in one minute's time, is that understood?"

His booming voice was met with silence.

"Now, today we are having, at the defense's request, a preliminary hearing in the matter of the *Government* v. *Bob Lee Swagger*, in which Mr. Swagger is accused of murdering a Salvadoran citizen, the Archbishop Jorge Roberto Lopez, on federal property, namely the presidential podium erected in Louis Armstrong Park March first of this year. For you spectators let me explain: this isn't a formal trial, it's a hearing to make certain the government has, in my judgment, enough evidence to warrant the formal trial. So there's no jury. The two attorneys will be arguing for my benefit. Furthermore, the defense is not entitled to bring evidence, but only to attack the evidence the government presents. Now, gentlemen, I want these arguments to be swift and clean. I don't want procedural detail cluttering up the proceedings. You may save the logrolling for the trial, assuming there is to be a trial, and before you object, Mr. Vincent, please note I only said *if* there is to be a trial. I'm not prejudiced. Now you may bring in the accused, bailiff."

And so Bob was led into the courtroom.

In a bright blue prison jumpsuit, with his hands manacled before him, and secured by a chain around his waist that was connected in turn to leg irons, he shuffled in, hair clipped short and face raw and white. He was calm, however, as calm as the last moment Nick had seen him, sitting next to Julie on the floor of Hard Bargain Valley, his face sealed off behind the war paint as Howard's SWAT team surrounded him.

God, he looked so, so *fallen.*

"Your Honor"—it was Sam Vincent—"is it strictly necessary to humiliate my client, who has yet to be convicted of a single crime and who was a decorated Marine hero of this country, by festooning him in chains like a common thief?"

"Your Honor," answered Kelso, just as fast, "Mr. Swagger has a known propensity for both extreme violence and escape. These precautions are merely prudent."

"Ah," said the judge, "Mr. Swagger, are you duly uncomfortable or humiliated?"

"Sir, it doesn't matter to me," said Bob.

"All right, we'll undo the manacles, but the leg irons stay. Is that an adequate compromise, gentlemen?"

"Yes, sir."

"It is, Your Honor."

"Bailiff, would you make the adjustments. Now, Mr. Kelso, your opening statement please."

"Ah, thank you, Your Honor."

Manfully, Kelso strode to the center of the courtroom.

"Your Honor, the government will demonstrate very simply that adequate proof exists to conclude that at approximately twelve-nineteen P.M., on March first of this year, Bob Lee Swagger did in fact fire a shot from an attic at Four-fifteen St. Ann Street in the French Quarter of this city, that, though aimed at the president of the United States, did strike and kill Archbishop Jorge Roberto Lopez, of Salvador, El Salvador. Mr. Swagger had the classic three-part *modus operandi* to accomplish such an act, that is, motive, opportunity and means, as we shall demonstrate. And that, Your Honor, should be that."

"All right, Mr. Kelso. Thank you. Mr. Vincent."

Nick's heart sank a little when the old man stood on rocky legs, and essayed a little sally past the defense table where he sat alone with Bob. It was a contrast to the team of bodies that surrounded Kelso and Howard at the prosecution table.

"Well, sir," he said, looking fully his eighty years, his rheumy blue eyes staring at nothing in particular, his suit a collection of bags that hadn't seen a dry cleaner but had seen more than a few pipe cleanings, his clunky black shoes unshined, "I s'pose you could say we'll show the other side and that this decorated war hero could not—"

"Objection, Your Honor, Mr. Swagger's war record isn't in question here and is irrelevant to the proceedings."

"He's got a point, Mr. Vincent."

"Well, hell, sir, if they say he's a shooter then damned if they oughtn't to point out it was the U.S. Marines that taught him to shoot and who gave the boy a chestful of medals for it."

There was an eruption of laughter at Old Sam's zinger.

"Well stated, Mr. Vincent. But since there's no jury here today and since I am in fact well acquainted with your client's military record, perhaps we could forgo, in the interests of moving into the meat of the matter, any further references to Mr. Swagger's wartime heroism, and perhaps that would encourage the prosecution to forgo any time-consuming pattern of objections."

"Well, I reckon that's a tolerable deal," said Vincent.

"Excellent. Mr. Kelso, it's time for you to open your case."

"Thank you, Your Honor."

Kelso began by introducing into evidence a letter dated December 15, 1991, addressed to the president of the United States, in which Bob Lee Swagger argued in a strident, faintly irrational tone that he deserved the Congressional Medal of Honor for his exploits in Vietnam.

The letter was projected on a portable screen that Kelso's minions quickly assembled.

"Your Honor, this document was what initially put Bob Lee Swagger on the Secret Service list of potentially threatening suspects and earned him an investigation, albeit a tragically inefficient one, by the FBI."

Nick winced.

Object, he protested silently. Make the point that Bob was on the C-list, felt to be the least dangerous and that even the Secret Service guys had said he could be skipped.

But Sam Vincent and his client sat mute at their table.

"Your Honor, I have here the depositions of four handwriting experts in the Federal Bureau of Investigation, the New Orleans Police Department, the New York City Police Department and one widely respected consultant, stating that they've identified—well, it varies, Your Honor—but between fifteen and thirty-one similarities in handwriting between this document and authenticated samples of Bob Lee Swagger's penmanship."

"Mr. Vincent."

At last Vincent spoke.

"Your Honor, I know I can't enter evidence, but if I could, I'd enter three depositions from handwriting experts in Los Angeles, London, England, and Chicago, Illinois, stating that the document is a forg—"

"Objection, objection, surely Your Honor can see that the defense is trying to enter evidence which is—"

"Objection sustained. Mr. Vincent, you do know the rules."

"Sir, I do and I apologize. But, the truth is in handwriting analysis there's just no way to know positively. You can have more experts than a mama possum has teats"—laughter from the spectators in the darkness—"and you won't get any two of 'em to agree. And let me point out one last thing; Mr. Swagger unfortunately didn't have the benefits of a fancy education like some among us. He's a product of public schools in rural Arkansas in the 1950s, with no college experience. Thus his handwriting, as you all can see, remained somewhat in the primitive stage; it looks to sophisticated people as if it were written by a child. Now the one thing most handwriting experts agree on is that such a script—it's called, oh, I think, 'infantile cursive' "—he said this as if he were just making it up—"is indeed the easiest for any kind of accomplished forger to imitate."

"All right, Mr. Vincent," said the judge, "I'll allow that, and keep it in mind, but please remember you are only permitted to attack the government's evidence, not introduce your own."

"Yes, sir."

"How can they win if they can't introduce evidence?" Sally whispered into his ear.

"He's got to show that their evidence doesn't add up to what they say it does," Nick said.

Meanwhile, Kelso struck back quickly.

"Your Honor, I'm not here to indulge in comedy or groundless conspiracy speculation, even when they amount to the same thing. I'm here to argue a point of law. And although this isn't the forum where absolute truth is to be decided, I think Your Honor will concede that I've made exactly what the law demands of me at this point in the proceedings: that is, I've established a reasonable argument for motive. It was enough for the Secret Service and the FBI to begin to monitor Mr. Swagger and it should be enough for the court."

"Young man, it's not necessary for you to tell me my job," said Judge Hughes. "But let's just say your observation isn't without merit, even if it was delivered to this court in a fashion dangerously close to contempt."

"I apologize, Your Honor."

"Then you may proceed with the second part of your argument."

"As Your Honor pleases," said Kelso. He retreated briefly to his table.

"We're not doing too well, are we?" whispered Sally.

"No, I'm afraid we're not. I thought this old man would have something *more* than tit for tat stuff."

"Nick, I'm scared."

"Just hang on. My part is coming up next and—"

But Kelso had returned to the center of the floor.

"Your Honor," he said, "I'd like to enter into evidence the sworn statement of a New Orleans police detective named Leon Timmons. Detective Timmons is not here because, tragically, he was slain in the line of duty last April. But it was Detective Timmons who heroically interceded as Bob Lee Swagger was—"

"Your Honor, I object," said the old man, stirring himself to Biblical wrath. "This here evidence is hearsay, beyond the reach of cross-examination. Moreover this 'heroic' detective has been named in several internal affairs reports of the New Orleans Police Department of having suspected ties with organized crime in the greater—"

"Your Honor, Leon Timmons won three commendations for valor under fire in his eighteen years with—"

"And he drove one of them damned German convertible sports cars that cost more than sixty thousand dollars on a salary of twenty-two thousand five hundred per year—"

"Your Honor—"

"All right, all right, gentlemen, quit your squabbling," Judge Hughes said with a groan. He paused. "Mr. Kelso, don't you have a *live* witness?"

"Shit," said Nick to Sally.

"Yes, sir."

"Then let's end this here. You put your sworn testimony into evidence and I'll read it at my leisure and if the issue is still in doubt, rule then on its admissibility."

"That's fine, Your Honor. I feel my next witness will clear up any doubts *anybody* will have about the viability of the government's case."

Suddenly a bailiff was standing next to Nick.

"Mr. Memphis. From Mr. Utey."

It was a note.

Nick unfolded it.

It said, *Last chance. As you can see, Bob is lost. You can still turn this to your benefit and the Bureau's advantage. Don't throw your life and that poor girl's away for nothing that can be helped anyway.*

"What is it, Nick?" Sally whispered.

So here it was.

The whole thing come to this.

His life could be so fine.

Bob was gone anyhow; that was clear. Old Sam Vincent was a cracker-barrel windbag. The evidence was overwhelming. RamDyne had won. He looked behind the prosecution table and saw Hugh Meachum sitting there, his face serene, his blue eyes opaque.

"The prosecution calls Mr. Nicholas Memphis."

Nick leaned to Sally.

"It's a note from a ghost," he said, crumpling it, and walked to the witness's box without looking at Howard.

Nick took the oath without a lot of emotional investment and tried to find a comfortable position in the hardwood chair. He could see Bob, ramrod stiff, all Marine, staring not at him but into space; and sitting beside him, his slouch carrying with it a suggestion of collapsed feed bags heaped in the barn corner, old Sam Vincent, his jowls slightly rising and falling as he breathed heavily, his eyes enormous behind the thick glasses.

"Your current employment, Mr. Memphis?" asked Kelso.

"I'm currently unemployed. As of yesterday."

"And until yesterday?"

Nick summed himself up quickly: twelve years, Federal Bureau of Investigation, special agent.

"And can you tell us your duties on the date of March first, of last year?"

"I was part of a multidepartmental task force assigned to a presidential security detail. I was—"

"Mr. Memphis, please just answer the question I ask without elaboration. You've done this before, no?"

"Yes."

"Good."

"But—"

"Mr. Memphis, what did these responsibilities entail?"

"I was parked in a car on St. Ann Street about five blocks from the speech site, Louis Armstrong Park, on North Rampart."

"I see. What was your job?"

"Uh. Well, it was a Secret Service operation, basically.

We were just on the farthest perimeter of the security envelope, pretty much as lookouts, that's all."

"I see. Now, please tell me what ensued at exactly twelve-nineteen P.M. that day. You are in your car and—"

"Well, it's a lot more complicated than that. See, there's *context*, it's very important, what came before, what came after, what I learned, what was involved, and just to isolate—"

"Mr. Memphis, you were asked a direct question. You answer with an essay on an irrelevant topic. What ensued at exactly twelve-nineteen P.M. that—"

Nick felt it all draining away. He'd rehearsed a dozen times, reducing the story into the smallest understandable parts.

"Your Honor, I have to explain, because—"

"Your Honor, I should explain the witness is here as a hostile. He's under subpoena and may soon be indicted under federal statutes for impersonating a federal officer."

"I just need—"

"Mr. Memphis, you've testified before," said the judge. "You know the rules. If you have a statement to make, I'll allow you to file it in writing at the end of the proceedings."

"Sir, I just feel—"

"Your Honor, he's got to answer the question."

I'm hurting him, Nick suddenly realized. *I'm coming across like a crazy man, and in doing that, I absolutely hurt the man I meant to help.* Kelso knew it. Kelso counted on it. Howard had prepped Kelso well on the weaknesses of Nicholas Memphis, formerly of the Federal Bureau of Investigation.

"Mr. Memphis, I'll have to hold you in contempt if you don't answer. I don't think you want three months in jail added to your current legal difficulties."

"I just want justice, Your Honor. I—"

"Mr. Memphis, I have to warn you once more. Answer the question, or I'll find you in contempt."

"Yes, sir. But if you would just let me put it in *con—*"

"Nick."

It was Bob.

"Nick, just tell the truth. Don't you worry about a thing."

His deep voice resonated in the courtroom like a mourning cry. It was followed by stillness.

"Mr. Swagger, if you make an interjection again, I'll find *you* in contempt, and I'll have you restrained and gagged," said the judge.

Nick saw how brilliantly the prosecutor had choreographed it. Put Nick in distress; gull Bob into breaking his stoicism; we both look like fools, locked in complicity, terrified of the truth.

Howard was watching intently, shaking his head as if to claim at this point the victory was too easy to take.

"All right," Nick finally said. He'd tried; he'd lost; they'd come so far; it was over; Bob the Nailer was nailed.

It was over quickly.

"I heard a shot. I got out of the car . . ." He told it simply, in the end identifying Bob as the bleeding man who'd jumped from the window, hit the roof and staggered down the stairs.

"Thank you, Mr. Memphis," said Kelso. "I'm finished, Your Honor."

"Mr. Vincent, do you have any questions?"

At last. Nick knew his time had at last come. Now he could get it out. Now he could—

Vincent said, "No further questions, Your Honor."

"You may step down, Mr. Memphis."

Nick looked at the old man in utter disbelief. He felt like throwing up. That was it? It was over? It was—

"Oh, one thing, Mr. Memphis." The old man seemed to be awakening from a dream.

"Uh, you say Detective Timmons was *already* inside the house out of which Mr. Swagger fled bleeding."

"Yes, sir."

"Hmmm. Did you see him enter? As I recall, there's only one entry to that courtyard."

"No, sir. And I was on station at 1000 hours."

"Damn, isn't that strange? Yet in his log he says he saw something suspicious at Four-fifteen St. Ann Street up near the roofline and entered the courtyard and—"

"Your Honor, I object," said the quick Kelso. "Detective Timmons isn't on trial here and counsel himself objected when I tried to introduce the detective's account—"

"Your Honor, I'm just an old country boy, but I'm wondering how this heroic detective turned himself *invisible* that day. That's a hell of a trick."

"Your Honor," Kelso pushed ahead, "let me *further* point out that Mr. Memphis has been dismissed from his job in the Bureau out of gross negligence and dereliction of duty. His screwups on this case are notorious throughout the law enforcement community. To offer him as any kind of paragon of professionalism, as the defense is clearly trying, is ludicrous beyond words."

Great. Now ritual humiliation in public added to everything else.

"He does have a point, Mr. Vincent. But I've marked your observation down for further study. All right, Mr. Kelso. Proceed."

Nick lumbered back to his seat, feeling the weight of ages on his suddenly frail shoulders. Another nail in the coffin.

He fought his way back to the seat next to Sally, and she leaned over and put a hand on his.

"You tried," she said.

"Catastrophe," was all he could think to say.

He looked up to see the judge announce an hour recess for lunch.

"Let's get out of here," he said.

On the way out, two or three news types hounded him, but he just bulled on by; more of them were clustered around the star of the hour, the charismatic young prosecutor, who gobbled up sound-bite-sized nuggets for the six P.M. news. Sam Vincent was nowhere to be found.

"Sally," he said, after they had sat in glum silence for a few minutes at a diner a few blocks away, the food claiming his last eleven dollars, "I think we have to talk."

"All right."

"I don't think we're going to win. In fact, I *know* we're not going to win. Maybe Bob specializes in getting out of tight spots but this time . . . well, the point is, it's not going to happen today. The noose is too tight. It's over."

"Nick, I—"

"And when he goes, I go, and when I go, you'll go. But it doesn't have to happen like that. I want you to call Kelso and volunteer to testify against me. Tell him I duped you, I seduced you, I used you. I won't deny it. It's me they really want. If you give them me on an espionage charge, something heavier than this stupid 'impersonating a federal officer' thing, they'll go for it in an instant. It's the smart move. Okay?"

"The smart move," she said.

"Howard only wants me destroyed, because I wouldn't give him his phony undercover thing. And there's this mysterious old goat named Hugh Meachum that I think works for the CIA or did or something like that, he's here to make sure it all stays contained. That's the point of the drill. I know they won't—"

"Nick, let me tell you something. Bob Lee Swagger may specialize in getting out of tight places, but you specialize in loyalty. You gave everything to the Bureau and everything to Myra all those years. I've watched you. I've been watching you for years, and how much you gave. And how I was never a honey to you; you were the only one who ever treated me like a human being, and you never came on to me, and believe me, A. B. Nick, you wouldn't *believe* some of the champions of the family value system that came on to me. And that's because at some point you are fundamentally the most decent man who ever lived. And now you've given your loyalty to Bob Lee Swagger. Well, Nick, I've loved you for half a decade and if all I get for it is today and tomorrow until we're both indicted and held without bond, then that's enough for me. I'll give you the loyalty you've been giving everybody else all those years. It's time for somebody to give *you* some loyalty."

"Sally, I—"

"And I'll bet you that old country boy Bob Lee Swagger has some sly left up his sleeve. I'll tell you this, Nick, I'm from the South and I've known men like that my whole life. They're not much damn good at anything except dying in wars and shooting helpless animals, Lord knows why, and outsmarting the law. They're sly, that's their talent. And I never met anybody who could outsly a sly old country boy and from what I've heard of Bob Lee Swagger, he's the slyest of them all. There's just no way a carpetbagging yankee like Howdy Duty or an old ghost like Hugh Meachum could bring it off. Nick, you've just got to believe in Bob Lee, do you hear me?"

He touched her arm. He wanted to kiss her. All that

radiance in those bright eyes. Dammit, she believed, where he himself had lost all belief.

"Come on, son," she said, "time to git back to the show. Got me a feeling there's fireworks to come."

The young man's name was Walter Jacobs. He was extremely clean-cut, balding, mild of face and demeanor, his eyes narrowly intelligent and beaming with goodwill behind his wire frames, his suit blue and crisp, his shirt white and crisp, his tie black and crisp.

And he was death.

He was the one who'd do it, finally, push it that last little bit.

"Your employment, Mr. Jacobs?"

"I'm a senior firearms technician in the FBI Forensic Ballistics Laboratory in Washington, D.C."

And so to means at last. Kelso, grunting to make it appear heavier and more lethal for the judge, bent to lift the means.

"And this is it?"

"Yes, sir," said Jacobs.

"Your Honor, I'd like to enter this rifle as state exhibit four, please."

"So mark it."

"And this."

It was a tiny, twisted piece of lead and copper—the base of a hollowtip bullet.

"Yes. Exhibit number five, Mr. Kelso."

"And this—the final link—as state exhibit six."

He held up a thin brass tube, 2.015 inches long, narrower at one end, rimmed at the other. It was an empty cartridge case.

"So marked," said the judge.

"Would you identify this exhibit please, Mr. Jacobs."

"Yes, sir. It's a customized Remington Model 700V bolt action center-fire rifle in .308 caliber with a Leupold 10× Ultra Scope. It was recovered in the attic of Four-fifteen St. Ann Street, in this city, on the date March first, 1992."

"All right. Can you tell us of the rifle's background?"

Quickly, Jacobs sketched the rifle's course from the Remington custom shop in Ilion, New York, to its special-order purchase through the Naval PX system by the commanding officer of the Marine Corps Marksmanship Unit at Camp Lejeune in 1975, where the paperwork said it was presented to Gunnery Sergeant Bob Lee Swagger, that unit, on the occasion of his disability retirement from the service.

"I see. Can you characterize the nature of the weapon?"

"Yes, sir. Someone has gone to a great deal of trouble and evinced a great deal of guncraft in making that rifle superbly accurate. The original custom rifle was very accurate, what we'd call a minute-of-angle rifle. But he has done things to refine it even more. For example, the original Remington barrel has been replaced by a custom-made Hart stainless steel barrel, with button-cut rifling. That work, incidentally, was performed by Hart Rifle Barrels of Lafayette, New York, according to company records, for Bob Lee Swagger, of Blue Eye, Arkansas, in June of 1982. The new fiberglass stock was manufactured by McMillan and Company, of Phoenix, Arizona; a stock of that model was sent to Bob Lee Swagger of Blue Eye, Arkansas. The firing pin has been replaced by a much lighter one of titanium from Brownells, of Montezuma, Iowa, to improve lock time thirty-five percent, that is, increase the speed between the trigger pull and the actual firing. The rifle has been bedded in Devcon aluminum and its screws have been 'pillar bedded,' meaning that they've been driven through a pillar of aluminum inserted in the stock. All of this, of course, makes the rifle more stable and therefore more accurate."

"Thank you. And now, the last two items."

Kelso held up the lead and copper scrap.

"That's what remains of a 200-grain boattail hollowpoint Sierra MatchKing bullet," said Jacobs. "It was recovered from the podium of the Louis Armstrong Park here in New Orleans, clotted with brain tissue and skull fragments."

"Is there enough left to make a ballistic identification?"

"No, sir. We were unable to get a rifling signature from the bullet, since it was so mutilated."

"I see. So what did you do?"

"Sir, we carefully sluiced the barrel of the rifle and took very careful samplings of copper and lead residue that remained in its rifling channels. We took copper and lead samplings from the bullet. Then, we made neutron activation analysis examinations of each metallic sample."

"What did you learn?"

"That the bullet and the residue were atomically identical, sir."

"Proving?"

"Proving that either that bullet, or one exactly like it, was the last bullet fired down that barrel. There were no other identifiable lead or copper tracings."

"Are these bullets common?"

"They're manufactured in small lots by Sierra Bullets of Sedalia, Missouri, primarily for thousand-yard shooting. The yearly production is less than five thousand. It's not a common hunting round. We found several boxes, including one recently opened, in the suspect's shop in Blue Eye, Arkansas."

"I see. And finally, the case. Would you characterize it, please?"

"Yes, sir. Well, sir, the case indicates a handload assembled with some care and skill. Both the outside and the inside of the neck had been turned, to guarantee smooth bullet release and concentricity. The primer, a Federal Bench Rest primer, had been seated precisely in the center of the primer pocket. The flash hole had been deburred for consistent ignition and the primer pocket cleaned and reamed for perfect depth and squareness."

"Could you mate it to the rifle?"

"Yes, sir. There are six tests and measurements that one can make to ascertain whether or not a shell was fired in the chamber of a rifle and ejected from it. These include neck diameter vis-à-vis chamber diameter, thickness, chamber imperfection pattern, rim indentations . . . and on and on. It passed all six."

"So it *was* fired in and ejected from that rifle."

"It would be mathematically impossible for it not to be."

"Thank you, Mr. Jacobs. What kind of case was it?"

"Sir, it was a Federal Nickel Match .308 case. Federal doesn't make them anymore but we found several boxes of them in Bob Lee Swagger's shop. And we found Federal large Bench Rest Rifle Primers. We identified the powder residue in the case as IMR-4895. We found an eight-pound keg of IMR-4895 in Mr. Swagger's shop, half gone."

"Thank you, Mr. Jacobs." He turned. "Your Honor, I think you can see the chain. We have motive—resentment of the president as evinced in the letter. We have opportunity, as Agent Memphis's testimony placed Swagger in the sniper's nest at the time of the shooting. And we have means—his rifle, custom built, painfully assembled over the years into the most efficient killing machine ever made. We have the bullet from the rifle.

We have the shell ejected from the rifle. And a good man is dead. And there sits his killer."

"We're screwed," said Nick to Sally.

"The prosecution rests," said Kelso.

"Mr. Vincent."

"Your Honor, I have no— Oh. Just out of curiosity. Mr. Jacobs, how does the rifle shoot?"

"I beg your pardon?"

"How does she shoot? If you're examining a rifle to see if it killed a man, don't you have to have some idea how it shoots?"

"I can assure you, sir, it has all the hallmarks of a rifle customized for maximum accuracy."

"Yes, but how does it shoot?"

Jacobs was suddenly a bit uncomfortable.

"Your Honor," said Kelso, "I object. This has no bearing on—"

"Mr. Kelso, you introduced the rifle to evidence, not Mr. Vincent. Objection overruled. Answer the question please, Mr. Jacobs."

"Well, sir," said Jacobs, "I assume it shoots very well."

"Whoa, son," said Sam Vincent. "You *assume*? Now does that mean, you haven't *fired* the rifle?"

"Yes, sir. There was no cause to, given the fact that the recovered bullet was too badly damaged to read the rifling signature."

"So you can't say how accurate this rifle is, not ever having fired it. You can't testify that this rifle is capable of the kind of accuracy you say it is."

Nick held his breath, wondering if the old goat had come up with just the faintest opening.

"What's going on?" whispered Sally.

"See," Nick explained, "because there was no ballistic signature on the murder bullet, they couldn't shoot it, because they didn't want to have to say in court they failed to get a match. They just passed on the test altogether. I don't know where this is leading."

Jacobs held his ground.

"Sir, I've examined thousands of rifles in my time, and I examined that one minutely, including taking it completely apart and examining it for function and reliability, and I can say—I can guarantee you—that everything in that rifle is consistent with a weapon of extreme accuracy. There was no point in shooting the rifle, as we had no sample of its rifling to test."

"Or maybe you *did* test it and it didn't match," said Sam Vincent.

Kelso was on his feet screaming.

"I object," he yelled. "Counsel is impugning the integrity of the FBI's ballistic laboratories, an institution with a worldwide reputation for integrity."

"Or maybe the FBI *tampered* with the rif—" Sam started.

"That'll be quite enough, Mr. Vincent," said the judge. "Objection sustained. There's no evidence to suggest tampering."

"Sir," said Jacobs, "may I make a statement?"

"Go ahead," said the judge.

"Sir, I've been testifying in cases for over ten years and nobody has ever suggested that our lab would tamper with evidence. On my word of honor, I guarantee that that rifle is exactly, precisely the way we found it, except for disassembly and the barrel swatching process I've already described. It has not been altered in any way at all."

"Seems to me he has you, Mr. Vincent," said Judge Hughes.

"No further questions, Your Honor," said the old man, and limped back to his chair.

"Your Honor," said Kelso, springing up, as Jacobs left the stand. "That finishes the state's case. I believe I've delivered on my promise, Your Honor. Now, the defense insisted on a preliminary, to discredit my evidence, and if you'll allow me to point it out, he hasn't *scratched* it. He hasn't *dented* it. Your Honor, isn't it time to declare this farce over and set a trial date?"

It was the contempt in his voice, as much as the triumph, that made Nick hate him.

"Mr. Vincent?"

"Your Honor." The old man had bestirred himself. "Your Honor, I confess my best shot didn't pay off. I'd hoped to prove that the FBI's failure to test-fire the rifle proved the case couldn't be made, but I just couldn't budge that smart young feller over there."

He had a sad moment; it was solemn in the courtroom.

Sally nudged him.

"What?"

"He's staring at you."

"Who?"

"Your friend."

And so Bob was. And when their eyes met, Bob's face suddenly lit into a big grin. Then he winked.

"What's going on?" Sally asked.

"I think Bob the Nailer's about to blow some smart boys to hell and gone," Nick whispered, his breath suddenly hard to find in his chest.

"But," said the old man, "the government has proven completely that this here rifle"—and he moved with surprising swiftness, the palsy gone from his limbs, his gut sucked in, his glasses gone—"this *death* rifle shot and killed Archbishop Jorge Roberto Lopez on March first of this year. That's their whole damn case and damned if it ain't airtight. A cat couldn't get out of that damned bag!"

With a swift hand he picked up the rifle from the prosecutor's table and flicked open the bolt. "Yep," he said, booming, "Bob took a bullet, a cartridge, just like this one"—and from his pocket he pulled out a gleaming brass cartridge—"just like this Winchester Ranger 168-grain .308 hollowpoint—"

It suddenly occurred to the judge that the cartridge was live.

"Mr. Vincent, that bullet is *not* to be inserted in—"

But Sam slapped the cartridge into the chamber and drove the bolt home. The sudden overwhelming power of the loaded rifle, that utterly transforming alchemy by which a mute piece of equipment, after insertion of the little missile of brass and powder and lead, becomes an almost living presence, filled the courtroom.

Kelso didn't even bother to object. Two bailiffs quietly put their hands on their revolvers.

"Mr. Vincent," said the judge, "you now have a loaded weapon in your hand. I formally order you to unload it quickly, and no nonsense about it, or, sir, I will find you in contempt and lock you up for the rest of your life. Bailiff, if Mr. Vincent doesn't comply—"

"Your Honor, Your Honor," said Old Sam. "I have no intention of firing this here murder gun that the FBI and the prosecution have proven Bob Lee Swagger killed the Archbishop Robert Lopez with, no sir."

He held the rifle aloft, its muzzle skyward.

"No, sir," he said, "no, sir, I have no intention of firing it." Then he smiled. "On the other hand," he said, "I didn't say nothing about pulling the trigger."

He pulled the trigger.

In years that followed, Nick would recollect that the loudest shot in the long and violent story of Bob Lee Swagger was also the quietest. But at the time, he had no way of knowing that. Like everybody else in the room, he watched the old man's finger constrict on the trigger and, anticipating the hugeness of the explosion caused by the crazy old man in the constricted space, he felt his face crack into a flinch.

Click, went the rifle, no louder than a pencil dropping on the floor.

Silence. Then chaos.

"Order, order," shouted the judge.

"Your Honor," shouted Kelso, "I object, I don't know what the point of inserting a dummy cartridge into—" And then he shut up himself, and shot a look at Howard.

"Your Honor," said Sam, "it wasn't no dummy. I could point out the dummies in here, but this cartridge isn't one of them. You could feed a thousand, a million live cartridges through this rifle. Because it does everything the FBI says it does, except one. It don't shoot."

Quickly, he ejected the cartridge to the floor, then pushed the bolt-retaining lever in front of the trigger and released the bolt. He set the rifle down on the prosecution table, and held the bolt up. Then he pressed the bolt against the tabletop to release the spring mechanism and in five expert seconds broke the bolt down to its components, one of which he held aloft.

"The firing pin, Your Honor," he said. "As the young man pointed out, it's a titanium firing pin, for faster lock time. What he didn't point out, because he didn't notice, was that it ain't four point five-six-five inches long, as the Remington specs call for. No, sir, it's four point four-six-five inches long. Ain't no way it's long enough to reach the primer. Now if you looked real careful, you'd see that a man who knew all about rifles took this little sucker and cut it in two with a file. Then he removed just one tenth of an inch of metal from the pin shaft. Then he welded it together again, and you'd have to measure it with a set of Jap calipers to tell the difference, but the one thing sure as death is that it ain't long enough to reach the primer. Just by a hair, but close don't count. It don't shoot. It don't go bang. Now why would he do that? If Bob Lee Swagger were a sly man, you might say that at some time in his past when he was shooting for some people, he noticed that somebody had removed one of the spent casings on his handloads and replaced it with another. It bothered him. A small thing, ten cents' worth of brass, that's all. But it bothered him. And so later he took out the firing pin and he performed that surgery and then he put it back, because he suspected something strange was going on in his life. And maybe all these months he's known he had absolute physical proof that he could not have shot the archbishop and the FBI and the government didn't know diddly. And maybe he used that time to find out who those men are, and what dark deeds they'd done in the past. Your Honor, you may have noticed that on the first day of deer season last month in Arkansas, there was an astonishing number of accidents. Three men killed on one day? Amazing, what with hunting accidents way down these days on account of blaze orange. But you know, Your Honor, sometimes justice happens in strange ways that men and courts can't quite understand.

"And so who fired the shot that killed Archbishop Jorge Roberto Lopez? You'll have to ask Bob Lee Swagger. Maybe he'll tell you. He won't tell me. But we do know this. Someone else fired that bullet from another rifle. 'Cause this one don't work. That's what the irrefutable evidence says. So, Your Honor, I ask you. Is there a case here? Or are we trying the *wrong* case?"

The judge asked the two attorneys to stand.

He looked at them both squarely.

"Mr. Kelso," he finally said, "what are you doing here? You have a murder to solve and you're nowhere near solving it. You haven't even started. Bailiff, please release Mr. Swagger. He is free to live his own life now.

I'm dismissing all charges. And I think that should do it. I think we can all go home now."

The reporters exploded out of the courtroom to file the day's astonishing events. In this ruckus, almost unnoticed, Bob stood, smiled easily, shook Sam Vincent's hand, then came over to Nick, his bonds at last off.

"You did good, Nick. You can spot for me any day."

"You did good yourself, old man."

"Aren't we a damn team, though? You sure you weren't a Marine?"

"No, I wasn't."

"Well, you take care now. It was fun."

"It was."

Bob Lee walked away, and within seconds, somehow, was gone. It was the sniper's gift. To disappear, leaving no trace, gone suddenly and totally.

Nick turned to Sally, but instead found himself looking upon the ruined face of Howard D. Utey.

"Howard, you weren't even close. You didn't even muss his hair. He just blew you away." Over Howard's shoulder, he could see the old man Meachum standing in the shadows, watching. Nick almost called out to him, but Meachum stepped back and he too vanished.

Then he turned to Sally.

"You want to get out of here?"

"Boy, do I."

"Where to?"

"Oh, I think we could figure something out."

CHAPTER THIRTY-NINE

The scandal was a flame. It burned hot and bright and it devoured those who attempted to control it. Howard was unceremoniously retired by a humiliated Federal Bureau of Investigation before the week was over, as were the other three members of the Lancer Committee; the U.S. Attorney's Office reassigned young Philip Kelso to a far western state, but he refused the assignment, resigned, and went into private practice. The real shocker, however, was Hugh Meachum, dead on the third day after the hearing by coronary aneurysm. His heart simply exploded, as if hit by a bullet.

When he heard, Nick thought: He got them all. Every last one of them.

He was spending a long, glorious week just being

with Sally, in her apartment mostly, but with a few other stops, when at last a phone call tracked him down. It was Hap Fencl.

"Quite a mess here, bub."

"Yeah, well," said Nick.

"Know where I might find a good, slightly used special agent? We got some snappy cases going down, need a guy with experience."

"Wasn't I fired?"

"Oh, Nick, gee, some guy may have had an idea like that, but he's long gone, and I don't think you could find anybody in the personnel office who knows where the paperwork went. Nick, seriously. This is where you belong. You were right. Howard was a mistake. They come along, sometimes. But they destroy themselves. It's a good outfit. Guys like you make it good."

"Oh, hell."

"Come on, Nick. Nothing special, just street work, New Orleans, the same salary, back pay. Some guys in Washington want to talk to you about this RamDyne thing, so you may as well get paid for it."

Nick breathed heavily. He just wanted to be an FBI agent, that was all he'd ever wanted.

"Okay," he finally said, "see you tomorrow."

"And Nick. Marry that damned girl, will you?"

"Well, dammit," he said, "I did. Yesterday."

"Congrats. See you, partner."

So Nick went back on duty, and spent his honeymoon in Washington, two weeks of telling his RamDyne story over and over again, as a crack team of hotshots tried to track down the elusive truth. That unit is due to release its report. It will happen any day now, you may be sure of it.

It would have helped matters immensely, of course, if they'd ever found Dr. David Dobbler. But they never did; he was either dead in the fastness of the Ouachitas, or perhaps living by his wits under a new name in some Southern California resort town. Nick always favored the latter explanation.

Of RamDyne, no trace remained. Its staff dispersed, its seedy headquarters languished and is now the location of a small software concern; those who spoke to the FBI were lower-level people, who knew nothing. Colonel Raymond Shreck's body went unclaimed; it was buried in Arlington National Cemetery, not far from John F. Kennedy's, because after all, the colonel had won the Silver Star and the DSC in Korea and another Silver and three Bronze Stars in Vietnam. John D. "Jack" Payne was buried in the United States Army cemetery in Baton Rouge, Louisiana. He, too, had been a hero.

And James Thomas Albright, or Lon Scott, his secrets lost forever, went into a mausoleum outside Danville, where his remains joined those of his father and his mother, which he had had disinterred and brought down from Vermont. He willed his collection of bench-rest rifles and shooting memorabilia to the National Rifle Association, and the Tenth Black King now resides in its National Firearms Museum in Washington, D.C., testament to a time when skill with a rifle was the most gentlemanly of all pursuits and men like Art Scott represented their country proudly with Winchester's best in their hands. The Association had little use for the other effects, including a curious collection of fired 162-grain .264 caliber bullets from some bizarre project or other in the early sixties, found in his safe deposit box. His corporate portfolio, amounting to over seven million dollars, went to the National Association of Quadriplegics.

Bob Lee Swagger was another instant MIA. When all state charges were dropped as a consequence of the collapse of the federal case, he vanished from public sight almost immediately with the woman Julie Fenn. But he paid his debts, in the currency of his choice.

An ex-big game hunter in Oklahoma was astounded to discover a package delivered to his doorstep. Opening it, the old man cackled with glee.

It was a pre-'64 Model 70 in .270 Winchester.

No note accompanied the weapon, only a tag.

"This rifle once belonged to Bob Lee Swagger," it said. It was signed Bob Lee Swagger.

And one day, a month after his return from Washington, Nick answered a knock on the door to find a UPS guy with a package about three feet long that weighed about seven pounds. He signed for it, took it into the basement and opened it.

It was the Ruger Mini-14.

"Nick," said a note in careful, almost childish handwriting, "am moving on. Thought you might want this as a souvenir of our days on the lam. You sure you weren't a Marine?"

No signature.

Nick looked at the damn thing. A small, handy, neat little rifle, once owned and used by Bob the Nailer. He shook his head.

"Honey, what is it?" Sally called down.

"Ah, just a deal from a guy I used to know," he said and went over and slid it behind the water heater, where to this day it remains, rusting.

They came over the last rise.

In the desert, the town looked like a patchwork of bright and dark shapes, flung across the living radiance. It was hot and dry and above the sun blazed down without mercy.

"It's not much," she said. "No mountains, no trees, just scrub pine and little sticky things that will kill you.

And hot. It's so hot out here most of the time that people live on iced tea and air-conditioning."

"It looks like rough land. Not too many people around, though, is that right?"

"Hardly any," she said.

"And lots of room to move and nobody to pay you mind?"

"Only me," she said.

"Sounds pretty good," he said. "Now let's stop somewhere and get us a dog."

"That would be fine," she said. "We can raise him with this damned baby I seem to be carrying."

ABOUT THE AUTHOR

STEPHEN HUNTER is the author of thirteen novels. He is the chief film critic of the *Washington Post* and won the 2003 Pulitzer Prize for Criticism. He is also the author of one nonfiction book and two collections of film criticism. He lives in Baltimore, Maryland.

"Hunter passes almost everybody else in the thriller-writing trade as if they were standing still . . . worth every extravagant rave."

—Daily News, *New York*

STEPHEN HUNTER

POINT OF IMPACT

____978-0553-56351-1 $7.99/$10.99 in Canada

"Suspense that will wire you to your chair. Hunter is damn good."

—STEPHEN COONTS

"A novel that will keep you turning the pages long after you should have turned off the light . . . great entertainment." —*Milwaukee Sentinel*

"Stephen Hunter has done for the rifle what Tom Clancy did for the nuclear submarine . . . score it a bull's-eye." —*St. Louis Post-Dispatch*

"Gripping . . . the tension of POINT OF IMPACT never lets up."

—*The New York Times*

THE DAY BEFORE MIDNIGHT

____978-0553-28235-1 $7.99/$11.99 in Canada

"A breathtaking, *fascinating* look at what could happen—given the possibility of an atomic 'given.' A wrap-up you'll never forget."

—ROBERT LUDLUM

"Rockets toward a shattering climax like an incoming missile."

—STEPHEN COONTS

"Nonstop action and mounting tension." —*The New York Times*

"The one to beat this year in the nail-biter class . . . an edge-of-the-seat doomsday countdown thriller." —*Daily News,* New York

Ask for these titles wherever books are sold, or visit us online at ***www.bantamdell.com*** for ordering information.

SH FIC 2/07